Praise for *Unbreakable*

"Military science fiction with a kick-butt female lead."　　—*Kirkus Reviews*

"Bauers has created a gritty, complex story Heinlein would have been proud of."　　　　　—James L. Cambias, author of *A Darkling Sea*

"W. C. Bauers gives us everything we want in our military science fiction, but never allows the hardware and action to overshadow Paen and everyone else caught in the cross fire."　　　—Dayton Ward, *New York Times* bestselling author of *The Last World War*

"A promising protagonist, a colorful band of brothers, and plenty of powered-armor battle action."　　　　　—*B&N Sci-Fi & Fantasy Blog*

BOOKS BY W. C. BAUERS

Unbreakable
Indomitable

For my sons:
Andrew, Nate, and Caleb.
Do hard things.

ACKNOWLEDGMENTS

Thanks to Lt. Col. Gary Foster, U.S. Army (Ret.); Cmdr. Mark Gabriel, USN (Ret.); and SSgt. Stephen Smith, U.S. Army. To John Duff, for your friendship and encouragement. To Evan Ladouceur for continuity and support. To my agent, Cherry Weiner, for keeping me grounded. To my editor, Marco Palmieri, and to Tor Books. To Stephan Martiniere for incredible cover art. To my family and friends for their ongoing support. To the freedom-loving women and men in uniform across the globe who stand in the gap.

IF I AM NOT FOR ME, THEN WHO IS FOR ME? BUT IF I AM ONLY
FOR ME, THEN WHAT AM I?

> —Moses Maimonides, twelfth-century teacher of the
> Torah, Pre-Diaspora

YOU MAY NOT BE INTERESTED IN WAR, BUT WAR IS INTERESTED
IN YOU.

> —Leon Trotsky, Bolshevik revolutionary and Marxist
> theorist, Pre-Diaspora

THE TRUE SOLDIER FIGHTS NOT BECAUSE HE HATES WHAT IS IN
FRONT OF HIM, BUT BECAUSE HE LOVES WHAT IS BEHIND HIM.

> —G. K. Chesterton, twentieth-century poet and
> philosopher, Pre-Diaspora

INDOMITABLE

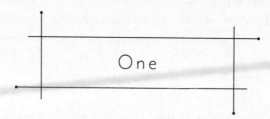

One

A round the size of Promise's trigger finger hit her like a maglev. It tore through her mechsuit and mushroomed in her chest, just above her heart. Miraculously, it didn't go off. Promise stumbled backward and off the cliff's face, into thousands of meters of darkness. Neuroinhibitors flooded her system almost as fast as the pain. *This is it* flashed across her mind as her body flatlined. *Tomorrow I'm hero-dead.*

Her vision grayed out and she lost all feeling in her hands and feet.

Promise rag-dolled in her mechsuit . . . fell and fell and fell, perilously close to the cliff's face. Her heel caught an outcropping several hundred meters below. Her AI, Mr. Bond, sealed the hole in her chest, and patched and packed it with cauterizing goo. Then Bond isolated the round kissing her heart in a null field, in case it decided to go off on its own timetable. Removing it was out of the question, and beyond the mechsuit's capabilities. A Marine Corps cutter would have to brave that. And there were more pressing matters to attend to. Her heart had stopped beating.

The mechsuit intubated her and zapped her pumper. One, two, three . . . six times before her heart's arteries and connective tissues remembered how to work in concert. A single stroke came followed by another, and then a stable *thrum thrum thrum.* Promise gasped, and came to. Her heads-up display blared with error messages she couldn't process. Her ears weren't discriminating sounds. Her body felt disemboweled, as if someone had ripped her soul clean out and now someone else was trying to stuff it back in but the fit was wrong. Insert leg there. No, not there, *there*. The tube down her throat was the worst violation. Mercifully, Bond pulled it out.

"SITREP," Promise said, the words a faint, hoarse whisper.

"You're in an uncontrolled descent. There's an armor-piercing explosive round in your chest."

"Is the APER hot?"

"Negative."

Promise exhaled, blinked hard, but still couldn't make sense of her HUD.

"Today is a bad day to die." Her voice was stronger now, the sky a starless void. "Why aren't my lamps on?"

"Stand by," said Bond at the same time that her proximity alarm howled.

Promise's forward lamps lit several milliseconds later. She gasped, and threw her hands out in front of her, which sent her tumbling backward end over end. Meters away, the rock face somersaulted in and out of view.

"Could . . . have . . . warned . . . me," she said through clenched teeth. Down became up became down until she couldn't tell the difference between them anymore.

"I tried, Lieutenant." Bond sounded mildly put out. "Tuck your arms to your sides. I'll right you."

Her mechsuit's ailerons bit into the wind, stopped the tumble, and reoriented her: head down, feet up, knifing toward the watery deck. The distance opened between her and the wind-carved face at her six o'clock.

"Altitude?"

"Forty-five hundred meters."

"LZs?"

"There's an island up ahead, ten degrees to starboard, three klicks out. Because of the headwind, you'll cover one-point-three klicks before splashing down."

That means a long swim . . . if I survive impact. "Comm the gunny."

"Your comm is out. The APER pulsed when it hit you, and the pulse knocked out most of your systems, including your heart. *My* secondary shielding held. *You've* lost weapons, scanners, countermeasures, braking thrusters, and the gravchute. You're going to hit hard."

"Suggestions?"

"Bail out."

". . . Of my armor? You've got to be kidding."

"You tweaked my personality chip to make that impossible, ma'am." Bond sounded a bit too sure of itself for Promise to be sure her tweaking had fully taken hold.

"Mr. Bond, I don't believe *my* tweaking worked."

Her AI made a *tsk*ing sound, three times. "Let's debate that later, ma'am, during my next inspection. Your beegees were recently upgraded. Use your microgravchute embedded in the fabric between your shoulder blades." Her beegees, or standard-issue mechsuit underarmor, were good for a lot of things. Prevented chafing. Absorbed energy fire. Made using the head while suited tolerable. Barely. The microgravchute was going to come in handy. But first she had to bail . . . out of her armor . . . which was the only thing keeping her alive at the moment.

"It's double-shielded and should still work. Theoretically. I lost my link to it so I can't tell if it's operational. You'll have to manually activate it."

"And if it doesn't work?"

Not one *tsk* now. "Passing three thousand meters."

This is going to be fun. "Did I see lights overhead while we were flipping?"

"Someone went over the cliff's face with us," Bond said. "I can't tell friendly from foe, not without my scanners."

"It won't matter if we botch the landing," Promise said. She stretched her limbs to slow her fall, and then made a slight correction with one hand, and rotated onto her back. "Open up on three and stay level. I'll rise. You fall away."

"Roger that," Bond said. "Good luck, ma'am."

"On my mark." She counted down from three. "Mark!"

Her mechsuit's chest, arms, and shanks unsealed. The air chilled her to the marrow. She felt the slightest movement upward before the suction ripped her out of her suit and into the open sky. For a moment she felt like a leaf blown about the air by an unrelenting gale. She wrestled the wind for control for several seconds. Far below her the lamps on her mechsuit grew dim.

Promise spread-eagled to kill as much speed as possible. She pressed her right thumb against her pinkie for a two-count. Her mechsuit's lamps vanished. *Bond just splashed down.* She flexed the thumb again. Prayed the drive-by-wire backup transmitted the impulse from her thumb to her mini-gravchute. She was nearly panic-stricken when the chute deployed a second later and dislocated her left shoulder.

Her descent slowed to a survivable fall before reaching an all-stop. Her night vision intensified until the darkness around her lifted. The sun crested the horizon. Howling winds fell silent. Promise looked down, looked between her mechboots, looked at the endless indigo ocean for as far as the eye could see. Her arms flailed widely for something to grab hold of as the fear of falling warred with her other senses; contrary to the laws of physics, she was standing on air. No, she was floating. Flying, maybe? Somehow she was hundreds of meters above the watery deck, holding station. After a few moments of abject terror she willed herself to calm down.

I'm not falling. I'm safe. Relax, P, you can figure this out.

A far-off object entered her field of view. A door perhaps, maybe a person. It was moving toward her. The door became a human silhouette and then a heavily damaged mechsuit: armor crushed; helmet lost somewhere in the clouds. The driver's eyes were open, lifeless. Now she could see the rank on the driver's armor and her bloodshot eyes. Then another mechsuit floated into view. Promise turned her head and saw not one but three lifeless bodies, all suited, all closing in. None wore helmets. Their faces were cadaver blue. Their hair waved gently in the air though no breeze stirred it. With nothing to grab ahold of or push off from, somehow Promise was able to rotate in the air and look behind her. The sky was raining dead Marines. Above her. Below her. The nearest boot opened his mouth to speak.

"Lance Corporal Tal Covington, present." The voice howled like a windshot cavern. Covington's eyes rolled up into his head and began to bleed. Then his body blew apart.

Promise threw her hands up without thinking, slammed her eyes shut to blunt the bright flash of light that followed. A moment later it dawned upon her that she was still alive, not blown to quarks. When she dared to look, Covington was still floating in the sky, two meters away, but his body was rent asunder. The explosion had frozen in process milliseconds after happening. Covington's armor was cracked a thousand ways, his organs and bones stitched together with little else but air.

To her right, Promise heard labored breathing, followed by an anguished cry that punched her squarely in the gut. A blast of heat swept over her, blistering the side of her face, her lips, and the inside of her mouth; the taste of death was on her tongue. Turning, she saw a mechsuit engulfed in fire. The wearer was desperately trying to put the flames out with what was left of his gauntlets. She couldn't look away from the hands. Metal and flesh clung stubbornly to skeletal hands. Then, as unexpectedly as the blaze had appeared, it simply went out. The smoking remains of a scorched mechanized Marine came to attention, and a blackened skull opened its mouth. Bits of charred flesh dangled from its upper lip. "Corporal Vil Fitzholm, present."

"Private First Class Molly Starns, present," came from Promise's opposite side. Starns started convulsing. She ripped her tongue from her throat and threw it at Promise. Starns's head rolled to the side and off of her shoulders. Bits of connective tissue refused to let go.

"Staff Sergeant Moya Hhatan, present." Hhatan was floating dead ahead of Promise. "All boots present and damned for eternity." Hhatan's lips curled upward, exposing shaved canines stained with blood.

No, this isn't possible, Promise thought. Hhatan was trying to swim through the air toward her. *I watched you die. I tried to save you but your wounds . . . and the enemy was so close. You sacrificed yourself for me. Told me to go and then . . . I ran away.*

"I'm so sorry, Staff Sergeant," Promise said. Hhatan was nearly on her. "I tried, really. I did my best, I couldn't stop them all." Promise raised her hands palms-up in front of her and kicked her legs to try to get away. "Please. *Please . . .* you have to believe me."

Staff Sergeant Hhatan drew a Heavy Pistol from her holster and took aim. "You don't deserve to live, Lieutenant." Then something peculiar happened. The staff sergeant's face grew young. Years of experience melted away, the eyes changed from blue to green. "You left me on Montana." The voice morphed so quickly that Promise barely registered the change. Now complete, Hhatan's appearance was for Promise a looking-glass mirror. "Your time is up. Good-bye, Lieutenant."

Promise heard her own voice say, "I'll see you in perdition."

Hhatan's gloved finger tensed around the trigger of the Heavy Pistol, took up the slack. The air cracked in two. Muzzle fire blossomed. When Promise opened her eyes the bullet had traveled half the distance from Hhatan to her. A second later it was a meter away, and then half a meter off. Promise screamed as the bullet pierced her temple, drilled through the crown of her skull, and tore her mind apart.

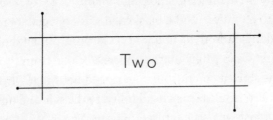

APRIL 14TH, 92 A.E., STANDARD CALENDAR, 0549 HOURS
REPUBLIC OF ALIGNED WORLDS PLANETARY CAPITAL—HOLD
MARINE CORPS CENTRAL MOBILIZATION COMMAND

The screams told her to wake up.

First Lieutenant Promise Tabitha Paen bolted upright, fully alert, First Wave blaring in her mastoid implant. The band was surfing high across the nets with "Alternate You," a throwback of classic metal and new-groove rage, set against a track of cosmic background noises. Week-one sales had topped all previous records. Promise dropped her feet over the side of her rack and hit the cold polished deck of her government-assigned quarters. Back straight, shoulders squared, and eyes focused dead ahead. She started counting "One, two, three . . ." as First Wave's lead singer screamed in perfect pitch. "There's another you who's stalking true, better run the 'verse, better strike-back-first!" At forty-nine, Promise fell over, laced her hands behind her head, and stopped when her abs gassed out and her "alternate you" found her "jumping dreams" while her "real self screams."

"Enough." Promise shook her head to clear out the dissonance and pursed her lips. "Um . . . play Chiam's Sonata in G Minor." Melody flooded her ears as her pulse settled down to normal.

The nightmares are getting worse, she thought as she rolled again onto her arms, pushed up, and started counting down from fifty. *Forty-nine, forty-eight, forty-seven . . .* To this point, the nightmares had been a rehash of her battles on Montana. She'd watched her Marines die again and again and again, each death more gruesome than the last. *Forty-three, forty-two, forty-one . . .* Perhaps it was her penance for failing them, for leaving so many dead on her birth world, or so she thought. *What doesn't kill you makes you stronger, right?* At best that was a hollowed-out truth. What failed to kill you still exacted its own pound of flesh, and not even sleep offered an escape. The nightmares were definitely getting worse.

A jolt of pain caused Promise to cry out at *twenty-nine*. She collapsed onto her side, clutching her hands over her pounding chest. Surely there was a gaping hole in her heart that must have turned black by now. Perhaps all that remained of it was a deathly hollow, carved out by the worst kind of flesh eater. Survivor's guilt.

I know because most of my first command is dead, she thought.

Her dead wouldn't stop coming to her mind. *The Skipper is dead, Lance Corporal Tal Covington shielded me from that blast and got hero-dead, Staff Sergeant Hhatan is dead because I left her behind, my mother—dead, father—dead, all turned to dust except for me.*

Tears pooled in her eyes. "Sir, if you're so good, how could you have let this happen?"

Promise willed herself up off the floor and on with her morning. She had a busy day ahead of her. The gunny was expecting her in less than an hour. She didn't bother drying her eyes as she force-marched herself to the head, shedding clothes as she went. "On." A bad memory flashed across her mind. Promise drowned it out by turning on the water as hot as she could stand it. A quick dunk under the faucet rinsed most of the night terrors away. She blindly felt for her towel on the wall. Dried. Stood up straight and punched her reflection in the face. Crack. The woman in the mirror was familiar except for the glass fractures—same eyes colored like sparkling ocean, same pale skin—but where Promise's hair was short, the reflection's was long. Where Promise was angles the woman in the mirror had curves. She was old enough to be Promise's mother.

"Warn me next time." Promise forced herself to breathe.

"Sorry, munchkin. I came as fast as I could." Sandra Paen was dressed in a silk robe with a low neckline. An ornate tail curled over her shoulders, and coiled around her heart. Promise drew a circle around her breast, mimicking the coil of the dragon's tail in the mirror.

"You remember." Sandra's hand was over her heart.

"How could I forget?" Of course Promise remembered the robe. It was the same one her mother had worn shortly before her death.

The gold band on Sandra's hand caught the overhead light. The band symbolized a bond that was supposedly unbreakable. Life had proven otherwise.

"Look, Mom. Now is not the time. My unit has morning PT. I'm needed out there. I have to go."

"The gunny can handle it." Sandra dared Promise to deny it. Sandra reached out of view and came up with a towel. "You need to talk about the dreams," she said as she dried her hair.

I already have. BUMED cleared me for duty, Promise thought. She didn't feel like discussing this particular matter. Besides, her mother was adept at reading minds. Well, hers anyway.

"That's not what I meant and you know it. You told the psychobabbler what he wanted to hear, not what's really going on inside of you." Sandra hung her towel on her side of the mirror and folded her arms.

Promise glanced at the empty hook on the wall and knew she was going mad.

Sandra cleared her throat. "Correct me if I'm wrong."

I told them enough . . . and I didn't lie. A Marine never lies, but that doesn't mean I have to tell the whole truth either. I've got this.

"For how long?" Sandra asked. "We both know you're running on damaged cells. What happens when they fail?"

I'll survive. Promise knew it was a lie. She was as close to lying as she had ever been comfortable with. *It's just a thought. I'm not responsible for every thought that crosses my mind.*

How long could she hold it together? The question was unanswerable. Promise had started seeing visions of her deceased mother shortly after her father's murder, just before she'd enlisted in the Republic of Aligned Worlds Marine Corps. Raiders had hit her birth world, Montana. Her father's pacifism had gotten him killed. She'd been too young, too inexperienced, too far away, and too frightened to help him. She'd tried to outrun the pain ever since. *How's that working out for you, P?* She never knew when her dearly departed mother would appear and read her like a well-worn book, but it was always at the most inconvenient of times.

Look, I need to get in my morning run. If I swear I'll talk with someone will you let it go?

"Yes."

Good. Talk later.

Promise turned away from the mirror and opened a drawer on the opposite wall. She selected a fresh pair of skivvies, and her PT uniform. After dressing, she removed the two polished onyx bars of a first lieutenant from the small box in the corner of the drawer, and pinned one to each side of her collar. When she turned back around she nearly jumped out of her skin.

"I love you, munchkin, you know that, right?"

"Yeah, I know," Promise said aloud. *And you know I hate being called that. I'm tired of telling you because it never makes any difference.* She heard her mother's laughter echoing in her mind, and then Sandra was gone. Promise couldn't help smiling, and she shook her head. "Don't stop laughing" was one of her mother's mantras.

Promise took a deep breath and told herself that the morning could only get better. *I'm sure some of my Marines talk to their ancestors too. I know some of my boots pray to them. This isn't as weird as it seems. I'm doing fine. Right.* Promise raked her short-cropped hair. A swipe of gloss completed the battlefield makeover. She grabbed a pair of socks and her boots and headed for the door.

Hold's rising sun peeked over the horizon as she stepped outside, inhaled the cool morning air kissed with a hint of rain. She reached over and activated her minicomp, which was strapped to her arm above the biceps, flicked to the next screen, and selected a preprogrammed sequence called "Dawn Up":

One—molded soles for running uneven terrain.
Two—activate Stevie.
Three—send Stevie for the usual: extra-hot caf with cream and sugar, and egg and chorizo roll.

"And turn the music off. I want to hear what I'm running through."

The soles of her boots morphed for light trail running, the sides with extra support for her ankles. Promise set off at a modest pace and looked left, nodding over her shoulder. "Right on time, Stevie. Stay on me." Stevie's humanoid metal carcass dropped back on her six, and settled into a slow hover on a plane of countergrav. It cradled a thermos of extra-hot caf in one hand and a breakfast roll in the other, fresh from the chow hall. Promise's pulse rifle was slung over its back, the muzzle pointed skyward.

In the next seven and a half minutes, Promise covered two klicks to the Saint Sykes training field, over hills, through a light patch of woods, and past Great-Grans's house. The RAW-MC's old lady was actually Lieutenant General Felicia Granby and her house was the RAW's Central Mobilization Command. CENT-MOBCOM wasn't much of a house either, just an unpretentious four-story seated on a foundation of one hundred underground levels. Grans was something of a legend in the Corps. She was pushing eighty and hadn't deployed in over a decade but still rated expert with heavy weps, and she held the record for most orbital insertions by a RAW-MC officer. Two hundred sixty-eight . . . and counting. Grans was lethal in a mechsuit. Out of mech she owned a near-vertical side kick and twelve grandchildren who didn't mess around. Eleven were Fleet Forces: eight Marines and three Sailors. The twelfth was the black sheep in the family. Johnny. He'd become a man of the cloth and was now a bishop in the Episcopal Church. The general's scarred hands had molded the RAW-MC over the last two decades, and more than one boot had assumed the position and taken a wallop in the ass from Lieutenant General Felicia Granby.

Promise sighted the open window in the upper story's northwest corner—Great-Grans's office—and Grans's personal ANDES standing watch below it. Only the truly brave approached the stoic sentinel and made a bet with Great-Grans. Promise slowed to a jog and fast-walked to the ANDES. She raised her sunglasses so the mech could scan her eyes. "Morning, Lieutenant Paen," said the ANDES in a perfect imitation of Great-Grans, grizzled voice and all. "Want to play Great-Grans says?"

"I'm game," replied Promise. Grans liked challenges and she liked to hand them out too. If you volunteered to play, Grans came to you on her terms, and it might be tomorrow and it might be a month from now. The record was five years.

"Grans will comm you at her convenience," the ANDES said.

Right. "Thank you, ma'am," Promise said, and pulled down her shades. "I'm off to the range."

As Promise took off, a gravelly voice boomed from the heavens. "Ooh-rah, girly—send one downrange for me." Promise almost ran off the path and into a patch of basil thornwood. Grans herself had been listening.

Promise arrived at the earthen track feeling at ease, limber, ready to face her Marines. The hulking girth of Gunnery Sergeant Tomas Ramuel crested the hill a moment later. Victor Company was struggling to keep up with the veteran senior noncommissioned officer. And, Promise noticed at once, the gunny looked pissed. *Uh-oh.*

Ramuel and Victor Company jogged past Promise and circled the field. Her Marines were dressed in PT uniforms with pulse rifles cradled in their arms. All except one. Private Atumbi had forgotten his, again.

Promise's eyes narrowed and zoomed on the Marine's face. "Figures." *Why can't he remember his wep?*

As Victor Company circled back to Promise's position, the gunny called out his first preparatory command. "Company, double time, march!" The company dropped out of a steady run and into step with the gunny, at a slight jog. A squat Marine fell out of formation and promptly threw up.

Private Race Atumbi was admiring Private First Class Jupiter Cervantes's backside when the gunny's order came, and his reaction time was far too slow to avoid a collision with her. When the company slowed, Atumbi plowed through Cervantes and burst through a platoon of Marines, sending every one of them to the deck.

Cervantes ended up on top of Atumbi. "Don't get any ideas," she said as she backhanded him across the mouth.

"Hey, *chica!* What was that for?"

"For your wandering *ojos.* Keep your eyes on target and off of me."

Cervantes stood first, and then offered a grudging hand to Atumbi. Her grip was like a vise, and she kept squeezing until he cried out. "What was *that* for?" he said, rubbing his hand, which now hurt worse than his throbbing jawline.

"So you don't forget." Cervantes looked pleased with herself as she shoved Atumbi forward. He fell in beside the Marines he'd just knocked down, and Cervantes joined him on his right.

"Where did you get a grip like that?" Atumbi asked as they jogged.

"Bion-*ics,*" she said, and held up her right hand. "I don't regen. I lost the original in a training *accidente.*"

Atumbi took a closer look at the skin's color. It was slightly off but pretty good for synthetics.

Colorful metaphors and insults erupted all around Atumbi as he found his place in formation.

"You fool. The gunny's gonna make us frog-jump around the field."

"Hey, Atumbi, you make me believe in reincarnation. No one gets so stupid in one lifetime."

His one-word nickname earned in boot camp—a solitary, cold dismissal—rolled off the lips of the woman who'd caught his eye. "Trip."

He brushed each aside with the dirt on his PT uniform. Jupiter's next words knifed the deepest. Cervantes eviscerated his manhood, shot through two magazines without so much as reloading. *"Tirar de su cabeza fuera de su asteroide."* His Spanish was north of rusty, but he caught the gist. Because they'd come from her they cut him to the core.

Atumbi's stomach sank when he realized the gunny had turned around and was marching backward with his eyes on him. They weren't quite smoldering. Then Ramuel did an about-face and started singing "The Old Lady."

Here we go again, Atumbi thought.

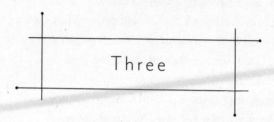

Three

Gunnery Sergeant Tomas Ramuel ran astride Victor Company in a sweat-stained shirt and shorts, his pulse lightly elevated. He'd just finished chanting, "Gimme some, gimme some. PT! PT! Good for you and good for me!" It was a legendary cadence in the storied history of the RAW-MC. In fact, the United States Marine Corps from the wet-Navy days, back eight hundred years ago, had sung the cadence too. This reminded Ramuel of the one about Ho Chi Minh and something about crabs and the seven-year itch. He couldn't remember it all or place the time period it was from, but he was pretty sure that this guy—HCM—had been a real SOB.

From the corner of his eye Ramuel saw a Marine fall out of formation and throw up, which made him smile. Looking over his shoulder, he found two stragglers about a quarter klick behind the rest of the pack. *Good,* he thought. *Still there. Still toughing it out. Still loving the suck. Good, girls and boys.* He grunted in satisfaction as he turned around and pounded over the next few meters of caked earth.

Ramuel clicked his tongue as he ticked through his repertoire, until he came to a personal favorite. *"The Old Lady." Oh yeah.* Ramuel cleared his throat. "Hmm . . . la, la, la." His deep baritone voice bellowed out the first verse. A collective groan rose from Victor Company, and then Victor Company echoed the response, a bit less enthusiastically and a bit more off-key. Back and forth it went, first the gunny and then the unit.

I saw an old lady humping down the street.
I saw an old lady humping down the street.
She wore a gravchute pack and mechboots on her feet.
She wore a gravchute pack and mechboots on her feet.
I said, Hey, Old Lady, where you going to?
I said, Hey, Old Lady, where you going to?
She said, I'm going to the RAW-MC Atmo School.
She said, I'm going to the RAW-MC Atmo School.
I said, Hey, Old Lady, I think you're too old.
I said, Hey, Old Lady, I think you're too old.
You'd better leave drops to the young and the bold.
You'd better leave drops to the young and the bold.
She said, Listen, Private Atumbi, I'm talking to you.
She said, Listen, Private Atumbi, I'm talking to you.
I'm a trainer at the RAW-MC Atmo School.
I'm a trainer at the RAW-MC Atmo School.

As the cadence ended, Ramuel barked out, "Company, forward, march!"

Victor Company eased into a brisk walk about fifty meters from Promise's position, all eyes staring past her. To his credit, the aforementioned Private Atumbi was in sync with the rest of company, mostly, but on the wrong foot.

The right flank overtook Promise, and the gunny called out, "Company, halt!" Ramuel's voice soared upward on "Pythons, right, face!"

Promise looked to her left, at Gunnery Sergeant Tomas Ramuel, her de facto second-in-command, and saw a plume of steam rising from between his ears. Ramuel was either overheated or pissed off. Promise was almost positive it was the latter of the two. After the gunny's "Order arms!" every Marine was supposed to shift his or her rifle to the right side, with the butt of the rifle resting on the ground. Promise counted three boots with their barrels scraping the deck instead of pointed skyward. Then there was Atumbi, who didn't have a rifle at all.

"Marines need feet to pound ferrocrete." Promise's voice carried over the field. "The gunny said order arms, not shoot the jane or jack beside you in the boot. Get it fixed. Now!"

Promise schooled her face to unreadable and began to walk the line. She stopped when she was standing in front of Private Atumbi's row. Promise motioned for Atumbi to step out of line. But Atumbi's eyes were locked on the aft compartment of the Marine in front of him, Private First Class Cervantes, and Atumbi had a dumb expression plastered on his face, and empty hands instead of a properly righted pulse rifle.

Promise cleared her throat to get his attention. "Private, I believe you're missing something."

Atumbi still wasn't paying attention.

This is going to be fun, Promise thought. She cast the gunny a look. *Shall we?*

The gunny nodded back. Yelled, "Atumbi! When the lieutenant speaks, the obligatory response is to listen. When the lieutenant speaks to *you* the obligatory response is 'Yes, ma'am.' When the lieutenant points out your mistake the obligatory response is 'I'm sorry, ma'am. I screwed the pooch, by the numbers, ma'am!'"

Now the private was looking unnaturally pale, which was odd for a man with skin as black as cinders.

Private First Class Cervantes matched eyes with Promise and muttered under her breath. "You need to listen better." Then she looked over her shoulder and shifted her weight slightly. Atumbi's head suddenly disappeared behind Cervantes's smaller frame. When he came up for air, his face was pained and his shoulders were hunched forward.

Promise scowled at Cervantes and raised a finger. Mouthed, *That's one.* Then she caught the gunny's eyes. "Hmmm . . . one of my Marines is not like the other. Gunny, I believe Private Atumbi forgot something important."

"We left before sunrise, ma'am. I should have double-checked."

Cervantes opened her big mouth. *"Estúpido imbécil—"*

"Enough, Jupiter!" Promise glared at Cervantes and raised another finger. *That's two.*

The gunny piped up, growled really. "Cervantes, you don't want to get to *three.* Shut your mouth or Atumbi's fate will be your own."

"Thank you, Gunny," Promise said, the full weight of her gaze on Cervantes, who was now looking quite pale too. "All of you. Keep your traps shut." The words edged out as sharp as a force blade. "I'll worry about Atumbi. You worry about you. Clear?"

Every boot in Victor Company looked dead ahead. Not a single jane or jack dared speak up and earn three klicks for the trying.

Cervantes nodded and broke contact.

Good, Promise thought, and then back to face Atumbi. *Now to fix this mess of a Marine.* Atumbi was coated in sweat and dirt and trying very hard not to cry. "Private, you've been in the RAW-MC for what, six months now? Let's start with something easy. Please repeat the Third Directive."

Atumbi groaned out a response. "Ma'am, ah, yes, ma'am. The Third Directive says . . . that . . . uh . . ."

Promise cocked her head; spoke just loud enough for her entire command to hear. " 'I don't know, ma'am' is a very good place to start . . . Private."

"Yes, ma'am." A tear rolled down Atumbi's face. "I don't . . . I don't know, ma'am."

"Lance Corporal Van Peek, the Third Directive if you please."

Nathaniel Van Peek's cobalt eyes and runway nose met her gaze, and he nodded. Van Peek was one of the few surviving members of her original command, and one of her heavy-weapons experts. One of her Montanan Marines. Promise approved of the sideburns and trimmed mustache, both new additions to his otherwise baby-faced appearance. They'd aged the young NCO by several years, clearly distinguishing him from the average green-as-get-you-killed privates.

"Yes, ma'am. The Third states, and I quote, 'A Marine must keep his rifle with him at all times. Failure to do so will result in immediate disciplinary action at the commanding officer's discretion.' Ma'am."

Promise nodded and looked from Van Peek to Atumbi. "So, Private, what happened to your rifle?"

Private Atumbi's eyes imploded. "I . . . I left my gun back in the barracks, Lieutenant."

Really. Promise smiled. "You left your *gun* in the barracks." She cocked her brow, planted her free hand on her hip, and raised a fist to her mouth like she needed to cough. Did so twice. She took the time to compose her thoughts, until she was sure every trace of amusement was wiped from her face.

"You left your *gun* back in the barracks? Did all you Pythons hear that? Private Atumbi left his *gun* behind, back in the barracks."

"That's because this *chica bonita* took it from him."

Promise snorted and raised two fingers, and cocked a third for good measure. "Shut your askhole, Jupiter, or this *chica* will have you running laps around the field for the rest of the morning."

Promise heard muffled chuckles and hushed swearing, but decided to let the small break in discipline go.

"Lance Corporal Van Peek, where's your gun?"

"Hanging on my lifeline, right where the *Maker* put it, ma'am. I get that right?"

Promise dipped her head toward the lance corporal. It was always the Maker, and never God, so said her father anyway, and a lot of Montanans too. As for getting the location right, well, if a jack didn't know where his gun was located he had bigger problems to deal with than the ire of his commanding officer.

Promise shot a sideways glance at Private Atumbi. The young boot would soon enough recognize the slight twinkle in her eye, assuming he didn't get himself shot first, either by the enemy or by a firing squad . . . for jar-headed stupidity.

"Private Screech Ashburn, where's your gun?"

Ashburn flexed his square jaw and his eyes dropped like stars. "Where it was this morning, ma'am, mounted to my front bulkhead."

Time to wrap this up, P, or the entire conversation is going to get away from you, Promise thought to herself. Before she could say more, Cervantes cleared her throat hard, making her intentions plain as the business end of a pulse rifle.

Promise sighed and closed her eyes. "All right, Jupiter, where's *your* gun?"

"What? Jupiter's got a gun?" came from one of the rank and file near the back of the formation. Promise rolled her eyes, immediately regretting that she'd asked in the first place. She wondered if she was encouraging lax discipline. Well, she'd lay that to rest in a mike or two.

Cervantes shook her pear-shaped hips before returning to attention. "Plumbing's a bit different, *Teniente*. I keep mine *alta y estrecha*—high and tight, ma'am."

"Just like a lady." Promise glanced down at Cervantes's rifle. "Hand your wep to Atumbi. He's going to borrow it and then return it to you later today in pristine condition."

Cervantes froze. Promise could see the stubborn mule in her posture and fire in her eyes. She didn't so much as raise her voice when she said, "Thank you, Jupiter."

Cervantes ground her jaw and did as she was told.

"Company dismissed." Promise took a deep breath and walked over to her Mule. She took the mug and breakfast roll from Stevie's clawed hands with anticipation. The first sip nearly burned her tongue. "Mm, cream and sugar are just right, Stevie. Thank you. Better pour a cup for the gunny too. After that run he's going to need it."

Gunnery Sergeant Ramuel rounded on Atumbi as soon as he heard the lieutenant say "dismissed." He drew his finger and stabbed Atumbi in the chest. "Not you. Ten-hut! Feet together. Eyes off the deck. Chin up. You're a disgrace to the company and the Corps. You are letting the lieutenant down. You are letting your sisters and brothers down. You are letting your platoon sergeant and your toon down. You are letting *me* down." Ramuel's neck was a red, splotchy mess. "And what's worse, you are letting *yourself* down. What am I going to do with you, Private?"

The sun peeked through the cloud cover, bathing Ramuel's face in light. His scowl thawed and his lip curled upward with a delicious thought. Ramuel threw a questioning look at Promise. "Ma'am, with your permission."

Promise waved him on as she took another bite of her chorizo roll. "Do whatever you think is best, Gunny. I'll watch."

"Son, someday you'll forgive me for this," Ramuel said. "You might even thank me for it. Now, strip."

Atumbi looked left and then right, then at the lieutenant, who simply nodded back at him.

"Better listen the first time, Private, or it *will* get worse. That's a guarantee. Here, I won't look." Promise turned around and took another bite. "This is really good."

Atumbi looked horrified. "Gunnery Sergeant?"

"Now! Son, down to skin. You have twenty seconds to comply. Trust me, you don't want to find out what happens when I hit zero. Twenty, nineteen, eighteen . . ."

"Chrono's ticking," Promise said over her shoulder with a mouth full of egg and spiced sausage. She washed it down with a sip of oh-so-good caf.

They were the quickest twenty seconds of Atumbi's life, followed by the longest hour of PT in the 'verse. For a full sixty mikes, Private Race Atumbi ran around the perimeter of the Saint Sykes training field, his rifle held high and his gun held low, chanting at the top of his lungs:

"*This* is my rifle.
This is my gun.
This is for offing targets.
This is for fun."

After Victor Company dispersed, Promise waved the gunny over and offered him a cup of hot caf.

"Chit for your thoughts, Tomas. Here, it's just the way you like it."

Ramuel took an angry sip. "Ma'am, I apologize. What you witnessed was disgraceful. We are barely what I would call a company. We will work double-time to shore up our deficiencies. I take personal responsibility for—"

Promise raised her mug of caf to cut him off. "Tomas, I know. Relax and drink yours while it's hot. A lot of our privates and PFCs were rushed through boot camp and the School of Infantry. BUPERS's decision to cut weeks from both schools is coming back to bite us in the tail. What do they expect us to do? Teach them to shoot properly, at distance, after we deploy?"

"They need more time, ma'am," the gunny said after gingerly sipping his caf. "Even a few weeks could make a huge difference. I've paired each greenhorn with a veteran and ordered extra range sessions. I'm seeing improvement, but they shouldn't have been sent to the fleet in such a poor state of readiness to begin with. They don't all deserve the title of Marine. Not yet." Ramuel scowled. "This isn't the Corps I came up in."

"This isn't the Corps of five years ago, Tomas. Did you hear about Vermont?"

"Yeah, I nearly punched a wall," Ramuel said. "Five hundred Marines, dead and gone. How did a hovtruck laden with micronite get through the gate at Fort Clark?"

Fort Clark was on the northern continent of the planet Vermont, about seventy klicks from the planet's capital. The Fifty-First Regiment called Vermont home; almost five thousand Marines, with supporting LAC wings, and a full task force of battleships and battlecruisers in orbit, and that didn't count Vermont's militia and system defense forces. Vermont had joined the RAW seven years ago and the vote for incorporation hadn't been close. Over two billion souls. Seventy percent of Vermont's population had turned out, and sixty-four percent had checked yes. A sizable minority had said no and some had picked up arms to make their point clear.

"The preliminary report looks pretty damning," Promise said. "The Marines at the main gate didn't do a thorough inspection of the vehicle. The driver's I-dent was forged. The truck floated up to the south barracks and detonated its payload shortly after midnight when everyone was asleep. It was a massacre."

Promise saw Atumbi rounding the far side of the running track. "We're trying to mass-produce Marines, be too many places at once, garrison planets when we're designed to fight small wars. Don't blame yourself, Tomas. Do what you can. Keep them training. Keep the pressure on and look for reasons to reward them. They need us covering their six even as we kick theirs."

"Yeah, I know you're right, ma'am. But I don't have to like it."

"Nope. But you have to love the suck." Promise punched him lightly in the shoulder. "I'm visiting *Kearsarge* at the end of the week, and then reporting to the colonel. I'll take the matter to him personally and see if I can buy us some time, okay?"

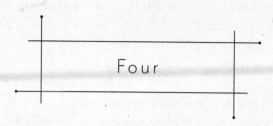

Four

Lieutenant Colonel Price Halvorsen, commanding officer of Charlie Battalion, Fifth Brigade, Twelfth Regiment, stood at ease in his cabin, aboard the Republican Naval Ship *Nitro,* and surveyed the warships of Battlecruiser Squadron Six through the screen on the bulkhead. Halvorsen's deep blue eyes focused on the nearest battlecruiser moored in space, the RNS *Phoenix.* At two-times magnification, it easily fit into the space between his massive thumb and forefinger. The *Phoenix*'s twin, the *Chou-Roon,* was out twice that distance, and looked more to the colonel like a faint star than an Osiris-class heavy BC—the pride of the fleet and, as it happened, that of BATRON-6 too. Massing 152,000 tons, and with a beam length of 553 meters, Osiris-class battlecruisers were nearly twenty percent larger than their older Mandrake-class cousins, with almost half again the throw weight in missile tubes. And BATRON-6 was fortunate enough to have two of them among its six total elements.

Halvorsen's gaze drifted upward, past Hold's partially eclipsed and heavily cratered moon, to a patch of space occupied by two aging Mandrake BCs: *Kearsarge* and *Rio Grande. Kearsarge* was the closer of the two warships. He placed his palm against the simulated viewport, which winked to life and confirmed his identity. He drew a perimeter around the small warship and spread his hands until the *Kearsarge* nearly filled his screen. To an untrained eye, *Kearsarge* looked like just another warship. In the colonel's estimation, the vessel had outserved its usefulness, particularly when measured against an Osiris. Fewer docking lights roughed out the vessel's hull. Only three bays meant fewer LACs to ferry his Marines around, and fewer lifeboats to evacuate the hundreds of souls aboard her should the worst happen. Halvorsen shuddered at the thought.

RNS *Izumo* was the sixth and final element of BATRON-6. The newly retrofitted Mandrake BC was on its shakedown cruise out beyond the Kuiper belt and not due to report in for another week.

At that particular moment, Halvorsen's astrophobia decided to make itself known. The colonel began to pick at the seam of his regular-dress navy-blue trousers. He forced himself to stare into the void several minutes more, though every fiber in his body longed to turn the screen off and turn on every light in his cabin. Being aboard ship, out in the drink, confused his internal compass, and on occasion made him nauseous. He'd settled on a small admission of weakness by leaving his desk light on when he slept. That and he'd seen the ship's doctor, who'd prescribed astrophobia patches, or "A-patches," to help him get his deck feet while in space. To his knowledge, none of his officers knew about it, not even the first sergeant, and Halvorsen planned to keep it that way. He made a mental note to slap on a fresh A-patch before he left his cabin. Seeing the aging Mandrake battlecruiser out there reminded him that man had tamed space with metal, that a warship's many fail-safes made interstellar travel nearly as safe as landlocked living.

Too bad our elected officials didn't give us the hulls we needed.

The Senate Uniformed Services Committee had approved the Osiris-class battlecruiser to replace the Mandrake. The appropriations bill had gone to the Senate floor only to be amended and sent down to the House of Planets, and then cut in half by a hastily formed coalition of Socialist Reformers and Neo-Isolationists. The end result was typical. The Navy got left with one-third of its requested warships, and a half-kept promise to modernize and extend the life expectancy of the aging Mandrake BCs.

Halvorsen grunted. *That was some son-of-a-broken-promise. The Mandrake is a good ship, though, tough, a real scrapper.* A thin smile crossed his face, and then worked its way up to his eyes. *She's not pretty—that's for sure—but she's got some pleasant surprises under her skirt. System-jumps hard too, like my alpha unit on my homecoming night after a long dip in the pond. If you treat a Mandrake BC right, and warm her up proper, she'll get you to your next waypoint in one piece, and boot you out the airlock with your seabag and a smile.*

A two-tone sounded in the colonel's mastoid implant, at the same time that a tiny vessel emerged from the bowels of the *Kearsarge*.

"Yes."

A pleasant, confident-sounding soprano replied. Halvorsen heard the wry humor in her voice. "Colonel, she's launching now. ETA—seventeen mikes."

"Perfect timing, First Sergeant. I'm watching Lieutenant Paen's LAC as we speak."

"Understood, sir. The holotank is queued and the caf is hot."

"Excellent, Samantha. I'll be up in ten."

Halvorsen chewed his lip as he mentally reviewed his agenda for today's meeting with Charlie Battalion's company commanders. Charlie BAT hadn't operated at the battalion echelon for the past two standard years, largely because of the manpower shortages being felt across the Republic of Aligned Worlds. Too many member worlds kept demanding stronger system pickets and Marine contingents to defend them. The protectorates and countless allies kept screaming about the ever-present threat of piracy and homegrown terrorists. The RAW's chief rival in this part of the 'verse, the Lusitanian Empire or LE, kept provoking the Republic while carefully avoiding all-out war. The Corps had done its best to cope by spreading its assets across the 'verse.

We need more time, he thought. *Charlie Battalion isn't ready.*

His company commanders sorted neatly into the "knowns" and "unknowns." He had high confidence in three of them. Captain Lili Chen and Captain Ffyn Spears were veterans and good friends. Spears had commanded Victor Company before getting seriously wounded on Montana. First Lieutenant Nia Massillon was a newly promoted company CO, and she'd reported for duty with glowing letters of recommendation from several officers he'd personally served with, women and men he would gladly entrust his life to. Then there was Victor Company, which was a virgin-green mess. The company's overall lack of experience didn't overly concern him. All boots had to start somewhere. But Victor Company's CO troubled him deeply. She was a highly decorated maverick who'd blazed in-system to her last post, won her battlefield commission with questionable heroics, and nearly gotten her first command obliterated. Scuttlebutt said First Lieutenant Promise T. Paen was an unbalanced, unbridled, good-as-get-you-killed mustang, and he wanted nothing to do with her.

Yeah, but BUMED green-lit her for active duty. That counts for something . . . even though she deployed with forty wolves and returned with over thirty in body bags. She must have a high-and-mighty rabbi somewhere in the hallowed halls of BUPERS. That or we're desperate for boots.

Lieutenant Paen was the colonel's only "known unknown." Paen had deployed to the planet Montana as a platoon sergeant in Victor Company. She was field-promoted when her captain was killed and Lieutenant Spears—now Captain Spears—was wounded in a confrontation with a mess of pirates. After that, Paen had squared off with a Lusitanian commodore named Samuelson, a light task force of Imperial cruisers, and a full-strength battalion of Imperial shock troops over Montana's pile of sand. On paper the Lusies should have won and Paen should have surrendered instead of fight it out. Instead, Lieutenant Paen had bled and bluffed her way to a truce at the expense of her command. She'd nearly gotten every one of her Marines killed.

And now I get to meet the infamous Lieutenant Promise Paen. Perfect.

The colonel hit the head and doused icy water on his face. He pushed up the sleeve of his blouse, changed his A-patch, and righted his trousers. His short-waist jacket fit squarely across his broad shoulders. Out of habit he spun the onyx star cluster on his dog collar, which shone brightly against the backdrop of his white blouse and navy-blue regular-dress uniform. He buttoned his jacket and tucked his beret under his arm. Satisfied, he left his cabin, turned toward the bow of the vessel, and walked ten meters to the lift marked LD3-SSC, which promptly welcomed him. "Main deck."

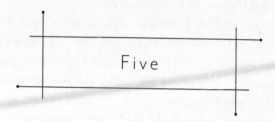

Five

APRIL 19TH, 92 A.E., STANDARD CALENDAR, 1016 HOURS
REPUBLIC OF ALIGNED WORLDS PLANETARY CAPITAL—HOLD
RNS *NITRO*, PARKING ORBIT WHISKEY-ECHO 6

First Sergeant Samantha Fuji, the senior noncommissioned officer in Charlie Battalion and Lieutenant Colonel Halvorsen's command advisor, was waiting outside the lift's bulkhead door. When it opened, Fuji's delicate brows knitted together as she read the colonel's expression. The colonel strode across the threshold and onto the deck, and Fuji fell in on his six o'clock, a half pace behind him. Fuji's rank insignia rode both shoulders proudly: three inverted gold Vs up top and three below, set against khaki flash. Her stripes arched left to right in metronome precision as she matched the colonel's much longer stride.

"You're looking . . . determined, Colonel."

Halvorsen looked over his shoulder and grunted. "Is it that obvious?"

"I've known you long enough to tell when something is bothering you, sir."

"I suppose that's why I keep you around, First Sergeant."

Fuji snorted. "Well, sir, someone has to look out for your best interests. May I ask the colonel who managed to piss him off this time?"

Strips of recessed lighting lit the gunmetal-gray passageways of the *Nitro*. Every ten meters they encountered a seam in the bulkhead wall, where a door could close to seal off a section of the vessel from a fire or hazardous chemical leak, or to lock down the ship to thwart a boarding maneuver, or to isolate a hull breach should the *Nitro* suffer a loss of atmosphere. Navy ratings and officers ducked in and out of bulkhead doors and paid respect as the colonel and the first sergeant passed.

On Republican warships, passageways running stem-to-stern posted white double-lined arrows along the bulkhead walls, at eye level. The arrows always pointed forward, toward the bow of the vessel. Passageways running starboard-to-port posted blue arrows, which pointed outboard, toward the vessel's hull. All of which ensured that only a civilian could get lost on a warship, or a "delta-sierra" seaman who wasn't squared away.

The deck plating clanked underfoot as they walked, Fuji taking nearly two steps for every one of Halvorsen's. The colonel hesitated as they came to a fork in the passageway, allowing the first sergeant to take point.

Fuji followed a blue arrow to starboard. "This way, sir."

A warship's decks bore clear, pedestrian labels, which suited Halvorsen's "kilo-india-sierra-sierra" attitude perfectly. The command deck was always the "main deck," and the main deck was always situated at the core of the vessel, with upper and lower decks labeled accordingly—UD1 or LD1, for instance. Warship nomenclature sectioned vessels into roughly three parts, A to C, forward to aft, with a starboard "S" or port "P" qualifier. Larger vessels went up to D and E sections, and sometimes F. He'd gotten on the lift from Lower Deck 3–Starboard Section C (LD3-SSC) and met the first sergeant on the Main Deck–Starboard Section C (MD-SSC).

At periodic intervals, the colonel looked up at the arrows near the seam between the overhead and the bulkhead to gather his bearings. Three turns later they were near the holotank, far away from the ship's all-Marine compartments and deep into "squid" territory. He realized, much to his own consternation, that the first sergeant hadn't looked up at the arrows once. He wasn't sure how to get back to his own quarters, and this put him in an even worse mood. The *Nitro* wasn't his post. He was just a passenger on the Navy vessel, being ferried to his next duty station. That's what Marines did: Marines Always Ride in Navy Equipment. He didn't need to know the bowels of the ship like his own backside. The passageways were well marked anyway. So what if an astro-patch was riding his port side? None of it set him at ease. As they passed from Section C into B, he slowed without thinking.

First Sergeant Fuji came to an all-stop, turned around, and cocked her head upward. At 163 centimeters, the first sergeant was on the shorter side of average for a female Marine. Fuji's oval eyes twinkled as they met her superior officer's gaze.

"A certain lieutenant on your mind, sir?"

The colonel crossed his arms and sighed. "Well?"

"Her jacket is . . . interesting."

"And?"

First Sergeant Fuji waited for a young rating to pass, and then she stalled for time. It wasn't uncommon for the battalion commander to ask his "first shirt" what she thought about a Marine under his command, particularly when said Marine was just reporting in for duty. In another Marine Corps, Fuji would have held the rank of sergeant major. But the RAW-MC preferred small unit sizes, and smaller units had pushed the chain of command downward. That meant first sergeants in a very real sense ruled the roost at the battalion echelon.

Fuji clearly sensed there was more behind the colonel's question than a cursory inspection might reveal, and that made her weary. In fact, she feared the colonel harbored significant doubts about his new company commander. Perhaps Lieutenant Paen's upcoming one-on-one with the colonel was actually a come-to-Jesus meeting. If so, she pitied the lieutenant for it. Regardless, this wasn't Fuji's maiden jump across the 'verse. Commenting on a *superior,* however young and inexperienced she might be, well, *that* wasn't done lightly, not even by a first sergeant. Particularly not to a disgruntled light colonel with friends on the RAW-MC's selection board for the rank of captain.

Fuji folded her hands behind her back and decided to humor the colonel. "Would you care to clarify what you're after, sir?"

"What happened to your ability to read my mind?" Fuji shrugged. "Okay, fine, what's your frank assessment of her?"

Fuji stalled again. "Have you spoken with Gunnery Sergeant Khaine?"

Halvorsen grunted, not at all pleased. He knew exactly where Fuji was going with her question, and he didn't like it at all. Not one bit.

Nhorman Khaine served in the billet of the battalion gunnery sergeant, or the "battalion gunny." Khaine directly reported to First Sergeant Fuji. Fuji was in many ways Halvorsen's right hand. Likewise, Khaine was hers.

The battalion gunny was an enigma in other military traditions. In fact, the RAW-MC was the only Marine Corps in the 'verse with that billet, the only Corps to field companies of forty mechanized Marines, the only Corps with gunnery sergeants serving as senior enlisted noncoms at the company echelon.

Battalion gunnies like Khaine functioned as a intermediaries between a battalion's gunnery sergeants and the battalion first sergeant. If there was a problem with morale in one of Halvorsen's companies, or a serious disciplinary issue to be addressed, or any number of other issues that might arise in the day-to-day operations of a battalion of Marines, Khaine would likely hear about it long before he did. And Khaine could always play the part of the "good gunny," allowing Fuji to be the heavy when the situation warranted it.

Halvorsen smiled grudgingly. "I'm still thinking, Samantha."

"Understood, sir." Fuji did her best not to smile back at her commanding officer.

Halvorsen knew that Gunnery Sergeant Khaine knew more about Lieutenant Paen than probably anyone else in the battalion. Khaine had actually served with her when she was a mere corporal in his platoon. That was Samantha's real point, after all.

Still, Samantha has a valid point. Khaine saw her in combat, he admitted. *That counts for something. It still doesn't mean she's fit to lead a company of my Marines.*

"No. I haven't spoken with the gunny," he said with a hard edge to his voice. "And I don't intend to. Any more questions?"

"No, sir." Fuji stood to her full height. She wiped every trace of emotion from her face and met the colonel's eyes without hesitation. She stared just long enough to make her point too.

"All right, Samantha. I'm putting you in an awkward position and I can see you don't like it."

"Sir, with respect, I'd rather not comment on Lieutenant Paen until I've had a chance to meet with her first and form my own impression."

"I respect that, and normally I'd agree with you. In this case, I'm worried about a potential weak link in my chain of command. There's little time before we deploy. I need to be well out ahead of any . . . personnel difficulties that may arise. It's fine and well to make your own first impressions. I'm sure you realize we don't always get that luxury."

Fuji stiffened. "Of course, sir."

"In that case, I'd value your assessment of her . . . now."

The first sergeant looked away, momentarily lost in thought. "At first glance . . . she's impressive. Dedicated and daring come to mind too." Fuji pitched her next words carefully. "The Silver Star isn't handed out casually, sir."

"Humph. Those aren't the words that come to my mind."

Fuji pursed her lips. "I suppose other words come to mind, depending on your point of view. Her actions on Montana were quite . . . brazen."

"That's one way to put it. Reckless also comes to mind." His eyes narrowed. "I see. So your assessment is . . ."

"Undecided, sir."

"Smart answer, Samantha. I told you there's a reason why I keep you around."

"And I believe I said something about looking out for your best interests, sir. If I may speak boldly, sir, you really need to speak with Gunnery Sergeant Khaine about her, and Captain Spears for that matter. The captain field-promoted Promise to second lieutenant after he was wounded on Montana. The gunny saw her in action. Both men had high praise for their lieutenant."

"*Their* lieutenant?" Halvorsen crossed his arms. "Aren't you just the event horizon calling the gravitational hole black?"

"That's not fair, sir." Fuji scowled respectfully. "The gunny was Promise's platoon sergeant before she made sergeant herself, and he fully endorsed her promotion. He used to be her superior and now he may have to follow *her* orders. His perspective is uniquely valuable. So, I sought it out. Lieutenant Paen went from corporal to first jane in two standard years. That's not a record—particularly with the Corps expanding so rapidly—but it's still fast. All I asked him was how he thought she was holding up under the acceleration."

"And?"

"He said two things. First, she's the real deal. Secondly, I should ask her myself, with respect of course."

Halvorsen grimaced. "Point taken, First Sergeant. I'll do that." He looked down the passageway, and squared his shoulders. "I suppose I better go and meet her?"

"Indeed, sir, you should." The first sergeant kept her feet planted.

The colonel had moved several paces down the passageway before he realized that Fuji hadn't budged. Then he turned around and threw her a questioning look.

"Something *else* on your mind, Samantha?"

"Because you asked, sir, yes."

Halvorsen noted the concern in her eyes.

"There may be more to Lieutenant Paen than either of us realize. I queued up her last fitness report. Frankly, sir, what I heard on the vid impressed me. But, and there is one, she's locked down tight—too tightly I think—like someone who's afraid of losing control. She may need to learn to bend or at some point she might just break. At the moment, sir, that's my best assessment of Lieutenant Paen."

Halvorsen nodded and turned thoughtful. "Anything else, First Sergeant?"

"Because you asked again, sir, yes. Have you seen Victor Company's range scores?"

"Yes, I have. And?"

"They're pathetic. At least two toons of privates and PFCs are scoring subpar." Fuji's eyes filled with disgust. "We're pushing our boots too fast, shortening training times, cutting through fat into bone. The lieutenant's unit isn't ready to deploy. She needs more time."

"You just had to go and remind me of that. I know, Samantha. I've already filed an official complaint. Lieutenant Paen is going to have to make do, just like the rest of us. Ours is not to reason why."

"Ours is but do or die. I know, sir." Fuji looked the colonel squarely in the eye. "That's what I'm really afraid of."

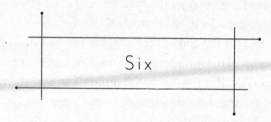

Six

Promise swam the tube between the shuttle and RNS *Nitro*. *Nitro*'s bays were full-up with LACs and support shuttles, which explained why Promise was boarding through *Nitro*'s fore collar instead of stepping off a gangway in one of the battlecruiser's expansive boatbays. Swimming the tube was a mildly disorienting experience that reminded Promise more of falling down a shaft than floating through zero g between two vessels under artificial gravity. A host of emotions flooded her mind as she put out a hand along the inside of the tube and pushed off to make a course correction.

Her newly reconstituted command was barely stitched together, the seams so weak even minor stress might tear Victor Company apart. She had more than her share of janes and jacks fresh out of boot camp and the School of Infantry. And they'd been rushed through. She planned to have words with the colonel about that. No reasonable commanding officer could expect a company full of untried, unblooded soldiers to operate smoothly in toons of five mechanized Marines, or together as a company. Not like a veteran unit could. Unit cohesion was hard-won and earned toon by toon, shoulder-to-shoulder, and hardened by training that either held true or tore apart in the close fight. *But I've got a real problem. V Company is full of green-as-get-you-killed privates and PFCs, some with poor marksmanship scores. I can't call them all riflemen, not yet. And it's not just poor scores, others nearly failed the long-range portion of their final evolution. A few are borderline proficient in mechsuit combat techniques, but they were allowed to graduate anyway instead of being bumped back an evolution for extra training. The Corps may be strapped for boots, but skimping on training like this is going to get a lot of my command killed.*

As Promise neared the end of the tube, she reached up and grabbed the bar marked OVERHEAD, swallowed hard, and swung herself into RNS *Nitro*'s standard gravity. Her timing wasn't quite right, and she nearly toppled forward before getting her feet planted beneath her. The junior officer of the deck was waiting with a datapad.

Her heels came together with an audible clap that echoed across the boatbay. She honored the colors, and then pivoted toward the officer of the deck and snapped a crisp salute.

"Permission to come aboard, ma'am?"

Suspended high above by invisible cables was the flag of the Republic of Aligned Worlds. It depicted the known 'verse spinning on its axis, in the protective embrace of a female seraph, wings unfurled. The feathers were vaguely reminiscent of the billowing sails that had once harnessed the wind to deliver men-of-war to battle. Around the flag's four edges were the names and planets of the charter member worlds of the RAW. Next to and below it hung the Navy's own standard.

"Permission granted," Second Lieutenant Elizabeth Jiles said, returning Promise's salute. Jiles wore navy-green utilities with black piping along the sleeves and trousers, and two gold bars on each collar point. Jiles's rank was equal to that of a Marine Corps first lieutenant, or an O-2, just like Promise. There was a slight twinkle in Jiles's eye. "Lieutenant Paen, welcome aboard the *Nitro*."

"Thank you, Lieutenant." Promise removed her beret and tucked it under her arm. "You run a tight boatbay. That was an extremely fast lock-and-tube."

Jiles's gray eyes brightened visibly. "Thank you, ma'am. We do our best. If you'll follow me." They crossed the flight deck of Boatbay 2 and passed between the lengths of two docked vessels, the nose of a Navy launch on the right and the cockpit of an assault-class light attack craft on the left. Both were battened down and had the look of polished alabaster. Each vessel bore markings stenciled in black and gold on the nose. The assault-class LAC was nearly three times as large as the much smaller transport shuttle and powered by dual fusion plants, a primary and a backup. As they neared the launch's engines, Jiles came to a stop and turned to face her. A gunnery sergeant in RAW-MC navy-blue regular dress, with three gold hash marks above the cuff of each sleeve, stepped out of the shadows and into full view.

Promise's heart nearly stopped when she caught sight of him.

"I believe you know the gunny," Jiles said. "We've been playing cards together for a while. The other day we got to talking about the strain being felt across both our branches. How the Lusies keep pushing our boundaries, like they did on Montana." Jiles gave Promise a telling look. "So, ma'am, I tell the gunny that we need more Marines like that Lieutenant Paen from Montana, the only Marine Corps officer to ever command a Navy warship. Then the gunny says he happens to know her." Jiles cocked an eyebrow. "Turns out he wasn't kidding. When I told him you were on today's arrivals he asked if he could meet you in the boatbay." Jiles saluted once more, and held it for a good second longer than protocol dictated. "It's a real honor, ma'am. I'll be back in five minutes. If you'll excuse me."

Jiles walked behind Gunnery Sergeant Nhorman Khaine and disappeared from view, leaving an expressionless Khaine in her wake. He too saluted, though he exaggerated the upswing and clicked his heels together a bit harder than protocol dictated. Promise responded in stunned silence. The gunny stuck out his hand and grasped hers enthusiastically. Only then did he smile. "Lieutenant Paen, it's so good to see you."

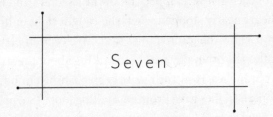

Seven

APRIL 19TH, 92 A.E., STANDARD CALENDAR, 1025 HOURS
REPUBLIC OF ALIGNED WORLDS PLANETARY CAPITAL—HOLD
RNS *NITRO*, PARKING ORBIT WHISKEY-ECHO 6

She didn't see the hug coming or she would have dodged it.

Promise went rigid in Khaine's arms as the space between them emptied out. They'd had a few close calls together when Khaine had been her platoon sergeant, back when she was a lowly stripe. She almost pushed out of Khaine's embrace, too. And then she didn't. Her arms relaxed and her hands found his shoulder blades. She leaned in ever so slightly, her head just under his chin. "You would have been proud of your toon. They fought . . ." Promise's voice grew thick as the memory of Lance Corporal Talon Covington surfaced. Tal smiling, holding his railgun over one shoulder with ease. Covington had been their toon's heavy-weapons expert, and he'd thrown himself on a grenade to save Promise's life.

Khaine patted Promise's back as she shook in his arms. When they pulled apart, reality was a blur of emotion.

"I hope you don't mind the breach in protocol, ma'am." Khaine cleared his throat a couple of times and sniffed a liter of recycled air. "The last time I saw you, *you* were my subordinate. Now just look at you. It only took you what, two years to go from corporal to first jane? Congratulations. I couldn't be more pleased. Took you long enough. How was Officer Candidate School?"

"For the most part, OCS was straightforward and uneventful." It took Promise a moment to look him in the eye. "I enjoyed the history and command theory. Major Jeff Garaund's course on pre-Diaspora wet navies was my favorite." Promise grew thoughtful. "Did you know preindustrial sea powers used to press their sailors into service, often after they were captured from enemy vessels? No Hartford Accords or Terran Conventions or even a basic outline of what we consider commonsense, humane rules of warfare. Talk about barbaric."

I know that smile. He's humoring me. Fine, not everyone's a history buff.

"The PT, on the other hand, left a lot to be desired." The gunny's expression changed immediately, the sort of look that said he knew what coming and was looking forward to the tale. "When I was your corporal, I ran a lot of klicks, uphill and downhill in utilities and boots with a pack strapped on my back, hugging my rifle, every day no matter the weather, and if I wasn't running with my company I was at the range or humping my gear back from it." Promise smiled. "At OCS, we almost ran buck naked—just PT uniforms—covering ground in shallow-treaded 'civvies' better suited for a morning stroll. I went into OCS conditioned. A lot of ninety-day wonders thought fifty push-ups were unreasonable. Seriously! They had a mental block they couldn't see past. I'm embarrassed to say my time for the five-klick actually increased because I spent most of my waking hours in class, drafting reports, drawing up operational plans, and when I wasn't in class my nose was in a book. I loved every minute of it—don't get me wrong. Unfortunately, my muscles paid the price. Seems to me the bars have it a bit too easy."

"That's because us noncoms work for a living."

Promise wagged a finger at him. "A fact I doubt you will ever let me forget, Gunny."

"Not a chance."

Khaine hadn't expected such emotion to come out of him, and he certainly hadn't planned to hug the lieutenant. *What was that about? A substantial breach in protocol is what it was. Thank God we were sandwiched between two craft, in a relatively quiet part of the boatbay.* The gunny thought back to the day Private Paen had reported to him for duty. The smartly pressed uniform that could have stood on its own, and a face like a still lake. Except for the eyes. He'd been pleased for Promise when she'd made private first class, and lance corporal, and then full-screw. Their relationship changed the night he overheard her cries, and found her in her rack in the throes of a nightmare. He almost woke her but stopped himself at the last moment. That battle had been hers to fight. When she finally woke, he'd handed her a drink with a sedative in it, and asked her if she needed to talk. The murder of her father was still fresh. Grit-on-discipline could push pain aside for only so long. She told him she couldn't keep going like this. He assured her that she could.

The first lieutenant standing before him was just as neatly turned out. Smart-looking regular-dress uniform and polished bars. The same calm face, plus a noticeable scar above the left ear. The eyes were still weary. But they'd hardened with confidence.

"Well, Lieutenant, you have a meeting to keep with the colonel. I don't want to make you late."

"Yes, about that, Gunny . . ."

"Ma'am, may I offer you a bit of advice?"

"Always."

Khaine searched her eyes a moment longer before speaking. "Colonel Halvorsen is a straight shooter. He can smell BS from a klick away. He dislikes being aboard ship even more. The colonel does his best to hide that fact. It still affects his mood when he's operating in the drink. Most boots in the company don't have a clue. You're one of his company commanders and that puts you squarely in the need-to-know. Don't ever let on to him that you do know, don't take his foul moods personally, and don't ever make him repeat himself. Understood?"

"Roger that. Thank you, Gunny."

"You may not thank me afterward, ma'am." Khaine took a quick look around the bay before turning back to Promise. "Permission to speak freely?"

Promise raised a weary eyebrow. *I thought you were.* "Okay, granted."

"I'm going to be blunt with you, Promise. Charlie Battalion has heard the scuttlebutt about you, and some took the time to read up on the matter; at least what the Bureau of Public Affairs released to the nets."

"What scuttlebutt?" Try as she might she couldn't keep the edge out of her voice.

"You *are* a ballsy, can-do Marine. And, you did a lot of good on Montana. I couldn't be prouder." The gunny canted his head. "Others resent your success. Their ilk will always be with us. Some believe you're a loose warhead. A glory hound who threw her command against a no-win situation. Only things didn't turn out that way. The naysayers chalk it up to blind luck, which proves what they know."

The gunny's revelation lit Promise like an inferno.

"I remember that look," Khaine said. "Think before you speak, Promise. That's why I wanted to talk with you before you saw the colonel."

Promise did her best to sit on her temper, turned away. Her hands started to shake anyway. *I lost a lot of good people on Montana and nearly got myself killed, more than once, defending my star nation and her people; families and children who had to leave their homes because a megalomaniacal Lusie commodore invaded their homeworld.* "You know I'm not a glory grunt, Gunny."

"Not even close. But, I'm not the one you have to convince."

Her head snapped around, nostrils flaring. "The colonel?"

"Safety that temper, ma'am. It will not serve you well. The colonel is *not* your enemy. He does not resent your past successes or wish to see you fail in the future. He just has reservations. The first sergeant came to me with questions. I told her you have my confidence and suggested she take the matter up with you personally. You may not want to hear this but I'm going to say it anyway. Halvorsen is your CO, and it's his responsibility to figure out what sort of Marine you are. The competent can-do jane I know you to be, or a glory-sponging jackass."

The gunnery sergeant held up his hands. "Easy, ma'am. I said he's still trying to make up his mind. Look at this from his perspective. You took a severely understrength company of mechanized Marines and a few LACs, and fought off a full battalion of the same, plus twice the number of LACs, and a light CRURON of Lusie warships to boot. A lot of bars and stripes think you're some kind of tactical witch."

Promise snorted. "Hardly."

"Careful, it just might stick. I suggest you consider cultivating that image. I'm not telling you to make stuff up." Khaine grew thoughtful. "When the boots under you think you're capable of more, it tends to raise the bar higher for everyone under your command. On the other hand, I've heard rumors too, and if they are even partially true some of the brass think you lost your battlefield perspective . . . and got lucky."

Promise's voice shook as she spoke. "All I did was *my* duty."

"I know. Remember that when you see the colonel. There's Lieutenant Jiles now. She will escort you to the lift."

As Promise turned around, the gunny pitched his voice low, and just above a whisper.

"Promise, don't ever forget who you are. Don't ever let anyone else forget it either."

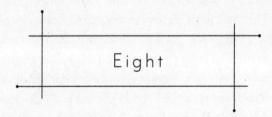

Eight

"Come."

The bulkhead door to the main deck's holotank opened. Promise stepped through it and into a dimly lit expanse. The floor was carpeted and muffled her steps. As the door closed behind her, the darkness pressed in from all directions, and made her feel small. She keyed her minicomp to find the room's schematic and realized her mistake the moment the screen glared to life. *I should have used a red light.* For a moment she couldn't see a thing. *Breathe, P, take it easy.*

Her other senses reached out to compensate, peeling back the black one pitch at a time. Her ears detected the ever-present hum of a warship emanating from the deck and the overhead. Her feet sensed the ever-so-faint tremor reverberating beneath her, no doubt emanating from the warship's massive fusion engines. The air smelled flat and recycled. Slowly her eyes adjusted until she could make out the opposite bulkhead on the far side of the room. She followed its curve to the end of a row of tiered seating. Then the next row down came into focus. The back of the nearest chair sat five meters away. Promise started scanning, row by row, until she was sure the room was empty and she was in the wrong place.

"Over here, Lieutenant," said a hollow, gruff voice. A hand popped up about halfway between her and the floor of the tank. Promise might have missed the wave altogether except for the minicomp on the speaker's wrist, which was lit up like a navigational buoy.

"Center aisle, eight rows down, on the left." Then the hand disappeared.

She found the steps and saw the back of the colonel's head a moment later, then stopped in the aisle and came to attention.

"Sir, Lieutenant Paen, reporting for duty, sir!"

"At ease, Lieutenant." Lieutenant Colonel Halvorsen saluted without rising from his chair, and motioned to the seat one over from his. "Take a seat," he said. "I do some of my best thinking in here. The lights are different, less artificial, and easier on my eyes. I'm told it has something to do with the tank's optics."

The colonel hadn't asked her a question or invited her to comment. And Promise didn't know the man at all. Unsure of how to respond, she took the advice of her dearly departed father. *Keep your trap shut and listen good.*

She had no sooner sat than her chair shifted beneath her; a bit more low-back support. The seat narrowed and the armrests came up. The headrest rose and tilted in until it brushed the nape of her neck. The seat warmer surprised her. She fought the urge to relax and instead forced herself to remain more or less at attention, back rigid, hands folded in her lap.

"Tell me something, Lieutenant. What is the primary duty of a Marine Corps company commander?"

And there it is, she thought. *Direct like an energy wep. The gunny was right—he's trying to make up his mind about me. What would my father have said? Oh, right—bite your tongue young lady, or your words will come back to bite you in the tail.* She drew in a slow, measured breath, just as she'd do if she were on the shooting range. The neutral smell of sanitized oxygen swelled in her lungs. Her nose twitched when she detected the slightest hint of saffron in the air. All at once her senses opened up and reached out for confirmation. *Mom?*

"Present," Sandra Paen said. "I suggest you stay in the present too. Mind the gunny's words and the colonel's. Go on, answer him."

Not funny, Promise thought back. She was a big girl and she could handle matters on her own. She didn't need her hand held. She thought she saw an arm wave from the corner of her eye, same row she was seated in, from the opposite side of the aisle. She looked over and saw nothing there.

"Munchkin, why do you keep asking yourself what your father would have said or done? He's not here anymore."

The voice was now as close as a whisper and there was no mistaking who it belonged to. She really didn't know what to call her talks with Sandra

Paen. Sometimes it was just her voice in Promise's head, knocking around like a stray memory. Other times she could swear her mom was really there, with her in the moment. Was her subconscious merely projecting itself into her daily affairs? Had her dearly departed mother somehow reached out from beyond the veil? Had something inside of her cracked? If she was truly honest with herself, a part of her feared that. Did it really matter? Her mother was right. Dad wasn't here anymore.

Mom, I appreciate it. Really, I do. You've got lousy timing.

"My timing is usually spot-on. But, if you really want me gone, I'll go. Okay?"

Sandra stood up and entered the aisle. She shook her head and then headed up the steps.

Wait!

The colonel cleared his throat. "Lieutenant? How long do you plan on keeping me waiting?"

Great. Promise took a deep breath. *So much for first impressions.*

"Lieutenant?" Now Halvorsen sounded put-out.

"I'm sorry, sir. I'm not one for giving pat answers. As to your question, sir, experience has taught me the primary duty of a company CO is twofold: to protect her command and to accomplish her mission, sir."

"True, and paraphrased from the Regs." The colonel didn't sound impressed. "But that's an oversimplification of battlefield realities. A Marine with your experience should know that by now. Regs are static. War is nothing of the sort. Please elaborate."

Promise heard the sleeves of the colonel's regular-dress jacket crease. She canted her eyes enough to see him rubbing at his face with both hands, hard.

Wonderful.

"That dark place just showed up," Sandra said from the seat next to Promise's, causing her to nearly jump out of hers. "Maybe he's tired, dear. It is after all still early in the hundreds of hours. Why can't you Marines tell time like normal people? What is it? Zero dark forty? You need to get some sleep. The bags under your eyes are growing, dear."

It's thirty, Mom. Zero dark . . . oh, never mind.

"You take my point," Sandra said.

Taken. Please.

"Stop brooding." The voice in her head started to laugh, which pissed her off even more.

"Tell me this, Lieutenant," Halvorsen said after a long pause. "Can you really protect your Marines and complete the op at the same time, all of the time?" The colonel's question sounded genuine enough, without a hint of challenge in it.

He has significant reservations about my ability to command. The gunny was right after all. This is about Montana.

"You're assuming, dear," Sandra Paen said.

No, I'm not. Have you heard anything the man has said? I've only just reported in and he's already upset with me, Promise thought back.

"Easy, kiddo. Maybe he's just getting to know you. He is your new commanding officer, after all."

Promise put a hand to her brow to knead the side of her temple. The three-way conversation was giving her a headache, dredging up bad memories. Memories of Montana, memories of the Marines she'd lost there, memories of her mother's death. *You weren't there to raise me, Mom. Stop trying to do it now.*

Silence. The presence in her head retreated until Promise was fairly certain she was alone.

Mom, MOM. Ah, come on, Mom. I didn't mean . . .

"Lieutenant, I get the feeling you're distracted. Is there some other place you need to be?"

Promise shifted in her seat and nodded. "Yes, sir. I mean, *no,* sir."

This is just wonderful. What did the gunny tell you? Don't make the colonel repeat himself and what did you do, twice?

"Lieutenant."

"Roger that, sir. I mean yes, sir. I'm listening, sir. Just thinking about how best to respond . . ."

"And?"

P, get a grip, P. What is wrong with you?

Promise took the sort of breath she would before pulling the trigger of her sniper rifle, deep and full of more oxygen than she needed, and then she drew in a second and exhaled normally, squeezed the trigger to take up the slack, and fired. "You asked if a CO can simultaneously protect her soldiers while completing the op, all of the time. If I may be so bold, sir, you're essentially asking if the two ever come into conflict. I know some officers who would answer that question in the affirmative. Well, sir, I'm not one of them." Her voice came out with a bit of an edge, and hearing that made her wince.

"Well, thank you for enlightening me, *Lieutenant* Paen. Care to elaborate on that?" Halvorsen kicked his feet above the chair in front of him and folded his arms across his chest.

Promise felt the hairs on her neck stand at attention. She had already mussed the conversation, so she grabbed it by the flight stick and went full-throttle. "Well, sir, a CO must send her Marines into harm's way. That comes with the job. Some come home wounded, and others are carried by sixes. But the orders must still be given. Not giving them would be a dereliction of duty."

The colonel didn't exactly laugh. "So the mission trumps all?"

"On the contrary, sir. Duty requires me to keep faith with the Marines under my command. They expect me to send them out with the orders that give them their best possible chance of completing the mission and coming back alive. To do that I must learn my Marines' strengths and weaknesses; help them utilize the former and overcome the latter. Coming back alive is never promised. Knowing your CO is watching your six should always be a given."

"What about the ones you lose?"

"We bring them ho . . ." Her voice jammed in her throat. She couldn't say that because she tried her best and still failed to make it happen.

"Home," the colonel added for her after a moment. "We always bring them home. *Semper fi*, Lieutenant. Too many don't ever make it back, do they? We've both sent soldiers to die. Tell me, how do you live with that?"

That's right. I sent a lot of Marines to die on Montana. Lost most of my unit in the process. So how did I live with that? She wanted to say as well as anyone could have but the moment she thought that she hesitated. *Oh, I don't know. I talk with my deceased mother about it. Colonel, meet Sandra Paen.* Her anger was getting the best of her. So, she opened her mouth and said exactly what she was thinking.

"Sir, with respect, if you have a question about me please just go ahead and ask it."

"Excuse me, Lieutenant. I thought I just did." The colonel turned his head and his eyes bored into her. "It sounds to me like you're the one who needs to get something off of her chest. You didn't ask to speak freely, but since you already are, please don't stop now."

"I'm sorry, sir." Promise grasped for words. "You're right . . . right to have reservations about me . . . right to ask about the Marines I lost in combat."

The colonel's tongue clicked like he was going to speak. Before he could get out a word Promise cut him off. "Please, sir, please hear me out. How could you not? After Montana, the scuttlebutt flew through the battalion. She's a maverick, out for glory, reckless. A loose tactical warhead. There might be a shred of truth in there, somewhere. I didn't take kindly to a Lusitanian commodore invading my birth world, and I took it personally, sir. How could I not? The Montanans are my people. I did my duty and protected good people who couldn't defend themselves. And I got a lot of my Marines killed in the process. You want to know how I live with my dead, sir. By remembering them. I remember them every day of my life. I see their faces before lights-out. I dream about them. BUMED says to give it time. Well, sir, it's a slow fade. Maybe that's the true burden of command, living with your dead. Frankly, I wouldn't wish it upon anyone."

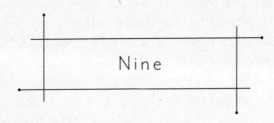

Nine

APRIL 19TH, 92 A.E., STANDARD CALENDAR, 1036 HOURS
REPUBLIC OF ALIGNED WORLDS PLANETARY CAPITAL—HOLD
RNS *NITRO*, PARKING ORBIT WHISKEY-ECHO 6

Price Halvorsen hated to admit when he was wrong. His first impression of Lieutenant Paen had taken an unexpected turn. He'd come to the holotank with his mind made up about her only to find the loose warhead analogy didn't quite fit. She was brash and aggressive, but he found no trace of the overconfidence that usually accompanied that sort of Marine. *Maybe she's just rattled. I tend to do that to my junior officers. And she's been through the grinder.*

"Lieutenant. Let me show you something."

The colonel typed several commands into his minicomp. A moment later a solar system sprang to life about two meters above the holotank's deck. A sun appeared and then one by one nine planets materialized in different orbital planes. "This is the Korazim system. The fourth world from the sun bears the same name." The colonel selected the third planet from the sun, an angry red globe. The name SHEOL appeared in a holographic tab to the planet's right. "This lovely world will be our home away from home for the next six to twelve months." Then the tab disappeared and Sheol swelled until it filled the holotank. A sea of red clouds shrouded the entire planet.

"Sheol is a world very much at odds with herself," Halvorsen said. "Her nickname is Camp Hell-No. Believe me, it fits. Virtually nothing grows there because of the heat and the marginal standard atmospheric conditions. The SAC will make your lungs pay. The water is loaded with toxic concentrations of heavy metals. Masks are not mandatory for short trips outside, though they are highly recommended. Rebreathers are required for runs and ops unless you're suited up. If you see the sun you've seen a rare sight. The days are violent. The nights shake you in your rack. We tried terraforming the planet to the tune of eight trillion chits, all because of this."

The colonel held up a small chunk of indigo rock in his hand, and handed it over to Promise. "Here, see for yourself.

"Sheol is known for two things: its violent tectonic activity and its rare earth ore. The rock in your hand is worth more than I make in a month. At least it was before we found a whole bunch of it on Sheol. It's mined on a number of core worlds and a few verge planets too, in the LE and the RAW, and a few other star nations. It only exists in trace amounts on the other worlds. Thanks to Sheol now we've got a boatload of it."

"What do we plan to do with it?" Promise said. Asking questions was a good way to cool off and she had a lot of anger to bleed.

"Up-armor everything: mechsuits; warships; LACs, you name it." Halvorsen tried to hold off a sneeze.

"Bless you, sir."

"Thanks. It's called Mizienite after the man who discovered it. We're calling it M-steel, and M-steel is nearly as hard as anything we can create in a lab, but it's too brittle in its naturally occurring form. Heat it to its melting point, though, and things get interesting. Slip a bit of carbon into the gaps and you've got yourself a miracle alloy that's thirty percent stronger than peristeel."

"And no one else has much, right, sir?"

"Exactly, which means, in case I need to spell it out for you, we must hold Sheol at all costs. CRURON-18 and BATRON-32 are already in orbit around Sheol, and a level-three orbital platform is partially completed; another three months and it will be fully operational."

That's a lot of firepower, Promise thought. *If Sheol is this important, it doesn't sound like enough.*

"We're relieving Able Battalion from the Seventh. Able has been on post for over fifteen standard months, upgrading Sheol's planetary defenses and installing a comm net throughout the system. With the big find came a host of new problems, which I will explain in a moment. Able's Marines are tired, overworked, and understrength. We are going in to relieve her with a full battalion of mechanized Marines. In a few months, I'm told, we will be brought up to brigade strength. Between you and me, don't count on it. That's why our task force is loaded down with remotely piloted platforms with both surface-to-air and antiarmor capabilities."

"Glorified drones," Promise said with disgust. "RPPs will never replace boots on the ground."

"Agreed," Halvorsen said. "You can't replace a flesh-and-blood Marine." Now he was smiling.

"Ooh-rah."

Promise resisted the urge to reach out and touch the terrestrial planet's outer atmosphere. She inhaled sharply as she and the colonel suddenly plunged through thick layers of clouds and into an ashen, lifeless sky. The rocky surface looked like dried blood.

"Welcome to Hell, Lieutenant." The colonel paused for a long moment. "If there is one, Sheol is as close to it as I hope to come. It rains a lot of acid. The atmosphere corrodes everything. The ground is unstable. In the distance—nine o'clock—is the city of Nexus. Nexus sits on a floating, quake-resistant foundation. Otherwise, it wouldn't be there. The soil may be worthless, but the Mizienite beneath the ground is a verge system's ticket to the stars, which brings me to the domestic terrorists."

"Domestic?"

"Indeed. The Greys are from the planet Korazim. They are system-grown. A lot of them came to Nexus with the guilds, under the pretense of finding work in Nexus or in the mines. Then they started blowing things up. The Greys accuse the Republic of raping Sheol and screwing the Korazim system out of the tax revenues while giving the jobs to out-of-system skilled labor. There might be a hint of truth there."

He went on. "The terrorists call themselves the Grey Walkers—we call them the Greys—and they have virtually brought mining on Sheol to its knees. Korazim is an independent system. With the full backing of the RAW, a number of Republican firms pooled their resources and leased the mining rights to Sheol from the Korazim government for the next thirty years. Our mining corporations are on the planet legally. Fifteen percent of their profits go straight to the system's pockets. We are not screwing anyone. The Greys see themselves as the savior, and the Corporate Congress the villain. As far as the Greys are concerned, any target is fair game."

"Military and civilian," Promise added with disgust.

"Unfortunately, yes. Five weeks ago we lost three crawlers and two mine shafts. Hundreds of miners and civilian contractors died in the last year alone. Able Battalion's wounds are company-sized. There's about a million souls living in Nexus: contractors and research firms, scientists, a couple of university branches, and a host of small businesses and venture-capital firms, plus all the service and support outfits to keep everyone fat and happy. That's a lot of warm bodies to target. That's why we're deploying.

"The Grey Walkers' commander, Walker Greystone, is a fierce guerrilla fighter known for his unorthodox battlefield tactics and megalomaniac ruthlessness. The man was a history teacher in his first life. Mr. Greystone apparently blows his top more frequently than the volcanoes on Sheol do. He's at the top of our most-wanted list and we have orders to shoot him on sight. We've been authorized to use enhanced interrogation techniques on his people: cold; heat; noise; sleep dep; bad music; reduced calories; and the infamous grab-and-hold. If that doesn't make the terrorists cream their skivvies we may up-pressurize select, high-value targets, if the threat risk is deemed critical. There's nothing like a little simulated high-altitude pulmonary edema to induce panic. Between you and me I hope we get the chance to take some Greys sky-high."

Halvorsen paused and turned in his chair to face Promise. "I don't have to tell you how badly the Lusitanians want this planet. Marine Intelligence believes the Lusies are fronting the Greys, and that together they will do almost anything to halt our mining efforts. One way or the other—Greys or Lusies—we are going to take fire."

"I've faced the Lusies before, sir. The thought of facing them again doesn't exactly excite me," Promise said with a tight smile, "but between you and me, sir, I wouldn't mind a few more targets. They nearly put me in the morgue." Promise pointed to the scar above her left ear. She turned in to the light of the holotank to give the colonel a good look.

"Back on Montana, right? An explosion cracked your brain bucket and your skull." The colonel shifted toward her. "So your AI jacks into your brain-box and starts driving *you*." Halvorsen gritted his teeth. "How did it feel to have your AI mucking around in your jelly?"

"It's a total blur, sir. I don't remember a thing."

"Probably best."

"Sir, perhaps now's a good time to bring up a somewhat sensitive matter?"

"You mean because I'm in such a good mood. Well, don't let it fool you. It won't last."

"Then all the more reason, sir."

"Shoot."

"Victor Company isn't ready to deploy, sir. If I'm being honest, we aren't ready for a lot of things."

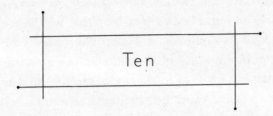

Ten

"What?" **Lieutenant Colonel Halvorsen's** good mood was now nowhere to be found. Sheol's light filled the holotank and the red-stained whites of his eyes, which could have melted through six centimeters of peristeel plating.

There's the colonel the gunny warned me about.

"That is not what I wanted to hear, Lieutenant, especially when I was just beginning to like you. Explain yourself."

"Sir, as you know, my unit has only just reconstituted. I've got a handful of toons fresh out of boot camp and the School of Infantry. They came to me pretty green and—"

"Sounds like life in the RAW-MC to me, Lieutenant Paen. There's never enough boots to go around, let alone veterans to keep tabs on the newbs. The Lusitanian Empire continues to increase its military expenditures, which is forcing us to do the same just to keep parity. This brings us back to Sheol's military importance. In some ways we are already on a war footing, which says nothing about the uptick in worlds seeking formal admission to the RAW, or the defense needs of our protectorates, or our antipiracy operations and force protection for interstellar commerce. I suggest you learn to love the suck."

"Aye, aye, sir." Promise steeled herself for a diplomatic fight. "I love the suck, sir, yes I do, love it like a RAW-MC screw." She sung the words to the familiar cadence, chin held high and proud.

Halvorsen's lip twitched but otherwise he said nothing.

"Boot camp used to last fifteen standard weeks, sir. Now it's eleven, and BUPERS is pushing for nine. The School of Infantry has been shaved down too. I know we're strapped for manpower, but I have 'slick sleeves' that barely passed their weapons evolutions and others who couldn't take a piss in a mechsuit if their lives depended on it."

"I'm fully aware of the Corps's manpower needs and the . . . unprecedented steps we've taken recently, including a reduction in training times, to hit our quotas. I have my own reservations about that. Under the circumstances, I fully support the powers that be, and so should you. You take my meaning?"

"Sir, I mean no disrespect. My concern is for the safety and operational integrity of my command, and that of Charlie Battalion." *Colonel, please hear me out, please.* "I have Marines with subpar range scores, sir, and a few with marks significantly below a passing grade at long distances. Scuttlebutt says our drill instructors are being leaned on to pass subpar Marines through their evos, instead of recycling them, to help the Corps meet its goals. I can't believe that's the case, sir. But, the rumors are circulating the vents, about scores across *all* competencies being averaged together to generate an overall passing mark, particularly for Marines with subpar rifleman skills. Not in the RAW-MC, right, sir? Marksmanship is still as important as it used to be, correct, sir? With respect to the powers that be, I have a half dozen boots who can't consistently hit a silhouette at five hundred meters while prone, with a compensated Triple-Seven carbine racked to a bipod. With optics, sir, and an AI-assist. Why were they allowed to graduate with their class?"

Halvorsen wanted to blow his top and tear the lieutenant a new one. Promise was treading on dangerous ground. Questioning the brass like this was a one-way ticket to a short-lived career. If she kept it up there was no way she would ever make it past the rank of major. And she was taking a significant risk by speaking so freely with him, because he could kill her career with a single efficiency report. *But I can't very well scuttle her career because she's right. She shouldn't have to make the argument in the first place. I don't know many full birds who'd risk the ire of their COs by going on the record.*

The caliber of the average Marine private had fallen measurably over the past few years. Too many greenhorns—and one was one too many in Halvorsen's estimation—were joining the fleet with glaring training deficiencies. A Marine who couldn't shoot at distance was a liability. A handful of sergeants had personally griped to him—off the record, of course—about the substandard skills of the Marines they were seeing coming out of boot camp and SOI. One particular staff sergeant had bemoaned the decrepit state of the Corps and the amount of time he was spending hand-holding green-as-get-you-killed privates. "I shouldn't have to teach them the basics, sir," the noncom had said. "By the time they get to me they should have the fundamentals habitually beat into their hides. And, they should know to keep their fingers off the trigger until they are ready to fire."

After a long moment, the colonel grudgingly nodded his head. "Lieutenant, what would you like me to do about it?"

"Could you buy me another week of training, sir? Even two, before we ship out. Victor Company needs more range time, and I'm afraid I need more than a few standard days. If we deploy now, we risk compromising the battalion and the mission."

"In a perfect 'verse how many weeks would you like?"

"Six weeks, sir, but I can do it for you in four," Promise said.

Halvorsen snorted. "And we leave in less than two. Lieutenant, you're asking me to delay our deployment by at least two weeks. Sheol is mission-critical. The brass won't sign off on this. And we're not just talking about delaying Victor Company but the entire battalion, and BATRON-Six too. That's six battlecrusiers plus screen elements. What's my excuse to Commodore Rebondir for delaying her departure?"

Promise faltered. "Sir—I, I really didn't think . . ."

"No, you didn't think, did you . . . and you should have. I'm not blind or unsympathetic to your concerns. However, you're going to have to live with them and shore up your company's weaknesses. That's what company commanders do. Understood?"

Well, P, you tried. "Yes, sir. I understand . . . and I will. You can count on me, sir."

"I'll comm you by twelve hundred hours tomorrow with new orders. I need to call in a favor, probably more like three." Halvorsen didn't sound at all happy about that, and Promise realized she was going to owe the colonel a massive favor. She decided then and there to pay it back if she was ever in a position to. "Under the circumstances, and given your unit's current situation . . . and the fact that you've just reconstituted after substantial losses, I think the extra time is warranted. *Kearsarge*'s captain owes me a favor. I'm sure Captain Shen can find a reason to keep the yard dogs crawling over her hull for a bit longer, for at least a few days more. Maybe longer. Captains tend to get a wide berth in dock, and a lot of deference. And rightly so. Somehow, I'll buy you your extra drill time, Lieutenant. You deliver me a company of riflemen."

"Aye, aye, sir."

"In the meantime, I have an idea." Halvorsen stood and nodded toward the exit. "Lights. I need to hit the head before the rest of my company commanders arrive. Walk with me."

The holotank died as the overhead lights kicked in, bathing the stadium in near-blinding light. Promise stood and nearly jumped out of her skin. She'd forgotten her mother was still there. Sandra had said little after Promise and the colonel had gotten into it, which wasn't like her. Sandra looked up at Promise from her seat and winked before she faded out. Promise said a quick *thank you, Momma* and fell in beside Halvorsen, walking back up the steps and toward the holotank's exit.

"Sometimes you need to light a fire underneath a unit to get it to pull together." The door opened and Halvorsen paused just inside the exit. "I'm sending you to the Island."

"Sir? With all due respect that's not exactly what I had in mind." *That's a no-win situation. I need to teach my Marines to win before they lose.* "We're not ready, sir."

"I know," Halvorsen said. "Better to fail in training than on the battlefield. Defeat has a clarifying effect on a unit's state of readiness." The colonel gave her a hard smile before storming out of the holotank and into the passageway. "We're going to break Victor Company down so we can build it back stronger." The colonel paused at a fork in the passageway and looked up to get his bearings. "I hate navigating in a warship," he muttered under his breath. Then he rounded the corner and disappeared from sight.

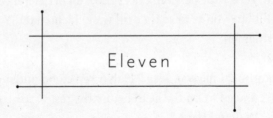

Eleven

Three silhouettes ghosted downrange and stopped at the twenty-five-meter line. The circular morphing plates began to dance in a predetermined pattern, at an arm's length from each other, while hovering on a plane of counter-grav. The leftmost disk suddenly leapfrogged up and over the center disk. Then the middle disk slid underneath and to the side. Now the first disk was into the middle position. Then the rightmost disk leapfrogged too. Back and forth they went.

Promise focused on the front sight of her pulse rifle with her naked eye, timed the next leap, and squeezed the trigger as the "morph" hung in the air before entering its downward arc. Her standard-issue Marine Corps, 3rd Evolution, Extended-Range Pulse Rifle, or MC^3-ERP (pronounced McEerp), loosed a bolt of energy downrange. The morph's bull's-eye glowed bright yellow for a two-count before returning to its normal mat black. *Solid hit, P. Now, do it again.* She switched targets and quickly triple-tapped. Her pattern framed the bull's-eye in an equilateral triangle, from twelve o'clock down to the four and over to the eight. The McEerp hummed as it cycled. Several short bursts of directed heat warmed Promise's arms as energy vented along the length of the rifle's ported barrel. Promise switched targets and drilled the third morph on its upward arc. Switched again and tap, tap, tapped as the morph rose and fell, until it looked like a slotted spoon. When the weapon's trigger locked in the forward position, Promise pressed the bullet button just behind the trigger assembly, and let the cell drop free. She grasped another from her bench, heard the click of a fed-up pulse rifle, and seated the weapon against her shoulder.

"I hate frog-fire drills," said Promise's guardian. Lance Corporal Kathy Prichart stood behind her at a parade rest, staring downrange, and her mouth was half full. "In a firefight, targets don't move like that."

Promise gave her guardian one of those looks over her shoulder. Every company commander had a guardian to watch her six while she was watching everyone else's. If there was a beam or penetrator out there with Promise's name on it, Prichart's job was to kill the shooter or take the hit, and Kathy had taken more than a few for Promise in their short time together. It wasn't like Kathy to complain about range time.

"That's true, Kathy, but that's not the point of the exercise." Promise turned back to her target. "Frog-firing teaches you to flash-sight moving targets. In battle, your targets don't stand still either, or say, 'Hey—kill me first.' F-sighting is a critical skill, and one not easily mastered."

Kathy raised a scoring optic to her eyes and nodded in approval. The optic was linked to the morphs and Promise's pulse rifle, and had recorded every hit and miss. "Not bad, Lieutenant. Tight groupings. Though we're in close and I know you can do better. Let's take the range out a bit, ma'am. Okay?"

Promise quick-locked a holographic scope to the rail of her rifle, and left the "irons" up to cowitness, and stabilized the rifle on the bench rest. Distance-to-target floated in her peripheral vision. When the targets hit fifty meters she raised her right hand over her shoulder and waved downrange. "Come on, Kathy, at least try to make it challenging for me."

"All right, ma'am. How about seventy-five?"

"That will do."

The pie plates retreated to their new positions and began to move in a line, more slowly this time as they shuffled in concert from side to side. Promise squeezed her right eye and her scope zoomed until the disks appeared to be no more than seven meters away. The plates morphed and stretched. Circles became squares and then rectangles with necks. Now three heads-on torsos floated before her reticule and each had a set of eyes glowing bright yellow.

"How about the cross-fire drill, ma'am?" Kathy raised two fingers to her temple and began outlining the exercise along the plane of her body as she spoke, top to bottom and shoulder to shoulder. "Noggin, nads, beater, breather. On my mark. Three, two, one . . ."

I hate this drill, Promise thought as her trigger finger took up the slack.

"Mark!"

Just before Promise fired, her first target jerked to the left and her shot went wide. Promise could have sworn it ducked its head too . . . if that was even possible for a morph. She supposed it probably was, and then tapped out four follow-up shots.

"Three out of four isn't bad, ma'am."

"Did you do that?"

"Do what?" Kathy cleared her throat. "Battle is unpredictable. The target ducked on its own."

"Right. Let's go again."

"Roger that. On three."

Promise bounced from cutout to cutout, four quick taps apiece. She took a bit more time on the brain to guarantee the kill, and quickly blew through the beater, breather, and balls. Then she set the rifle down and pushed back from the bench, pleased with her work.

"Not bad, ma'am." Kathy racked her hands on her hips. "Okay, say your rifle just jammed. You're pinned down with no way out." The three silhouettes quickly shrank back into circles, canted forward like they'd dug in imaginary heels, and rushed Promise's position. Then they multiplied and three became nine. "Here they come, ma'am. They are returning fire. You're running solo. Help is three mikes out. What do you do?"

Promise didn't hesitate. She drew her backup, racked the slide, and sidestepped the bench as the plates hit sixty meters. She advanced on the targets at a quick step with both eyes open and locked on the front sight. When the range dropped below fifteen meters, she opened up from left to right. Each disk shattered upon impact. The booms shook the firing range and hammered Promise's eardrums. Then she realized she'd been had. She looked down at her senior in her hands and shook her head, partly because she found the humor in the situation and partly because she should have known better. And her ears were ringing. The slide was locked to the rear and small flecks of gold littered the ground. She turned around to find a newly assembled group of smiles and frowns, and kicked a stray shell out from underfoot before walking back to the line. The warning signs posted in multiple locations across the range could not have been clearer. ENERGY WEAPONS ONLY.

"I hope y'all enjoyed the show?" *"Y'all"? My birth world is bleeding through.* It happened, just not often, and Promise intended to keep it that way.

Victor Company's platoon sergeants and senior noncoms had assembled at a respectable distance. They were early, which made Promise wonder if something was afoot. They were her aces in a house of flexi cards. She caught the eyes of her second-in-command, Gunnery Sergeant Tomas Ramuel, and shrugged her shoulders while mock-offing herself with her off hand. The gunny was leaning against a post underneath the range's portico, arms crossed, face wrapped in a look that was coldly aimed at Lance Corporal Kathy Prichart. Ears smoldering.

"Stunts like that get people killed, Lance Corporal," Ramuel said as Promise walked up.

Kathy blanched but didn't break away. Nodded. "Gunny, I was only trying to have some—"

"Next time, don't. Understood?"

"Yes, Gunny."

"Go easy, Tomas, I'm just as much at fault. I knew better," Promise said as she stepped underneath the portico, racked the slide of her GLOCK, and holstered the weapon.

"Ma'am, at least get a mini pulser fixed to the rail of that . . . antique." Emphasis on "antique." It was not a real weapon in the gunny's estimation. He'd said so as diplomatically as a gunny could. "That thing is dangerously underpowered. It won't serve you in a stand-up fight." The gunny went to say more but decided against it and clenched his jaw.

"Noted, Gunny. That's not a bad idea. I'm a bit of a purist when it comes to my GLOCK." Promise pursed her lips. "I'll consider it. Okay?"

The gunny dipped his head.

Well, Tomas isn't too happy. I don't blame him either. I'm not too happy with myself. Or my guardian. Kathy and I didn't display proper range etiquette. Not by a long shot. This could go in my jacket.

Promise carried her senior whenever she could, which wasn't often, because of the Regs. For starters, her GLOCK-27 subcompact semiautomatic was about seven centuries out of date. It wasn't even considered a firearm by any modern definition of the term. It predated the Projectile and Pulse

Weapon Proliferation Act of 2633, which meant her senior was exempt from most regulations. But it was still potentially lethal and it could still kill. Promise had no intention of ever testing the limits of that law, which meant she carried her senior on the range and in the privacy of her quarters and that was about it.

Her GLOCK was an old-world semiautomatic pistol made in pre-Diaspora times. It was a dirty weapon that fired bullets that blossomed, fueled by antiquated powder that stained the hands. Many generations of the women in her family had owned and operated the smooth black relic. When her mother died young, the semiautomatic became Promise's. It was about all Promise had left of her mother's things, and wearing it settled her nerves; connected her to her ancestors and robbed life of some of its uncertainty too. Promise was grateful for its presence now as she appraised her Marines. They had a very long day ahead of them and she was about to drop a bit of news she knew they wouldn't like.

Lance Corporal Kathy Prichart stood at the center of the group of Marine noncoms. She wore a tank shirt and running shorts, exposing sinewy arms and legs. The ankle of her left leg reflected sunlight, metal and polymer from toes to shin, a souvenir from the Battle of Montana because she didn't regenerate. Her ocean-colored eyes were impossible to miss, just like the hair on her head, which changed color depending upon the lance corporal's mood. Today, it was morphing-target-yellow. Kathy held a power stick in one hand and quickly raised it to her lips.

"Sorry, ma'am," Prichart said, mouth half full yet again. "I guess I wasn't thinking."

"You have that right." Promise spoke as sternly as she ever had to her guardian. "Kathy, I just drew my senior without thinking, on an *E-only* range. I'm going to be busy this afternoon with the accidental discharge report. The ADR won't get done until the range master is through ripping my head off, and those practice plates are coming out of my meager pay!"

"No worries, ma'am. I've got you covered. I worked it out with the range master ahead of time," Prichart said. "See." The range master's white booth stood in the distance like a small pillbox. "Staff Sergeant Heckler wanted to see your senior in action. You know how rare those things are."

Promise turned around as the door of the range master's booth opened. A Marine dressed in utilities stepped out and waved back at her. *That must be Heckler.* Even though the staff sergeant was a good ways off Promise could tell the woman was smiling. Then she gave Promise two vigorous thumbs up before disappearing back inside.

"We'll, she's heard my G-Twenty-Seven's report," Promise said. "Why don't you invite her to the range tomorrow? Say eight hundred hours . . . for a private shooting lesson. Please ask her to be early. The antique ammo is on the RAW-MC. *You* may go replicate me some more."

"Aye, aye, ma'am. That's very generous of you. The staff sergeant will be thrilled."

"She will owe you one, no doubt."

"Something like that, ma'am." Prichart looked like a Marine caught with contraband.

"Mm-hum, why does this feel like a setup?" Promise asked.

"Said the target to the sniper." Sergeant Maxzash-Indar "Maxi" Sindri, one of her platoon sergeants and closest friends, stood next to the gunny. Maxi just reached the gunny's shoulder, and barely measured up to the Marine Corps's minimum height requirements too. He had a big, hidden temper that emerged when someone tried to kill him, or wound his pride. Unless you were inside his circle of friends, or you didn't know any better, you kept your mouth shut about his height. "Maxi, wear extra socks so you can see out the visor of your mechsuit" or "Maxi, I said ten-hut!" He'd give you that smile, and knock you to the ground. Maxi and Promise had non-com days to fall back upon, and Promise could have gotten away with more than most if she'd wanted to. There were moments when Promise regretted the distance her commission had created between them.

Next to Maxi stood Sergeant Richard Morris, an unremarkable-looking man with brown hair and brown eyes. Morris would have made a good spook, because his face was utterly forgettable. Morris was a good man. He'd fought hard on Montana, and Promise trusted him with her life.

Beside Morris was Lance Corporal Nathaniel Van Peek. The lance corporal was as tall as the gunny, only thicker in the back and shoulders. Van Peek had almost bled out on Montana. He was, in many ways, a walking miracle.

Maxi, Kathy, Nathaniel, Richard, and Tomas made up the old guard from Promise's pre-Montana days. Her Montana Marines. They had fought and bled together on Promise's birth world, and owned the wounds to prove it. Some wounds, like Kathy's ankle, were more visible than others.

On the opposite side of Kathy were four newcomers to Victor Company. Four women as different from each other as light and dark, and all of them were wolves. Blooded. They'd all killed in combat before joining V Company, and Promise needed their experience badly. Their faces showed a mixture of genuine surprise, uncertainty, and condemnation over the range incident involving Promise's GLOCK. Firing rounds on an E-only range was a serious infraction. At the moment Promise couldn't recall which number. *Maybe the twenty-first. Regardless . . .* All ranges had five-meter-tall earthen berms for absorbing beams. The berms were equal to the task for bullets too, but sensitive Marine ears were definitely not, and the Corps went to great lengths to protect them. That, and a round might ricochet off a target plate or the ground, and create a friendly-fire incident.

"Relax, sisters," Prichart said. "No one's getting thrown in the brig today. Look around. There's no one here but us. I reserved the range ahead of time. And those were not standard E-range pie plates either. The lieutenant just destroyed a trio of breakaways."

Understanding spread across the lined face of Staff Sergeant Gail Ghorn-Oguomalandashi, the seniormost newcomer to V Company. She nodded gravely, dark eyes shifting from Kathy to Promise. Then a tight smile crept across her mouth. "Try that on me, Lance Corporal, and you *will* be incarcerated."

Prichart stiffened and looked straight ahead, nodded sharply. "I'll remember that, Staff Sergeant Ghorn-Oguo . . . ah . . ."

"See that you do," the staff sergeant said. "The range master and I go back a ways. Staff Sergeant Heckler has always been a trickster. She got me once, got me good too, back when we were lowly PFCs on our second tour in the verge. Mine was a dummy walkie-talkie. It ran right up on my six and through my legs. Turned around and started squawking in Standard. I jumped on top of it to save the Marines beside me but it never went off, and then it spoke words I will never forget. Someday I might tell you what it said, maybe after I've had a bit too much to drink." The staff sergeant looked mildly amused. "It seems the two of you have a similar sense of humor, Lance Corporal. Please call me Staff Sergeant Go-Mi. It's easier."

And a bit self-serving, Promise thought. To be fair, the staff sergeant wasn't coming across that way, and the woman had a point.

Kathy met Staff Sergeant Go-Mi's gaze directly and realized she was being toyed with . . . partly at least. The other part of Go-Mi was dead serious.

Kathy dipped her head in defeat. "Yes, Staff Sergeant Go-Mi. If I ever do play a trick on you, I'll make sure to wipe my tracks completely."

"Be sure to do that, Lance Corporal. Payback is sweet." Go-Mi nudged the pale-looking sergeant at her shoulder. "Portia, I believe we're going to fit right in here."

"Yes, Staff Sergeant, I believe you're right." Sergeant Portia Dvorsky spoke with a heavy accent and lively blue eyes. Her PT uniform hugged her womanly frame, and her standard-issue tank shirt was barely adequate to the task. Porcelain pixie features betrayed an Old Earth Russian heritage. Next to her stood Sergeant Carol Keys, a broad-shouldered woman with a plain face and large hands. Beside her stood Sergeant Hema Lu. Lu's blond hair contrasted sharply with her bronzed skin and brown eyes.

Promise motioned to the waist-level ferrocrete table situated behind the firing line. "Circle up, Marines. We've got a lot to cover."

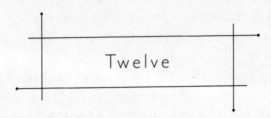

Twelve

Promise set her minicomp in the center of the table and lightly touched the opaque screen. A short sequence of commands brought up a holographic map, which blossomed above the device, consuming about a cubic meter of air. At the center of the map rose a tall snowcapped mountain carpeted in lush green up to the tree line. The mountain's base flowed outward toward a ring of sandy beaches, and dropped below ocean level into a shallow walk-up reef. One side of the mountain was blown out. Tense eyes absorbed the dormant volcano. Promise heard a throat clear, a sharp inhale, and a not quite subvocalized profane invocation.

"Yes, Marines, it's *that* mountain." The volcanic peak was called Mount Bane for a reason. For decades it had served as the principal assault testing ground for frontline RAW-MC units. Mount Bane had humbled the most adept Marine company commanders. One-hundred-percent unit casualties weren't unheard-of. *And that scares the mess out of me.* Promise continued, "Victor Company's scheduled for a surgical strike on the island." Promise cleared her throat. She reached into the map and grabbed the leeward face of the mountain, slid it left to expose the volcano's interior. The cross section showed dozens of levels. "The command center is located here. As you can see, the entire island is heavily guarded by Android Enemy Soldiers and surface-to-air platforms. The beach is a kill zone. The sky is a kill zone. But, the water is perfect for swimming."

Promise looked up at the gunny and nodded. Ramuel grunted in response and shook his head no, giving her a look that said, *You've got to be kidding me.*

"I'm deadly serious, Gunny." Then Promise scanned the faces of her Marines, one by one, until her eyes came to rest upon Maxi's. He was on the opposite side of the holomap and turned slightly toward her, so the unit patch on his utility shirt was clearly visible: a snake coiled around a warship, crushing it to death. "Pythons, it's our turn. I realize tomorrow's exercise is just a training op. I know you will give it your best. The women and men under your command, particularly our greenhorns, may be inclined to slack. Don't let them. Tomorrow, we go to war. We are going to run the operational plan for the rest of the afternoon, and then run it again as a full company later on tonight, down to the smallest detail. Let's win this one now. It's going to be a long night and an even earlier morning, and tomorrow will kick with a vengeance. Time to love the suck."

"Operation Doomtouch," said Sergeant Morris wistfully. "If you make landfall, you're a lucky jane or jack."

"Luck has nothing to do with it, Sergeant. Success hinges on our planning and preparation," Promise said in a neutral voice. "I suppose providence has a hand too." Promise reached into the map and collapsed it. "My goal—my expectation—is zero-failure. We all make landfall together. We all come home. Questions?"

"If you say so, ma'am," Morris replied.

Promise had fought beside Morris on Montana and they'd barely survived, and then they'd buried the rest of Victor Company together. Morris knew firsthand what a no-win situation felt like, and Operation Doomtouch had all the hallmarks of a royal FUBAR. *Not on my watch, though. Not if I can help it.*

"Ma'am, I'm with you—you know that," added Morris after a long moment. "But, this operation rubs me raw. It's designed for failure. What good is running an op that's unwinnable?"

"Just because it hasn't been done before doesn't mean it can't be done, Sergeant."

"Ooh-rah, Lieutenant."

"That's the spirit, Lance Corporal Van Peek," Promise said as she turned to the much larger man standing beside her and reached up to slap him on the back.

"I assume you'll want a HALO drop?" The gunny brought them back to point, arms crossed as he scrutinized Promise through the holographic display from the opposite side of the briefing table.

"Yes, with a splash at the end." Promise smiled with her eyes.

"I was afraid you'd say that, ma'am."

Promise parroted the gunny's body language. "Don't give me that look, Tomas. That's what tanked air is for. We can walk the bottom and swim the pipes. No one's tried it before. The powers that be won't be expecting a blue space approach."

"Yes, that's true, Lieutenant, they won't expect us in the blue. But walking in drink will slow us down considerably. If we're detected, we're bait."

"That's why I brought this." Promise looked over her shoulder. "Stevie?"

Promise's Mule hovered over on a plane of countergrav and handed her a nondescript box with a serial number stamped on both sides. The close infantry-support platform was dressed in desert camouflage and fitted with webbing on its front and back.

"Thank you, Stevie." Promise gave her Mule a gentle pat and shooed it off.

Staff Sergeant Go-Mi looked at Promise strangely. Sergeant Maxi was standing opposite Go-Mi and read her expression, started to laugh, and raised a hand to his face to clear his throat. "She goes easy on her Mules, Staff Sergeant. Actually, Stevie is her first issue—her one and only—and that was six standard years ago. The two are attached at the hip."

"I'm rather proud of that fact, Sergeant," Promise said with an edge that didn't match the twinkle in her eyes.

"I know, ma'am," said Maxi, who turned and winked at Promise.

"Wow, I'm on my seventh Mule with twelve standard years in the service," said Staff Sergeant Go-Mi. "Ma'am, with all due respect, is Stevie humping your gear or is it the other way around?"

"Told you," Maxi said.

"And Sergeant Sindri is on his sixth Mule and it only took him six years to beat the living daylights out of the first five," quipped Promise.

"What?" Maxi said with perfect innocence. "Mechs were designed to grunt it out for us."

"Didn't the Corps put you on notice? Next one is on you if it doesn't last through Christmas, right?" Promise said.

"Thanks, Lieutenant. Thanks a lot."

"That's why I'm here, Sergeant."

The gunny's sigh brought the conversation to a halt. "All right, boys and girls, shall we get on with it?"

Promise nodded. "The gunny's right. We drop tomorrow and we're dropping into blue space."

"This just gets better and better," replied Gunnery Sergeant Ramuel.

"Come now, Tomas. You aren't afraid of a bath, are you?"

"I don't like the idea of not being able to swim. Mechsuits don't have fins, ma'am. They don't float either."

"I *know,* which is why, before I was so rudely interrupted, I brought this." Promise held up the box that her Mule had humped over for her. She set it on the table, cracked the top, and pulled out a metallic disk that looked like a giant-sized egg separator. "This is a multidirectional hydrodisk."

The gunny looked unconvinced.

Promise set the disk on the table and activated it. For a moment nothing happened. A soft hum grew into a ramping sound followed by several clicks. Four rungs deployed and the disk enlarged to twice the size it had been moments ago. "The handholds and outer ring make up the M-HYD's base." Promise grabbed both to demonstrate. "The inner circle is tethered to four retractable tow cables. When deployed underwater, the M-HYD's forward assist advances several meters ahead of the user, and generates propulsion. We will slave these to our AIs. All we have to do is hold on while they pull us through the water."

Staff Sergeant Go-Mi cocked her head. "Ma'am, I would love to know how you got your hands on forty M-HYDs without tipping your hand. Tomorrow's assault will be carefully monitored and those are not standard issue."

"That is a superb question, Staff Sergeant. Turns out some brass will be monitoring our drop too." All eyes were on her now, wide as saucers. "Sergeant Sindri, would you care to answer the staff sergeant's question?"

"Yes, ma'am." Maxi turned to Staff Sergeant Go-Mi. He made a show of stretching to his full height and grew uncharacteristically serious.

"The explanation you seek, Staff Sergeant, won't be found in the good old RAW-MC."

"You went off-grid."

"I would never, Staff Sergeant. I simply went off-base and into town. Deep Sea Six was having a sale on thermal suits and rebreathers, and ten percent off everything else."

"And you blew all your pay," Promise said.

Maxi looked guilty as charged, and shrugged. "Um, DSS really does have everything. You should see the place. The cathedral ceiling is breathtaking, with a top-rate holosphere. I literally walked through the jaws of the Devil Dog on my way to the men's." The Devil Dog was a famous constellation faintly visible from the surface of the planet Hold, and across the planet's solar system. The view from Hold's only moon was particularly gratifying. The constellation consisted of ten stars, the nearest being twenty-two light-years away. Drawn together, they outlined the profile of a fierce canine (assuming you filled in the teeth with foam and drool, and added flaming eyes and a snarl).

"Just off the men's is the longest row of poles and tackle in the 'verse. Even the literature says so. I picked up a sonic spear—the Mac-Seven—perfect for the modern underwater enthusiast."

Promise felt a headache coming on. A few standard years ago she'd pushed Maxi to invest a portion of his monthly pay into a multisystem index fund. Thankfully, he'd heeded her advice and his portfolio had grown consistently, even beating the market most years. Without Promise, he would have been a very broke sergeant.

"I placed the order for the hydrodisks too, on the lieutenant's orders. They arrived four days later via jumpship, which is stellar service by any standard."

"And how did you . . . how did we . . . how did the company pay for forty hydrodisks?" asked Staff Sergeant Go-Mi.

"We didn't. Deep Sea Six donated them to the RAW-MC, specifically to our company. DSS has a large parent company with a significant R-and-D department, and its weapons division is courting BUWEPS." Maxi nodded to the hydrodisk before them. "That there is the M-HYD Model A, and we will be testing it in a simulated combat environment for some very senior brass."

"You're leaving something out. Do tell, Sergeant," said Staff Sergeant Go-Mi.

"Ah, well, I suppose I should mention that my great-granny sits on the board. She's RAW-MC too, First Sergeant Ahana Sindri, retired in 53 A.E. She will be observing the op tomorrow."

"That bit of information is need-to-know." Promise swept the faces of her platoon sergeants to make the point clear. "It will just make our cubs anxious so we're not telling them. Clear?"

Verbals and nods all around.

"Crystal," said Ramuel.

"During the last few days, you've all stepped up, trained hard, encouraged and pushed and prodded the greenhorns to step it up too. We've made real progress and you are to thank for that. Even Private Atumbi is showing promise." The looks she got back told her her platoon sergeants needed some convincing. "All right, point taken. He will get there." *I hope.*

"Tomorrow we deploy as a full company and find out if all the hard work has paid off. I know we will do ourselves proud. Mount Bane is designed to teach Marines to face the very real possibility of failure. Complete, utter failure. We all know a traditional assault on the island sets us up to fail by the numbers. We have to think differently, and train our least-experienced boots to expect the unexpected too. Teach them to adapt, and flex under pressure."

Promise looked around the circle and locked eyes with each Marine in turn. Nodded to, reassured, and challenged every one. "We can do this. It will be fun."

"Are you bringing your senior, ma'am?" asked the gunny.

"Of course, Tomas. Regulations allow good-luck charms on an op. Don't worry. I'll have a standard-issue sidearm on me too."

"I wear a cross, ma'am." Ramuel let himself smile. "Don't you think you're stretching the Regs just a bit?"

"No. Why?" Promise feigned innocence. "Did you know GLOCKs can fire underwater?" she replied without missing a beat.

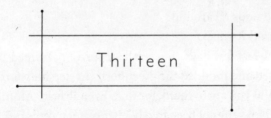

Thirteen

Lieutenant Promise Paen stood near the rear of the forward compartment of the Maku-class light attack craft and watched the chronometer on the forward bulkhead wall tick down to "drop."

"Ten mikes out," she barked over a sea of noise: mechboots shifting on the deck plating, mechsuits jostling in webbing, raucous humor, and the hum of the LAC's dual fusion engines.

Promise strode through her Marines, steadying herself on the overhead racks as she threaded the aisle, to counter the rough turbulence battering the LAC's hull outside. The maglocks in her boots were engaged to keep her anchored to the deck. A tropical hurricane had decided to vent its fury along their approach to Mount Bane, and the pilot had taken full advantage of the storm to mask the LAC's signature from the island's scanners, which meant flying through soup. After a brief, peaceful stint in the eye of the storm, they'd plunged into 150 kph winds that were giving the LAC's countergravity matrix a workout.

In the midst of a particularly rough patch, Promise dropped onto the empty bench next to Private Ed Kartoom, to help him fix a feed problem with his standard-issue FS-7.77 or "Triple-7" Carbine. Like all of her Marines, Kartoom wore the RAW-MC's standard-issue Kydoimos-6 Mechanized Infantry Combat Battlesuit, or mechsuit: the interlocking plates of peristeel molded to the wearer's body, flexed where necessary like the skin of a snake. Ergonomic compartments along the thighs and forearms housed spare cells, magazines, throwing grenades, and snacks. An external mount on each hip took a sidearm. Every spare millimeter of internal capacity was crammed with enough tech to prosecute a small war.

"It won't cycle, ma'am." Kartoom stabbed the small display mounted to the carbine's frame, directly above the trigger. "I've run all the diagnostics and can't find the problem." Kartoom looked about ready to break the carbine over his knee.

"Here—hand it over. Forget the screen. Use your head for something besides a helmet rack." Sharp words, she knew. She tempered them with humor and smiled at Kartoom as they bit into his hide. "See." Promise popped the magazine and pulled the charging handle. She saw the problem at once. "I believe you have a bad magazine. Uh-huh, like I thought. See, the casing is bent inward at the top where it fits into the mag well. It's not seating properly, so your penetrators aren't feeding up the ramp like they should. Toss it and grab another. Safety on, Private." Promise pointed to her head. "Remember, tech is only as good as you are."

A bit farther down the aisle Promise spotted Private Mary Chang. Chang was looking paler than usual, and sweat dripped from her nose. "Chang, get your head down . . . between your knees. *Now.*" Promise grabbed an empty crate from an overhead smartrack and tossed it on the deck, and then kicked it hard toward Chang. "Incoming!" Several outstretched boots quickly pulled back as the crate screeched across the LAC's deck plating, showering sparks in its wake. Staff Sergeant Go-Mi stuck out a mechboot to apply the brakes while Sergeant Sindri pulled out a smoke and made a joke of lighting it. A ghost-stricken Chang lunged for the crate, cheeks bulging with spew.

"Nice save, Lieutenant," said Staff Sergeant Go-Mi. "We've all been there, Chang. Hang tough. One day you'll look back on this and laugh."

"Ain't that the tru*uuu*—" Chang said before heaving again and again and again.

"Feel better, Private?" Promise took a knee beside Chan, and then looked up into the young woman's stricken face. She'd smelled worse in the barracks, which didn't say a whole lot for Marine hygiene. "You just need to get your drop legs underneath you. They'll come in time. Swallow. Good. Now, stick out your tongue."

Promise popped a hatch on her thigh compartment and withdrew a stim. "Hold still, this will sting a bit. And don't bite me or you'll break a tooth on my gauntlet. There." Promise thumped Chang on her shoulder plate. "You're already looking like yourself, Marine. Don your helmet and have your AI check your vitals. Keep your faceplate up, in case . . ." She was already moving when she heard Chang's helmet lock tight.

Just then the LAC dropped suddenly, and it was enough to break the pull of her maglocks. Promise instantly thrust her hands up to prevent her skull from rapping the LAC's overhead.

"See," said Kathy. "If you won't strap in at least don your helmet."

Promise fumbled with the helmet latched to her waist, finally got it un-hooked, and pulled her head through the collar. She flexed her jaw to equalize the pressure in her ears while her HUD spooled up. Flipped her externals to on and said, "Happy?" Then she headed toward the front of the compartment.

With her armor on, she grew about twenty centimeters boot-to-crown. She was less than a meter across at the shoulders, thick in the waist, and heavy as a small boulder. Armor and an EMP-hardened mesh and triage capabilities and synthetic muscles all had to go somewhere. Promise had never cared much about the way she looked up-armored. She'd never under-stood the janes who obsessed about how their derrieres looked in mech— nothing in the 'verse could help her flat aft anyway. Promise had modified her mechsuit to accommodate her senior and three spare magazines inside the right thigh compartment, and if she was going to have one pear-shaped hip she figured she might as well have two, so she'd thrown extra cells in the left compartment and a couple of walkie-talkies. The "run-baby-run"s were a lot of fun to throw and if your trajectory was off, the grenade would stand up on its own and sprint toward the target before going boom. Because she was flat on top, she'd shaved the chest cavity down a bit too. It was a small price to pay for a smaller side profile while maintaining her suit's ability to shrug off damage. She reached the bulkhead door to the LAC's cockpit, which was sealed for flight, and pivoted on the balls of her mechboots, grabbed an overhead rung for stability, and sized up her command.

"All right, Pythons, drain it, dump it, pack it up, wolf it down. We go in five mikes."

Thirty-nine heads turned to face her. Her order simultaneously traveled over the company net, resonated in the mastoid implant of every jane and jack in Victor Company. Powered gauntlets and helmets locked and sealed, weapons racked and cycled, fingers flexed, and more than a few Marines blacked out their visors and said a hasty "thank you, Jesus" in the privacy of a vac-and-sound-sealed suit as they took care of business and grunted out a load.

Promise made a point of tapping her visor, which turned clear, so her people could see her smiling eyes as they bounced through atmo in the minutes leading up to drop.

At T minus three mikes to drop, she barked out, "On your feet, Pythons. Take a rail. Double-check your gravchute and your buddy's. Private Atumbi, sound off."

Atumbi stepped out of line and waved from midway back. *"Here, ma'am."*

"Private, please tell me you brought your rifle to the big show?"

The battlenet lit up with cackles and colorful metaphors. *"Bet he brought his gun too,"* said Sergeant Sindri.

"I'd certainly hope so or the private will need a medic," Promise added dryly.

"Both are racked and ready, ma'am," said Atumbi.

"More than I need to know, Race. Finger off the trigger, okay?"

"Roger that, ma'am."

"Platoon Sergeants—roll call and report, by toons."

One by one, the boots of Victor Company pinged the battlenet and reported in, green to go, first to their respective platoon sergeants. One by one each platoon sergeant reported to Promise directly. When all of the all-present-and-accounted-fors were received and dutifully logged, Promise slaved the company battlenet to her heads-up display for a final review of the operational plan. A small 2D aerial map of the island and the surrounding waters appeared on her heads-up display and on the HUDs of very boot in Victor Company. Promise dropped a ring around Sector 53 and a ring around their current position, and tasked Bond to track time-to-target in real time.

"Remember, we are dropping to two-zero thousand meters, seven klicks out from our target. We will fall to one-five-hundred meters before deploying gravchutes. Your bubble will activate immediately once you clear the LAC's drop ring. Until we hit the drink, you are to maintain comm silence."

Promise pinged Private First Class Jupiter Cervantes and gave her the deck. "Jupiter was jumping long before she joined the Corps. Family business and such. She's already logged more drops than most of us will in a full career and she recently made Senior Parachutist. Before joining Victor Company, Charlie Battalion, she was with Whiskey BAT—the Demon

Wings—where she logged over thirty-five HALO combat drops, and five orbital insertions. She is our acting jump master for today's op. Jupiter, please give us a one-mike rundown on the gravchute and the bubble."

Private First Class Cervantes chimed in. *"Aye, aye, ma'am. The bubble is your run-of-the-'verse null field. Cancels all comm traffic in and out, and masks your signature. Once it's penetrated, either by incoming fire or returning fire, there's no going back, and you're roscado—screwed. Mount Bane's ground cannons will take you out in the span between two heartbeats. Keep your pie hole shut and your pads off the trigger and let the bubble mask your sig while you're in free fall. Next comes the gravchute. It's a whole other animal. It's touchy at higher altitudes. Keep a light touch and no matter what you do pull your chute before minimum ceiling. Pass it and your chances of survival drop precipitously. Wait too long and it's hasta la vista, chiquita."*

Promise took over. "Thank you, PFC," Promise said. "Any questions? Now's the time. Anyone? No? Good. Go-time."

The forward drop ring opened in midcompartment, revealing scattered, backlit clouds and thousands of meters of empty blackness below. "Marines, stay on your platoon sergeants and you'll reach the LZ. Alpha toon, on me. We go in thirty."

Promise walked to the yellow jump ring and grabbed the handhold just above her head. When the chrono hit five seconds, she gave the obligatory thumbs-up to Kathy and the other four boots of her toon, dug her mech-boots into the deck's grated plating, and surrendered her mortal body to the sky.

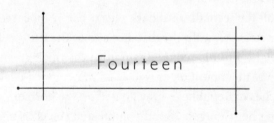

Fourteen

"All systems nominal, ma'am," Bond said as she fell below nineteen thousand meters. "Your heart rate is slightly elevated but well within acceptable parameters. I'm detecting increased cortisol levels in your bloodstream and a slight rise in your core body temperature. Would the lieutenant care for some music?"

Not this again.

A cumulonimbus shaped like a warship drifted into her flight path. She punched through the aft hammerhead and was through in seconds.

"Actually, the lieutenant would prefer to hear the howling of the wind."

"I'm sorry, Lieutenant. Would you confirm that request?"

"You heard me correctly, and while you're at it, dial the temp down five degrees. I'm hot."

"Aye, aye, ma'am. Patching through the howling of the wind. Dialing your suit's internal temperature down five degrees."

At least Bond's hardwired to my mechsuit and not to me, thought Promise. At least she could pull her helmet off and leave Bond on the shelf if she wanted to. And if her AI tried to link with her mastoid implant she could always take a message.

She fell several thousand meters more, knifed into a dense cloud formation. "Twelve thousand meters, ma'am."

"Acknowledged. Run another diagnostic."

"Aye, aye, ma'am. Running . . . stand by."

Promise fell and fell and fell.

She ticked off the seconds until dark-blue ocean reappeared beneath her thousands of meters below. In the distance and to the left was Mount Bane. Even at this height, Promise could distinguish the thick green canopy that ringed the base of the mountain as well as its snowcapped peak high above. Two small patches of Republican gray floated on the horizon.

As if reading her thoughts, Bond volunteered the class and tonnage of each vessel. "Choong Mo–class destroyers, RNV *Yi Lee* and *Yu Lee*. Each displaces seven thousand two hundred tons."

It took Promise a moment to remember what the "V" in RNV stood for. Wet Navy. Republican Naval Vessel. She'd never been aboard one before.

"Designate them neutrals, Zulu One and Two. I don't expect them to participate in today's exercise. All the same, monitor their position and alert me if it changes."

"Aye, aye, ma'am."

Her mechsuit's AI, Mr. Bond, was a Class-2 Semi-Autonomous Reasoning Grunt, or SARG for short. Bond spoke proper twentieth-century European English because Promise had told it to. Bond also liked to make a fuss about her. She'd first heard the voice in 2D action-and-adventure vids, dating back to Earth (pre-Diaspora). They starred a male spook who worked for a long-deceased organization called MI5. *Or was it MI6?* She couldn't remember which. Promise had immediately fallen for Bond's voice and uploaded his speech patterns to her AI's personality matrix. Bond could read the field manual for the Marine Corps, 3rd Evolution, Extended-Range Pulse Rifle and make it sound almost sensual.

Promise's eyes flicked up to her altimeter reading. *Too fast.* She flared her arms and legs, and raised her head in a classic box-man position. The ailerons along her armor—back, forearms, and legs—bit into the wind to stabilize her fall. Promise raised her right arm, banked right until the diamond-shaped waypoint projected on her HUD was once more centered within her field of view. She fell below eighty-six hundred meters.

"Diagnostic complete. All systems nominal."

"Confirm weapons systems are in games mode."

"Games mode confirmed. Governors are green. Your beam strength is set to point-zero-niner of standard." That was considered flash strength. Not enough to hurt armor at any distance.

"What's the status of my bubble?"

"Intact—no detectable rifts. Radiation bleed is less than one one-thousandth of one percent, well below detection level."

"Run the diagnostic again and—"

"Your cortisol levels are still elevated," Bond said. "Would the lieutenant care for something relaxing now?"

Most of the time, Bond referred to her as "ma'am." Lately Promise had noticed its preference for her rank and the third person when it tried to handle her.

"No, thank you. The lieutenant is fine. Just run another diagnostic."

She passed six thousand meters.

"Running . . . *third* diagnostic in progress." Bond sounded put out. As if it were saying, *I do know how to do this after all. It's part of my programming.* Instead of saying that, it simply replied, "Stand by."

"I didn't ask you to keep count."

"I am programmed to record minutiae, such as how many diagnostics I've run on the lieutenant's systems, ma'am."

"Well, stop it."

Bond fell silent. When it didn't report about completing the third diagnostic, Promise sighed. "And?"

"And what, ma'am?"

"The diagnostic."

"Yes, ma'am, I ran it. In fact, I ran three. You ordered me to stop reporting the results."

"I told you to stop counting."

"Exactly."

"Fine, please report your findings."

"I found the same results as before, ma'am. Nothing. Shall I run a fourth and find nothing again, or play something relaxing?"

This is ridiculous.

"Fine. Play something appropriate to the situation. Um . . . anything by Heroes of Mass Destruction will do."

"HMD will do?" Promise's AI nearly choked on its programming.

"Dutifully."

"Fine, ma'am. My aim was to help you relax. Perhaps the lieutenant would—"

"I *am* relaxed."

She fell below five thousand meters to the first verse of "Hammer Drops Final." A dozen bands had covered the cult classic since the twenty-second century. The most recent iteration included a postapocalyptic dedication:

In Memoriam of Earth—The Latest Living World to Bite
the Cosmic Dust

A rolling drumbeat set to distant explosions swelled in Promise's mastoid implant. Then the explosions stopped and a single-word mantra barely louder than a pitched whisper began:

"Hammer, hammer, hammer falls, hammer drops final.
Hammer, hammer, hammer culls, hammer drops final.
Whoa-ho, the hammer falls, hammer drops final.
Hell-o, the hammer falls, hammer drops final."

"Ooh-rah!, ma'am. That was inspiring."

"Shut up." Promise shook her head, had to quickly flutter her hands to adjust her fall. It took a moment for her to realize her ailerons hadn't automatically kicked in. That was part of Bond's job. "You're being passive-aggressive."

"I wouldn't know what the lieutenant means?"

"Very funny."

"Passing three thousand meters," her AI said.

Promise smiled. "Ready gravchute. On my mark." Promise knew that the moment her chute opened her bubble would immediately burst, and she'd be vulnerable to enemy fire. That's why her stealth suite would kick in at exactly the same moment. Stealth wasn't perfect, and it certainly wasn't as good as her mechsuit's cloak, but the cloak wasn't authorized for this op and stealth was more than sufficient for the task at hand.

"Aye, aye, ma'am, gravchute and stealth standing by. Awaiting mark."

Promise passed twenty-five hundred meters. Then her bubble burst without warning and several Marines broke comm silence. Panic flooded the battlenet.

"What just happened?" asked a male voice.

"'Ell if I know," replied a female. *"I've just—wait—oh 'ell, three o'clock, oh*

'ell no, oh 'ell, I'm locked up, repeat I'm locked up—incoming! All points scatter, repeat all points . . ."

The voice dropped out of the net. An icon on Promise's HUD changed from green to red. Platoon Sergeant Hema Lu, KIA.

"One-Alpha to all points, cut the chatter. Report through your platoon sergeants and—"

"Que demonios?" There was no mistaking that voice. Private First Class Cervantes was speaking her native tongue again, words that made as much sense to Promise's untrained ears as "blankety-blankety-blank-blank." Then Cervantes dropped out of the net and her icon turned red too, before it disappeared.

That's not right. We're being jammed.

Promise barked over the battlenet, "One-Alpha to ALCON, dive dive dive. Deploy gravchutes at minimum ceiling. Repeat, deploy chutes at Mike Charlie, over."

"I'm hit," replied another female. "My HUD just died. I—"

A Marine zoomed by Promise and sent her cartwheeling through loosely spun cotton. She lost all sense of down as the sea and sky blurred together. And either the horizon was punch-drunk or her gyroscope had malfunctioned. Her mechsuit should have righted her and hadn't. Then a bolt of panic hit her gut because her AI should have warned her about the near-collision, and it hadn't. I'm dropping blind.

Promise clenched her teeth to keep from biting her tongue. "Bond, my scanners are down. Get them working, now!" She found Mount Bane staring at her upside down, and locked on to it with her eyes as if her life depended upon it. Left, right, over, and down. A half mike later she more or less had her bearings and a throbbing headache.

Another Marine tumbled past her. I think that was Chang. Two more streaked into view, arms and legs spread-eagled. Promise winced as three Marines collided and their weapons went flying. The sky was raining boots. Mount Bane was living up to its name.

"Ma'am, I can now confirm you're jammed," Bond offered. "I can't do any more from this elevation. You need to get down, now."

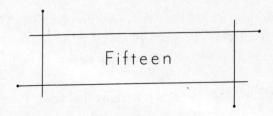

Fifteen

"I'm locked up," **said** a frightened male voice over the battlenet. Possibly Kartoom's. *"Flight of birds headed down my throat. Diving, diving, diving—"*

Promise's HUD should have thrown a ring around Kartoom and displayed a window of data on her HUD. Name, rank, proximity, health. That sort of thing. Instead her HUD looked like snow, so she shut it off. Now she was leaning on visuals alone. Maybe that was Kartoom diving to her right and maybe it wasn't. Either way she approved of the last-ditch maneuver, was pleased to see the boot thinking with his head. Promise breathed a sigh of relief. He was going to make it. Once she reached terra firma she wouldn't be alone. If she could pull a couple of toons together perhaps there was a chance of completing the operation. But she knew the odds of that happening were about nil.

"They got me. My HUD just blacked out." Definitely Kartoom, and he sounded nearly apoplectic. *"I can't raise my visor. Can't see anything. I'm—"* Kartoom's voice fell out of the battlenet.

"Kartoom, calm down," Promise said over the company-wide channel. "It's just a sim. Your chute *will* deploy." Because this was a training simulation, Promise knew Kartoom could hear her even if he couldn't respond. She imagined how he felt at the moment, falling through sky in complete darkness. Suddenly her HUD cycled and a claxon sounded in her head. There was no time to worry over Kartoom, because a ground-based launch had just locked her up.

"We've dropped below their jammers, ma'am. But you're target-locked. Impact in seventeen, sixteen . . ."

"Fire decoys on my mark. Hold the chute." She tucked into a ball to minimize her signature. Two simulated birds blipped on her HUD and closed the range. When they were almost on top of her, Promise flared her arms and legs to kill her speed. On three she yelled, "Mark!" Her HUD turned white as the missiles detonated below. Another claxon went off. She was way past minimum ceiling.

"Deploy chute, maximum gravity and thrusters, now. Now, *now*, NOW!"

Her gravchute blossomed overhead and unfurled to either side. Maximum gravity soaked up her velocity as her chute went taut. Her vision grayed out. Promise had never deployed her chute at such an extreme speed, or at such a frighteningly low ceiling, even with a grav assist. The experience nearly ripped out her soul. Life stalled out. The sea rolled gently beneath her in a light breeze.

"Assault configuration," Promise heard her AI say because she couldn't make her brain make her mouth form the words. Current shot through her gravchute and turned it into a fixed wing, which was capable of moderate subsonic speeds. Her mechboots sculled the water and for a moment she thought she was going in. At the last possible moment she leveled out and started gaining altitude. Her comm barked to life.

"*. . . do you read, over?*" The voice broke in midsentence, strained and hoarse. "*Two-Alpha to One-Alpha, do you read, over?*"

Kathy, Promise thought. Her guardian had made it. Thick words formed on Promise's tongue. "One-Alpha . . . reads you . . . loud and clear, over."

"*Copy that, One-Alpha. I'm on your six, will overtake, over.*"

"Negative, Two-Alpha, maintain position, stay on me, over," Promise said as her head cleared.

"*Roger that, One-Alpha, maintaining position, over.*"

Promise queued Victor Company's roster as she flew. Thirty-four red icons burned angrily on her heads-up-display, all KIAs. An additional three boots glowed yellow, MIA. Promise saw Lance Corporal Kathy Prichart out of the corner of her HUD. Prichart's ellipse-shaped gravwing was knifing through the wind. A moment later, a nine-o'clock shadow drew Promise's head around. Staff Sergeant Gail Go-Mi's winged profile was a sight for sore eyes. The staff sergeant nodded as she took the lead position, reached over her shoulder, and drew her pulse rifle, bringing it to bear.

"All points, report."

"This is Two-Alpha, over."

That's Kathy, Promise thought. *One.*

"One-Charlie reporting, over."

That's Staff Sergeant Go-Mi. That's two.

As the seconds ticked by Promise's heart sank into the sea.

I make three. Three left out of forty. What a disaster. She watched the sea undulate below, the rises and crests of an indeterminate force of nature that had just swallowed her command. Thirty-seven boots in the drink. Of course, her Marines weren't really dead. They were simulated casualties, sitting in seventy meters of water, butt-prints in the sand. When the exercise ended the powers that be would thaw their suits and send the retrieval boats to bring them home. Cervantes's face appeared in her mind's eye, mouth spewing bilingual curses while fish nipped at her faceplate. Promise couldn't help smiling. Her next thought wiped the humor from her face. This op was eerily reminiscent of Montana. Being ambushed, losing most of her Marines, and facing another no-win situation. *Except this time everyone lives to fight another day.*

"All right, we are three," Promise said, breaking proper voice procedure. Because what was the point. "I believe this op calls for forty boots, which makes us slightly understrength. Time to head home."

An object pierced the waves below, drawing Promise's attention. For a moment she couldn't believe her eyes. A massive wing tipped to one side and water sheeted off of it. Then there were three and they all rose together. Promise called it a small miracle. Kathy would later say it was just plain luck. Sergeant Go-Mi would tell the tale for years to come, about the time a trio of mechanized mermen leapt out of the sea, just like in the movie *Neptune's Crossing.* Except they weren't mermen at all, but real men, real flesh-and-bone mechanized Marines, flying gravchutes with simulated damage. And their siren calls were RAW-MC war cries.

"*Ooh-rah,*" said Sergeant Richard Morris. His chute was teetering badly from an imaginary torn wing and damaged gravmatrix.

"*Get some,*" added Private Race Atumbi in an uncharacteristically confident voice.

Good for him, Promise thought.

"Where do we go?" asked Gunnery Sergeant Tomas Ramuel as water sheeted off his mechsuit.

Promise and a resolute, reinforced toon of Marines growled out the response. *"To hell and back. Ua! Ua! Ua!"*

"Finally, the boys have arrived." Promise dropped a ring around a small atoll a few klicks northwest of the main island. *"There, let's put down while we wait for our ride. I need a SITREP. What just happened?"*

"I pulled the trigger, ma'am." To his credit, Atumbi's voice didn't so much as waver. *"I did it, ma'am. I got jumpy and gave us away. It was all me."*

"Gaawd bless, Private, didn't I tell you to keep your—"

An intruder overrode the comm, locked Promise out of command. *"That's enough, Lieutenant. I'm calling the op. A retrieval boat is en route. This op is over."* The last face Promise expected to see appeared on her HUD. Lieutenant General Felicia Granby.

It was one thing for Promise to call the op and quite another for the general to do it for her. The mule in her kicked without thinking. "Permission to carry on, ma'am." The words were away before Promise could weigh them properly.

"Lieutenant, you can't be serious?" Lieutenant General Felicia Granby said. *"Girly, you're down to a reinforced toon of Marines. What do you expect to accomplish with that?"*

"The mission, ma'am. We're enough."

"Uh-huh. And your plan?"

The irony of Great-Grans's question caught up with Promise a few seconds later, because at that moment, a schematic marked TOP SECRET appeared on Promise's HUD.

"Ah, Great-Grans—one moment, please."

"Take all the time you need, girly."

Promise muted the general. Asked her AI, "Where did this schematic come from?"

"Unknown, it wasn't part of the OPLAN or in any of the mission briefs."

"What about the RAW-MC's archives? Look under Corregidor Island or Mount Bane."

"Stand by while I query . . . interesting . . . I just met by a very angry AI that insulted my programming and showed me the sign, as if I can't read what it says."

"What sign?"

"It's in a classified file ringed with lockouts." Her mechsuit's AI was try-ing to describe in physical terms what it had only seen in virtual space. In reality, the lockouts looked more like the annual rings of a tree. The sche-matic was at the center of the tree inside the pith, or the tree's heart. "It's a DACT."

Promise rolled her eyes. "A Don't Ask, Can't Tell." The Corps wasn't without a sense of humor. A Marine stomped past a DACT at his or her own peril, because after all, you'd been warned. Violating a DACT could get you a permanent billet inside Camp Vimerling breaking rocks for the rest of your term of service.

"This schematic didn't just appear. Someone gave us the information." A window popped up on her HUD with a list of specific suggestions. "Well, what's the harm in at least trying?"

"General?" Promise said after taking Granby off mute.

"Still here, girly. Whatcha got for me?"

"A plan, ma'am."

The general laughed freely over the voice-only link. *"How 'bout that. And?"*

"We're going to skim the water." Promise read the mystery bullets one by one. "We'll fly under the island's intruder net, minimum grav, and use the wind at our backs." Promise focused on the upper right portion of the schematic, which was hard to miss because it was pulsating. There, an un-marked entrance to the mountain. The schematic said it was lightly guarded by two ANDES and easily accessible by air. "There's a rock face on the lee-ward side of the island. I . . . believe it's largely unprotected. We can scale that to the access tunnel above," Promise said as she followed the tunnel in-side the mountain, "and see where it goes." *And see where it goes?* "With your leave, of course."

"Climbing in mechsuits?"

"No, in skin with gravbelts for safety, ma'am." Fifth bullet down. "Standard-issue gear does come in handy from time to time."

"You'll be awfully light."

"All I need is my pulse rifle and a backup, ma'am." *And a wing and a prayer.* "All we have to do is reach the control tower and hit the little red but-ton to end the exercise and take the W." According to bullet six there was a little red button too. *This is insane.* "We're good to go, ma'am."

"Is that all, Lieutenant? The ANDES may not make it so easy for you. And the island defenders know roughly where you are. You're compromised."

"Not if you provide me with a bit of cover, ma'am." Bullet seven had suggested she ask. You just asked the general to break the rules, said her by-the-book self. No, just bend them a bit, said her break-the-Regs alter ego, because there's a time to follow Regs and a time to chart your own course.

"Ha—you show your true colors, Lieutenant."

"I would never suggest that you—"

"Shut up, Lieutenant. I like your idea." Emphasis on "your," which made Promise think it was actually the general's. "Permission granted. I've thought for some time we needed to shake the simulation up. It's grown stale and the defenders complacent. Stay on the comm. Wait one."

The general placed Promise on mute and commed the control room located inside Mount Bane. A second window opened in Promise's HUD, and the face of a young man appeared. He looked competent and wore the single inverted gold V of a lance corporal (not to be confused with the single flat stripe, or "runway," of a PFC). His eyes widened with recognition, causing him to sit up straight as a board.

"Good morning, General Granby. How may I help the general?"

Promise noted the one-way feed. He couldn't see her.

"Victor Company has suffered crippling casualties in today's exercise and has been asked to return to base. We won't reset the op for at least an hour. Please stand down the mountain and get something to eat."

The lance corporal didn't seem surprised, but his disappointment was obvious. "Aye, aye, ma'am. That's too bad. We were looking forward to squaring off against Lieutenant Paen. After what she did to the Lusies on Montana, well, we thought this one might get interesting."

"Me too, Lance Corporal. We all have our off days. Lieutenant Paen is no different. She'll just have to try again, perhaps sooner than later, mmm? I hope it's the former. I'll leave you to it, then."

"Yes, ma'am."

"General Granby, out."

The water below was choppier and Promise could see a coral reef as they approached the atoll.

"There," Granby said.

"Thank you, ma'am."

"Don't thank me yet. Deal with the private who blew your op and teach him to keep his finger off the trigger." Granby cleared her throat. "Mount Bane no longer expects you. So you'll have the element of surprise. Don't blow it.

"I didn't tell the lance corporal you were ordered to stand down. Merely that you were asked to call it a day. You're not the only one getting schooled today. In war, Marines often see what they want to see and end up misreading the battlefield. The Corps does a good job of teaching us to look for the enemy in hiding, not so the enemy in plain sight. If the lance corporal is sharp, he's going to figure out something is amiss. Hopefully not too soon. Lieutenant, a suggestion?"

"By all means," Promise said.

"You'd best hurry before he pushes the green button and blows you away. You are to use every advantage at to your disposal to take the installation and secure the control room. That's an order." The general smiled. "And Lieutenant, be brilliant. Granby, out."

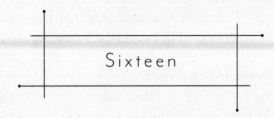

Sixteen

APRIL 24TH, 92 A.E., STANDARD CALENDAR, 0559 HOURS
REPUBLIC OF ALIGNED WORLDS PLANETARY CAPITAL—HOLD
PUGILIST SEA, CORREGIDOR ISLAND WARFARE TRAINING CENTER

"This place crawls." **Sergeant** Richard Morris sounded teed off.

From his tone of voice, Promise didn't have to guess what he was actually thinking. *Lieutenant, back at the firing range, I told you so.*

"Or at least it will when those things reactivate," Morris added a moment later, gauntlet pointing at the ledge above.

Promise turned to look at Morris and punched him in the shoulder plate a bit harder than she'd planned to. The sergeant lost his balance and fell over in the wet sand.

"Sorry, Rich. I didn't think you'd topple so easily."

Morris lay on his side, laughing, in a sandy depression ringed by one-and-a-half-meter-tall greenie. *"Thanks a lot, ma'am."* He started choking on his laughter. *"I needed that."*

Beside Morris were Promise and Lance Corporal Kathy Prichart. Kathy's rifle was up and tracking. Promise's HUD was zoomed to nine-times magnification. At their backs lay the beach with the sound of rolling surf. The remaining points of Victor Company were submerged in a nearby tidal pool, roughly thirty meters away. The pool was shallow enough that Gunnery Sergeant Ramuel had had to sit down to fully submerge, legs straight out in front of him. He'd nearly mutinied when Promise split the remains of Victor Company into two understrength toons of three points each—Alpha and Omega—and left him behind.

"Because we started this op and we're going to finish it too," she'd said.

"And how are we supposed to topple them?" Morris asked as he took a knee in the sand and brushed off his gauntlets.

Up ahead lay Mount Bane's leeward face. Reaching the ledge above meant a near-vertical climb while two ANDES stood watch. The ledge was sizable, perhaps large enough to accommodate a small shuttle or VTOL, though Promise wouldn't have tried a landing, not with her meager piloting skills. According to the mystery schematic on her HUD, an access tube emptied onto the ledge and back-flowed deep inside the mountain fortress. Promise's HUD calculated the distance from the ground to the ledge—130 meters—and then calculated the safest route to the top, which zigged a good bit and zagged across half again as much rock, all angles and faces. There was no way she was climbing that in or out of mech.

"The ascent is impossible, ma'am." Now Morris sounded ticked off.

"Pull out your gravbelt, Sergeant." Promise removed hers from one of her mechsuit's side compartments. Two interlocking plates formed the belt's thick rectangular clasp.

"Bond, establish a link and make it rise."

"Aye, aye, ma'am."

The belt rose on a cushion of countergrav, and floated out of her hands. "We're going to strap these on, and make ascent."

"And leave our mechsuits behind? With respect, ma'am, you've got to be kidding."

Promise had read something in Morris's jacket about his fear of heights. Perhaps he was rattled. Phobias did that sort of thing, even to veteran operators.

"Well, Sergeant, your belt can't handle your weight and your mechsuit's too. You could try to jump the cliff. A full boost might get you there. Though you'll probably signal our position to every ANDES on the island. You could free-climb the ascent. But I wouldn't try it. Got another idea?"

"How do you plan to deal with the ANDES once you scale the face?" Morris asked.

"Mr. Bond, would you kindly explain that to the sergeant?" Promise slaved the company battlenet to her HUD so her boots could watch Bond's presentation.

"Yes, ma'am." A window opened on Promise's HUD and a full-body avatar of her AI appeared to the side, standing at attention. Balding and well into his sixth decade, Mr. Bond wore a thin monocle and tan utilities.

Her AI nodded sharply at her and motioned to the left. On cue, a large white-board and a tray of markers appeared. Bond chose blue and set to work.

"*What am I looking at, ma'am?*"

"*The answer to your question, Sergeant,*" Bond said as he wrote, "*is quite elementary. These are Mount Bane's access codes.*"

"*Access codes?*" Prichart, Morris, Go-Mi, and the gunny said in unison.

"Access codes," said Promise.

Atumbi mumbled something under his breath.

"I heard that, Race." Promise spoke with a confidence she didn't feel. "And, no, we are not in over our heads."

"Have a little faith," said Maxi.

Morris's visor cleared, revealing a scrunched-up face. "*You're gaming the games—ma'am?*"

"I'm seizing the initiative, Sergeant. Today's exercise simulates desperate circumstances. Today we blew our cover, and most of us died on-the-drop. On average, assaulting units lose forty percent in the air, and another thirty on the beachhead—and those are the lucky ones. No unit has ever success-fully pierced Mount Bane's defenses and taken the control room. This exercise is meant to be lost." Promise grew quiet. "Not today. During my comm with the general, I received a short-burst transmission with a sche-matic of the island and the stand-down commands for the ANDES and the island's perimeter defenses."

"*Why did the general give you that?*" replied Sergeant Morris.

"We don't know that she did," Promise said, though she believed the gen-eral had. "Scuttlebutt says Great-Grans hates this exercise. Hates the whole idea of a no-win op. Well, I'm with her there. Maybe she's making her point. Or someone else is for her. Right now I don't care. We have sentries to neu-tralize." Promise fashioned her right gauntlet into a weapon and pointed toward the ledge, pulled the invisible trigger, and held it for a solid one-count.

Nothing happened. Promise pulled the trigger again, and then a third time.

"*Is that thing loaded?*" Prichart asked.

Very funny. "Bond?"

"I sent the stand-down codes and the ANDES acknowledged receipt. I'm just as mystified as you."

Without warning, the leftmost ANDES's head snapped up. It spun on its synthetic heels and walked to the second ANDES, and picked it up around the waist. Turned, and walked to the cliff's edge, and threw it over.

"ANDES overboard," said Prichart.

The members of Alpha toon heard the ANDES skip down the mountain face over their suit's external pickups. The crash was spectacular.

"*So much for camaraderie,*" replied Sergeant Morris. "*Look—this is getting interesting.*"

The first ANDES was examining its forearm, which housed a small pulse cannon. Then it opened its mouth and . . .

"*You've got to be kidding me,*" replied Kathy.

Looks like the scuttlebutt about Great-Grans is true, thought Promise.

Because the ANDES's weapon was also on games mode, it inflicted no real damage to its synthetic self. The ANDES still dropped to the ground like a real suicide.

"All right then." Promise broke concealment. "Crack your suits and shed 'em. Strap on your belts. Bring your rifle, a pistol, and all the cells you can carry. Leave everything else. This won't take long."

"*What else aren't you telling us, Lieutenant?*" asked the sergeant.

"As soon as we hit the ledge I fully expect a proximity alarm to go off. I wasn't sent the codes for that."

"*Wonderful.*"

"*That's the spirit,*" replied Gunnery Sergeant Ramuel. He, Sergeant Sindri, and Private Atumbi were moving up from the pool, and their mechsuits were slick with water. The gunny pulled off his helmet and racked it to his side about the time he reached their position. He dropped his arms and planted his feet a shoulder width apart. A seam materialized along the length of his battle armor, from crotch to sternum, and then down the length of each leg, stopping just above the ankle. Then the gunny stepped out of his mechsuit. He was wearing his black beegees, or underarmor one-piece, and a high-and-tight. Gold Vs on khaki flash rode each shoulder. Below the left shoulder lay the Pythons' unit patch: the bright green and gold snake was coiled around a warship in the throes of death. The gunny's branch tab covered his heart and his individual name the opposite side of his chest.

"I've never heard of Marines assaulting a fortified installation in beegees, ever." The gunny looked himself over with disgust. "Might as well be in skivvies, ma'am. These patches are nothing but bull's-eyes."

"That's why I brought blackouts. Just in case." Promise stepped out of her mechsuit and stretched her arms over her head. "Ah, that feels better." Then she pulled a wad of patches from a thigh compartment, and tossed several to the gunny. She had enough to go around. "Heads up."

I hope I'm right about this. Promise looked out into the great beyond, mouthed, *Sir, a little help and a lot of cover, please.*

"You brought blackouts?" Ramuel couldn't hide his surprise. "That's not fair, ma'am. With respect, you should have warned us."

Promise quickly applied the blackouts to her underarmor. "The enemy rarely does. There, I'm dark. Problem solved."

"Ma'am, I've transferred the stand-down codes to your minicomp, continual squawk." With her helmet off, Bond's SITREP came through her mastoid implant. *"It will be short-range inside the mountain. Maybe fifteen meters. Remember to give the codes time to work before you count the ANDES out."*

"Roger that." Promise didn't bother looking over her shoulder at her mechsuit, at the ghost in her suit. She glanced at her minicomp to confirm receipt of the codes before strapping it to her arm. "Squawking confirmed. Thank you, Mr. Bond. Please hold down Fort Paen while I'm away."

She sighed as cool ocean air washed over her body. "At least beegees breathe." Promise tapped several commands into her minicomp and picked up a foot. Her boot reconfigured itself for standard duty, with an aggressive tread and a noise-canceling sole. "Set your belt for a one-meter-per-second rise. Stay on Lance Corporal Prichart. Move out."

Seventeen

APRIL 24TH, 92 A.E., STANDARD CALENDAR, 0608 HOURS
REPUBLIC OF ALIGNED WORLDS PLANETARY CAPITAL—HOLD
PUGILIST SEA, CORREGIDOR ISLAND WARFARE TRAINING CENTER

Promise hugged Kathy's six as they entered the mountain fortress, quick-timing it with the rest of her Marines in a single-column formation, the gunny at the rear. The mystery schematic had revealed the entrance they were using, suggesting it ran deep inside Mount Bane. The map's value ended there. From this point forward the map was a fog.

Remember, it's just a game, P. That brought her little comfort.

Her thoughts drifted from Marine to Marine, until she got to Kathy. *You've grown attached, P, and you know better. It's Lance Corporal Prichart.* Promise knew she should think of her plucky subordinate as a promising noncommissioned officer first, someday maybe even a "Top Three" SNCO. The markers for greatness were there: competence; dedication; unwavering loyalty; and a zeal that encouraged her toonmates to step up their game. Deep down, she worried about losing Kathy. Combat was a master thief, stealing what the heart could not replace. "An officer must maintain a healthy distance from her subordinates." She knew the regulation, why it was drafted in the first place. Commanders needed their wits about them on the battlefield, thoughts unburdened by personal affections. But Promise couldn't shake it. Kathy had somehow slipped through a chink in her armor, and past the wall she'd erected. *Never let them in.* She glanced down at Kathy's artificial foot, remembering her guardian's near brush with death on Montana. *Focus, P. Keep your thoughts centered and you'll keep her safe. Stop going to a dark place.*

The farther in they went the more the cavern walls narrowed, the more her nerves took hold of her thoughts. If they ran into trouble, Kathy would take the brunt of it. What if Mount Bane's defenders misunderstood what was happening and responded with lethal force? She should have thought of that. If they got pinched by the enemy, they could be goners. The entrance had been a tight fit, barely a shoulder's width across. She might have scraped inside in her mechsuit. Maybe. Now she doubted it.

"Safeties off, stay alert," she subvocalized. The tunnel's sides were low-lit and smooth like volcanic glass. Her feet slipped more than once. Rounding a corner, she saw a recessed floodlight and the base of a flight of rough-hewn steps. The stairs rose quickly, leveled off, and circled to the right, at which point they dropped down four more steps.

Kathy slowed, stepped blindly into the next passageway. She disappeared around the corner for a moment, before reversing direction and coming back into view. The muzzle of her rifle didn't as much as quiver. "Clear."

This tunnel seemed to go on forever. Promise kept looking over her shoulder, counting her Marines. She tapped a quick set of commands into her minicomp, scanned for embedded weapons pods and electronic security measures. Nothing on visual. Nothing on thermals. No energy output detected. *Not very fortressy.* She longed for her AI, but communicating with Bond was impossible through all of this rock. She kept expecting the enemy to appear, or a siren to wail, or a weapon to drop from the overhead and catch them by surprise. She was storming a secret military installation without challenge? Where was everyone? Mount Bane was a secure installation on a classified island, patrolled by wet-Navy destroyers, on the RAW-MC's capital planet. First Fleet under Admiral Yi Soon Singh was out there. Not to mention the platforms strategically covering the system's jump points, laden with weapons pods, energy beams, and myriad point defenses, and a substantial LAC screen. *Nothing is getting through all of that. So why are we getting through here?*

Promise was so distracted she almost missed Prichart's all-stop and ran into her. Her guardian raised her left fist and motioned dead ahead, to the left turn approaching. A large, blind corner. Kathy skirted the wall until she was about a meter from the L. Promise followed behind her and put her hand on Kathy's shoulder, squeezed to let her know she was ready. Then they proceeded to "slice the pie," with Kathy in a crouch and Promise in the over-guard position. They worked quickly, one lateral step at a time along a circular arc. They stepped, aimed, and cleared a piece of the pie. Step-clear. Step-clear. Until they were through. Promise's rifle jerked upward and she nearly stroked the trigger at the woman standing in their way.

Her heart missed two beats. *Warn me next time. I thought we covered that.*

Sandra Paen blocked her path, no more than a meter from the business end of Kathy's pulse rifle. She wore RAW-MC standard-issue beegees and the single gold star of a brigadier general pinned to each side of her collar. "How's my girl?"

Busy. When did you make flag rank? Promise's thoughts dripped sarcasm.

Sandra looked down and smiled. "What a pleasant surprise. Mother's prerogative, I suppose." Sandra's bluegrass eyes glowed faintly in the low light. "Why so uptight, munchkin? I've seen Lieutenant Promise Paen kick in death's door and storm Hell's inner sanctum. This," Sandra said dismissively, "is just a test. A little game. Bond was right. You're nervous like an unbroken pup. Why?"

Kathy looked up and over her shoulder and raised an eyebrow. "You okay, ma'am? You seem, I don't know, off."

"Fine, just feels tight in here." *And crowded.*

Kathy nodded. "Things open up ahead, ma'am. Suits in motion?"

"Let's make some commotion."

"Ooh-rah," Kathy said as she motioned the column forward.

Kathy walked through Sandra Paen first, and as she passed, Sandra turned and fell in step with her daughter.

"She's a good girl. Faithful like an adopted stray."

We have that in common, Promise thought.

"True. The Corps became your family, and hers. Though that's not the whole of it."

Working in tandem, Promise and Kathy cleared two more L-turns before running into another ANDES at the next intersection.

"Things are about to get interesting, wouldn't you say?" Promise gave her mother a do-you-mind-if-we-do-this-later look. *Please.*

"Roger that, munchkin. Later it is, plan on it." Sandra folded her arms and looked down the bridge of her nose. "Just remember to keep your finger off the trigger until it's time to shoot, okay? God help Private Atumbi. That kid's gonna off himself if he's not careful. Or someone else."

Promise smiled and shook her head.

"Ah—there's my girl. It's about time you showed up to the dance."

The truth was Promise did feel better. *Thanks, Momma.*

"That's why I'm here." And then she wasn't and Promise was alone with her Marines and her doubts. They were quieter now, pushed to the side, where they couldn't get in her way.

"He looks harmless enough," Kathy said.

Two meters of fortified peristeel stood at attention. Officially, the RAW-MC referred to all ANDES as "it," not "he" or "she" because ANDES were mechs, not flesh and blood. Sometimes Marines slipped. Close quarters and war bred familiarity, even when it came to tech, not to mention the ANDES' humanoid appearance. Regarding AIs and Mules, the Regs were a bit more accommodating. Mechanized Marines were allowed to name their AIs and their Mules as long as the labels were economical, decent, and didn't undermine discipline. AIs and Mules were also tech. But there was tech, and then there was the tech you lived, breathed, and sometimes died with. That changed things.

So, officially *it*—the ANDES—was standing at attention just outside the lift, and it appeared to be powered down. At least, Promise hoped it was. Her minicomp should have bathed the ANDES in stand-down codes.

It never hurts to make sure. She swiped her minicomp's flatscreen and hit TRANSMIT again. Took a tentative step forward, and then another, until she was standing beside it, looking up.

It towered over her, covered from head to toe in gray reflective alloy. Scale-like panels covered its arms and legs. They could blunt heavy energy-weapons fire and deflect high-yield penetrators. The head roughly resembled that of a human. Instead of eyes there was a seamless visor. Embedded in each forearm were twin pulse cannons, business ends just visible above and behind the wrists.

Kathy walked up to the sentinel and knocked on its chest. "It appears off, ma'am." Satisfied it wasn't going to shoot her, Kathy approached the lift and stopped abruptly when her minicomp chirped. "I believe we've come to the end of the line, ma'am. The I-dent port on the wall just challenged me. Did Great-Grans give you a code for that?"

"No."

"Then I guess it's time to earn our keep."

Down a side corridor, something metallic crashed to the deck and someone hollered out in pain. Kathy, Promise, and the other Marines instantly hugged the walls, and crouched in defensive-fire positions. They heard a male curse a blue streak. He promised to kill someone named George because George had apparently left his tools in the middle of a passageway, particularly where it was poorly lit. A female voice started laughing. "Buck up," she said. "It's just a little bruise and you've got plenty of padding. You're a *big* boy. You can take it."

Promise thought she detected a third set of footfalls too. "Remember, point but don't shoot," Promise subvocalized over her mastoid implant. "If we score now we give away our presence."

The voices rounded an intersection. "You've never missed a meal," said the female, "and you need to watch where you're going."

"I don't intend to miss breakfast either," said a deep male voice. "Let's get this over with."

"You two fight like lovers," said the third.

"Eew!" replied the woman.

"What? I'd make a great catch," said the older-sounding male.

"There's *so* much of you to enjoy," said the female.

"Shut up, you bi—"

"You *what?*"

"Blowhard."

"Afraid to say it? You're nothing but a fat pig *and* a coward."

"All right, you two," said the younger-sounding male. "This won't take long if you don't make it take more time than it should. Cut the chatter and fix Five and Six so we can go eat, okay? It's probably a glitch in their programming that a simple reboot will fix. The lieutenant said to handle it and *then* hit the chow hall. Okay?"

"Not utility carts," said the female.

"George should have put his gear away," said the older man. "I'm going to give him a piece of my mind. Oh, that's right. He ran upstairs to get breakfast. I bet he's hovering over a hot plate now. And I'm not, no thanks to the lieutenant."

"Your lieutenant has a lot to learn about working with civilians," replied the female. "I like a full stomach before the day starts. My contract stipulates three squares a day. Three *squares*. Starting with a hot breakfast. Technically, my shift hasn't even started yet. I need a cup of hot caf before I get a raging migraine."

"We'll break your fast just as soon as the ANDES are back in the net, okay?"

"Very funny, Corporal. *Roger* that."

The trio stepped into view. They were turned away from Promise and her Marines. One was dressed in tan Marine utilities and jackboots and wore the rank of corporal. The other two were dressed in civvie coveralls. Promise couldn't read the corporal's last name from her position, but she could see two gold half Vs on his shoulder set against khaki flash. The corporal held his minicomp to the I-dent port and turned to the side, motioning the others to enter first as the lift doors opened. That's when he caught sight of the business end of a Marine Corps standard-issue sidearm leveled at him. His eyes went wide as his hand jerked to his holster. Staff Sergeant Go-Mi rushed the lift, weapon trained on the corporal. "Ah, ah, ah, not so fast." But the corporal was faster. He pivoted to the side and struck Go-Mi's wrist, knocking her pulse pistol from her hand. As the corporal drew, Go-Mi rushed him and the two grappled for control of the weapon. A second later it discharged.

Promise pushed between the corporal and Go-Mi as the other Marines took up flanking positions on either side of her, weapons trained on the corporal. "Enough! Corporal, stand down," Promise ordered. "We have you outgunned."

"Fan-frogging-tastic. I'm dead," the corporal said as he looked down at the games tag on his chest, which was blinking red. "With all due respect, Lieutenant, you'd better explain yourself before I comm this in."

Eighteen

APRIL 24TH, 92 A.E., STANDARD CALENDAR, 0617 HOURS
REPUBLIC OF ALIGNED WORLDS PLANETARY CAPITAL—HOLD
PUGILIST SEA, CORREGIDOR ISLAND WARFARE TRAINING CENTER

"Welcome to the afterlife, Corporal," Promise said dryly. She offered him her hand.

He stood his ground and raised his chin in defiance.

Promise dipped her head. "Fair enough." Then to both civilians: "Please stay calm. I swear not to kill you." She gave the woman and a heavyset man a thin smile before returning her attention to the simulated casualty. The corporal's name tab said FENWAY. "I'm Lieutenant Paen, commander of Victor Company." Promise ignored etiquette and stuck out her hand. After all, as far as today's game was concerned, the corporal was technically dead and the Marine Corps bible said nothing about saluting corpses. "I'm sorry to drop you this way. Unfortunately, it was necessary. If you're a willing soul, your death can service a higher call."

The corporal formed her last name silently, and then his eyes narrowed in thought.

"Pythons don't bite, Corporal."

Recognition hit the corporal's eyes and he came to attention.

"Lieutenant Paen, it's an honor to meet you, ma'am." Corporal Fenway's arm rocked upward, his eyes focused in the distance at a regulation three centimeters off her right ear. "You did the Corps proud on Montana, ma'am. It's about time we stood up to the Lusies."

"Thank you, Corporal. As you were, um, before I shot you."

The corporal's brows knitted together. "How did you get in here? We beat you. I watched your Marines splash down on the scanners. No disrespect meant, ma'am."

"None taken, Corporal. The Marines before you are what's left of my company. I should be saying 'well done' to you and the island's defenders. As you can see, there's still a remnant of Victor Company, and we have an op to complete. I intend to take this mountain and push the little red button." Promise cocked her head in thought. "Care to be in on it?"

The gunny stepped to the front and cleared his throat. "Tell you what, Corporal. You let us pass and I'll explain it to you over a round of beer. On me. Name the drink. Do we have a deal?"

"I'm sorry, uh . . ." With the gunny's rank insignia and name tab blacked out Fenway was at a loss.

"That's Gunnery Sergeant Ramuel," Promise offered. "We had to take precautions."

Fenway stuck out his hand. "Gunny, even if I wanted to, you know I can't officially help you, or the lieutenant."

The corporal's eyes fell out of focus, a telltale sign that he was being commed. "Too late, ma'am. That's the lieutenant wanting to know why I got shot." The corporal looked down at his weapon, which was now locked down and useless, and shook his head in disgust. "I'll be on KP duty for a month."

"Then you'd better take that comm and change his mind, Marine," Promise said.

"Aye, aye, ma'am." The corporal actually came to attention again and took a deep breath before looking away. "Lieutenant, this is Corporal Fenway, go ahead, sir."

Corporal Fenway winced, seemed to shrink into himself. After an agonizing minute, Promise made a knifing gesture across her throat.

"One moment, sir."

"All right, ma'am. I've just put Lieutenant Cahill on hold." Fenway's expression made it obvious he didn't think much of Cahill. "I'm going to pull a crap assignment after this is over. Something tells me you're going to make it worth my while. Aren't you, ma'am? That bit about my death serving a greater purpose, right?"

"Don't worry, Corporal. When this is over, I'll tell Lieutenant Cahill I held a pulser to your head and made you do it." Promise drew her sidearm and waved it in the air. "See."

Promise had been an NCO before the field commission was thrust upon her, and her company lieutenant had been a wise man with an ear attuned to his noncoms. When he spoke, she'd listened. It had worked both ways. Respect was the foundation of the Corps and it flowed like time in both directions. Wise officers—especially inexperienced lieutenants—knew they knew next to nothing about the RAW-MC. The Corps had its share of puffed-up officers who thought they knew it all, and made sure everyone else knew it too. If Promise had to guess, Cahill was one of those.

"Lance Corporal," Promise said to Kathy, "please relieve the corporal of his weapon and minicomp. Corporal Fenway is now our prisoner. Zip-tie his hands and feet until the end of the exercise. Sorry, Corporal, now you have absolutely no choice in the matter."

Fenway gushed relief and thrust out his hands. "Thank you, ma'am. I'm grateful."

"Now, Corporal, we need to take the lieutenant off comm-hold. Wait one." Promise looked over at the female civilian who'd been standing in the corner with her arms crossed, taking it all in. "Would you kindly remove your laser cutter from your belt, set it to its lowest setting, and shoot the corporal?"

"You want me to what?"

"Shoot the corporal," Promise said. "Just do it and I'll explain after, okay?"

"The corporal did keep me from my breakfast. Fenway, hold still." She hit the button. "There. Happy?"

"Thank you," Promise said. "Just humor me for a moment." Then she turned to Fenway. "Corporal, here is what you are going to say, 'sir's all the way." The corporal's smile spread over his face as Promise told him. "Understood?"

"Yes, ma'am!"

"Good Marine. Take the lieutenant off hold . . . now."

The corporal immediately winced again. "Sir . . . yes, sir. Sorry, sir! If you'll allow me to explain, sir? No, sir, I am not trying to rain piss on the lieutenant's otherwise pleasant morning or ruin his fresh-brewed caf, sir. No, sir, I did not just off myself with my own pulser, sir. Sir, if I may . . . I can explain, sir. Sir, the civvies you assigned me are upset about missing breakfast. My tag recorded two direct hits, sir. I was shot with a laser cutter, sir. That's pretty creative if you ask me. No, sir . . . you didn't ask me, sir. Yes, sir . . . I'd say she's quite mad, sir." The corporal smiled and relaxed his shoulders. "Yes, sir. I will make a full report of the incident. No, sir,

I don't intend to press charges, sir. I'm sure I can patch things up with her on my end, sir. Yes, sir, I will remind her of that, sir. Roger that, sir. We are headed to fix the ANDES at the lieutenant's leave. Yes, sir, we will get them back in the net. Thank you, sir. And thank you for your understanding, sir. Corporal Fenway, out." The corporal wiped his brow with his shackled hands and muttered something uncomplimentary under his breath.

"Well done, Corporal," Promise said, slapping Fenway on the shoulder.

"Ma'am, I just lied to a superior officer."

"Did she or didn't she just shoot you?" Promise reminded Fenway. "Now shut your trap so you can't incriminate yourself." She turned to the civvies and gave them a once-over.

"You're not tying me up." The female holding the handheld laser cutter was still pointing it at Fenway. "Corporal, just what is going on here? You just incriminated me. Thanks a lot. You too, Lieutenant. Who are you anyway?"

"Sarah, this is Lieutenant Paen," said Corporal Fenway matter-of-factly.

"So what? Her name means nothing to me. Should it?"

The corporal pursed his lips. "How many Marine Corps lieutenants do you know named Promise Paen?"

"Corporal, I said shut it," Promise said with a smile. "I appreciate your courtesy, but I will take things from here."

"Sorry, ma'am," said Fenway.

"No need to apologize. Now, for you two."

Recognition dawned upon the woman's face. "You're the lieutenant from that planet. What's it called again? Something with an M—Montezuma, Mariana . . ."

"Montana," Promise volunteered.

"That's the one. You're the savior of Montana."

Promise's face hardened, and she heard the gunny clear his throat. Kathy's weight shifted toward the woman. Promise put a hand on Kathy's shoulder and shook her head, *no*. They all hated the word "savior" because they'd lost so many on Montana, and the loss was always with them.

The corporal seemed to notice the tension in the room. The female civvie plodded along, oblivious to the hot button she'd pushed. "Well, now. That changes things. I'm Sarah Krantz, android maintenance tech for the Wynn Claxon Corp., subcontractor for the RAW-MC. I work on the ANDES." She extended her hand. "You disabled my mechs, didn't you?"

"Sorry about that, Ms. Krantz. Please make repairs out of the lieutenant's budget." Promise grasped the woman's hand and smiled. "How about that breakfast?"

"Finally, a little courtesy from the RAW-MC." Sarah spread her arms wide and gave the corporal a stern look. "See, that's how it's done." Then to Promise: "Thank you, ma'am. Please call me Sarah. You Marine types sure take your games seriously, and your titles too."

"Yes, we do, Sarah. Speaking of games, I need to reach the control room and push the little red button. Up for a little ruse?"

Sarah chewed her lip in thought. "I don't know—Lieutenant Cahill isn't that bad. But, you—you're Lieutenant Promise Paen. Well, what are they going to do to me? Fire me for becoming a hostage in a war game." Sarah unclasped her utility belt and handed it to Kathy. "Go on—take it." She undid the front of her coveralls, stepped out, and tossed her clothes to Promise. Her skivvies were civilian-grade. Royal-purple separates finished with enough white lace to cover her vitals. Unlike her face, her construction was far from plain.

Promise heard a couple of mouths pop open behind her.

"Mouths closed, gentlemen." Promise took the coveralls from Sarah and quickly dressed. "Thank you, ma'am. My men are in your debt."

Sarah placed her hands on her hips and gave the gunny a once-over. "You—comm me later and we'll call it square. Make that an order." She winked at the now-blushing Tomas Ramuel and jerked her head down the corridor. "Take the lift to the twenty-third floor. Exit and head left through two more corridors; take the third one right, and then an immediate right. You'll probably need this." Sarah pulled her minicomp out of the cup of her bra and handed it to Promise. "When you get there you'll understand why." Then she turned to her civilian colleague with mischief in her eyes. "Strip."

As the lift doors opened, two ANDES swiveled round to meet them.

"I-dent please," warned the one on the left in a pleasant-sounding voice.

Promise stepped into the lift's threshold and held up Sarah's minicomp to the I-dent port on the sentinel's chest. "Here you are, sentinel."

The ANDES considered Promise a moment, and then ducked to peer into the lift. It suddenly jerked upright, turned to its left, and walked across the corridor and into the opposite wall. The wall cracked and the ANDES went still. The second ANDES sat down and put its head in its lap.

"Everyone out," Promise ordered.

"That one's flexible," Kathy observed as she crouched next to Promise, rifle scanning for hostiles.

Private Atumbi and Sergeants Morris and Sindri crouch-walked around Promise and into the open, scanning for targets. Maxi kept to the wall nearest the lift and moved forward several meters, toward a set of double doors. Found them locked. Staff Sergeant Go-Mi and Gunnery Sergeant Ramuel maintained overwatch positions from their partially concealed positions just inside the lift.

To his credit, Atumbi's approach was close to textbook: He was balled up to present the smallest target possible, and he was leading with his fixed sights. The only sign of self-doubt was the sweat on his brow, which on a more experienced Marine might have been overlooked completely. Atumbi and Morris reached the wall opposite the lift, and took up defensive-fire positions. After scanning the corridor, they signaled Maxi, and Maxi motioned the all-clear. Only then did Promise walk into the open.

Kathy and Promise were dressed in civvie coveralls. Kathy's were large enough to fit two of her in each leg, and the material scuffed as she walked.

"Can you be any louder?" Promise did a quick three-sixty. "Kathy, I need eyes in the sky."

Kathy stuck out her tongue and then took a knee. She pulled two disks from a thigh compartment and slid them across the deck. Maxi did the same but in the opposite direction. Before the disks had slid to a halt, the tops opened. Four swarms of whiskers took flight. The insect-sized probes hovered for a moment before forming into flights and accelerating away. Almost immediately the map loaded to Promise's minicomp began to update.

Still no challenge, Promise thought. *I have a bad feeling about this.*

"Wait, I've got two tangos headed our way," Kathy subvocalized over her mastoid implant. "Twenty meters and closing . . . in that direction."

"Kathy, you're with me. Maxi, I want to know what's through those doors." Promise pointed to the doubles that were locked. "Everyone else, hide."

Promise walked back toward the lift where both ANDES were. She held her minicomp out in front of her and started talking loudly with her free hand and an affected drawl. "Beats me. I've scanned these two twice and can't locate the problem. This one's gyroscope and optics must be shot through. That one crapped out on the floor. We're gonna need a gravsled to haul both to the shop. I knew we should have brought one with us. Told you so myself."

Kathy's mouth dropped open. "Ah—right, ma' . . . Mary. What a pain in the rear! Guess I was wrong. I'm sorry. . . ."

Promise shook her head at her guardian. Gave her a look that said, *Is that the best you can do?*

Kathy shrugged her shoulders, turned, and walked over to the ANDES sitting on the floor. She kicked it in the side, and then again in the head. "Stupid frogging ANDES! Armored-up but no one's home."

The two tangos rounded the corner, hands on their sidearms. A medium build lance corporal named Childs wore light makeup and neatly trimmed brows. A balding sergeant named Korviscante took the lead. "Just what do you think you're doing?"

"Taking out my frustration on this worthless piece of tech," replied Kathy from down the hall. She looked back at her CO and smiled. "Lieutenant Cahill told us to fix them. Well, when I get done, they're going to be in a world of hurt."

"Uh-huh. I don't recognize either of you. I-dent please." The sergeant's hand twitched at his sidearm. "Slowly."

Kathy walked up to the senior noncom with her minicomp outstretched as Promise reached into a deep front pocket to fish out hers too.

"Here is mine," said Kathy.

"And, here is mine, Sergeant."

The sergeant's pulse pistol was nearly out when he got shot. His chest tag started blinking red.

"That was fast, Sergeant. Well done." Promise leveled her pulse pistol at him and motioned to the floor. He slowly pulled his weapon and tossed it. "What gave me away?"

"Your accent vanished."

"Perceptive." Promise held out her hand. "Lieutenant Promise Paen of Victor Company."

Korviscante and Childs came to attention and saluted. "Ma'am, we weren't expecting you."

Promise returned the salute and shot them both again, paying deference to the sergeant's higher rank first. "Kathy, tie them up. Sorry to drop you this way. But, I intend to take this station and . . ." Korviscante's eyes glazed over. "Oh, that would be the lieutenant on the comm, right?" Korviscante nodded slowly. "Okay, Sergeant, here's what I want you to tell Lieutenant Cahill."

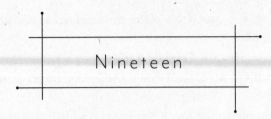

Nineteen

"This is strange," said Atumbi. "Why would the Corps build a passageway to nowhere?"

"The Navy Corps of Engineers built this place," said the gunny.

"Oh."

"Now, now, Gunny. Our Navy brethren aren't the ignorant irradiated spacers we make them out to be, at least not all of them," Promise said. She scrunched up her nose in thought. "Give me a hand." Promise set her mini-comp on Kathy's outstretched palm. A holomap of the twenty-third floor appeared above it. A small blinking icon winked to life a moment later, marking their location on the schematic. They watched as the whiskers scouted unknown passageways, updating the map's blacked-out areas with the exact positions of doors and the internal dimensions of offices and various other rooms.

"The control room is supposed to be here. It's not," Promise summarized. "It has to be here, unless . . ."

"That sergeant you shot fed us bad intel," Kathy said. "Can't blame him for taking it personally."

"We did zip-tie and stuff him in a utility closet," Promise added thoughtfully. "That might have been a bit much."

"What about this room?" asked Kathy. She stabbed a large rectangular-shaped area near the center of Floor 23. Maxi's icon wasn't far away. "One of the whiskers stopped here but didn't enter. Why?"

"Maxi, please check it out," Promise subvocalized over her mastoid implant.

"*Aye, aye, ma'am. Stand by.*" One mike later Maxi had the answer. "*I found the head.*"

"Oh, good. Nature calls," replied Kathy.

Staff Sergeant Go-Mi looked down the bridge of her nose, clearly not amused.

"*I found a morgue full of ANDES too,*" Maxi added. "*I walked in, cued the lights, and found myself surrounded by assault-class drones. I nearly creamed my skivvies.*"

"Any signs of static defenses?"

"*None. Not a single blip. Except for the ANDES in the closet, this floor appears to be empty. I checked a couple of offices and a maintenance hatch on my way back. They were all unlocked, and the hat racks were empty too. I found some personal effects, framed stills mostly. I also found a small arms locker, which was locked tight—no surprise there. And I found this.*"

An image of a small menu appeared in the air, adjacent to the holomap. "*It loaded to my comp when I stepped inside a Sergeant Tiller's office,*" said Maxi. "*A Captain Copenhagen is making flapjacks.*"

Promise read the menu's header: "Flapjack and freshly brewed caf, 0615–0700 hours. Come while it's hot." Toppings included local berries found on the island, fried eggs, syrup, and crisped bacon.

"Let's drop by when we wrap this up," Kathy suggested. "I'm hungry."

Promise glanced at her chrono. "Your stomach can wait. We have seven mikes to find the control room and press the little red button before breakfast is over. Stop pouting, Kathy. You'll survive."

"*This* isn't right, ma'am," Staff Sergeant Go-Mi said. "Where is everyone?"

"Isn't it obvious?" said Kathy, clearly annoyed. "They're at breakfast."

Go-Mi was not amused. "This entire enterprise is a waste of time. Ma'am, can we please get on with this?"

"Let's take a closer look at Atumbi's passageway to nowhere," Promise said. "Gunny, Atumbi—watch the mouth of the p-way. Shoot anything that enters."

"The walls are taller here. I wonder why." Promise followed the three-meter-high rock face to where it joined with the overhead.

"Looks like a dead end to me," said Kathy.

"Looks like a Navy corridor to nowhere," said Maxi.

"Looks can be deceiving." Promise pulled Sarah's minicomp from a thigh pocket and tossed it in her hand. "Sarah said I would need this. Why?" Promise touched the screen, and nothing happened. She turned it over in her hand and shrugged her shoulders. "This isn't coded to me. What am I supposed do with it?" Promise walked to the wall and ran her fingers across the uneven rock. "Where's an I-dent port when you need one?"

"Ma'am, it just appeared, right there." Private Atumbi pointed to the left-facing wall, at about eye level, to a small recess in the rock, just inside the mouth of the passageway.

"That wasn't there a moment ago," Kathy said. "I think there's a projector in the wall."

"Good work, Atumbi." Promise held Sarah's minicomp up to the interface.

They all turned when a low hum began emanating from the dead end behind them. A seam appeared in the rock. It became a step, and then two steps, and soon an entire flight of stairs lay before them. And they could hear someone coming down.

"Maybe that's Lieutenant Cahill."

"If it is his timing is perfect." Promise commed the lieutenant over her mastoid implant.

"Who is this?" The voice echoed down the stairs and into the passageway, and the footfalls stopped.

"Lieutenant Promise Paen."

"Ah, Lieutenant, so sorry about today. Better luck next time."

"I certainly hope so," Promise subvocalized. "Your defenders did well. Congratulations."

Kathy spun her pointer finger in the air and looked up. "Here they come now." When the whiskers flew by and up the stairs, Kathy turned around. "Stay on me."

They took the stairs one at a time, up one flight to a landing and a switchback, up a second flight to another landing with a small window to the outside. Beaches and ocean stretched out far below. They encountered Cahill on the third flight and almost knocked him over. He wore tan utilities and the single gold bar of a first lieutenant on each collar point.

"Sorry about that, Lieutenant," said Kathy, who offered him her hand and yanked him to his feet when he refused to take it.

"Just what is the meaning of this?" sputtered Cahill.

"Lieutenant Cahill," Promise said, extending her hand, "I'm Lieutenant Promise Paen. I'm afraid you're my prisoner for the duration of this exercise."

"We'll see about that." Cahill reached for his sidearm, but not before Sergeant Morris had a hand on it.

"I'll take that, sir." Morris drew the weapon and tucked it into his web belt.

"Lieutenant Paen, I don't know what you hope to accomplish—"

"Lieutenant Cahill, I'm a bit pressed for time. Let's do this up top. Everyone up." Promise motioned up the steps with the business end of her pulse pistol.

"I will not be manhandled. This is my installation. Remove your hands from me this instant, and point that thing somewhere else or . . . or I'll have you court-martialed."

"Not today, Lieutenant," said Promise. "After you, sir."

To Promise's surprise, the nexus of the mountain was little more than an excavated chamber with rough-hewn walls. Three workstations and four folding chairs sat facing a wall of clear armorplaste. A small table sat against one wall with a cup and the remains of Cahill's breakfast on it. A broken-down ANDES stood next to it. The lack of security was appalling. Mount Bane's exterior was all bravado and balls, ANDES standing guard and ground-based launchers searching the skies. Inside the mountain was a paper tiger.

"Where's the little red button?" Promise's Marines fanned out around the room. The gunny and Private Atumbi took positions at the mouth of the stairwell to cover their six.

"I don't know how you got in here, Lieutenant Paen, and it doesn't matter. The game is over. You're nothing but a cheat."

"Lieutenant Cahill, like it or not I have my orders. This installation is now under my control. You are hereby relieved of command. Please surrender your minicomp to Sergeant Morris, and stand down."

"How did you get into my mountain? You, you're . . ." The lieutenant's ears were noticeably flushed. "You're not supposed to be here. *You*," he said, pointing at Promise, "were ordered back to CENT-MOBCOM by General Granby. I heard her give the order myself."

"Why don't you play it back to be sure you heard right," Promise suggested.

"I will."

The lieutenant stomped to the center workstation. His hands danced across a flatscreen. Above it a segmented holoscreen appeared and several tiers of date stamps blossomed on the right panel, in bold colors. He scanned down the first tier of dates and returned to the top of the second. He was halfway down it when he stopped. "Ah-ha, here it is." The lieutenant stabbed the date stamp with his pointer finger, dragged it to the left panel, and spread his fingers wide. General Granby's voice instantly filled the room.

"Victor Company has suffered crippling casualties in today's exercise and has been asked to return to base. We won't reset the op for at least an hour. Why don't you stand down the mountain and get something to eat."

The lance corporal spoke next. *"Aye, aye, ma'am. That's too bad. We were looking forward to squaring off against Lieutenant Paen. After what she did to the Lusies on Montana, well, we thought this one might get interesting."*

Again, Granby spoke. *"Me too, Lance Corporal. But, we all have our off days. Lieutenant Paen is no different. She'll just have to try again, perhaps sooner than later, mmm? I hope it's the former. I will leave you to it, then."*

"Yes, ma'am."

"General Granby, out."

Lieutenant Cahill turned around, looking vindicated. "What do you have to say for yourself now, Lieutenant Paen?"

"Is this what the academy is churning out these days?" Sergeant Morris nudged the lieutenant's shoulder with the business end of his rifle.

"Careful, Sergeant, or I'll have you on charges of insubordination and assaulting an officer."

Promise shook her head at Sergeant Morris, and raised a hand for him to back off before she returned her attention to Cahill.

"Lieutenant, bear in mind that you're a POW for the duration of this exercise."

"An exercise that *you're* carrying out against orders!"

Sergeant Morris raised his weapon. "Sir, your minicomp or your wrists. Your choice?"

"I will not stand down, Sergeant. As you just heard, you were ordered back to HQ by the general. I'll see you busted down to corporal for this."

"Lieutenant," Promise said as patiently as she could. "The general never *ordered* me to do anything. All she did was *ask*. I asked to continue the mission, and the general approved my request. That is not on your recording.

You may comm her personally to confirm its truth. I'd replay the conversation for you myself. Except I can't seem to reach my AI at the moment. Nevertheless, we just heard what she said to your controller and she couldn't have been clearer. Play it again. Please. Because you are so adept at following orders, I believe you will be able to clearly discern the nature of the general's."

During the replay, Cahill's jaw clenched. He turned back to look at Promise. "You're arguing a technicality."

"Words matter, Lieutenant. In fact, the First Directive specifically mentions this fact. Lieutenant, do you remember the First?"

The lieutenant crossed his arms. "Don't mock me."

"Sergeant Morris, if you please."

The sergeant cleared his throat. "'A Marine never lies to a superior or violates his word. If he does, he betrays the Corps, his fellow Marines, and himself. A Marine's word is her bond. What she thinks she says. What she says she does. What she does defines her.'"

"Sergeant, relieve the lieutenant of his minicomp. Kathy, tie him up. You are authorized to use appropriate force if he resists you."

"You have no right." Cahill looked ready to lunge at Promise. "Lieutenant, I will have you up on charges, all of you. Do you hear me?"

"And shut him up too."

Promise walked up to Cahill and pushed his chair out of the way, with him still in it. He lunged for her sidearm but was a microsecond too slow. Morris grabbed the lieutenant's hand, bent it backward, and brought the man to his knees.

It took Promise a moment to find the main comm. Her words echoed across the floors and lifts, the offices and mess hall of Mount Bane, causing tables of Sailors, Marines, and civvies to pause in midchew. "This is Lieutenant Promise Paen of Victor Company, Charlie Battalion, Fifth Brigade, Twelfth Regiment. Roughly one hour ago, my unit assaulted this installation and was presumed neutralized. Obviously, V Company is alive and well. We have secured this installation and the control room. Lieutenant Cahill was ordered to stand down and chose to resist instead. After an unfortunate tussle, we regret to inform you he is now in our custody and care. If I understand the mission brief correctly, upon entering the control room the attacking force may claim the victory by pressing the little red button." Promise lifted the clear plexi lid and pressed the red button. The room went dark for a moment. "This exercise is over. Enjoy your breakfast. Lieutenant Paen, out."

The ANDES standing in the corner of the room was used to being ignored. Second-gen, Mercury-class-B12 android enemy soldiers hadn't been used for years. Spare parts were impossible to find. This particular Mercury was missing armor plating on the right chin and thigh, probably removed years ago with the weapons systems. The faceplate was cracked, the lower abdomen open to air. Abandoned and long forgotten, no doubt, except for the bits of dried carbonscreen someone had stuffed into its bowels. And, in spite of the regs against naming ANDES, the Mercury's name tab said JOE BREAKDOWN.

Breakdown happened to be an amnesiac. It knew to answer to its proper name and the shortened version of it—Down. "Get Down to do it" was commonly heard in the main control room, after one of the bars had issued an order that the stripes didn't particularly care for. Like refilling the caf or trudging down to the utility closet for spare sani because the head had run out.

Earlier that morning, when Promise transmitted the stand-down codes, Breakdown had responded like the other ANDES. Except it encountered a problem. After decommissioning, the ANDES's combat matrix had been wiped and its memory links severed. This meant Breakdown didn't know what to stand down from. When it sought clarification, it ran a diagnostic and found the problem. A small, long-forgotten reserve of nanites restored the ANDES's connections to its backups, at roughly the same time that Sergeant Morris subdued Lieutenant Cahill, the lieutenant of the watch.

It was then that Breakdown remembered its original programming, and it responded as it had originally been designed to do. With lethal force.

Sergeant Morris didn't see the sentinel turn toward him and draw back its fist.

The ANDES looked down at Morris, now crumpled on the floor, blood gushing from his head.

An unidentified woman dressed in beegees threw herself over Morris's body. Her screams echoed across the control-room floor.

"Medic!"

Twenty

I wish they would back off. Promise batted another hovercam out of her way. "No comment." The newsies were everywhere. Warm bodies and mechs, pressing in from all directions.

"A statement. Just a word, ma'am, please."

I'll give you a word. Promise wanted to shoot the hovercams out of the Senate rafters, and if she'd had her pulse rifle with her the temptation might have been overwhelming. She was barely halfway down the main aisle of the Senate floor and far short of the brick-red carpet the newsies had to stay off of. Red like a sea of blood. Sharks patrolled the waters and she didn't dare show fear or they'd smell it and eat her alive. Overhead a swarm of hovercams clicked and jockeyed for the best aerial position as flashes of light burst from the sky. Logos for TransWorld News and Universal News Corp. and the *Hawk*. The noise and the barrage of light were stretching her thin. One of the hovercams got too close. Boom. The flash temporarily blinded her, and triggered a memory she'd worked hard to lock down. She saw the ghost of a Marine jumping on a grenade meant for her. Boom. Another specter came, a downed Marine near death, mechsuit crushed, autodestruct enabled in a final act of defiance. Boom. She was standing in a sea of decaying corpses. Then they started to rise and claw at her legs. She swore she could feel a bony hand tearing at her calf. *It's not real, P. None of it is.* Boom. "Just a word, ma'am." Boom. *Get a grip, Marine.* Boom. The room began to spin.

"All right, all right! Leave the lieutenant alone." A striking woman with jet-black hair and high cheekbones pushed through the newsies and put her arm around Promise. Several men in tailored suits followed close behind her, and then spread out to form a human wall. "There will be time enough to interview the lieutenant . . . after her testimony."

"There will be?"

"Of course, Lieutenant. Here, drink this. You don't get to come to the mountain without paying the price. Senator Terra Jang, at your service." Jang was older than Promise but not by enough to be her mother, and her tailoring was exquisite. "Now, let's get you to your chair. Everyone, please step aside. Now!" Jang barked like a gunnery sergeant in a sea of privates. "Better. Thank you all. I will be holding my own press conference after the hearing and you are all invited. Drinks and hors d'oeuvres will be served."

"Thank you, Senator," Promise said as she wiped her brow.

The flashes and clicks and "over here, ma'am"s retreated to a manageable distance. Promise stepped onto the red carpet and took a deep breath, felt her senses return and with them her better judgment. *Never fully trust a bureaucrat, particularly one you don't know a stitch about.*

"Ah, here we are." Jang motioned to a long rectangular table. Each end had its own small touch screen and a pickup. In the middle sat a tray with water and drinking glasses. "You're going to do splendidly. Orphans like us must stick together." Said like it was a badge of pride. "You've got more than one senator in your corner. Okay?"

Promise's eyes narrowed as she considered Jang's revelation, and took her seat. *Interesting.* Jang nodded. "Our stories matter, Promise. It's up to us to make sure they get told. Don't hold back, ever. We will talk later. Plan on it."

We will? The noise level on the Senate floor had grown so loud that Promise couldn't hear herself think. She turned in her chair and saw hundreds of unfamiliar people; dozens were staring at her. *Looks like a full house.* Maxi and Kathy were in the balcony somewhere, which looked just as packed. Promise was about to give up on them when she saw a white flag waving back and forth from the third row back. *Very funny.* Maxi and Kathy were dressed like she was. Regular-dress blues, standard glittery and ribbons. She desperately needed a familiar face, even if theirs were too far away to make out.

A moment later, a young woman in a smartly pressed suit approached from Promise's right side. "Lieutenant Paen, I'm Valentine Aliri. Senator Jang asked me to check on you. Is there anything you need?"

Need? Promise's shell shock must have been apparent. Aliri smiled. "Don't worry, ma'am. It's your first time. Here." Aliri leaned forward and activated the screen on the table in front of her. A holographic window opened above it, at a comfortable reading level. Promise's statement appeared a moment later in large script.

"Don't worry about them—" Aliri looked over her shoulder, nodded to the wall of newsies and hovercams, and then looked back at Promise's speech. "Only you can see it. Feel free to edit on the fly. If you lean to the side it disappears. See? Keeps the newsies from scooping your speech."

"That's very useful," Promise said.

Senator Terra Jang appeared in an adjacent window and briefly made eye contact with Promise. Below Jang a file appeared with the names and party affiliations of senators she was about to testify before. All very useful.

"Thank you," Promise murmured. "My mind's gone to mush. I've been trying to keep all the names straight. Ms. Aliri, thank you for your assistance, and please thank the senator for me too."

"My pleasure. And please call me Val. The senator likes to keep things on a first-name basis. Do you need anything else, ma'am?"

"No, I'm fine, I think. And please call me Promise."

"If I may, Promise, breathe in through your nose. It will help."

"Like a runner. I should know that."

"Exactly." Val looked up as someone shouted her name. "This place can get to you if you let it. So don't."

"Roger, that."

Promise turned her attention to the holoscreen and Senator Jang's dossier. She quickly scanned it and then swiped it aside. Keyed a file and quickly discarded it, and then another. Movement on the Senate platform drew her attention. A few senators had already found their seats. There was Senator Jang taking the steps now. Jang's seat was off to the side, which made sense, Promise thought, given Jang's junior status on the Homeworlds Alliance Committee. Promise returned to the dossier and dug a bit further. One of Jang's op-eds caught her eye.

ANTI-SLAVER'S GUILD SAVED MY LIFE

A quick scan of the article and she knew Jang's orphan story was absolutely true. Her parents had died when she was young. An unscrupulous uncle had sold her to a sex ring at the age of seven. She'd been trafficked until thirteen. Escaped with a life-threatening virus. Jang had clawed her way back to health, and attended school, landing an internship with Justice Brick on the high court. The more Promise read the more she liked Senator Terra Jang. *But don't like her too much. She's still a poli—*

Bang.

A gavel crashed and the hearing was called to order by a frail-looking gentleman wearing a dark-gray suit and a bow tie. The man appeared in Promise's holoscreen and seemed to look right through her. His name floated to the right. Senator Harold McIrney.

"Lieutenant Paen, thank you for appearing before the committee this morning." Senator Jang's dossier vanished and McIrney's replaced it. He was the chair of the Homeworlds Alliance Committee, in his eighth decade, a high-ranking member of the New 'Verse Democratic and Labor Party. The challenge in his eyes was impossible to miss. "We look forward to hearing what you have to say to us regarding the tragic accident that claimed the life of Sergeant Richard Morris, one of your platoon sergeants, and we hope to learn the truth of why your unit took the actions it did leading up to the sergeant's ill-timed death."

Promise nodded and squared her shoulders. A shiver of sharks was circling, and Promise feared Senator McIrney was leading the pack. McIrney introduced his fellow committee members and gave an opening statement. Then he addressed Promise.

"Before we ask you *our* questions, I believe you prepared a statement for us to hear. Yes?"

"Yes, Senator McIrney."

"The floor is yours, Lieutenant," said McIrney. "You have the committee's undivided attention." Then McIrney clasped his hands together and leaned forward.

"Thank you, Senator." Promise took a sip of water and said a quick prayer. *Sir, morning glory. I could sure use some grace.* "Before I read my statement, I'd like to thank the Homeworlds Alliance Chair and Committee and the Senate Frontier Defense Chair and Committee, and the honorable senators present, for the opportunity to testify today. I've given much thought to my comments, regarding the fateful events of the day in question. I wish to make it clear that I was Sergeant Morris's commanding officer. He was operating under my orders when he was killed, and I assume full responsibility for his loss."

Promise spent the next five minutes sketching the events leading up to Morris's death: her unit's losses; the mysterious stand-down codes and her conversation with General Granby; infiltrating the island; and her deep regret over the sergeant's death. "He saved my life on Montana. I wouldn't be here today if it weren't for his actions then. His loss will never leave me." Promise fought hard for her composure.

"Thank you, Lieutenant," said McIrney with a flat expression. "While I appreciate your candor and heartfelt feelings for Sergeant Morris, I'm not sure I agree with everything you said regarding the training operation you commanded. But, we will get to that in due time. For the present, I yield the floor to the honorable Senator Jang. Senator, the floor is yours."

"Thank you, Mr. Chairman." Jang turned to Promise. "Lieutenant, you're a credit to the Marine Corps and to our great Republic. You deserve even more for what you accomplished upon your birth world, Montana. And you have my sincere thanks . . . and that of your star nation."

McIrney and a few of the other senators on the platform went rigid in their chairs at the mention of Montana. Smiles forced, there and gone a moment later. Jang's comments had obviously touched a nerve.

"Thank you, Senator Jang," Promise said.

"I just have a few questions for you. So, let's take them one at a time, okay?"

Promise nodded. *Here we go.*

"First, did General Granby order you to continue the training operation before or after your unit suffered nearly ninety-percent casualties?"

"After, Senator."

"Secondly, did the general send you the stand-down codes for the island's defense?"

"Senator, I honestly can't be sure. It was not precisely clear to me where the codes originated from."

"Understood, Lieutenant. Then tell us what you believed at the time to be the case."

"At the time . . . yes . . . I believed the codes came from the general. Though I wasn't sure."

"Very good. Thirdly, did the general authorize you to continue the training operation after she'd commed the island and told the lance corporal on watch to stand down the island? I believe she told him to go get something to eat too. Does that sound about right?"

"Yes, Senator, but not in so many words. However, her intent was clear. That's as I remember things."

"Very good, Lieutenant," Senator Jang said. "As you know, Lieutenant, your actions on the day of Sergeant Morris's death have come under scrutiny." Jang looked to her right as she spoke. "Mr. Chairman, I'd like to read a letter from Lieutenant Paen's former commanding officer because it speaks directly to her utter dedication and experience in—"

"Senator Jang." McIrney's tone was patronizing. "If you wish to ask the lieutenant more questions then please continue. Otherwise, please yield your time to the next speaker. We have a tight schedule to keep this morning and much to discover."

"Mr. Chairman, this letter—" Jang held aloft a piece of carbonscreen. "—bears directly upon the events at hand."

"Senator Jang, we are here to question the lieutenant, not to grandstand. Since you have no further questions, the chair recognizes—"

"Mr. Chairman, I must protest your actions. My time is not up!"

The senator next to Jang leaned over and spoke something into her ear. A brief flash of anger crossed Jang's face. They exchanged words and then Jang closed her eyes, and nodded. When she looked up, a near-convincing smile was locked into place.

"If it pleases the chair, I yield the bulk of my time to the honorable Senator Oman," Jang said. She glanced at Promise, her expression unreadable. But the close-up of Jang on Promise's screen showed the worry in her eyes.

"The chair acknowledges the honorable Senator Jang has yielded the remainder of her time to the honorable Senator Oman. Senator Oman, the floor is yours. You have your time plus Senator Jang's remaining minutes to ask your questions."

"Thank you, Mr. Chairman." Senator Lucia Oman surveyed the Senate floor. Her cool, deep-set eyes bored into the pickup and out from the flatscreens positioned throughout the Senate floor, and via the nets across Hold, into every tuned-in home. The news bureaus were feverishly editing the feed in real time and transmitting just-in segments to the small fleet of private courier jumpships scheduled for all the major system nexuses. Departures in the A.M. and P.M. hours. The senator licked her lips and nodded.

"Good morning, Lieutenant. I don't expect to keep you long. I hope you'll be forthright and as direct as possible in answering my questions. Do that and you and I will get along famously.

"Sergeant Morris's death is a loss to us all. But his death was unnecessary and completely avoidable, Lieutenant Paen, and that is the basis for my questions today. I'm most interested in your exchange with Lieutenant General Granby earlier that morning. Please relay the contents of your conversation with her to your best recollection."

Promise had carefully prepared for just such a question. She consulted her minicomp and read from her notes, even though she could have projected them onto the holoscreen before her.

"Lieutenant, I know *what* was said between you and the general. I've seen the data feed from your mechsuit too. I'm far more interested in why it was said in the first place. Would you care to read between the lines?"

"I'm afraid I don't understand the senator's question."

Oman sighed over the pickup. "Of course you don't. Why don't we start with the facts and work toward the truth, okay?

"Lieutenant, is it true you petitioned General Granby to continue the Mount Bane operation, even though your company had suffered almost ninety-percent simulated casualties?"

"Yes, Senator, that is correct."

"Hm . . . that's telling. And is it true the general granted your request?"

"Yes, Senator, that is also correct."

"I see. And is it true the stand-down codes for the Mount Bane installation magically appeared on your, ah, your mechsuit's heads-up display. Your HUD as you call it?"

"I suppose you could say the stand-down codes appeared unexpectedly, Senator."

"Indeed. And did you know the general had sent them to you?"

"As I've already said, I had no specific knowledge of the sender's identity, Senator."

"But you had a hunch, didn't you? Were you aware of the general's antipathy for the entire Mount Bane program?"

"Not specifically, no."

"How about generally, Lieutenant?" The senator's eyebrows rose together.

"I believe the general has spoken freely on the matter, Senator." And General Granby had, on more than one occasion. Her distaste for the games was no great secret.

"Do you agree with the general?"

Promise's mouth opened reflexively. She forced it closed as her mind raced for a suitable answer.

"Ah-ha, now we come to the truth. You utilized codes you should not have possessed because you wanted to win the game, at all cost. You and the general are both decorated, skilled warriors, and a credit to our Fleet Forces. Each of you seems to have a history of rushing into overwhelming odds and bending the rules to suit your own purposes. Did you actually believe you could take the installation with, how do you say it, a reinforced *toon*?"

Promise hesitated. "I believed I had to try. War isn't fair, Senator. I simply utilized every advantage at my disposal."

"That may be true, depending upon your point of view, of course. But we are not at war, Lieutenant, a fact I must constantly remind some of my fellow senators of."

"We are not *yet* at war, Senator," Promise said, and she might as well have tossed a flash-bang into the room. A collective gasp rose from behind her. "Whether war comes will ultimately be a political decision, not a military one. My job is to prepare for war should it ever come. That's why we have the games."

The blood drained from Senator Oman's face. "Yes, and that's why we have this committee, to make sure leveler heads prevail. Tell me, Lieutenant, do you believe in an unwinnable scenario?"

"Are you referring to the overarching philosophy of the Mount Bane war games?"

Oman hesitated a moment. "I am, yes. Why?"

"Then, with respect to you and my superiors in the audience, no, I do not. There must always be a way out. There must always be a path to victory. There must always be hope, even in the face of overwhelming odds. Training Marines to lose is a mistake."

"So you do agree with the lieutenant general."

"I sympathize with her position, yes, but arrived at my own opinion independently."

"And her methods. Do the ends justify her means?"

"She changed the game's parameters. In war, our enemy will do nothing less than that if it means achieving victory."

"And here we are again, back to war. Lieutenant, need I remind you we are enjoying an unprecedented time of peace across our core member worlds."

"And how about our protectorates, ma'am?"

"You're referring to your birth world, Montana." Oman's words carried a dangerous edge to them. "You have a bit of history with unwinnable odds, don't you, Lieutenant. How many Marines did you lose on Montana?"

"Senator Oman!" Senator Jang was standing now. "With all due respect, you are out of line." A swell of outrage rose from the Senate floor, though Promise couldn't be sure how much of it was for or against her.

"Sometimes, Lieutenant, battles are manufactured, not simply fought." Oman was almost shouting. "War is the most costly game and it rarely solves anything. One should not court it."

Two more senators stood in protest, their voices carried by the pickups across the chamber. The chairman banged his gavel again and again, but to no avail.

"Mr. Chairman." Senator Terra Jang was leaning into the pickup. "We did not call Lieutenant Paen to testify in today's hearings just to second-guess her past command decisions or question her patriotism to the Republic." Jang's voice shook with anger. "The lieutenant is a highly decorated Marine Corps officer and a national hero. She deserves to be treated as such." Jang had a roll of carbonscreen in her hand and was waving it menacingly at Senator Oman.

"I remind the honorable senator from Glasgow that *she* yielded her time to *me*," Senator Oman said. "You are free to request supplementary minutes from the chair after I and the rest of our colleagues have each had a turn to question the lieutenant. Thank you, Lieutenant Paen, for your service to our star nation. Mr. Chairman, may I suggest a short recess before we continue?"

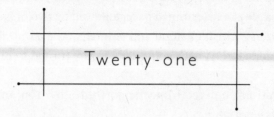

Twenty-one

Promise found her seat in the upper gallery of the Republic of Aligned Worlds Senate chambers, two rows from the front. She sat on the cushion's edge to get the best possible view. Politicians, reporters, government workers, and military brass flooded the main level of the RAW's upper house of government. The Senate was circular in shape, with an outer and an inner ring comprised of delegation boxes and virtual pickups. Plebiscite worlds—mostly from the verge—sat farthest away from the center platform, where the Senate president and the committee chairs presided over half the daily affairs of the Republic's governance. Core worlds comprised the inner ring of the chamber. The outer ring funded eighty percent of the government and wielded twenty percent of the power, while the inner ring generated twenty percent of the Republic's tax base and got to spend the other eighty percent too. You could have cut the enmity between the two with a knife.

Myriad delegation flags hung from the overhead, casting intermittent shadows across the Senate floor. Clusters of Marine Corps noncoms and officers ferried about in regular-dress uniforms, their white berets tucked beneath their arms. A sizable delegation from the Navy had turned out in its telltale regular-dress greens.

All at once a flight of hovercams converged on the north entrance.

"What's going on?" Kathy popped a handful of dried fruit into her mouth and leaned forward.

"There—the screen on the wall is zeroing in." Promise inhaled sharply. "That's Fleet Admiral Ben-Ziser, the chairman of the Joint Chiefs." The admiral took the aisle at a determined pace, followed by two of his senior staffers. Several dozen politicians stood and pointed at the admiral.

"I don't understand. What's going on?" Kathy turned to Promise for an explanation.

"The admiral just entered from the north, Kathy. You understand the significance of that, right?"

Kathy shrugged and popped a hard candy into her mouth.

"Don't you know anything about Republican politics? The uniformed services—we—are supposed to be apolitical. I know. Not in this 'verse. Tradition says we always enter from the west side of the Senate building. We do not take sides in political turf wars." They exchanged telling looks. "It's against Republican law."

Admiral Miles Ben-Ziser was almost to the military's box, situated next to the interplanetary high court's.

Promise continued. "The west entrance is largely symbolic. But time has set this custom in ferrocrete. The New 'Verse Democratic and Labor Party and the Conservative Socialists always enter from the south. Centrists, the military, and the high court enter from the west, where leveler heads are said to prevail." Promise rolled her eyes. "The minor parties—some would say the fringe parties—enter from the east." The eastern parties included the War Hawks, the One 'Verse Alliance, and the Universal Catholic League, among others. "The Conservative Coalition and all of the hard-line, pro-military, pro-defense senators enter from the north. The admiral just made a political statement, and it won't sit well with the Congress."

"Okay, I get it," Kathy said. "Sounds minor if you ask me. What's the big deal?"

"Who sets the Fleet Forces' annual budget, Kathy?"

"Oh."

"Right."

The gallery noise died to a low-level murmur as the main screen switched to the west entrance. Heads turned like a wave across the Senate floor as Lieutenant General Felicia Granby entered the spheroid chamber, and walked down the politically correct radius, from the west. All cameras and pickups on her.

"She got her directions right," Kathy said.

"Doesn't matter." Promise shook her head. "Whatever happens won't change her fate. It's just a show. I was merely the opening act."

Scuttlebutt said Granby's fate was already sealed. The general was being benched.

". . . **you advocate war when** we're at peace." Senator Oman was visibly angry. "You'd spill our star nation's precious blood to sate your need for conquest. Well, let me tell you something, General, our republic does *not* deserve your wrath. And whatever their faults may be, neither do the Lusitanians. What's needed now is time, diplomacy, calmer heads, willing hearts. You have faith to move mountains, I give you that much. But, you've forgotten a more excellent way. A warrior like you probably wouldn't understand that."

General Granby stayed in her seat. Hands folded, she spoke evenly into the pickup.

"'. . . if I have a faith that can move mountains, but do not have love, I am nothing.'"

"I believe the senator is quoting from the Good Book. I tend to agree. However, the senator has forgotten one important fact. Love does not exist in a vacuum. It has obligations to fulfill."

Granby closed her eyes and spoke.

> "Love is patient, love is kind. It does not envy, it does not boast, it is not proud. It does not dishonor others, it is not self-seeking, it is not easily angered, and it keeps no record of wrongs. Love does not delight in evil but rejoices with the truth. It always trusts, always hopes, always perseveres, always *protects*.

"We must protect ourselves, Senator. Our citizens deserve nothing less from us, and if we fail in this regard, what does that say about us as a star nation? As a people?

"Diplomacy has failed us, Senator. We have given our trust, spent our hope, and persevered through gross injustice. We have been patient. Releasing our territorial rights to plebiscite systems has failed us, Senator. We continue to give and the Lusitanians keep taking. We have been kind. Considering our star neighbor before ourselves has failed us, Senator. We have not boasted. We have refused to malign the Lusitanian Empire in the nets even when harsher words were deserved. We have not dishonored them, Senator. We have gone to extraordinary lengths to avoid war and bloodshed. We have not been self-seeking. We have not been easily angered. We have overlooked a long list of wrongs. And now we come to the naked truth. We must *protect* ourselves.

"The Lusitanian Empire does not respect our territorial boundaries or our sovereign laws. She has repeatedly tossed aside our overtures of peace. She has maligned us in the nets and boasted of her superiority instead. She is dishonorable, self-seeking, easily angered. Have we so soon forgotten the gross treaty violations—dare I say blatant acts of war—that occurred in the Montana system and on the planet itself, a Republican plebiscite world, just this past year, or the—how did you put it, Senator—ah yes, the 'regrettable incidents' upon half a dozen of our worlds before that? Have you forgotten the precious Republican blood they spilled? Have you forgotten their queen's indifference to our diplomatic overtures?"

The general stood and looked to her right and left before turning around to appeal to the entire assembly. "Every time we back down they grow emboldened. And our diplomats offer them another olive branch and another system and another living world and more innocents instead of the guilt they deserve." The general clenched her fists, and then to everyone's surprise she slammed the witness table. "We are negotiating from a position of weakness. Weakness, I say! Please, Senators, all I'm advocating is we reinforce our flanks, enlarge our ranks, and redeploy our assets to make the Lusies think twice before violating our borders again."

"You—you're a warmonger, General." Senator Oman's voice shook. "We need cooler heads in the military, not bullish, careerist, myopic generals preoccupied with their own greatness."

Granby straightened her uniform. "You, Senator, are a feckless coward, a simpleton, and a pacifying fool." A number of Marines and Sailors were on their feet and they looked ready to mutiny. "You advocate we wait and talk. Talk has soundly failed us, Senator. And wait? What are we waiting for? Another attack? More of our own dead and wounded? I say the time for a war footing is now. Now, Senator. Now! Before it's too late."

Senator Oman's words drowned in a sea of murmurs as General Granby turned toward the exit to leave. "You have not been dismissed, General! General, do you hear me?"

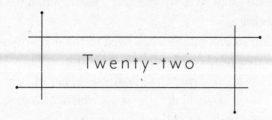

Twenty-two

Lieutenant General Felicia Granby spent the last day as the commander of CENT-MOBCOM hiding her true feelings. Changes were coming, at jump speed, changes far beyond her control. There were units to equip, ready, and deploy, and emerging threats to consider in multiple sectors. Notes to leave for her successor. Gear to procure, receive, and inventory. Classes to steer toward graduation. And last orders to give before the change of command, which she wouldn't be present for. "The task is taller than ever," she'd said to her staff earlier in the day. Her final stand-up meeting. "You're prepared to handle them. I have complete faith in you. The Corps needs you now more than ever to help it prepare for what's coming." *Even as my career ends.* She'd seen the recognition in their eyes. Several had wanted to say more. She'd held up a hand to avoid their questions. It was enough for them to know she was taking the fall for Sergeant Morris's death. And, she supposed, she was at fault for that. Still . . .

The truth came down to guns and butter. General Granby was a war general. She'd been doing what she could to prepare the Corps for the inevitable. The Lusitanian Empire had its eyes on Republican-controlled space, particularly the metal-heavy worlds in the verge. The Republican Press Corps and a glut of politicians warned that a war between the LE and the RAW would be the war to end all wars, that conceding a few systems here and there was far preferable to an interstellar conflagration, that peace was possible in our time. It was all utter foolishness. Did they not know history? It was long past time for the president, the Congress, and the Joint Chiefs of the Fleet Forces to wake up to the dangers pressing upon the Republic, and adopt a war footing.

The RAW-MC's commandant belonged to the prepare-and-wait camp. Granby had butted heads with him on several occasions. Her fight with Senator Oman before the Senate had finally done her in.

Be honest, Felicia. Your mouth got you cashiered. Doesn't matter if you were right. You can be dead right and still wrong.

The general sank into her office chair. She hadn't picked a fight with just any senator, either. Senator Oman was a senior member on the HWAC, and a minority leader in the Senate. Head of the New 'Verse Democratic and Labor Party. Watching Oman stand in protest and turn red with anger had been immensely satisfying, at least in the moment, even as a claxon had sounded in the back of her mind.

Be honest, Felicia. It wasn't worth it.

Oman's party had a standing arrangement with the Conservative Coalition, which was a motley alliance held together by two imperatives: securing interstellar trade routes and preserving the upward curve of the gross systems product. Oman's ilk had voted to give the defense department enough money to build a strong deterrent—at least on screen—and that had kept the pro-military parties in check. The balance of power was shifting. Scuttlebutt said Oman had threatened to pull her votes from several pieces of legislation, including a defense reauthorization bill that the Corps desperately needed, unless she got her way, and Oman's way had included the head of a three-star general.

There was a knock at her door.

"Mm?"

"Ma'am, the commandant just commed. He's fifteen mikes out."

"That was nice of him." Granby tapped her fingers on her glass-like workstation in time to the ticking metronome mounted on the wall. For the first time in a long time, perhaps for as long as she could remember life in the Corps, she had nothing pressing to do and all the time in the 'verse to do it in.

"If you say so, ma'am." Sergeant Major Shaun Lake stood at ease, one foot inside the office of the commanding general, Republic of Aligned Worlds Marine Corps Central Mobilization Command. Lake's hands were tucked into the small of her back. Like the general, she was dressed in her navy-blue regular-dress uniform and white blouse. Seven gold stripes rode each shoulder, three up top and four below; the gold star cluster nestled between the chevrons and the rockers. Her short-waist jacket hung open at her sides. Four hash marks cut across both sleeves, one for every five years of service. Lake was well on her way to a fifth. Minimum glittery and ribbons covered her heart. The sergeant major looked hard at the personal case on the floor beside the general's desk, and the full crate of personal effects next to it. Lake took her time scanning the empty walls and shelves of an office she'd spent more time in during the past three years than with her husband and children in their base housing. When she finally looked back at the general what she saw gave her pause. Granby's eyes were as black as her obsidian dress shoes, and they looked pissed off.

The general clasped her hands together on her desktop, forcing a tight smile. "Please come in, Sergeant Major." Granby dipped her head and smiled. "This is still my office and you're still my senior noncommissioned advisor . . . and friend."

"To the end, ma'am," the sergeant major said.

"Appropriate words, Shaun. To the end . . . and right off the galactic cliff. Never thought I'd see the day. Figured a beam would get me before *that* happened." Granby gave Lake an apologetic look. "That was an awful thing to say at a time like this." The general held up a hand in apology. "We must have some compassion for the commandant. After all, he had a warhead named Oman pointed at his budget, all because of me. He needs well-equipped boots and retrofitted mechsuits and the lift capability to ferry them around the 'verse, all the AIs and drones he can talk the Congress out of, and the flexibility to build the Corps of the future. He's not asking for much, is he?" Granby inhaled. "What he does not need is an uppity three-star who can't keep her mouth shut. He didn't have a choice."

"If you say so, ma'am," Lake said after a long moment. "It's still wrong benching you like this."

Granby waved her hand dismissively. "Never believe your own press, Sergeant Major. You might start thinking you're indispensable."

"General, I—I know you don't. . . ."

"Thank you, Shaun. I do know and I am grateful, truly. Now, you have a career to tend to, which no longer involves me. I will not see yours plummet into oblivion because of my mistakes. I've already spoken with the commandant about it. You will not be put out to rust in some backwater, godforsaken command. As long as you don't create a fuss. Let me go quietly, let this go, here, now. Please."

Lake nodded while making it clear she wasn't happy. "I won't forget. I don't believe I can."

"Believe me," Granby said, "I certainly won't."

The sergeant major actually laughed. "I don't doubt it, Great-Grans." Lake bent down to grab the general's things.

"Leave them for now. There's plenty of time."

"Yes, ma'am. Let me know when you're ready and I'll see to them."

Granby reopened a file on her workstation and swayed in her chair, grasping at stray thoughts. The vid to Sergeant Morris's next of kin had taken her far too long to record. She hadn't needed to make the vid or send it at all. That was Lieutenant Paen's job.

So why did you, Felicia? And why go back to it now? It won't change anything.

Her hand brushed her mop of cropped snow-white hair. It contrasted sharply with the dark-navy hue of her regular-dress uniform. She tried to rub the tiredness from her eyes. Her jacket and pants were badly crumpled by the lateness of the hour, and fresh worry circled her eyes. A half-drunk cup of caf sat beside her workstation, long since cooled. She'd picked at her cuticle until it was a raw mess.

Because he was my last and he didn't have to be. The admission was so painful she couldn't voice it, not even to the sergeant major. Morris was the last casualty of her command, the last boot to fall under her direct orders. She didn't want Morris's service record tarnished by politics. *Or by my foolhardy choices.* She sat up straight, hit REPLAY. "I regret to inform you that . . ." Her voice had caught in her throat and she'd almost edited that part out of the vid. The emotion had been so genuine it had caught her by surprise. She could at least give Morris's family as much. The vid continued. "Your son was a credit to the Republic and the Marine Corps. He was . . ." She'd gone on to praise the sergeant's life and accomplishments without overdoing it, a skill mastered with far too much practice over decades of death notifications. The wall of multicolored ribbons over her breast reminded her of the whens and wheres and hows.

She skipped to the end of the vid and hit PLAY.. "Mr. and Mrs. Morris, I wish I were there with you now, to thank you for your sacrifice and your son's. His presence will be missed. He was a fine Marine and a credit to you, his platoon, and his star nation."

Her words had no doubt hit the Morris family like a twin blow to the jaw. The realities of interstellar travel made personal notifications simply impossible. The words would never be enough. They never were.

She brushed the stars on her collar points and felt herself drifting off to a dark place. Perhaps the Morrises lived out in the country on their world, with plenty of open space. Their home took shape in her mind. An old-fashioned brick walkway greeted them each morning, and a screen door let in the cool morning air. She imagined taking the steps, slowly, testing each one for weakness. The creak of the porch as it bowed beneath her. Three swift knocks. The door opens and the father looks out. *He knows,* and nods to himself, steels himself for the worst.

"Hello, sir. Are you home alone?"

The mother tries to come around him. "Honey, what is it?"

He turns to block her view. She pushes past him and stops abruptly, hands rushing to her mouth.

And the pain lasts a lifetime. I'm so sorry.

At the end of the vid she'd inserted a final message. "Mrs. and Mrs. Morris, I'm reminded of an ancient saying engraved at both ends of the All Souls monument, just outside of National Cemetery here on Hold." The monument curled more than one hundred meters across a manicured lawn, flanked by a small lake on either side, and ringed with sitting benches and shade. The monument was made of smart plexi and looked like reflective black stone. Visitors were encouraged to bring personal vids, stills, and holographic mementos to pin to the wall. Pots and loose earth were available for planting flowers. The unclassified portions of a Marine's jackets were available for the public to scroll through and remember, unless sealed by the family or for another reason. "I can think of no more fitting words to honor your son with," the general said before she recited the inscription from memory.

> *Our fallen paid the highest price, displayed the greatest love,*
> *by laying down their lives for their friends.*

Her recording to the Morris family had traveled by jumpship, arriving in the Kelbakk system two days after she'd recorded it, to Aael's World, and with it the sergeant's flag. A Republican Marine, probably from the planet's central recruiting office, had delivered the news and presented the flag with her deepest sympathies. An identical standard had covered the sergeant's casket at his military funeral at National Cemetery. There was a time when the ceremonial flag was precisely folded into a triangle, and handed to the next of kin. The Diasporas had erased that tradition.

On any given day, there was always a Marine flag traveling by jumpship across the known 'verse with the news no loved one wanted to hear. Sergeant Morris hadn't left a spouse or children behind. Small consolation, that. How many others would never be born because of her foolish actions? Granby knew the question would haunt her. Her stubborn pride. Her determination to prove the futility of a no-win scenario, her desire to silence a mountain, and her willingness to toss the Regs aside to suit her own agenda. One of her Marines was down because of an accident between a man and a machine, caused by human error, and the error had been hers.

Stop digging your grave, Felicia. Don't dishonor the sergeant's memory that way. He deserves better. Shoulder back. Head held high . . . until the end. Now, you have one last vid to record. There are a few things Lieutenant Paen needs to understand about politics and war. Whether she knows it or not, she's painted a target on her back. I helped her do it, and now she's in Oman's sights. The least I can do is give her fair warning before she gets herself shot.

Twenty-three

"He's here, ma'am."

"Thank you, Shaun. Please send him in."

General Granby took a deep breath, got to her feet, and tried to smooth the wrinkles out of her short-waist jacket. She looked around her office one last time, and told herself she'd done all she could with the years she'd had. She could let go now. Someone else would fill her boots. The Corps would survive without her, and General Bao was a good man. CENT-MOBCOM would be in good hands, just not in her hands. Her office was packed. Faint outlines on the walls were all that was left of her career. Fifty-four years in uniform and it had finally come to this. She traced the edge of the workstation as she walked around her desk, and then she walked out the door of her office. Bao's office now.

Commandant Habakkuk Raghavan stood just outside with his arms at his back. He wore a gunmetal-gray buzz that showed off his scars. He was conversing with the sergeant major. When he caught sight of Granby, he did his best to smile.

"General."

"Commandant. What brings you to my neck of the 'verse?"

"One irritating senator who shall remain nameless. I warned you, Felicia. Didn't I warn her, Sergeant Major?"

"Yes, sir. I believe you did, on multiple occasions. If you'll excuse me, sir, I'll see to the general's things."

Raghavan turned toward the woman who might have become the commandant of the RAW-MC, had things turned out differently. "It seems like only yesterday we were at the academy together, squaring away our racks just so, slogging through mud and live fire drills. How did it ever come to this? I swear I never saw this coming, Felicia. Not the bench. An official reprimand in your jacket? Yes. I'd have gladly given it to you myself, even taken a star, but not this."

"Me either, sir. Well, that's not entirely true. My words were brash. I gave Oman the reason she was looking for. You saw the look on her face when I turned around and walked out of the Senate chamber."

"Walked? More like stormed through. It was hard to miss." Raghavan smiled.

"It was almost worth it."

Raghavan nodded toward the exit. "I'm afraid it's that time. I'll walk you out."

General Granby fell in beside the commandant, matching his much longer stride. They passed a row of workstations, now sparsely manned considering the hour. The occupied chairs swiveled as the two passed by. Several sergeants and a handful of corporals watched in disbelief as their CO was escorted out of the building by the highest-ranking officer in the RAW-MC.

"It's been an honor, ma'am." A lance corporal was standing at attention by his workstation, arm canted at his brow.

The general stopped and returned the honor. "No, the honor was mine. Carry on."

"What they're doing to you is . . . it's total . . . ," said a burly staff sergeant who couldn't think of anything professional to say. He clicked his heels together, and puffed out his chest.

The general couldn't help noticing the moisture in his eyes, and put a hand on the staff sergeant's shoulder. "Yup, I'm afraid that it is, Staff Sergeant . . . all of those things and more. But, you have an amazing opportunity to set a positive example in the midst of this. Don't let it change you. Let it go." The general looked over his shoulder. "They . . . are watching."

After a few more good-byes and best wishes the general reached the main lift. Once inside, she clasped her hands behind her and closed her eyes as they descended to the ground floor.

"I'm sorry about this, Felicia. If there was any other way, I would have found it. Those bastards insisted I escort you off the premises personally,

before the change-of-command. You run a round-the-watch operation."
Raghavan scoffed. "They didn't specify the exact time. I did my best."

The lift doors opened at the ground level.

"We go back a long time, you and me. If I weren't the commandant, you
probably would be. And if it had been up to me, your little stunt on Mount
Bane probably would have gone unnoticed. Sergeant Morris's death was
tragic. It was an accident and it was not your fault. I shouldn't need to tell
you that."

"We both know my actions played a part." Granby sagged against the
wall. "This time I pushed too far."

"Yes, you did . . . and how I wish you hadn't. I need you at CENT-
MOBCOM scanning readiness reports and fighting for every kiloton of
gear we can get our hands on. Not sipping tea at that pile of fortified rock
you call a country home. There's always a chain of command. I suppose you
could link any decision one of my officers makes back to me because I'm
the head of the Corps. But, that's ridiculous and you know it."

To her relief, the corridor was clear. It led to the back entrance of the
building. "An aircar is waiting outside." The commandant paused at the
I-dent, and turned to face her. "You read Lieutenant Cahill's report."

Granby's face hardened.

"The little prick went around proper channels when he submitted it. He's
already been reprimanded. I know. It's not much. Imagine my surprise when
the HWAC released the report to the chairman of the Joint Chiefs, and then
Admiral Ben-Ziser personally commed my office and demanded an explanation from me."

Raghavan got a funny expression on his face. "This stays between you
and me. BUPERS is going to misplace Cahill's file while he does a double
tour in the verge."

"Rank has its privileges." Granby didn't smile. "He deserves a lot worse."

"I know. Cahill's report set you up."

"He had help," Granby said.

"No doubt. Oman and her cronies have been after you for years."

"Habakkuk, take the stars off for a moment, okay?" Granby opened her
collar to massage her neck. "Do you believe I screwed up? I'm not asking the
commandant of the Marine Corps. I'm asking you. You. Hab, we run war
games on the island three hundred sixty days a year. I simply threw an unknown into the mix."

"I was afraid you'd ask me that." Raghavan took a deep breath and looked away. "Yes. Yes I do. You violated the parameters of the games and in doing so you risked the welfare of the Marines involved. I might have given you a commendation for original thinking after ripping you a new one behind closed doors." The commandant's smile was strained. "I'm sure you see that giving Lieutenant Paen the stand-down codes for the ANDES and the mountain's defensive grid crossed the line." Raghavan held up his hand to stall Granby's retort. "Whether it needed to be crossed or not is another matter, and beside the point. Suppose one or more Marines thought they were dealing with a massive intelligence breach and a real attack, not just a mock battle. Suppose lethal force had been used by one of our own instead of one of the ANDES. What then?"

"We can't hand-hold our boots. Isn't part of our job to train them to cope with the unexpected?"

Raghavan shook his head. "Yes. But, it's also your job to keep them safe."

"Given a long enough time line, the survival odds always drop to zero."

The commandant sighed. "Felicia, it doesn't matter."

"You know what?" Granby said, dabbing under her eyes. "I wouldn't change what I did, even if I could." The RAW-MC's flag waved in the background next to that of the Republic of Aligned Worlds. A company of Marines jogged by in the distance, singing cadence. "You need to take a hard look at the games, Hab. Lieutenant Paen was right. Training Marines for failure is a mistake."

"Well, it's not supposed to be your problem anymore. I'm retiring you. Except I refused."

Granby's head snapped up. "What?"

"I'm placing you on reserve status, quarter pay, until I can get you back in uniform. It's the best I could do."

"How?"

"A lot of favors. I called in every favor I had. Now I've got red on my ledger. Don't make me regret it. Keep your head down. Keep your mouth shut. Take up gardening. Work with indigents. Go see your grandkids. Cook dinner for your husband for once in your life. I don't care. Just don't raise any Cain, at least not until after I call you up. Might take me a while to get you back on active duty. Senators have long memories."

Raghavan scanned his I-dent, then swung the door outward and walked

Granby to the waiting aerodyne. The sergeant major was standing beside the aircar with a gravsled laden with the general's things.

"Hab, do me a favor?"

"Seriously?"

"Keep an eye on Lieutenant Paen. She's a good Marine. We need more officers like her. Would you see to that for me?"

"One day I'm going to look back and regret this. Sure, Felicia. Anything for you."

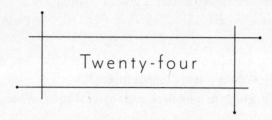

Twenty-four

Promise stood inside the transport's open-air cargo bay, feet perched two shoulder widths apart at the edge of the bay, one hand gripping the overhead rail and the other on her hip. As the transport floated to a stop, she picked up her seabag and tossed it overboard. Then she jumped to the deck to retrieve it. She was headed to Guinevere for a vacation. The colonel had dropped that on her like a bomb the afternoon before.

"A special pass? Why? Why *now?* Sir, we're preparing to deploy."

Colonel Halvorsen had called her into his office the morning after she testified before the Senate. He hadn't looked happy to see her. "You need to disappear for a few days. Don't ask questions and don't make waves. Understood?"

"No, sir, I don't understand. With all due respect, I have way too much to do before—"

"Stop! I don't . . . want to hear it. Do you know what a pain in the ass you are?"

"Sir, I really don't know how to take that. I asked for more time to train my company, not for special passes so they could take time off from training. Permission to speak freely?"

"Permission denied. Do you even know how to disappear, Lieutenant?" Halvorsen's hand flew upward before she could answer. "Wait, don't answer that. Look, Promise, a lot is going on," he'd said, and rubbed his face hard, "and you are not in the need-to-know."

It was the first time the colonel had used her first name, and hearing him use it now knocked her off-balance.

"General Granby was benched for her stunt on the island. The *only* reason you're still in uniform is because she gave you a direct order. But 'I was simply following orders, sir!' only goes so far. Believe me. Matters could have turned out differently for you. Be grateful for how they did turn out differently. That's why I want you off Hold and away from the newsies while this mess calms down. That's all I'm going to say. Leave. Now. That's an order."

"For the record, I protest in the strongest possible terms."

"Noted, now make yourself disappear. Dismissed." Halvorsen grabbed a datapad and tried to look very interested in whatever was displayed on the screen.

"What about my unit?"

Halvorsen looked at the overhead and sighed. "Same song, different key. Every boot in Victor Company gets a special pass too. Yours is already in your queue. Enjoy the vacation because it's the last one you'll see for a very long time."

Promise saluted and stormed out the door. She was halfway down the office corridor when the colonel barked at her to come back.

"Lieutenant, for what it's worth, Sergeant Morris's death was not your fault," the colonel said, surprising her. "I barely knew the man but he was well liked and he'll be missed."

Seabag now slung over her shoulder, Promise consulted the map on her minicomp and looked up to get her bearings. The gray ferrocrete looked freshly poured. Rows of LACs lay in their cradles, hatches popped to ingest cargo. Mechanized Marines scurried about, doubling as stevedores, hefting enormous weights with ease. Promise watched a suited Marine deadlift an enormous crate of ordnance and head up a gangway. Then she turned toward her Mule.

"Come on. I don't have all day." Her Mule was still strapped to the side of the transport behind her, and it appeared to be stuck. "What have I told you? Don't move until we come to a stop. Otherwise you'll get twisted up. Honestly, Stevie, I should have you scrapped."

The mech dropped its head and chirped an apology.

"Right. I'll believe that when the sun goes nova. Here, hold still."

Stevie bobbed to the ground before stabilizing on its own plane of countergrav. Promise held out her seabag. "Take this to the shuttle on Pad Three. I have a few stops to make first." She glanced at her chrono. "We don't lift off until sixteen hundred hours. I'll see you at fifteen thirty." She had plans to kill the remaining hours. Promise shoved the Mule with her boot. "Move out."

The mech disappeared into a mixed crowd of Fleet Forces personnel: Marines wearing tan utilities; Sailors wearing greens; and civilian workers dressed in solid blue, gray, and black coveralls. A variety of Mules and other bots painted myriad colors darted among their human counterparts. Promise consulted her minicomp and pivoted around. The port's control needle towered high above the other structures, and cast a long shadow across the tarmac. Afternoon showers were in the forecast. A good-sized thunderhead had already built in the east. Promise could see the haze in the distance and what appeared to be a warship, earthbound. Beached like a whale.

She did a double take. It was unheard-of to see a warship sitting on the deck like that. RNS *Pylon*. A quick search revealed what had happened. *Pylon* had been in low-earth orbit, awaiting a new fusion engine. It had lost power and vented atmosphere out its port side, pushing the vessel out of its parking orbit and into Hold's gravity. The Navy held a press conference as the vessel overflew the city of Cormandy. Miraculously, *Pylon*'s crew managed to restore partial power and set her down in one piece, in an open field close to Joint Spaceport Mo Cavinaugh. Scuttlebutt said BUPERS planned to retrofit her, to test the feasibility of an atmo-capable warship. That sounded to Promise like a very bad idea. A drop-capable battlecruiser could haul a lot of Marines and gear, true. But letting a jump-capable vessel inside a planet's atmosphere was madness. What if something happened and the ship jumped?

Promise stood in disbelief. "That must have been some ride," she said to no one. "I hope the *Pylon* gets topside soon, and stays there for good."

A gust of wind pushed Promise off-kilter. The sky looked like she felt, troubled. It was time to do something about that. Time to get moving. She hiked a quarter of Mo Cavinaugh before she found the building.

The sign above the door was a rotating holo, shifting between the proprietor's name and samples of his artwork. A red and gold rising phoenix burst from a pyre of flames, climbed on invisible currents, and then plummeted into a lake. Out of the water came a double-edged dagger. The dagger turned on itself. Other letters materialized to spell the word "Tullivan." FATHER FRANCIS TULLIVAN, SPIRITUAL GUIDE AND TRADITIONAL AMERICAN TATTOOIST appeared in old-world script. Then the sequence reset itself.

She'd seen the word "American" in the histories. A constitutional republic. At one time it had been the only superpower on Holy Terra. Traditional American was a tattoo style popularized at American military bases during the 1930s and 1940s, and it was still alive and well in 92 A.E.

"Apparently he's the best." Promise squared her shoulders, removed her beret, and pushed through the door. The rough-hewn cross over the threshold was hard to miss. It made her think of her father, Morlyn Gration. He'd been so devout that Promise had found him nearly impossible to live with. Had it not been for the door chime she might have backed out then and there.

A choir of monks started chanting in a language she didn't recognize. The music was soothing, and Promise figured it couldn't hurt to at least meet the proprietor. If they didn't click she could always make up an excuse and leave, or schedule an appointment for another time and then cancel it.

"I'll be right with you," said a low voice from an adjacent room.

Sample tattoos covered every centimeter of one wall. Some color, others black and gray. Another wall was stuffed full of printed books, all spine-out and in no particular order. The exit was to her right, and the door on her left led into a well-lit hallway. Several placards hung by the entrance to the hallway. Two were certificates from the Celeste Wei Canvas Academy on Hold, one for a journeyman's course and another for advanced studies in the art of needle and laser tattoo work. Below them was a document from the Third Council of the Episcopal Church.

> *Father Francis H. Tullivan*
> *On the Day of his Ordination*
> *June 5th, 84 A.E.*
> *Solo Deo Gloria*
> *Signed: Mother Agatha Teresse*
> *High Reverend Mother of the Order of Saint Thomas*

A door creaked open and a woman stepped into the corridor and padded toward Promise in her bare feet. "Excuse me," she said as she entered the room. She was in her undergarments but didn't seem at all self-conscious. Clear bandages and ointment covered parts of her thighs, abdomen, and shoulders. Her body was nearly covered in ink except for her face and neckline, ankles and wrists.

She must have caught Promise's expression, because she said, "Today is touch-up day. The father has been my artist for close to a decade. He let me off easy this time. Only ninety minutes in the chair. I won't let anyone else touch this canvas." She cocked her head at Promise. "First time?"

"Sorry?"

"It's your first time, right? You look apprehensive . . . that's all."

"Oh."

"Don't worry—the father is good with ink. If needles bother you, the laser tats only take a few seconds. Don't get me wrong. They hurt like no other. But, if I were you, I'd go old-school. Once your endorphins kick in you won't want to stop. Trust me."

"Thanks for the tip. A little pain never hurt anyone, right?"

"That's the spirit," the woman said. She reached for a pair of coveralls hanging on the wall, just off the exit. She turned toward Promise and started to zip up.

"Cute tattoo."

"Thanks." She looked down and smiled. "Which one were you referring to? I have a catalog's worth."

"That one over your heart." The feet were so small Promise would have missed them if she hadn't been up close.

The woman froze.

"She . . . didn't make it. I carry her prints to remember her . . . so she's always near."

You had to pick the one tattoo this woman doesn't want to talk about. Perfect aim. Wrong target. Way to go, P.

"I'm sorry," Promise said.

"Don't be. I'm not. I'm glad you asked. Talking about her helps me keep going."

Promise didn't know what to say to that.

"Like you said, a little pain never hurt anyone. Losing her nearly undid me." Her eyes looked faraway. "But life's ahead. It has to be . . . or what's the point, right?"

"That's what I'm hoping," Promise said.

The woman nodded like she understood, retied her hair, and brushed something off a sleeve. "Nice chatting with you. Enjoy your time with the father. And go old-school. You won't regret it." As she walked out the door, a heavyset man in a burgundy robe walked in.

Twenty-five

"You must be my next appointment. Lieutenant Paen, right? I'm Father Francis Tullivan. Please call me Father or Father Francis. It's very nice to meet you."

The father took Promise's hand in both of his. They were the warmest hands she'd ever felt. He was middle-aged and bald, and his speckled beard swallowed his mouth and chin. What little neck he had was ringed with a white collar.

"It's nice to meet you too, Father."

"What brings you to my house, Lieutenant? Art or faith?"

"A bit of both, I think."

"Then you've come to the best possible place. Do you have a vid or a still I can look at?"

Promise pulled a small disk from her thigh pocket and handed it to the father. He set it on a small table, finger hovering over it. "May I?"

"Please, it's not encrypted."

A holographic montage filled the air above the table, stills of women and men and a few twos and threes. Many were relatively young. A middle-aged couple appeared with a little girl between them. A few stills showed the torso up; others were full-body. Most of the people wore RAW-MC uniforms. After a dozen or so, the father started stroking his beard. "Exactly what am I looking at, Lieutenant?"

"Some family and a lot of my company."

"I see. Such wonderful faces. Why do I fear they are no longer with us?"

Promise's throat went dry. She cleared it several times to get something out. "I wish things had turned out differently." She was crying now. "I don't really know what I'm after, Father. I can't keep doing this."

"Then don't. You don't have to, you know." The father smiled and motioned to a couple of chairs. "Now, you were saying."

"Recently I lost one of my platoon sergeants. A year ago he helped me pull a toonmate out of harm's way. We were taking heavy fire. We were so badly outnumbered, just a few of us survived. He made it out then, only to die during a training mission . . . all because of me." The image cycled again and Promise cupped her mouth.

"That's him, isn't it?"

It was all she could do to nod.

The father laid a hand on Promise's shoulder and squeezed gently. "Ah, I see. A brother of the close fight. God rest his soul."

"Yes." *He was in every sense of the word.* She took a moment to collect herself. "Are you former military?"

"I was in another lifetime." The father looked up. "*He* enlisted me. You know, we have this silly little notion about death that's definitely not from Him. We've had it for millennia, back to the dawn of time. We tell ourselves to say good-bye to our lost ones so we can move on. The truth is that's the biggest bunch of nonsense, and it eats at the spirit. It's impossible to let go. The human heart wasn't designed for good-byes. We were designed for forever. Death wasn't part of the original plan."

"Then how do I keep going, Father? I feel like I'm coming unraveled. The flashbacks and nightmares won't stop. I barely sleep anymore. I'm becoming afraid to try."

"You don't. At least not like you're thinking." The father folded his hands across his stomach and filled his chest with air. "Instead of moving on, think of making space in your life for your pain. You have to do life with it. Give it a place at the table. Tell it, 'You're welcome here.' Only then can you begin to heal.

"Someday, we will all come to the end of ourselves. It's inevitable, even if the scientists say otherwise. I happen to believe in life after death, and if you ask me, the best stuff happens on the other side. On this side, we have the misfortune of outliving some of the people we love. More than I really care to think about, honestly." The father closed his eyes. "I overheard a bit of your discussion with Katia, the woman who just left."

"I didn't know."

"Don't feel badly, Promise. Do you mind if I call you that?"

"No, not at all."

"Katia has seen her share of loss too. A parent losing a child is one of the worst kinds of loss imaginable. For her the cycle of life was reversed. Your occupation guarantees you a double portion, probably more than that." The father looked genuinely hurt for her. "I'm afraid it's simply impossible to move on from death. You must learn to move with it."

"I don't know where to begin."

Father Francis opened his arms wide and smiled. "That, my dear, is why you came to me."

"And you believe a tattoo can make a difference."

"Absolutely! I've staked my livelihood upon it. And His."

"I suppose you have." Promise's eyes went to the disk. "You've seen my Marines. What do you suggest?"

"Script, possibly." He frowned. "A lot of names get tricky. We'd have to make them small and the small ones don't age as well . . . unless you want your body covered with janes and jacks, space will be an issue. What about a symbol? Maybe something you shared in common with your sisters and brothers."

Promise raised her left shoulder. "How about my unit patch?"

"Hmm, it has possibilities. Snakes are a staple of the industry."

Promise caught the edge of a memory. She was a child, sitting on her father's lap. They were reading together from an old picture book. There were trees and animals, and a new sun was high in the sky. A snake and a man were talking to each other, and it wasn't going well. The next spread showed them fighting. She hadn't thought of it in years.

"What if I incorporate a field of stars into the background, one for every fallen soul?" Father Francis looked pleased.

"I think I'd like that."

"What if I work them into a pattern of concentric circles, like this?" Promise nodded.

"Good. Give me half an hour to draw it up. Help yourself to my library. I've always loved the printed word. Given the choice, I'll choose carbonscreen every time. Room Two is down the hall, second door on the right. There's fresh-brewed caf and a nice selection of iced beverages. Please take your pick."

Room Two was an oasis. Soft blues and greens covered the walls. The holographic ceiling swelled with clouds, and a flight of birds passed overhead. A slight current stirred her bangs and fresh caf filled her nostrils. Stringed music played as she doctored a cup with heavy cream and sugar. It was strong. The good stuff, she thought. She sat and the chair reclined, and molded to her back and legs. The heated seat was an added bonus. As she relaxed she noted the piece of framed art on the wall. At first, Promise thought it was a holographic still. A closer look made her think twice.

The scene depicted two armies enjoined in battle. Not all the soldiers were human. And everything was slightly out of focus, as if an optic had rendered the entire piece from a real battle, or perhaps a reenactment, and the optic hadn't known what detail to focus upon, so it ended up rendering the entire scene slightly out of phase. Even so, the details were as real as they were gruesome. Corpses were piled everywhere. Explosions and debris filled the air. The carnage was near-total, which made the man in the center of the painting seem at odds with his surroundings. He stood on a small hill, and his arms were outstretched and soaked with blood. Survivors on both sides were gazing up at him in shock. His face was a collage of browns, greens, blacks, and whites. His eyes were full of pain and they appeared to be looking straight at her. The plaque at the bottom said:

"Blessed are the peacemakers, for they shall be called
the daughters and sons of God."

The great Mediator, Promise thought. *One of the holy triumvirate.* Promise's father, Morlyn Gration, had believed in the Mediator, Maker, and Sustainer, what he'd called the three-in-one. "God is never alone, and because God is with us neither are we." He'd taken that belief to the grave. Promise wondered if her father was now in the presence of some great spirit. Perhaps looking down upon her this moment. She'd certainly never sensed his presence. And right now she wished she could in the worst way.

When it came to dogma, her father had been as devout in his faith as her mother was uncommitted. They'd agreed on little else except their love for each other and for her. Somehow they'd made it work.

Maybe that's where I got my love for doing hard things. Then Mom died. Then they came. She'd never forgotten the day her father died and she'd tried everything imaginable. It flashed to life. Her hands began to shake, so she set her cup down, and rubbed her hands together.

One of the alien soldiers in the painting caught her eye. It wore a cross around its neck. His neck? Her neck? Its features weren't what you'd call masculine or feminine. Would aliens be male and female or something else entirely? She thought if other sentients were out there, then the God of heaven must be their God too.

How do you serve something that you can't see? Or talk to. How do you tolerate a God Who tolerates so much death? She closed her eyes but found no answers there. Moments later she fell asleep.

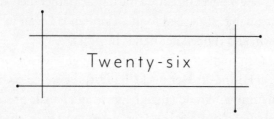

Twenty-six

Beating feet across the hot tarmac of Mo Cavinaugh gave Promise time to order her thoughts. They'd shifted beneath her like tectonic plates. Crashed together. Pushed up jagged questions she didn't want to face. The problem with learning something new was you were obligated to do something about it, ply the new knowledge, gain more intelligence (intelligence in the military meaning of the word and an officer of Marines had better be on the evolutionary ladder and on the upward bounce).

Father Francis Tullivan was on to something about making peace with death. *Our mutual friend. He got that right.* Maybe she'd have a summit and agree to peace talks. Greeting death with a kiss? That didn't sound appealing. Neither did growing old with bad memories weighing her down.

She'd nearly spilled her guts in the father's chair during two consecutive sessions, each close to two hours, as he'd pounded color into her skin. They'd talked about the church, the state, her Marines, her nonexistent love life, and even her parents. Father Francis was careful not to pry. When he finished, he'd slathered her skin in balm and clear wrap. Standing before the mirror, she felt lighter than she had in years.

"It's perfect." She tried to hold back the tears, and turned her shoulder for a better view.

"Let them come, child. Remember, it wasn't your fault. You were doing your duty. They were doing theirs."

Promise inhaled sharply. She'd heard the exact same words only days before, from the most unlikely source. General Granby's vid.

Because it wasn't marked priority it had sat in her queue for the better part of a day. It began, "Send one downrange for me, girly." A still of Great-Grans filled her screen, and then Promise hit PLAY. "Didn't expect me, did you? I wouldn't either if I was you. Make that your first lesson. Don't outgrow your britches." After that, Grans got straight to the point. "Watch your six, Lieutenant. Politicians have long memories. You just blipped on their scanners like an inbound hostile." Grans elaborated a bit, and then listed their mutual enemies.

I have enemies . . . in my own star nation.

Grans told her to grieve Sergeant Morris's death and not to hold herself responsible. *Not likely.* "Not your fault, Lieutenant. Don't even go there. You were just doing your duty, and so was he. Don't forget that."

Don't even go there. How do I not go there? Why do we talk about there as if it's a place?

"Well, I'm off for the country," Grans said. "My home away from home isn't far from here. The alpha unit and I have thought about downsizing for years. Each time we come close the memories convince us not to." Granby thought hard before saying more. "I may never see a uniform again. God only knows. Well, it doesn't matter anymore. Maybe it's time I put my big house to use." Granby brightened visibly. "Drop by sometime. Make that an order. And let me know if you ever need my help . . . such as it is. Good hunting, Lieutenant. Granby, out."

As Promise rounded the corner of the building, she stepped from the shadows and into the blinding sun. She raised her hand in time to avoid the mech coming straight at her.

Her ride up was a Starburst-class medium-range orbital shuttle, nicknamed the Blowfish. The body was more a cylinder than a plane or wing, which made the bulbous cockpit and nose look out of place. Crewed by five, just like a Marine Corps platoon. The engines took up the ship's entire aft compartment, and dozens of stabilizers poked out of the hull.

About two shuttle lengths away, Promise caught sight of a familiar profile. No, make that two. Lance Corporal Kathy Prichart and Private Race Atumbi were standing nearby, just off the middle hatch of the medium-range intersystem transport, watching passengers disembark. Atumbi was manning an empty hoversled. Kathy held a datapad and was wearing shades. Then she pointed to a tall Marine wearing tan utilities, and nodded to Atumbi. The newcomer stood in the shuttle's hatchway, and set his bags down to don his beret.

Now Promise was close enough to see the stranger's gross features, and they looked out of place. The nose was flat and smoothed-over, and the jaw was too big for the head. Too-pale skin more fitting for a corpse than a Marine. Kathy waved to Promise as the newcomer hit the bottom of the stairs. His name tab said MARGOLEASE. He wore a number of service ribbons and medals, including a purple heart surrounded by three stars and two suns. Promise's brows shot skyward. That was five total wounds-in-combat; stars for the injuries and suns for the fatalities. Resurrections were rare enough. But twice? It was only then Promise put three and two together. *Margolease has five WICs and he's been jumped twice.* That explained his appearance.

"And who do we have here?" Promise met Margolease's gaze directly even though she wanted to stare at him in the worst way. The man seemed to notice and dipped his head. His salute was as crisp as any she'd seen, and lightning fast.

"Sergeant *Jesus* Margolease, reporting for duty, ma'am."

"He's your new platoon sergeant, ma'am." Kathy held up the datapad. "His transfer papers just arrived." Kathy raised her shades and gave Margolease a once-over. "You're a lot to take in, Sergeant."

"Lance Corporal! Watch your mouth," Promise said. "Please forgive her, Sergeant. She should know better."

"Lieutenant." Margolease's tone spoke volumes. "Take a good look at me. Can you blame her?"

The man has a point. "Maybe . . . still doesn't make it right . . . or respectful. A man with five WICs has a story to tell and the right to tell it whenever he pleases. Drinks on me, anytime." Promise frowned. "Except not today. I'm being kicked off-planet."

"Rain check, then." Margolease extended his gloved hand. His grip was firm, measured, and Promise suspected carefully restrained. She held it a moment longer than protocol dictated. "I bet you crush rocks with that, Sergeant."

"Not quite, but I'm an undefeated arm wrestler."

"I'll remember that," Promise said as she looked into his eyes. They were his most human feature, though the left one was off somehow.

"The cornea and most of the rods and cones were destroyed in an explosion. The doc saved the eye but the optics had to be replaced."

"Zoom-capable?" asked Promise.

"Yes, with a micro-HUD hardwired to my brain."

"Really? Can you download telemetry or sync with your armor?"

"Negative, ma'am. Thank the Congress and the AI Acts for that."

"You're human," Promise said with surprise. "Those don't apply to you."

"I agree. I am human, and because I don't regen I'm now eighty-two percent synthetic. Wireless tech might leave me open to a virtual attack. My entire self is drive-by-wire through what's left of my original neural network. I'm safest that way and so are my toonmates. I can't even link with a coffeemaker. It was that or one-eye blind and a gravchair."

Promise couldn't help noticing his ears. *P, stop scanning the man's anatomy.*

"I asked for big ears, ma'am. You know, to hear better with, and the points were for style. Thankfully, my inner ears are fine, and so is my balance. Cochlear implants have a long way to go. I manage."

Margolease tapped the bridge of his nose.

"Crushed by the turret of a hovtank. I have rebuilt sinuses and a top-line filtration system. I can tolerate level-five contamination sites without a rebreather, at least for short periods of time. I can hold my breath for days."

"Sergeant, I'm happy to have you aboard." Promise nodded at Margolease and then at her Marines. "That's my shuttle over there. I'll see you next week."

"I hope you enjoy the trip."

"I'll try. Kathy, get the sergeant settled and take him to the chow hall. Strike that. Take him off-base and get him something edible. Charge it to my account. Private Atumbi, get his gear stowed. Sergeant Margolease, welcome to Hold."

"Thank you, ma'am. My friends call me Jay." The sergeant flashed a set of perfectly straight teeth. "Yeah, I'm walking on glass too. It goes with the image."

"What's your call sign, Jay?" asked Kathy.

"Lazarus."

"Dead man walking," whispered Kathy.

"Don't I know it," replied Margolease.

"I like it," said Promise. "You're going to fit right in. Welcome to the Pythons."

Promise slapped him on the shoulder and felt impossibly hard muscle shake off the blow. "Jay, I am really looking forward to working with you."

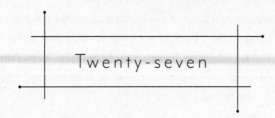

Twenty-seven

After two uneventful jumps and a surprisingly fast burn in-system, Promise stepped onto the deck of Kies, a newly renovated pleasure sphere with four-star accommodations and a round-the-clock casino. She was wearing one of the few off-duty ensembles in her locker: a pair of gunmetal slacks and a white blouse with three-quarter-length sleeves, and matching shoes. Promise had wanted something in a quiet system, not too busy, with as few people as possible. Kies was the only operational platform in orbit around Guinevere and it was far enough off the grid for the colonel's taste. And Kies maintained a small sister resort on the surface, Kies Black Sands. Other than that and a biogenic firm on the surface, the planet was undeveloped.

By all outward appearances, Guinevere was the model HAB planet. But looks were deceiving. A flu-like virus had attacked the initial survey team three months after landing, all but wiping them out. Something like that had never happened before on any other explored world. It ran contrary to the "locked ecosystem" theory. Until Guinevere, alien environs had shown early signs of cracking the human genome only after a generation or more had passed. Guinevere changed everything. Kies Inc. put a biogenic firm planetside for a small fortune when no one else would. In trade, the RAW gave Kies a planetwide lease for a hundred years.

Ms. Night met Promise at the bottom of the landing slip. Night was medium height and wore a cerulean dress slit up the thigh. In the right light, the dress changed to emerald green. She was human, not a mech. This helped explain Kies Orbital Tourosphere's four-star rating.

Promise's minicomp chirped as the attendant held out her hand.

"Welcome aboard, Ms. Paen. I see this is your first time with us. And you're staying the night. Wonderful." Night paused, eyes focused inward. "You're checked in and your I-dent is coded to your room. I'll have your bags sent up. May I generate your retinal key?"

"Yes, thank you."

Ms. Night looked at her intently. The white of her left eye turned black, and her pupil a solid green.

The focused burst of light caused Promise to blink. A second later, Ms. Night's eye was back to normal and she was smiling as if nothing out of the ordinary had happened.

"That's expensive tech," Promise said. "Your employer spared no expense."

"My colleagues carry readers. I served eight years in the Sector Guard before getting out. Mostly customs sweeps in backwater systems. It was incredibly boring except for the five days I can't tell anyone about." Night's smile reached all the way to her eyes. "This"—she pointed to her eye—"was courtesy of Aunt Janie. I believe the two of you have met."

"Guilty as charged."

Ms. Night glanced at Promise's hand. "Are you meeting someone, Ms. Paen?"

"No, I'm running solo." Promise smiled warily. "Why?"

"Comm me if you change your mind. We have other guests vacationing alone." She turned both palms upward. "And a small staff of highly trained courtesans. Sometimes it's nice to have company." She gave Promise a telling look. "Our questionnaire only takes five minutes and identifies over forty-two dimensions of compatibility. Access the panel over your vanity and follow the instructions. Our house AI, Gunnar, will be happy to assist you."

Promise's eyebrows rose. "I'll keep that in mind."

"I've uploaded a map of the station to your minicomp. Are you hungry? Most everything is closed for the night. Except for room service, which is open round-the-watch."

"Famished, actually. I've never been one to eat during transit. The shuttle food wasn't very good anyway. How's the pasta?"

"How's linguine with local surf and turf and fresh greens sound?"

"Perfect."

"That's why I'm here." Ms. Night nodded her head and smiled. "Done. I'll have it sent to your room."

"Actually, I'm not ready to turn in just yet."

Night's smile froze for a split second before relaxing naturally.

"Then I recommend White Kies, our tiki bar. It's open all night."

"A cup of caf will do."

"Cream and sugar."

"Please."

"Consider it done. May I help you with anything else?"

"I'd like to go for a run in the morning before I shuttle down to the surface."

"The observation deck is a must-see. Guests usually prefer the outer ring." Night pursed her lips. "I, on the other hand, run on Level Five. It has the most open space and the fewest tourists. You may link your mastoid implant to the ship's music library. We have over a thousand genres in our files and playlists to suit most every taste imaginable."

"Thank you. A bit of peace and quiet is just what I need. To be perfectly honest, I wasn't looking forward to this. My chain of command is very, well, never mind." *Now why did I tell her that?* "I'm sorry. I'm not at liberty to discuss it."

Ms. Night nodded like she understood. "Someone up the COG FUBARed and you took the fall."

Promise snorted. "Ms. Night, you are perceptive."

"I've had enough of Aunt Janie's school of hard knocks to last a lifetime."

"Oh, my room on the surface won't be ready until tomorrow afternoon, about fourteen hundred hours. Anything you can do?"

Night held up a finger and cupped her ear. "I know someone who—" Her countenance brightened. "Troy, how are you, handsome? . . . Yes, I know I still owe you dinner. Don't worry. I always keep my promises. I'll make it up to you. . . . Please, stop that, I'm with a guest." Night dipped her head, turned away. "Ms. Paen . . . Papa Alpha Echo November . . . yes, that's her, she's due in tomorrow and she'd like an early . . . Possible? . . . Noon isn't early. I'm sure she'd like to have lunch on terra firma . . . please do that . . . I'll hold." Night blew a puff into her bangs. "He always does this, puts me on hold and makes me wait when I know he's just going to get me what I want."

Night's eyes widened and she pointed to her ear. "Ah . . . yes . . . Troy, but I asked about Ms. Paen's early. Fine . . . I'll meet you for dinner on Tuesday. What will I be wearing? Let's keep that a surprise . . . just wear a tie . . . about Ms. Paen's early . . . eleven is perfect. Thank you, Troy. You're a peach."

Whatever Troy said last caused Ms. Night to blush.

"Ms. Paen, your room will be ready by eleven hundred hours. Your shuttle leaves on the half hour but please arrive fifteen mikes before that."

"Fantastic. Please thank Troy for me. And it's Promise."

"I'll be sure to do that, Promise." Night cupped her hands together in front of her and quirked her head.

Right. That. Promise fumbled for her minicomp and hit TRANSFER.

"That's very kind of you." Night tapped the side of her eye. "I have a micro-HUD in the same eye. I like to stay informed."

"It's been a pleasure, Ms. Night. You've been most helpful. I plan to let management know." The two shook hands and Promise's stomach growled. "Now, which way to the bar?"

Ms. Night watched Promise disappear into the station proper. She sat on a nearby bench and began typing into her datapad. A moment later she received an encrypted comm over her mastoid implant.

"Sir, she's in. . . . No, sir, I don't think she will be a problem. She's a loner. I was subtle. She got my point and she wasn't interested in company. But—" And Ms. Night took a deep breath. "—she could encounter the client. You know he likes to dine late." Night visually winced at her employer's response. "No, sir, I tried. She wasn't ready to turn in. However, she let something slip. Her superiors aren't happy with her at the moment. She's keeping a low profile and picked Kies for a distraction. . . . Yes, I'll keep an eye on her. I already have eyes in the sky. . . . No, sir, I seriously doubt it. Not unless she goes looking for them. And why would she do that?"

Ms. Night tagged Promise with two whiskers, and headed for her room. If Paen did anything she shouldn't, her probes would let her know. The odds of that happening were remote. And Night was tired. It had been a long day and tomorrow she was pulling a double. One of Kies's chief shareholders was due in the morning for a tour. Then more guests at noon. She had a banquet at six and everyone from the station chief to the lowly research assistant on-planet would be there, and she still had reports to file.

Best to get some sleep while she could. That's what she told herself before she entered her room, set her minicomp to wake her in an emergency, and tossed it on the nightstand. "Gunnar, something from the oceans, please." Waves crashing always did the trick. She fell asleep as soon as her head hit the pillow.

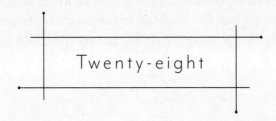

Twenty-eight

MAY 14TH, 92 A.E., STANDARD CALENDAR, 2145 HOURS
PLANET GUINEVERE, NIGHTSIDE
KIES ORBITAL TOUROSPHERE

Promise walked into White Kies after a brief stop at a small observation post along the outer ring of the tourosphere. The Clown Nebula was just visible to the naked eye. A dais sat near the viewscreen, which opened at the top. It was shaped like a bowl and contained a polished black orb. It warmed to Promise's touch. A well-dressed man appeared in a fitted trench coat with matching slacks and an old-fashioned pair of frameless glasses.

"Hello, Ms. Paen. My name is Gunnar, the station's AI. Would you care for a tour? If you'll just take a seat, there, we'll be on our way." Gunnar motioned to a comfortable-looking armchair that hadn't been there a moment before. Beside it was a small, circular table. On it lay a small visor that fit her perfectly.

"I'll let the kitchen know to keep your meal hot."

Promise opted for the spacewalk and the room about her shifted, and then she was looking out the visor of a vacsuit with a filtered view of the fifth planet. It ended up being ten minutes very well spent. Alterra boasted the most beautiful ice rings she'd ever seen. The experience wasn't quite complete and the gravity in her stomach kept reminding her of how hungry she was. With some reluctance, Promise killed the program prematurely and found her way to the bar.

White Kies was an oasis in the stars. Throughout the bar palm trees grew in pots, casting shadows over wicker tables and chairs. The roof appeared thatched, and sunlight winked through here and there. Just off the bar, groomed sands dotted with reclining beach chairs and tables completed the setting. Calypso and birdcalls played in the background. Promise opted for a seat at the bar, poolside, and leaned in so the terminal could scan her eyes. An attractive middle-aged bartender appeared a moment later with a steaming cup of caf and a tray of additives to doctor it blond. The second tray was piled high with finger foods.

"Ms. Paen, welcome to White Kies. I'm Tanin and these are on me for while you wait. The tartare is divine."

Tanin placed a cloth napkin and a full service on the bar top with expert care, and fussed a moment until it looked just right. Kind hazel eyes, framed in silvery hair, looked up at her. His muscled arms wrapped in a sleeveless tropical shirt fit the ambience perfectly.

"Let me know if you want something stronger." He smiled. "Your entrée will be a few more minutes. I just need to shell the clams."

Promise laughed as Tanin disappeared through a set of swinging doors at the back of the bar. She dumped and stirred and sighed as the caf went down extra hot, swiveled in her chair, and looked up as a thunderhead rolled across the overhead. A slight breeze stirred the room.

But for her and Tanin the bar was nearly empty. In one corner a young couple was playing a game of chance and an elderly gentleman appeared lost in a book. A short grunt came from the cage behind the bar. She turned to find a cheerless, four-legged creature with sad eyes looking at her. A bowl of fresh fruit sat at the bottom of the cage.

"Don't mind him." Tanin returned with her meal and a glass of water on the rocks. "He just wants your food, not his. Please don't feed him. He's partial to fingers."

"Thanks for the tip. He's pretty cute."

The creature scowled at the bartender before blowing Promise a kiss, and then he climbed a tree branch and disappeared into the foliage.

"Yeah, well don't let his eyes or charms fool you. He can con you with two, but the third is always on the meal." Tanin held up his left hand and waved his center digit. It was missing the first joint. "My souvenir from my first day on the job, and I don't regen. The previous barkeep didn't bother to warn me."

At this, a furry three-eyed head dropped through the leaves upside down, looked at Tanin with two eyes open and the middle one closed, and stuck out a long blue tongue at him.

"Laugh it up, Punk," Tanin said as he gave the beast his truncated middle finger.

"He's pretty smart, too. What's his name?"

Tanin looked at Promise squarely. "It's Punk, and believe me, he deserves it."

"Hello, little Punk," Promise said, and then she blew the fur ball a kiss.

A furry arm dropped into view, waved at Promise, and gave Tanin its middle finger before it disappeared.

Tanin scowled and shook his head. "I won't keep you two from each other. Holler if you need me. I'm on break for the next ten. I'll just be over there." He pointed toward a couch and screen in the far corner. A large wooden tribal mask hung from the overhead. "The Stellars-Grayclings game is on holocast and I'm only through inning three. I have box seats, too."

"Wait . . . isn't that an old game?"

"Ah, so you're a fan?"

"A friend of one." She was thinking of Sergeant Sindri—Maxi. "He gambles a bit and loves to talk sports. I've picked up a few things from him over the years. I don't recall the century."

"Twenty-sixth, during the Sector Series. A few planets tried to make a go of a mulitworld league. Unforeseen costs quickly bankrupted the venture. Such a shame. It was a marvelous series. The Stellars won in the sixth game, final inning."

"Well, enjoy." Promise held up her half-full mug. "Fantastic caf by the way."

"My pleasure," Tanin said.

Promise dug into a heaping plate of al dente pasta, shellfish, and something like squid. She got a shock when a tentacle latched itself to her back molar and refused to let go. She had to chew it to death. The food was well seasoned and on the raw side for her taste, but altogether satisfying. Promise gave herself permission to lick the plate clean.

I am on vacation. A few extra klicks in the morning should take care of that.

She was halfway through a second cup of caf when a man joined her on the opposite side of the bar. Tanin placed a tall beer in front of him without saying a word. Promise nodded when he looked up. He seemed lost in another place and looked right through her. He wore a fitted, white, short-sleeved shirt with KIES embroidered over the heart. The man worked out.

A lot.

She couldn't help noticing the ink on his arm. It was nearly a full sleeve. She thought she saw the coiled tail of something much larger too. Her hand snaked up her arm to her shoulder, which was still pretty angry from her time in the chair with the father. When the man cleared his throat, Promise realized she'd been staring at him.

"Sorry," Promise said from across the bar. "I was admiring your tattoo."

His eyes could have frozen space.

"Enjoy your stay on the tourosphere." He held her gaze a moment longer, until she looked away.

Tanin broke the awkwardness of the moment with a second beer and a plate of sushi. He placed both without saying a word. Then he skirted the bar to Promise's side, and grabbed a pitcher of water on his way around.

"One of your colleagues?" Promise asked in a low voice, nodding to the other man.

"Yes and no. We both work for Kies. He's corporate. I know what he drinks and eats, and to leave him well enough alone." Tanin gave her a firm look. "The rest isn't my business."

"I was just admiring his ink. I got my first before coming here." Promise patted her shoulder. "His line work is exquisite. Even from here I can see that. Do you know what the tail goes to?"

"A dragon. I've seen the rest and it looks cultural, from where I couldn't say."

"Local artist?"

"You'll have to ask him but I wouldn't bother. Name's Wade. I'm back to my game. Yell if you need something."

Promise finished her caf and keyed her minicomp. She added a hefty tip for Tanin and sent a quick thank-you to his queue. As she got up to leave, Wade pushed back too, and they locked eyes. This time there was a hint of something else in them. Wade gave her a reluctant nod, looked left, right, and behind him, and then headed for the entrance.

He just checked his sight lines and the exits. Strange thing for a corporate type to do. Unless . . . Beneath the shirt she noticed the slightest bulge, by the left kidney. Wade was packing. *And he's a leftie.*

Twenty-nine

MAY 14TH, 92 A.E., STANDARD CALENDAR, 2337 HOURS
PLANET GUINEVERE, NIGHTSIDE
KIES ORBITAL TOUROSPHERE

As Promise exited White Kies she caught sight of Wade entering the hotel Tribeca, on the opposite side of the concourse. A small kiosk of Kies souvenirs flanked the entrance. The lobby was open-aired, giving her an unobstructed view. And, given the lateness of the hour, deserted. She'd briefly considered staying at the Tribeca until she saw the nightly rate. The four-star hotel lay along the outer wheel of the tourosphere. The presidential suite was famous for its swimming pool that seemed to flow into space.

Just inside, Wade stopped at the hotel's caf bar and withdrew his minicomp.

Which reminds me. I said I'd make the best of this.

Promise glanced at her chrono, and then realized she had no schedule to keep but her own.

Perhaps, just this once, I'll take a lesson from Maxi and spend some of my hard-earned chits. But only a bit. As she reached the kiosk, Gunnar appeared in a white Kies uniform, and asked if she was after something specific.

"No, thank you. Just browsing."

"I have several items on special. Perhaps you'd like to see. . . ."

A small light-blue tote immediately caught her eye; then she scanned the price. *Oh, well.* The white and blue Kies souvenir cup was cheap enough, and it fit within her budget.

"We're running a three-for-two special, today only," said Gunnar. So she scooped up two more—one for Maxi and one for Kathy—and the lapel pin for her PT cap. She held out her bracelet to pay.

Out of the corner of her eye a man and a woman appeared from a door marked EMPLOYEES ONLY. Promise paid them little attention at first, until the man gently shoved the woman forward, causing her to stumble a bit. There was a brief exchange of words, but Promise was too far away to make them out. Her antennae shot up instantly.

The couple made their way to Wade, and a moment later ordered drinks. The man opened his hand and gestured toward the woman, palm up, from head to toe. Like Wade, he was middle-aged. His hair was braided and pulled back and tied with a lavender ribbon. The woman seemed younger, but from this distance Promise couldn't be sure.

The woman's dress was floor-length and hooded. When the older gentleman pulled the hood back and brushed the woman's face with his hand, Promise felt her gut knot up.

She was just a girl, perhaps a young woman at a stretch. The men shook hands and Wade headed to the lift while the ponytail and the girl stayed at the bar.

Promise moved to the minicomp cases on autopilot. She found an armband died a lovely shade of blue—for her morning runs—and a large bill hat to match. She purchased them and a Kies tote bag to carry it all in without checking the price. While she paid, the girl became agitated and shook her head. Their voices rose, and Promise heard the girl say, "No." Then she tried to pull away and Ponytail spilled his caf. He grabbed her arm and pushed her toward the lift at the back of the lobby.

Promise didn't think. She rounded the kiosk, purchases in hand, and jogged between the tables and chairs to reach the lift just as the doors closed.

"Thanks for holding it for me." Floor ten was already lit. "Eleven please."

A hint of a smile crossed Ponytail's thin lips. "First time on the station?"

Promise held up her bag stuffed with overpriced trinkets. The simple-script gold Kies insignia on the tote consumed most of one side. "Guilty as charged."

"My daughter and I spend a lot of time here." Ponytail's hand was still wrapped around the girl's arm. "I do a bit of consulting for Kies, so . . ." He trailed off as if nothing more needed to be said.

Right. Promise went fishing. "What sort of consulting?" Promise smiled at the girl, who promptly looked away.

"Mostly legal contracts," said the man. "Not very interesting I'm afraid."

The girl shifted her weight and the man pulled her closer to him, and then he pulled her hood on, covering her eyes.

"Forgive my daughter's rudeness. She ate something that didn't agree with her."

"Well, I hope you get to feeling better."

The girl nodded but didn't speak.

Maybe I'm being paranoid. Maybe she really does feel bad. For all I know, there's a perfectly good explanation for all of this.

"I'm off to the surface tomorrow morning . . . and I've had a long day of travel. Bed sounds good." She forced a yawn.

"Enjoy. Ah—here we are. Have a nice stay." The lift doors opened at ten.

Promise exited a floor above, found the stairwell, and descended as fast as she could, making as little sound as possible. As she reached the stairwell exit she heard voices approaching. Ponytail's was immediately recognizable.

"Try something like that again and it will cost you." His voice was gruff and pitched low.

Light spilled beneath the exit door, and then flickered as their shadows swept by.

"Mr. Wade is an important client, and he's very particular. You understand? *Answer* me, foolish girl."

"Yes." The one-word answer was clipped and full of pain.

"When he's done with you, meet me in the lobby like we discussed. Listen carefully to everything he says. I want a full . . ."

Promise lost the conversation as they moved farther from the stairwell door. She counted to ten and tried the door. To her great relief it opened without protest. As she slipped out onto soft butterscotch carpet, they turned the corner and disappeared from view. One hand to the wall, Promise advanced down the corridor until she came to the L, and then she peered around the corner. They were five doors down and still moving. Promise ghosted across the passageway and into the alcove. Two high-back chairs and a small table faced the viewport and the starscape beyond.

Down the hall more words were exchanged, a door opened, and a third voice spoke. Wade's. The door closed and a set of footfalls drew close. Promise slipped into one of the chairs and curled up, waited until the lift opened and closed. Surely the man with the ponytail had returned to the lobby like he'd said he would. A few moments later, Promise was at the door of Room 10312. "Now, go undress," she heard Wade's muffled voice say. Feet shuffling. Something hit the wall and shattered. She heard a defiant "No," and the sounds of a struggle.

Promise reached for the stunner concealed against her hip and passed it to her off hand. Fleet Forces were prohibited from carrying lethal weapons while off-base and out of uniform. She'd never have gotten her service piece—or her GLOCK, for that matter—through the platform's security anyway, even though the GLOCK was a registered antique and grandfathered under the RAW's firearms laws. Stunners were allowed with the appropriate permit. It would have to do.

She fished the cap from her bag and pulled it down to conceal her eyes, pulled the bag over her left shoulder, and pushed her hand and the stunner into the bag. Then she put her eye to the scanner on the door of 10312 and blinked rapidly to generate an error. She heard the error message sound, and wondered if it was enough to get Wade's attention. *Better kick the door just to be sure.*

"Why does this always keep happening to me?" She kicked the door a second time. "I *just* want to go to bed." She grabbed the handle and tried to force it open, jostled it in frustration to be sure Wade heard her. "I'm going to give Gunnar a piece of my mind. I paid too much to put up with this crap." The door clicked, and swung inward. Promise did her best to look surprised.

"Oh, I'm sorry. I must have the wrong room. What number is this?"

Wade was shirtless and dressed only in skivvies. His eyes focused upon her, and then his head tilted slightly. His tattooed dragon covered a third of his body and it seemed to be alive. "Wait, don't I know—"

Promise squeezed the trigger as Wade's eyes went wide in recognition. His body tensed immediately from the shock of the blast. She followed up with a hard kick to his groin. Wade stumbled back into the room, bent over in pain.

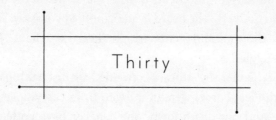

Thirty

Wade stumbled back several paces and almost went down on the plush carpeting. He somehow managed to get his feet beneath him and when he came up he was actually smiling.

Uh-oh.

"Is that all you've got?" He put his hands up, both palms out in mock surrender, and began moving backward toward the bedroom door.

"Don't move," Promise said, "and keep your hands where I can see them."

Wade took another step backward. Promise heard a whimper coming from the bedroom, and then the rustling of bedclothes. She thumbed the stunner to two-thirds of max and fired again. Wade grunted, and a bead of sweat broke from his hairline and ran down the side of his face. He steadied himself against a wall to keep from going down.

"It will take more than that to take me," he said with labored breath. "When I'm done taking you you'll wish you were dead too."

A normal man would have gone down, but Wade hadn't, and that led nowhere good.

He must be shielded, Promise thought.

Shields didn't come cheap. Some spooks had them, as did private security firms, and some crime syndicates too.

What have I gotten myself into?

This time she hit him will a full-power blast. The snarl on Wade's face turned into a pained expression that froze in place, face shocked open in white-eyed panic. Promise rushed forward and drove the stunner into the eye of the dragon over Wade's heart. She stroked the trigger twice more, half expecting to kill him. He landed with a heavy thud on the floor.

"About time."

Promise quickly swept the modest sitting room and secured the door, which also meant she was locked inside with no way out. She took advantage of the simple slide latch and dead bolt put there to set guests as ease. They were mostly decorative and useless, considering the biometric locks hidden in the door and walls. If Wade hadn't opened the door Promise would have needed a battering ram to get in. Without her mechsuit she doubted she was strong enough to kick the door in on her own. The small couch was easy work to move against the door. It wouldn't stop anyone from getting in but it might trip them up for a moment. Leading with the stunner, Promise approached the bedroom.

The girl was seated on a frameless bed with her knees pulled to her chest, gently swaying back and forth. Makeup and fresh tears stained her eyes, and her hair was a tangled mess. What was left of the top of her dress was hanging on her body by a thread.

When the girl saw Promise, she quickly wiped her eyes with the backs of her hands and sat up straight. "*You*. You . . . need to get out of here. Now. Before they come."

Promise lowered the stunner and knelt down beside her. "*You* first. I need to tie him up, okay?"

Quickly scanning the room, Promise's eyes settled on the girl's clothing, which was heaped against the base of the closet door. When she picked it up, something primal cracked deep within her, and a monster crawled out. Her fury tore the dress asunder until all that was left was thin strips meant for binding. She was panting hard when she turned her attention to Wade. Rolling him onto his back proved to be a challenge, because the man weighed a ton, far more than she'd guessed by the look of him.

Maybe he's a heavy worlder, Promise thought, *which would explain his resistance to my stunner.*

She bound Wade's hands and feet with the strips of the dress, and stuffed a ball of crushed cloth into his mouth to keep him quiet if he somehow managed to come to.

"My name is Promise," she said to the girl over her shoulder, as she finished up with Wade. She opened the bedroom closet and withdrew a fresh white robe with the Kies logo embroidered over the breast. "Here, put this on? We need to get you out of here."

The girl's eyes hardened. She held out her hand to take the robe, and then hesitated when Promise tried to give it to her. Her hand was shaking uncontrollably.

"I won't bite," Promise said.

After a moment the girl nodded. With only one arm for a covering, she slid off the bed and took the robe, and quickly dressed in its downy sleeves. Then she tied it closed.

"I can't leave," she said, meeting Promise's gaze. Her eyes were flushed with heat and fear and she spoke so softly Promise almost missed what she said. "I can't." Her words grew urgent. "They won't let me. Please, just go."

"Why?" Promise checked her minicomp and two minutes had already passed. They needed to move, now.

"There's nowhere I can go that they can't find me; where *he* can't find me." Now the girl was staring at Wade.

"Look, I can get you far away from here . . . to people who can help you . . . but you're going to have to trust me, okay?"

"We're already as good as dead."

"What about station security?"

The girl knelt down beside Wade. "He keeps a knife strapped to his thigh," she said as she reached between his legs. "See?" It was small, serrated, the sort of blade you tucked between two fingers before knifing someone in the gut. She wedged it between the bed frame and the mattress. "Now he won't find it when he wakes."

Promise's eyes went wide. *This isn't her first time.* She'd been foolish to assume as much. She simply couldn't understand why the girl would want to stay.

"Please, you have to leave." The girl began to cry. "Go, please."

"There's always a way out." Promise held out her hand. Up close, the girl couldn't be more than seventeen. "Believe me, I know."

She crossed her arms and took a step backward. "You couldn't possibly. You don't know what he's capable of."

Okay, time to change tactics.

"Gunnar?" The station AI did not respond.

"*Gunnar?*" Again, nothing.

"Station AI, this is Lieutenant Promise T. Paen of the Republic of Aligned Worlds Fleet Forces. Please acknowledge."

"He disabled it," the girl said. "He's paranoid about security. He's paranoid about everything.."

Some people felt uneasy with an AI always running in the background. A small percentage of citizens refused to use AIs altogether. They were in the minority and Promise had seen Wade with a minicomp. He didn't seem the type.

"Who is this guy?"

"Someone you don't want to mess with. When he wakes up I'll tell him you held me at gunpoint and asked if we had any valuables. Top drawer, over there. His chrono is worth a small fortune. Hurry before they come."

"I can't do that. I'm not leaving you here."

"Why? Just go. You're going to get both of us killed. *Please.*"

Promise took a deep breath and reassessed the girl, and the situation. *She's not thinking clearly. She's probably in shock. Then why is she so worried about herself . . . and about me? Wait . . . she's just trying to survive. She's doing exactly what Marines do in the heat of battle. Compartmentalizing. She's harnessing her fear to survive. How can I use that to my advantage and get her out of here?*

"I might survive the beating he gives me. You won't. I've seen what he does to his enemies."

Promise walked around the bed and grabbed the girl by the shoulders, shoving her up against the wall. Hard.

"Ow! What the 'verse?"

If this doesn't work nothing will.

"Get your hands off me. I thought you said you were trying to help." She spit in Promise's face.

Good, now she's fighting. "The man in the lobby is your procurer, isn't he?" Promise felt dirty just saying the word. "*Isn't* he?"

The girl tried to fight free, managed to get a hand loose and strike Promise on the jaw. The blow smarted and it made Promise smile.

"You don't like being handled, do you?" Promise grabbed her arm and bent it backward, and used the leverage to force the girl onto the bed, facedown.

"You're hurting me."

"Not as much as he's going to hurt you when he wakes up. How long before he's had enough of you? How long before he decides you're not worth it anymore? How long before you end up in a refuse bin dead and forgotten, or beaten so badly no one can recognize you, or pregnant and tossed out on your own?"

Promise twisted the girl's wrist until she cried out. "No, you listen to me. We're leaving. Either you walk out with me or I'll carry you over my shoulder, unconscious. Your choice."

P, what are you doing? You can't just drag her out of here, and you can't just pistol-whip her because you don't know this station that well and she probably does.

Promise triggered her mastoid implant and opened a link with the station AI. The girl had stopped fighting, was now still on the bed. Promise couldn't comm the AI or establish an emergency link with the station, and that set off all sorts of alarm bells in her head. Whoever she was dealing with had a military-grade dampener and that meant they could—

At that moment arching light appeared in the upper right corner of the entrance to the room, tracing the door's frame from top to bottom in seconds.

The girl swore and kicked her heel backward. Her targeting was off and the blow glanced off Promise's side. "Let go, please. They're *here.* You've got to let me go!"

The door fell inward and the man with the ponytail entered first, pistol at the ready. Because he was so focused on Promise, he didn't see the couch at first and nearly ran into it. A woman dressed like station security entered next and ran into the back of him. Their collision bought Promise precious seconds. She wrenched the girl off the bed and threw her toward the side of the bed farthest from the door. Then she dove for the wall. A moment later, the report of a flechette pistol shattered the silence, tearing into the pillows and duvet like a saw on flesh. Promise got a shot off before she slammed into the wall that abutted the door frame. Her shoulder took the worst of the hit and she heard something crunch. She'd aimed for Ponytail but hit the woman instead, dropping her to the floor.

All things considered, it was pretty impressive that she'd hit anyone with that shot.

Promise started counting. *One.*

A hand popped up from behind the couch and lobbed a disk into the air. It sailed through the doorway and disappeared into the bed's entrails. Promise slammed her hands over her ears and yelled, "Cover!" as the disrupter blew. Even with her palms buffering her ears the blast nearly knocked her out. Her vision grayed and she feared the girl was down for sure. A blast of energy holed the wall between the bedroom and the sitting area, and grazed Promise's upper thigh. She clenched her jaw and yelled at the girl, who was nowhere in sight. Then the closet door moved and the girl leaned out, a pulser in her hand.

Promise shook her head. *No good. It's bio-locked.*

More shots holed the wall and another struck the tote bag, which to Promise's surprise was still slung over her left shoulder. The smell of burning plastic stung her eyes and lungs.

The girl looked at Promise and then dipped her head toward Wade's bound hands.

That might work. Promise nodded, started ticking off fingers.

Three.

Two.

On *one,* she tossed the tote through the door frame and rolled into the opening. Ponytail rounded the couch and fired at her bag of kitsch while she placed him in her sights. The blast knocked him sideways. A potted plant and an end table cushioned his fall.

Two, Promise counted.

Stunner at the lead, Promise came up and moved out of the bedroom, toward the entrance to the hotel room. She heard doors slamming and footfalls outside the room and voices shouting. Still a good ways down the corridor someone barked, "Get back in your room."

"We need to move, now," Promise said as she stepped backward toward the bedroom entrance and looked behind her.

Suddenly a sharp pain enveloped her shoulder and radiated across her torso. For a moment she could hardly catch her breath. Time slowed. She turned toward the door as another man in uniform entered the room and fired again.

Promise's body folded beneath her. Her head hit last and lolled to the side, which gave her an unobstructed view of the bedroom. The girl was out of focus, on her knees next to Wade. Promise wanted to scream at her to take cover but she couldn't remember how to form the words. The girl forced Wade's weapon into his bound hands. Out of the corner of her eye she saw the man with the ponytail start to rise. Promise watched the girl raise the weapon, close one eye, and fire. The room grew dark and silence washed over her.

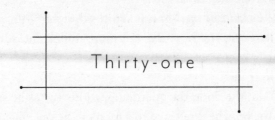

Thirty-one

MAY 15TH, 92 A.E., STANDARD CALENDAR, 1133 HOURS
PLANET GUINEVERE, NIGHTSIDE
KIES ORBITAL TOUROSPHERE
STATION SECURITY, CELL TWO

The cell could have been a lot worse. Promise lay on a too-thin mattress, eyes mere slits against the too-bright overhead lights. Her right eye was swollen and it hurt to breathe. Her side had taken the brunt of things, and her clothes were soaked in blood. At least they'd dressed her hand and thigh, and stopped the bleeding before tossing her in the cell. She still felt groggy from the hypo they'd pressed to her neck. When she bent her knee the pain brought her fully awake, and a soft cry slipped out. A few rounds of quickheal would have made short work of that, if they bothered with it.

"You're awake. Good, I'll go get the boss." Her guard outside sounded bored.

"Mind if I visit the head while I wait for my lawyer?" Promise asked.

"I'll think about it," said a tall man wearing a Kies shirt, sleeves rolled to the elbows. Promise was sure he was going to say no. Then a sigh. "Behind you, near the back," and to the station's AI, "Gunnar, the lieutenant needs some privacy. Some things I don't want to see."

Hearing her rank lifted her spirits. Not that she expected the uniform to shield her for long. Whoever these people were, they didn't seem like the kind that responded well to authority.

"My apologies, ma'am." The station AI actually sounded like he meant it. "It's not much, I know."

A rimmed seat slid out from the wall at the right height, and a privacy screen dropped from the ceiling.

You've got to be kidding me. "This is sanitized, right?"

The guard laughed. "Lady, you've got more important things to worry about than that."

"Anything to read?"

On the way out the door, the guard cupped his ear as he subvocalized, presumably to the boss he'd referred to a moment before. She instantly recognized the Mann 23 pulse pistol strapped to his thigh. It wasn't pretty, but it got the job done.

Limping to the cell door, Promise swept the room for a way out. Though she couldn't spot the pickups she was sure they were there, recording everything she said and did. The door was plexi and no doubt reinforced. Outside, she saw three spartan workstations, all empty. A close-up of a large sea creature hung on one wall, and the eyes could have been human.

She envisioned spending the rest of her vacation incarcerated, or worse. If she was lucky, they'd hand her back to the Marine Corps with a trumped-up charge, her word against theirs. She'd receive a formal letter of reprimand in her jacket, perhaps career-ending. Or she might go home in a body bag. *Unless I do something about it.*

Promise knocked on the plexi, three times. When the guard didn't appear she started pounding and yelling.

"Hey, knock it off in there. I'm on the comm."

"Hey, yourself. Tell me something. How does it feel to get off raping little girls?" The guard walked to her cell, fists clenched at his sides. He went to say something but changed his mind and sat back down.

Interesting.

"What? Oh, I get it. You were ordered not to touch. That's too bad. I was hoping to rumble."

"You've got nerve, Lieutenant, I'll grant you that." He gave her a once-over. "And pretty-girl potential. When the boss is through with you, then it's my turn."

"Lieutenant" again. Her rank was obviously providing her a bit of protection. She'd been in the nets recently. Maybe that was it. There was the matter of Montana and her battle with the Lusies, and her appearance before the Senate. At the moment, it was the only leverage she had.

"What are my charges? Assuming you're actually a station enforcer, which I doubt."

"They are legion, Lieutenant." Her guard crossed his legs and leaned back in his chair. "Breaking and entering. Assault and battery." His eyes narrowed. "Murder. Kidnapping. How'm I doin'?"

"Kidnapping?" She hadn't expected that.

"You tried to take Sephora without her guardian's permission."

"Sephora? Nice name for a pretty girl, isn't it?"

The guard clenched his jaw and looked away, and then he crossed his arms and met her gaze evenly. "You tried to take her without permission. She didn't want to leave."

"*Sephora* is being trafficked."

"It's perfectly legal work in this part of the 'verse."

"Not in the Republic of Aligned Worlds, it's not. Besides, what law gives a man the right to beat a woman or force her to have sex?"

"We may be in Republican space, but the RAW's laws do not apply here, *Lieutenant.* Our exclusive charter to the planet exempts us on this matter . . . and others. You presumed a lot and it's going to cost you."

There it was, and without the girl to back her story, this wasn't going to end well. Unless she called their bluff.

At this point, I have nothing to lose.

"How's the man with the ponytail?"

Anger flashed across the guard's face. "I believe I mentioned a murder charge. He was a good man."

"He was a coward and a rapist."

The guard cracked his neck. "When I get my hands on you—"

"Tell your boss he can either deal with me now on his terms, or deal with me later on mine."

"Is that a threat?"

"A guarantee."

She turned and walked two paces to her bunk, easing herself down so as not to injure her knee further.

A moment later, she heard the guard get out of his chair and walk out of the room. Promise didn't have to wait long before her cell door opened and a stranger entered.

"Declan, leave."

"Sir . . . I don't think that's a good idea."

"She's not going anywhere because she wants to live. Isn't that right, Lieutenant Paen?"

Promise opened her eyes to find a small man standing over her. As she sat up she realized he was one of the shortest men she'd ever seen, no more than one and a half meters tall. One of her platoon sergeants—her close friend Maxi—had at least five centimeters on the man, which wasn't saying much. Shorty looked early fifties, and wore the fashionable clothes of a much younger man. A low V-neck exposed toned muscles and several scars.

He rolled his sleeves to the elbows while appraising her wounds. "Now, Declan. Kill the pickups on your way out. I want this off the record."

"Thank you, Declan," Promise said without taking her eyes off of Shorty.

Declan slammed his chair into his station desk. "I'm locking you in . . . just in case."

"Fine, now go."

Shorty struck her as the sort of man who could slit a person's throat with a steak knife one moment, and then clean his hands and the blade before carving into his medium-rare sirloin the next. He casually leaned against the plexi door. "This is nice, yes? I've seen worse. The perspective shifts on this inside, doesn't it? I've made up my mind to let Declan have you. You have two minutes to change it."

For a moment Promise thought she'd miscalculated. The girl, Sephora, she'd been right about their predicament. They were both as good as dead. She envisioned Sephora lying on the deck; all the horrible things they'd probably done to her. Promise wanted nothing more than to curl up into a ball and cry. She'd only meant to help and instead she'd managed to kill the girl before her time.

"Ninety seconds, Lieutenant."

You came to me. Something has you worried.

"I want safe passage off of the station and the girl goes with me. Otherwise, you're going to regret this day."

The man's eyes widened in surprise.

"Watch your words as you value your life, Lieutenant Paen. You can't hide behind your uniform, not from me. I make bad things happen to people . . ." His voice trailed off. ". . . very bad things, very slowly. My men like to take their time, Declan in particular. One Marine can easily get lost in a 'verse as large as ours."

Shorty sounded like he was posturing. She got to her feet while making no effort to hide her injuries, and pulled nose-close with him. "You've obviously done some homework on me. I've tried to keep a low profile." Promise shrugged indifferently. "I'm due back on Hold in a matter of days. After that my unit deploys. A lot of people know I'm here: your people; the station workers; the ship I arrived on; my commanding officer. After the Senate hearing, even some of the Congress knows, including Senator Terra Jang."

Dropping Jang's name was a calculated risk. The senator was a stalwart anti-slaver. Jang's history with human trafficking was well documented, Promise knew. She prayed Declan's boss knew it too.

I hope he reads the news.

"Thirty seconds."

"When I don't return on schedule my superiors will send someone after me to find out why. You're a businessman in a line of work with enemies, and people know you're here. My people know I'm here. You don't want the Marine Corps Criminal Investigation Division snooping around. That could be very bad for business."

"You sound desperate, Ms. Paen. I believe we're done." He turned to go.

"Taking Sephora off your hands will be doing you a favor."

Shorty paused and then turned back to face her. If he was surprised that Promise knew the girl's name he didn't show it. His eyes flicked sideways. "Declan took care of her already."

No. The room started spinning and Promise fought the urge to sit down. "I thought Declan liked to take his time," she shot back.

His slight smile told her she'd struck home. "You can't prove anything. Still, the girl is a . . . minor inconvenience." Finally, they were getting somewhere.

"That's true," Promise said. "That's why I'm going to do you the favor."

"What can you possibly offer me?"

"My silence. And when I die doing my job on some forsaken, backwater planet, what I know about your operation won't matter anymore. I'm a mechanized Marine in a frontline company that's prepping for a long deployment to Sheol. We expect to take casualties. Do the math."

Promise grabbed her side as a sharp pain hit her. "I'll actually be doing you a huge favor," she said through gritted teeth. "Sephora doesn't want to be here any more than I do. If you kill her you'll have to kill me too."

"Don't tempt me, Lieutenant. I can think of ten different ways to do you . . . just off the top of my head. It's not complicated."

"Let's not circle round the issue. You're going to have to deal with the girl one way or the other, and you're going to have to deal with me, too. If I disappear there will be an investigation. What I'm offering you avoids *that* complication."

"Perhaps. Say I kill you and dispose of your body. Maybe no one comes looking after all. Say I stage your death, tag your corpse, and space you out an airlock, and then retrieve your frozen body and smash you into a million little pieces. Say I strap you into a capsule and drop you into the sun with the rest of the trash. Say I do the same to you and the girl. Death notices are easily forged. I'll write yours myself." The man looked up in thought. "Ah, how's this? As soon as you arrived, you shuttled down to the surface and hit the north shore. Regrettably, what passes for a shark on Guinevere dragged you under and had you for lunch. We never saw you again. I'm a good storyteller and everyone has a price. What then, Lieutenant?"

Promise didn't miss a beat. "The Marine Corps will still investigate. We never leave one of our own behind. Consider my brain-box." Promise tapped the base of her skull. "It's implanted in my cerebellum. If I die, it records the time, place, and cause of death. It's nearly indestructible. You can tamper with it but the Corps will know, and the Corps will want it back. They'll go diving."

The man scratched his head. "Maybe, assuming they can even find it. I've made a career out of solving difficult problems."

"Go ahead. Make me disappear. Incinerate me." Promise dared him. "When I don't report in on time my superiors will file a report. I'll be considered AWOL and the Corps will want to know why. Take it from me: I'm not the type to desert my post. Either way, the RAW-MC will come looking for me."

The man pursed his lips and seemed to give her words some thought.

"Why, Lieutenant? Why should I believe either of you won't talk if I let you walk? What prevents you from running to the senator you mentioned and trying to shut me down?"

"Like you said, the Republic's laws don't apply here. And, I keep my word. If either of us talked, I'm sure you'd make sure something unpleasant happened to us. Believe me, I very much want to live."

"How good is your imagination, Ms. Paen? What's to stop, as you put it, something *unpleasant* from happening to you in the future?"

"I'm going to lie." Promise knew her decision would eat at her for the rest of her life. "I came here on vacation, had a good time, and told the staff so in writing. I even wrote a letter to the management expressing my thanks. Draw it up, name whomever you wish. I'll sign it."

"I want more. You're also going to write to your commanding officer and you're going to explain your injuries as an unfortunate accident on the planet's surface, while telling him what a wonderful time you had. Please brag about our medical facilities and our staff. We took amazing care of you. We care a great deal about our military guests. By the way, thank you for your service. We've already created a backstory for the girl . . . in the event we need to dispose of her. Never deviate from the story for as long as you live. Do, and I'll have you both disappeared.

"One last thing, Lieutenant. Please listen very carefully because I want these words to haunt you in your dreams for the rest of your life." A thin smile crossed his face. "I know you're an orphan, just like Sephora. But, you do have friends in the Corps. Kathy and Maxi. Did I get their names right? They each have families. Little nieces and nephews and parents who love them dearly. I found their stills on the nets, and both look like upstanding Marines. I would hate to think something might happen to either one of them, or their families. Or to Sephora. Something unfortunate. Something unpleasant. Something permanent. Do we understand each other? Do we have a deal?"

"Yes, we have—" Her words caught in her throat and it took everything in her to get them out.

Thirty-two

A half hour later, Ms. Night opened Promise's cell, her luggage and a fresh set of clothes in hand.

"Size four, right?"

Promise raised an eyebrow as she hobbled outside. "Where's Declan? I want to say good-bye."

Night appeared tense, fidgety even. "We're stopping at Medical before you leave ... for your first round of treatment. You may change there." Night hesitated. "You're staying aboard for the next couple of days, for the rest of your convalescence. I put you in one of our best suites. You won't be permitted to leave your room or roam the facility. I'm sorry about that but there's nothing I can do. I wish things ... well ... I wish you the best, Ms. Paen."

"I would normally say thank you, Ms. Night. I'm afraid you don't deserve it. What about Sephora?"

"The girl will join you when you leave the station."

"What about my early check-in?" Promise couldn't have been more sarcastic.

"Ah—"

"Please thank Troy anyway."

Night looked like she wanted to say something more.

A nurse dressed in white scrubs with the Kies logo embroidered on the breast met them at the entrance to Kies Medical. Coastal scenes hung on the walls, and a holo of the human nervous system rotated on a dais. "I'm Nurse Haak," the nurse said to Promise, and to Ms. Night, "Will you be joining us?" Haak looked Promise over and gave Night a perturbed look.

"No, I need to settle some matters," Night said. "Ms. Paen, I'll be back for your signatures in a bit."

Signatures? Oh, right. You mean so I can falsify screenwork.

Promise tried to peel out of her clothes and found the blood had already dried. "Wait." Haak sprayed her wounds down, dampening her clothes while wicking away the pain. "They break it and I have to put it back together. Some days this job doesn't pay enough." Getting her pants off ripped open the wound on her thigh anyway, and Promise nearly passed out.

"They did a piss-poor job of dressing that."

"Tell me about it," Promise said between labored breaths. Haak caught her underneath the arm and walked her to an examination table. "Guess they got their kilo of flesh too."

"Best leave it at that." Haak shook her head. "The less I know about you the better. Call it an occupational hazard."

Haak cast a competent air about her. Stern eyes said she wasn't one for small chat. Her chin-length hair was cut in a bowl and it swung gently as she worked, every movement precisely measured. She reached for a side table and a small cylinder about the length of her forearm. "Let's wand the open wounds first. Then you point and I'll shoot, okay?"

Interesting choice of words. "It's a plan. My ribs are killing me."

"Good. They're up next."

An hour later Promise walked out of Medical feeling more like herself. She was freshly showered, and dressed more or less as she'd arrived, minus the bloodstains and most of the swelling. Ms. Night, a taxi, and a pair of armed guards were waiting at the entrance. The larger of the two helped her get her head down as she entered. "Careful, Ms. Paen." The driver turned around and offered her a beverage and a mint.

Rolling out the welcome mat. I guess we're all friends now, Promise thought. She kept her situational awareness about her. If either guard reached inside a coat pocket or into the waistband for a knife or hypo or some other weapon, she wouldn't hesitate. An elbow strike to the larynx—guard left. Then a back fist to the nose followed by a hammer fist to the groin—guard right. She'd grab the driver's ponytail from behind and snap his neck. The phantom crack of breaking vertebrae made her smile. They'd all be dead before they knew what hit them.

The pain in her ribs had subsided to a midlevel ache by the time they reached the hotel. The bruising had mostly faded, so someone would have to really look to see it. The blistering on her hand had been severe and would require several more rounds of quickheal. Haak had debrided the skin before spreading a gel across the open wound, which quickly set while retaining its plasticity. Then she'd "wanded" the site to promote healing. Her palm looked pretty raw. She figured she could kill with it if she had to.

The taxi drove into a service hatch at the base of the hotel and found its spot among a small fleet of hatch-back bubbles. A private lift deposited her twelve floors up. She was escorted to her room, a hand on each arm. A small tray of food lay on a stone table in a well-furnished sitting room. The napkins said THE PEPPER SEED, and there was enough food for two people.

"Am I expecting company?"

Ms. Night gave her an unreadable look and sat down. "The pepper seed is actually a nut-bearing tree on the surface. The nuts have kick. I'm not fond of them."

"Seriously?" Promise eyed the food, thinking it might be poisoned or something.

"Here." Night took a bite. "See. It won't kill you. Besides, we have time."

"Yes, about that. My vacation isn't due to end for a bit," Promise said. She turned her attention to the large viewport against the outer wall. Several vessels were docked outside. EN MOUVEMENT was stenciled in black on the largest vessel, a pleasure cruiser much like the one she'd jumped in on. Two rows of viewports ran the length of the ship from the cockpit to amidships, and she could see people moving inside. Her stomach growled; she wasn't yet ready to put solid food in it. Maybe a cup of caf. "How am I going to explain the change of plans? I'm supposed to be on the planet's surface." The cockpit lights came on and the caf nearly burned her tongue. She turned to face Night. "I just arrived, yesterday."

"We've taken care of that." Ms. Night stared off into space. "*En Mouvement* is one of our finest vessels. The morning after tomorrow, she departs for a quick tour of the inner system, and a brief orbit of Alterra. You'll be aboard. After that she returns here for the next group of guests."

Best get this out of the way before I throw up. "Better tell me the official story, then."

Night looked at her directly. "When you arrived, you stopped by White Kies for a late dinner, where you unfortunately came down with a bout of food poisoning. We felt so badly about it we gave you a tremendous discount on the intrasystem tour. While you recovered you took us up on the offer. You met Sephora as you boarded the *En Mouvement*. You hit it off and spent a lot of time with her during the cruise."

Promise sensed there was more and cocked her head.

"You'll still be billed for your stay and the tour but at a substantially reduced rate. The tour is, well, no-expenses-spared. The boss wants you off his station as soon as you've completely healed. After the tour, you'll stop by the tourosphere just long enough to switch vessels and then return to Hold with the girl."

"How much is all of this going to cost me?"

"We already ran the charge and you will be pleased to know it didn't bounce. You've saved up quite a lot for a lieutenant."

Wonderful. "What about Sephora?"

"The girl's contract with us ends the day she boards the *En Mouvement*. She's opted to spend her outstanding vacation and company credits on the same tour you're taking. She's worked at the Tribeca as waitstaff for the past two years. Her father was a maintenance worker and died in an accident. When he passed, she stayed on. She had no other family to speak of and we took her in." Night looked down and fidgeted with her nails. "I've loaded the details into your queue. You only get to read it once before it self-deletes. Here." She handed Promise a datapad. "That explains it all. Don't try to link with the nets or get out a message. We've deactivated your implant too. You're running dark until you board the jumpship for your return to Hold. We have assets in the Marine Corps so we may check in from time to time."

Night's admission was said so casually it took a moment for the words to register, and then Promise did a double take.

"Oh, I need a couple of signatures, here and on the next screen, and a retinal scan."

"This is the letter *I* wrote?" Promise asked.

"Yes. You're welcome."

The simple script logo of Kies Inc. appeared in the upper right of the screen; the letter was thorough. The hotel's concierge was mentioned, and the bartender at White Kies, Tanin. So were the resort on-planet and Troy who manned the welcome desk. He'd arranged for the early check-in she didn't get to use. And two sentences praised Haak from the medical clinic. Promise didn't disagree there. She cited all of them for "services above and beyond" her "every expectation." She'd be sure to pass the word around the Corps too. Declan was even mentioned, and that went down like a jagged pill. The date stamp was four days from now.

"Nice to see Declan getting his due." Promise read on. A minor mishap with a plate of undercooked surf and turf had sent her to the infirmary, the toxins nearly killed her. She'd been in her room and grown nauseous, fallen, and gashed her leg on a side table. She'd been boiling water for tea to help calm her stomach, and as she went down she'd reached out and brushed the hot plate and burned her hand too. She'd no reason to doubt the report except she knew it was all a fabricated lie. "The tour of the system was breathtaking and the ice rings around Alterra I won't soon forget." The last paragraph turned her stomach. "Everyone at Kies was wonderful, and in spite of being sick I've never been so pampered in my life. The staff was amazing. I'd tell you to hang on to Sephora but . . ." Promise put the tablet down for a moment and inhaled slowly, and slow-released her anger. ". . . but she's already told me it's time for her to move on. As it turns out we'll be on the same in-system tour for two days so I'll have the pleasure of her company for a bit longer. She was there when I needed her most, when I could barely get up to care for myself. You should give her a fat bonus as a sendoff."

Promise signed the document with clenched teeth, swiped to the next document. It was addressed to her commanding office, Lieutenant Colonel Price Halvorsen, and the date stamp showed the current date only later that afternoon.

MAY 15th, 92 A.E., STANDARD CALENDAR, 1500 HOURS
LT COL Price Halvorsen, RAW-MC
Commanding Officer, Charlie Battalion, Fifth Brigade, Twelfth
    Regiment
Queue: MM-1 160 021 533
Dear Colonel;
    I've been waylaid on Kies Tourosphere and never made it to the planet's surface. Of all things I ate undercooked shellfish and the toxins nearly offed me. Kies Medical is top-notch and I should be good-to-go by the time my liberty is up. I'm writing to keep you informed . . . just

in case. If my situation changes, you will know ASAP. Kies is comping most of my trip and if I'm up to it they've booked me passage on a two-day cruise of the system in the captain's suite. Not too shabby for a lowly jane. A nurse is accompanying me to monitor my vitals. I tell you . . . these folks are tops.

Plan on seeing me back on Hold, on time, green-to-go.

Paen, out.

LT PROMISE T. PAEN
COMMANDING OFFICER, VICTOR COMPANY, CHARLIE BATTALION,
FIFTH BRIGADE, TWELFTH REGIMENT

She signed the letter and shoved the datapad at Night. "Happy?" A medical report was attached, which would become a permanent part of her jacket in the RAW-MC, probably before she returned for duty and after it had passed the colonel's screen. It even fed into her reputation for getting into trouble, and if anything, it was going to make working for Halvorsen that much harder.

Just another link in my chain of recklessness. Touché, Mr. . . . ? She'd never learned the name of Declan's boss and still he'd read her like a book.

What choice did I have?

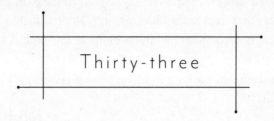

Thirty-three

"This is nice," Sephora said as the door between their rooms slid open.

Promise nodded without looking up from her book.

Her accommodations probably rivaled the personal quarters of a captain of a Republican battlecruiser, and maybe even a battleship. The small kitchenette included a fully stocked minibar and pantry. The formal sitting area was on the lavish side, even by captain's standards. Off it was a spacious bedroom with a sizable potted plant. Watering directions were mounted to the bulkhead.

> **"My name is Carlie. I like one deciliter in the morning and classical music at night."**

A 3D relief of an ancient wet-Navy galleon sailed across the headboard. Her simulated viewport was spectacular and if she hadn't known better she would have taken the view for the genuine article. The *En Mouvement* was up to one-tenth of C, far too slow for the visible stars to care.

Promise's nose was buried in a book of military history. *Third Diaspora Conflicts and the Rebirth of the Wet Navy,* by Schweikart and Grossman. It was a bit on the dry side, even though it'd won the Miron-Lee Prize for narrative history the year before. Promise was tired and struggling to concentrate, and she'd read the same page twice already. And Sephora was standing in the threshold between their adjoining rooms, hugging herself and waiting for permission, again.

"We've been over this," Promise said, slamming the book shut. She did her best to hide her opinion of the girl's dress. *I've seen more cotton in an aspirin bottle. Just make eye contact, P.* She did and nearly cringed. Sephora wore a sleeveless top that hugged the body like a wet T-shirt. Her crumpled skirt kept riding up. The ring in her lip chained to the one in her left nostril. Apparently, Kies had made her take both out when she worked.

"Fine, please," Promise said with all the patience of a lieutenant of Marines, "come in." She patted the cushion beside her. The urge to nap almost won her over. Days of too much inactivity aboard the tourosphere and the *En Mouvement* had siphoned her energy. She didn't want to think about what it was doing to her conditioning or run times. The ship's gymnasium was out of the question. She wouldn't leave Sephora for any length of time, not until she was satisfied the girl was emotionally stable and wouldn't try something foolish like hurting herself. *Considering what she's been through, how could she be?* She and Sephora needed to talk again, sooner than later, before they returned to the tourosphere and switched vessels for the return leg to Hold.

"Look," Sephora said, running a hand through her hair. "You don't have to do this."

Which isn't the same thing as telling me not to. "I don't have to do anything," Promise said. "Neither do you. You always have a choice. Come in. Sit down. Let's talk it out. Please."

Sephora did so reluctantly, but perched on the arm of the couch instead, knees toward Promise, skirt bunched up to her panty line.

"I don't bite," Promise said. "By the way, I can see your skivvies."

"My what?"

"Your . . ." Promise spread her hands. ". . . your pink panties. Where's the rest?" Sephora's legs went on forever, conjuring jealous feelings Promise did her best to shake. Muscular thighs and angles and blocks in all the wrong places were Promise's lot. In her RAW-MC utilities, Lieutenant Paen showed just enough to let you know the body underneath was female.

Sephora snorted and crossed her legs. "They're fuchsia, not pink, and I'm wearing a thong."

Right.

"P—*your* wardrobe needs help." Sephora gave her a once-over. "Why don't I take you shopping when we get to Hold? You have a cute shape. You shouldn't hide it."

My wardrobe? Wait a minute. I'm not hiding anything. "Thanks for the offer." Promise hoped she sounded genuine. *And then I'll look like a cheap escort. Um . . . no thanks.*

The previous two days had passed quickly enough aboard the *En Mouvement*, Promise arguing with Sephora about her future and getting nowhere for it. At least some of the pretense between them had fallen. The girl was even using Promise's nickname—P—and leaving her things in Promise's room. Sephora's dress was going to be a problem. They were heading back to Promise's current duty station, which meant that a lot of young janes and jacks shot full of hormones would be within striking distance, and some were downright predatory about it. Promise needed to explain the dress code on-base without offending the girl. Hopefully, Sephora had packed less revealing clothes. First, she had to get through the girl's emotional shields, and they were full-up.

Promise had boarded *En Mouvement* first, watched with disbelief as Sephora swam the tube in stilettos and a plunging diamond-cut halter top, her black mesh mini not quite covering her derriere. A Kies attendant had helped Sephora into the tube and got a unobstructed view of her stern and support structure as a bonus. As Sephora entered *En Mouvement*'s gravity she overcorrected, landing so hard one of her heels broke.

"Got you," Promise said, moving quickly to catch her.

Sephora had jerked her arm free. "I don't need your help."

Fine, you need space you got it. Don't take it personally.

A small family had reared back, censure written on their faces. They scrutinized Sephora and pulled their children closer. Sephora eyed them before blowing the little boy a girly kiss and the daddy a big-girl one. The wife muttered something and pulled her family down a passageway. Something like an apology crossed Sephora's face when she looked back at Promise. "Sorry."

"For what? They were rude. Well, they were rude first. You didn't have to be rude back."

"Whatever."

"Let's get you settled and grab some chow." *And into something less provocative.* "You've cut your hair." It was buzzed. "I like it. It's so . . . you."

"What is that supposed to mean?" Sephora said as she pulled off her other heel and tossed it in a nearby incinerator.

Promise turned to face her. "I don't know how else to say this so you'll have to forgive me. You like being a badass, don't you?"

Sephora crossed her arms and for a moment Promise feared she'd gone too far. Then the girl tossed her head back and roared. "You know, I think I'm going to like you."

The porter cleared his throat to get their attention. He wore a Kies jacket and slacks, and wandering eyes. "Welcome aboard, Ms. Nesbitt." His eyes might as well have been scanners. "If you'll follow me, ma'am. Ms. Paen."

Ms. Nesbitt? Promise cleared her throat. "Eyes in the sky, mister, and off my sister."

The porter sputtered out an apology. "Right, well, um, this way, please."

"Sister," Sephora said in a hushed voice as they followed the porter toward their cabins.

"It was the first thing that came out. You're not a pinup calendar."

Sephora looked surprised. "Thanks."

The first day aboard ship Sephora stayed in her own room. Promise checked on the girl for meals and a time or two to ask her if she needed anything. Otherwise, she tried to stay away, hoping the girl would come to her.

The next morning, Promise heard a light knock at her cabin's door. Opening it, she found Sephora standing in the ship's corridor, wearing a bit more than she had the previous day.

"You mind, I'm a little cold."

Obviously. Promise stepped aside as the girl entered her room.

"What's for breakfast?"

The tray of scones, hot caf, and crisp bacon had just arrived. "There's enough for two," Promise said as she pulled out a chair for Sephora and waited for her to sit. "How do you take your caf?"

"Black as space and scorching hot." Sephora turned in her seat to look up at Promise. "You?"

Promise smiled and squeezed her shoulder. "I like to enjoy mine."

"Very funny."

More small talk followed. They both liked action holovids, so they ordered snacks and watched two back-to-back in Promise's cabin. *Fleet in the Fire* wasn't bad. *Blood Ship* upset Promise's stomach and she had to cover her eyes more than once. It was about an AWOL cyborg with massive brain damage that went on a killing spree. A lowly Private Brigance got him in the end.

"Pulsers don't sound like that," Promise said. "You know, they're silent. They don't make *beaming* sounds." Sephora had rolled her eyes.

They even picked each other's roles. Sephora played the private and Promise the bloodthirsty cyborg. "You look like the type," Sephora said. "Up for a third. I hear *Freedom Down* is really great. I can be the president and you can be my bodyguard. Sounds fitting, don't you think?"

"Better than a ruthless killer cyborg," Promise said.

"You're a Marine." Sephora's face wrinkled. "Isn't that what you do?"

Promise wanted to backhand the girl and it must have shown. "You have a lot to learn about Marines." She might as well have struck true because Sephora shrank into herself. "Understand this. I kill when I have to, to protect the lives of others. I don't court death. Ever."

An awkward silence followed. Promise mentally kicked herself, knowing she had to break it now or things between them might never recover. She killed the screen and turned to face Sephora. "Look . . . I'm sorry for my tone of voice . . . and for scaring you."

"You looked like you wanted to kill me. Just like that 'borg."

"I know. That's a side of me I keep under wraps. Look, what you said hit close to home, okay? I can't blame you for thinking that way. Especially if all you have to go on are action vids like *Blood Ship.* I'd make a lousy 'borg." Promise smiled. "Besides, pulsers really don't make beaming sounds. They're silent killers."

Sephora glanced up at Promise. "You look like you've just seen a ghost."

"Bad memories, that's all."

Sephora slid to the cushion, her shoulders slumped forward, but her lips twitched in response. "I doubt I'd make a good president either. I'd probably get pissed and push the little red button over something stupid." She turned to face Promise. "I didn't mean to hurt you either."

Little red button. Promise did her best not to laugh. *It's like this girl is reading my mind.* She laughed anyway, and then Sephora joined her. Promise leaned over and mock-punched her in the shoulder.

"Friends step on each other's toes," Promise said. "It is going to happen so get used to it. Apology accepted. I'm sorry too. Look, we need to chat about a few things."

"No we don't. I'll just be a bother." Walls went right back up.

"No you won't. Just hear me out?"

The head nod was so slight Promise nearly missed it. "I can't walk away from this."

"Sure you can, it's easy. Just don't look back."

"Okay, let me rephrase. . . ." Promise took a deep breath. *Patience is a virtue . . . so learn it, P.* "I can't walk away from you. And I don't want to."

That brought Sephora's head around. "Why?"

"Because I know what it's like to be alone. Trust me, you don't want that."

"I've had enough company for a lifetime. Trust *me*, some alone time sounds good."

Promise flinched. The girl had been through the unthinkable, much of it at the hands of men like Declan and Wade. "Point taken. I—"

"More caf? I'll brew some." Sephora pushed off the couch and walked into the kitchenette.

"I'm not offering much," Promise said. "When we reach Hold, my unit deploys offworld, far from the sector. I'll be gone for months. I've never lived off base. It sounds nice, and I'll need someone . . . to watch the place for me."

"Hire a maid," Sephora said as she put the kettle on to boil and pulled two mugs from one of the overhead cabinets. The cabinets, the dishware, and the heating plate were all magnetized in case the vessel lost power. That way they wouldn't float into the air if the vessel lost gravity. "Better yet, buy a mech. They come cheap. I don't."

"I'm trying." Promise gave her a pleading look.

"Try harder."

"All right, how about roommates? At least until you get on your feet, and find work so you can pay your own way. Maybe you could go back to school too?"

"I've been schooled in the 'verse of hard knocks." Sephora slammed one of the mugs on the counter and gave Promise a cold stare. "I've got the bumps and bruises to prove it. I've got the basic idea. Thanks, Mom."

"Maker knows I don't want to be *that*. How about your friend?"

"You know nothing about me." Sephora's eyes withdrew to the teakettle as it blew steam. She turned to grab the sugar and banged her head on the cupboard door, stepped back, and slammed it shut in frustration. "Ouch."

"You're a survivor . . . like me." Promise sat forward with her hands clasped as if in prayer. "I was about your age when they came for my father."

Had her full attention now. "Who?" Sephora said, leaning on the counter.

"Before enlisting, they hit our homestead. Their vessel was several gens old—I recognized it later, after I was in the Corps. It's a cheap buy in a lot of verge systems. They wore third-rate battle armor, nothing like my mechsuit back on Hold, but more than adequate to the task." Sephora finished pouring her cup and went to work filling Promise's. "My dad never had a chance. They shot him because they—"

Sephora hollered out in pain and stumbled out of the kitchenette favoring one foot.

"In the sink, now." Promise was on her feet and had the cold water running full blast before Sephora could get her foot up and into it. "Keep the water on the burn while I find a medkit."

Promise found the small Kies clamshell in the bedroom, beneath the nightstand, and rushed back to Sephora's side. She filled a bowl with cold water and set it by the couch, and then helped Sephora hobble over. "Hold still so I can see what we're looking at."

"Oh . . . I don't feel so . . . ." Sephora's hands didn't get to her mouth before she tossed her movie snacks all over Promise.

"I've been doused with worse," Promise said. She used the blade of her hand to squeegee off the worst of it. "You know, it really doesn't look that bad."

Sephora's foot was a mottled red from the ankle to the instep, a few spots already blistering. "Try dropping through atmo with a platoon of green boots." Promise returned with another bowl. "Into this next time, okay?" She stripped off her slacks and shirt, and lobbed them into the kitchen sink. Sephora had turned as pale as the Kies-white sheets on her bed. "Let me get the wand. Head down. Deep, slow breaths. Good girl."

A few passes with the wand and the skin looked less angry. A few more and the color returned to Sephora's face. "I think we can skip the ship's infirmary. Besides, docs like to use medbots, and bots don't always stick the right instruments in the right places."

"Sounds like some of my former clients," Sephora said.

"Now I feel sick," Promise said.

"You—sit," Sephora said. She pointed to the seat beside her on the couch, and then she handed Promise the bowl.

"Aren't we a pair," Promise said.

"Yeah. Hey, I'm sorry about your dad, P. Really sorry. My mom ran out on us when I was two. I lost my dad in an accident on the tourosphere. He was working on a lift and fell down the shaft when his gravbelt failed. I was fourteen and Dad had bills to pay. That's why I started working. Wade was my first . . ." Sephora's voice trailed off.

Promise reached over and grabbed Sephora's hand. "I'm sorry too. I don't talk much about my father. He was a hard man to live with. He loved me. He didn't know how to show it most of the time. He didn't deserve what he got."

After a few deep breaths Promise was feeling better. Sephora's bluntness would take some getting used to.

"There was nothing I could do to stop them," Promise said, knowing full well she didn't fully believe her words, "and when he was gone there was nothing left for me either. No home. No family to speak of. Enlisting made sense. I needed to get away. Somewhere along the line I got tired of running. The Corps became the family I never had." Promise slipped her arm around Sephora's shoulders. "I'm not saying I can be that for you. Maybe I can help you get a head start. You're going to need help. Here, let me see your foot again. We'll need to wrap it so we don't pop the blisters. We'll hit it with the wand again in a few hours."

"Bowl."

Promise slid it over as Sephora spewed liquid.

"Okay—" It came out so fast Promise did a double take. "—roomie."

"For a tough girl, you sure are squeamish."

"Shut up," Sephora said, wiping her mouth with the back of her hand. "When we get to Hold let's go apartment shopping. I'll hold down the fort while you storm across the 'verse and break skulls for a living. I'll consider school but no promises. Job for sure. Something *not* in the service sector. My dad liked to fix things. Maybe I'll try that. Make sure you send a vid once in a while so I know you're still alive."

"Ah—that's sweet," Promise said.

"Stop it, or you'll make me puke again."

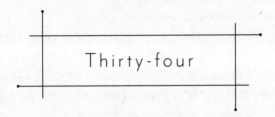

Thirty-four

As soon as they jumped in-system, Promise's minicomp chirped to attention.

"What was that?" Sephora asked. She and Promise were on the couch in Sephora's dayroom and both had their nose in a book.

"My commanding officer."

"That doesn't sound good."

Usually isn't. Promise looked up and tried to reassure her. "I'm sure it's nothing."

When they were thirty mikes away from making orbit around Hold, Promise commed the colonel directly. At such a short distance, the *Arosa Star*'s civilian-grade comm was more than adequate; it was certainly not FTL, but the lag was a small inconvenience.

"Why have you been off-net?"

Promise stalled for time. She couldn't very well tell the colonel about her encounter on Kies Tourosphere. "Solar flare?" It was a least a plausible explanation. "I'll have my implant checked when I get back to base."

"You do that. ETA?" Lieutenant Colonel Price Halvorsen didn't waste words.

"Fifteen hundred hours. Sir, I'm not traveling alone." She waited several seconds for Halvorsen's response, schooled her face to neutral and attentive.

Again, a small delay, and then the colonel's one-word response. "Explain."

And now Promise began wishing she had access to an FTL comm, because the lag was giving her plenty of time to second-guess what the colonel's message was about. Mere seconds filled her lack of information with several unpleasant possibilities.

Which brings up the First Directive—no lying to a superior officer. I killed a man too, at least I was partially to blame for his death, and I'm covering up a sex-trafficking operation. She'd thought a lot about how to explain Sephora's presence and she fully intended to tell the truth, just not all of it, which probably violated the spirit of the directive even if she was technically following its rule.

"I met a young girl during my vacation. She worked for Kies, and so did her father before he passed away. She helped nurse me back to health when I fell ill. Sir, she's an orphan at a crossroads. Sir, I know what it's like to be in her shoes and I want to do something about it." Promise paused, unsure of what to say next.

Halvorsen's next response followed several seconds later. "And you're telling me this because?"

The lag was a bit less now.

"She's moving in with me until I can secure a place off-base. May I have the rest of today to get her settled before I report for duty?"

The colonel's expression froze for a moment. When it did change, his face softened and he looked less like a colonel and more like . . . Promise wasn't sure like what. More human. Un-Halvorsen.

"What you do in your personal life is your business. We will talk more about this girl later. It sounds like what you're doing is admirable, Lieutenant. But—" And several seconds ticked by. "—don't forget your duty." The colonel held up a finger and stepped off-screen, putting her on mute. He came back a half mike later. "You've got the rest of the day to get her settled. Send me the girl's I-dent and I'll have a temporary pass waiting for her at the north gate. Report in the morning to the Square, at eight hundred hours. Regular dress and minimum glittery. Some of the brass will be there. Check your minicomp for directions."

The Square? "Brass, sir? What's this about?"

"Tomorrow, zero eight hundred. Be early."

Thirty-five

MAY 20TH, 92 A.E., STANDARD CALENDAR, 0722 HOURS
REPUBLIC OF ALIGNED WORLDS PLANETARY CAPITAL—HOLD
THE OUTER COURT OF THE SQUARE

Promise stepped out of the compact aerodyne and looked up at the cloudless sky. She raised her I-dent bracelet to the reader mounted to the aircar's door to pay her fare, and watched the yellow craft shrink into the distance. *Glorious morning,* she thought. A flock of gulls overflew her position in a V formation. They winged by, seemingly without a care in the world, their singular purpose oblivious to the craft she'd just exited. The aircar adjusted sharply to avoid a collision with the lead bird. *We're never going to own the skies, not like they do.* Her eyes fell to the outer court of the Square, the headquarters of the Republic of Aligned Worlds Department of Defense and the central hub of the RAW Fleet Forces: Marine Corps, Navy, Branch Sector Guard, and Department of Planetary Militias.

The RAW Special Operations Command and Bureau of Military Intelligence (including MARINT and NAVINT—you could insult BUMIL without disparaging a particular military branch, which came in handy during cross-branch socials) each took an entire floor. The Republic's Central Intelligence Agency and a few subordinate clandestine services on the plainclothes side of the fence called the Square home too, and they took up the top floor. The suits and uniforms didn't mix much. Theirs was less a friendly rivalry and more a cold war.

Beret smartly canted on her head, she inhaled and said a quick prayer. *Sir, please cover me.* Then she spun toward the entrance and through the first checkpoint.

"I-dent please," said the Marine Corps sentry. Like Promise, she wore her RAW-MC regular-dress uniform and white beret.

The grounds of the Square were covered with security drones, most no larger than a small bird, and you'd never find them unless you knew exactly what to look for. Four branch flags fluttered in the breeze atop five-story poles anchored in ferrocrete, their bases flooded by a man-made lake still as glass. Manicured lawns and grasses sprawled in every direction. Smaller flags—one for each of the planetary militias—ringed the perimeter of the lake for more than half a klick. Montana's was a recent addition. Multicolored fish swam through knee-high greenery while several species of bird bobbed in the morning sun. A hundred-year-old piece of artillery sat on a dais and still went boom every independence day. The antique two-seat supersonic to its right was banking sharply on its mount, while the dummy pilots inside gazed out the armorplaste and saluted passersby. A statue of the first RAW mechsuit stood defiantly in the sun. To Promise the thing looked more like a Merkava tank than a suit of mechanized armor.

The Square's flat gray façade complemented the flat navy blue of her regular-dress uniform, and its reflective windows mirrored the polish of her glittery and commendations. The grounds were full of women and men from every branch in their regular- or business-dress uniforms, and all wore the RAW-FF's white beret with the seraph, globe, and anchor cap badge. The white cover was the unifying dress symbol of the Fleet Forces. Otherwise the colors of their regular-dress slacks and short-waist jackets set them apart like mat-colored signal flares. Marines wore navy blue, Sailors wore dark green, and the Sector Guard wore dark brown.

The small group of red berets playing ball on a well-manicured lawn immediately caught her attention. Red covers were a rare sight, and worn only by an elite group of special operators, Marine Corps Force Space-Reconnaissance. Even the Navy and Sector Guard SPECOPS wore white. Seeing the red tops filled her with awe. They were the best of the best the Fleet Forces had to offer. You couldn't try out for SPACECON either. You were asked, if you were lucky.

As Promise neared the inner court of the Square, she caught sight of the Montanan standard fluttering in the breeze. Its reds, blues, and golds dipped her into her past and the memories it dredged up refused to be ignored. More flags ghosted overhead as the names and faces of her fallen surfaced, janes and jakes of Victor Company she'd led and lost in the defense of her birth world. Her Montanan Marines.

As she passed by the lake it became a war-torn haunt. Promise quickened her pace toward the tiered entrance steps and through the second checkpoint. The guard was a smart-looking private first class, not one of those rent-a-sentries. She scanned both of Promise's eyes and her I-dent bracelet, used her minicomp to wand Promise's body. A genderless holo appeared beside Promise that matched her every move. The guard approached the image and deft hands quickly stripped layers away down to the bone.

"You're clear, Lieutenant. Have a nice morning." The PFC saluted sharply before turning to the next in line.

Promise saluted a couple of majors and a captain on the way up, nodded at a good-looking first lieutenant who did a double take, and returned respect from some junior officers and sergeants. A RAW-MC colonel with his arms loaded simply nodded and said, "Lieutenant." A Navy captain recognized her, stopped in midflight, and turned to salute *her*. This drew a small crowd, most of whom looked clearly confused over why the captain was saluting a lieutenant of Marines. His "Thank you for Montana, Lieutenant" seemed to put their questions to rest. Promise's cheeks heated in the warm sea of recognition and she nodded politely, returned his salute as crisply as she could. Didn't think she'd ever get used to that.

As she entered the inner court, she pulled her cover and tucked it under her arm. Her glosses clacked across the hollowed floor and over the inlaid stars that formed the Deck of Heroes. Each star was embossed with the name of an honored warship, unit, or soldier from nearly three hundred years of Republican military tradition. Reading the names as she passed overhead helped calm her nerves.

There was the RNS *Janice-Krighton,* and the RNS *Dect,* three stars over.

Master Sergeant George Manuel 33 A.E.–69 A.E., RAW-MC.

1st Battalion, 5th Marines, with "Darkside" standing out in blocked quotes.

Because she was indoors, she dispensed with the salutes. The nods and "good morning, sir"s and "ma'am"s were simple common courtesy and she scolded herself to pay better attention. *Eyes up, P.*

Above the entryway floated a holo of the Fleet Forces' seraph, globe, and anchor. The ubiquitous symbol of the RAW Fleet Forces kept station in the air thanks to a small army of projectors mounted into the floor, the overhead, and the walls. Every Marine, Sailor, and Sector Guardian wore the seraph, globe, and anchor with pride, as a cap badge on the crown of the beret. Flanking it was a second holo, of the militiaman with a rifle on the shoulder. This symbol was a throwback to before FTL, before the First Diaspora, when Holy Terra's fractured nation-states had depended upon volunteer, part-time citizen soldiers to defend their homelands.

Promise thought hard for a moment. If she had her history correct, militias predated even the iron horse and the rifled long gun. Militiamen from across the RAW's core worlds and protectorates wore the militiaman's badge with obstinate pride. Its presence in the inner court of the Square was an important reminder of the history and genesis of the Republic. A large standing fleet force was critical to the safety and security of the Republic of Aligned Worlds. But the militia had made its existence possible. The militia had given birth to the RAW through an armed rebellion against the Terran Federation, in a desperate bid for self-determination.

A drone met Promise outside the inner court's central bank of lifts. "Good morning, Lieutenant Paen," said the reflective globe in a pleasant enough voice. "If you'll follow me." The drone didn't turn around so much as reverse direction.

Together they entered the northwest lift, which abutted the outside, and took it to Level 47 of eighty total floors. The lift floor was transparent and after a quick look down Promise swallowed and decided to look outside instead. The view of the grounds below swelled until she could see the sprawling tarmac and pads and runways of Joint Spaceport Mo Cavinaugh in the distance. There was the control tower, and over there lay dozens of dropships and smaller vessels in their assigned cradles. To Promise they looked like a fleet of children's playthings.

She watched an assault-class LAC lift off and climb vertically into the air before gradually pulling forward. Once clear of the spaceport, the LAC accelerated into the atmosphere and soon disappeared from sight.

Promise straightened her jacket and turned around as the doors opened on Level 47. She walked into an unmarked hallway with multiple access points. None bore distinguishable markings. The globe wished her a "good day" and reversed course again as the lift's door closed.

The RCIA's seal hung on the opposite wall. A seraph with daggers for wings was ringed by a gold circle and the words "Republican Central Intelligence Agency."

Well, I'm not in RAW-MC territory anymore, Promise thought. *Now what?* She looked left and right. Heard a door open and came round to see her old platoon sergeant step into the hall with a cavernous smile on his face.

"Gunny, boy am I glad to see you."

"Lieutenant, it's nice to be seen," said Gunnery Sergeant Nhorman Khaine. He stuck out his hand and gripped Promise's enthusiastically. "How was the vacation?" Promise's early years in the Corps had been in Khaine's toon, before he was bumped upstairs to Battalion. *That seems like a lifetime ago. Simpler times for sure. So, how was my vacation? Um . . . that's complicated.*

"I'd like to say uneventful, Gunny, but I have the feeling you already know better." Promise searched Khaine's eyes for any clues about why she was standing on Level 47, in RCIA territory. All she got was a cocked eyebrow and a headshake. No.

"What?" Promise smiled coyly, cocking her head in question.

"Would you like to talk about it?"

"I seem to recall you asking me that once before."

"Me too," Khaine said somberly. "That was a doozy of a nightmare." It had happened when Promise was a private, back when she worked for Khaine. Khaine hesitated. "How time changes things. Speaking of changes, this meeting is going to be a bit unusual because—"

The same door the gunny had stepped through only a moment before blew open and careered into the wall with a resounding clang, and the last person Promise expected to see stepped into the corridor. The indigo hair had been replaced with bright blond. She wore a severe A-line jacket and matching slacks, and café-noir stiletto heels. Her hawkish gaze target-locked Promise like a heat-seeking missile.

"I don't understand," Promise said as she looked from the woman to the gunny. "Ms. Night?"

"Not anymore, no thanks to you." Night stopped at the bleeding edge of propriety. "I was deep undercover for two years, trying to take down their sex ring, before you blew my operation. I would say it's nice to see you again but I try not to lie unless the job requires it." She didn't offer Promise her hand.

"Lieutenant, this is Special Agent Rayn McMaster. She's with the *agency.*" She would have to have been deaf to miss Khaine's warning. She thought she detected a hint of disgust in his voice too.

"You're a spook?" Promise balled her fist and nearly decked the woman then and there. "You can't be serious."

Khaine cleared his throat. "I'm afraid she is."

"Special Agent," Khaine said, "you're early. I was supposed to have time to talk with Lieutenant Paen."

"Plans changed." McMaster turned to Promise and planted her hands on her hips. "It's *Special Agent* to you, Lieutenant. I'm curious about Sephora. Tell me, how's the little bitch doing?"

"Agent McMaster! With all due respect, ma'am, you're out of line," Khaine said.

McMaster's lips curled slightly before she dipped her head toward the gunny. "Sorry, I'm glad she's out of that hellhole."

A hard edge formed around Promise's eyes and drained all the warmth from her words. Her weight rocked to the balls of her feet, fist still ready to break McMaster's jaw. "How could you watch an innocent girl being trafficked like that? Oh, that's right. You were just *following* orders."

"Believe me, there was nothing innocent about that place."

Promise's hand shot out.

"Lieutenant," the gunny warned, stepping between Promise and McMaster. "You haven't been properly introduced. Agent McMaster is—"

"On dangerous ground. At the moment, Gunny, I don't care who she is." Promise wrenched her arm free and dropped her arms to her sides. But she didn't back off.

"Perhaps I was out of line." McMaster's sneer didn't leave her face. "You wandered into matters that didn't concern you. *You* nearly got me killed. You blew an undercover operation with ramifications someone of your rank can't possibly fathom. It took me *two* years to gain their trust and you threw it away in a single night. As it is, I've been pulled from the field because our informant changed his mind. You almost killed him."

"Wade? He was your informant? The man got a lot less than he deserved."

The gunny had his arm around Promise now, and was using his body to block her from McMaster. "She's not worth it, Lieutenant."

"Wade isn't the only one who got off easy," McMaster said. "I should have left you in that cell to rot."

"Lieutenant! Agent McMaster, this stops now." The force of Khaine's voice caught both women by surprise. "That's better. Expect an official complaint from my office, Special Agent." Then, addressing Promise, "As for you, lock it down, *now,* ma'am. For the record, McMaster is on our side—she's one of us, a reservist in the Sector Guard. She's a lieutenant *commander.*"

Khaine's eyes were was almost pleading with Promise now. "You may be outside her chain of command but she's a superior officer and you'd be wise to remember that."

Promise appraised McMaster with new eyes. She'd almost broken the Second Directive—assaulting a superior officer. One punch and she would have faced a mandatory court-martial and been drummed out of the Corps. One fist relaxed, and then the other as she sagged into the gunny's frame. "Thank you, Gunny," Promise said softly before pushing away. "This isn't over." To McMaster, "Ma'am, I was hardly what you would call respectful. Please accept my apologies." Her words were far from sincere but at least she'd said them. "We obviously have our . . . differences. I'm personally invested in the girl's future."

McMaster dipped her head and smiled. "I'll bear that in mind, Lieutenant."

"Ma'am, please accept my apologies. My feelings for the girl may have clouded my judgment."

"That's the first honest thing you've said, Lieutenant. You screwed up, and now it's going to cost you."

Promise had the sinking feeling she'd just given McMaster what she'd wanted. Maybe not all of it. But certainly more than enough.

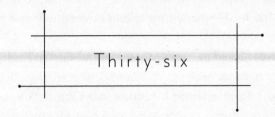

Thirty-six

Promise entered a utilitarian room with a holotank on one side and a white-board on the other. The oblong conference table was as black and smooth as obsidian, with the RCIA's seal inlaid at the center. At the table's head sat Commandant Habakkuk Raghavan, the senior officer of the RAW-MC.

Not good. Promise stiffened when she saw him and the glittery over his chest, which must have weighed a good kilo. Next to him sat a slight gentle-man with Asian features wearing a white shirt rolled to the sleeves and jet peppery hair pulled up in a bun. He was middle-aged with an almond-shaped face and as casual in his dress as the commandant was official in his. The jacket discarded over the back of his chair belied the nature of the build-ing they were in and the seriousness of the meeting. On the opposite side of Raghavan sat Lieutenant Colonel Price Halvorsen. McMaster rounded the table and sat beside the only other person in the room wearing plain clothes.

That explains who he is.

Halvorsen held up a hand, palm up, indicating that she would stand for the meeting. The gunny came around her and found his chair, and she got the impression that he sat as close to her as he dared. She came to attention and saluted, eyes a regulation three centimeters off the commandant's right ear, and waited for the other boot to drop.

"At ease, Lieutenant." Raghavan came forward and placed both hands on the table, palms down. "I'll be quick with the introductions. To my left is Assistant Director Cameron Suh of the Republican Central Intelligence

Agency." Raghavan didn't sound at all pleased. "I believe you know who everyone else is." Raghavan stared at Promise until she nodded.

"Very well, then." He paused for a long moment. "Please tell me, Lieutenant, why are you here?"

Promise's eyes flicked to Agent McMaster and then to Raghavan. "I seem to have stepped in it, sir."

Raghavan didn't quite smile; his brows rose slightly. "Explain?"

"Out in the corridor . . . a moment ago, Agent McMaster told me I blew her operation and nearly got her killed. Compromised an asset too, all for a little—well, I won't repeat what she called the girl. All for a young woman who was being trafficked. I'm sorry for blowing the op, truly. But, sir, with respect, I had no knowledge of the operation. I was fighting for my life . . . and for the girl's. Her name is Sephora. Frankly, sir, had I known about the agent's operation, I'm not sure it would have mattered."

"Really? Why wouldn't—"

"Commandant, you already have my full report," Agent McMaster said, interrupting the commandant. "Lieutenant Paen was clearly off the reservation and operating without orders. Her actions can only be construed as a dereliction of duty and—"

Raghavan held up his hand and gave Assistant Director Suh a stern look.

"Agent McMaster, now is not the time," said Suh. "Remember your place. You've said more than enough already."

"But, sirs, I must insist—"

"Enough." Suh hadn't even pitched his voice upward and the look in his eyes could have frozen a company of shock Marines in their mechboots. "Agent McMaster, impatience will not get you where you want to be." He cocked his head toward Promise. "Lieutenant, you were saying . . ."

Raghavan and Suh looked like men who had already made up their minds about her. In her peripheral vision she saw the colonel gently shake his head and McMaster fuming in her seat on the other side of the table. The gunny couldn't seem to find a comfortable position in his. Promise realized she had everything to lose.

"It wouldn't have mattered, sirs, because the girl asked me for help. Not in so many words," Promise added quickly when McMaster opened her mouth to speak. "She didn't have to say the words. She said them with her eyes, with the fear on her face. I saw her 'no' from across the room. I watched her being sold for the night. I watched her procurer—the man who eventu-

ally tried to kill me—grab her arm and force her to go through with it anyway. Her silence might as well have been a scream for help. She didn't have
a choice. I could not, *could not* stand by and do nothing." Promise was nearly
shaking now. "Apparently, the special agent could."

McMaster bolted to her feet. "I will not be spoken to that way!" Her fists
came down hard on the polished tabletop.

"Agent McMaster—sit." Suh's face went taut. "Lieutenant, you know
nothing of Agent McMaster, or of her past. Your words assume too much
and you do her a great disservice. Please think more carefully before you
speak again."

"Then, sir, may I ask your agent why she said what she did about the
girl—" Promise nodded toward the door. "—out in the hall, before we
walked in."

Suh's eyes hardened. "Let *me* do that."

"I've heard enough." Raghavan exchanged looks with the assistant director. "Cameron?"

Suh nodded in agreement. "I'm done here."

Raghavan pushed away from the table and stood. "The assistant director
and I already discussed this mess before the meeting started, and we agreed
then that the lieutenant didn't act maliciously, nor did she break any laws."

Raghavan spoke more for the benefit of the official recording than for
her, and while it irked Promise to be talked about as if she weren't in the
room, she also realized that the commandant was going "on the record" in
her defense. She took a deep breath and nodded. *Thank you, sir.*

"Everything Lieutenant Paen said here today only reinforces my original opinion of this matter. Contrary to Special Agent McMaster's official
charge, Lieutenant Paen did not go off the reservation because she wasn't
under orders . . . except to get some R and R. She didn't follow that order
very well," Raghavan said icily, "but that's not justification for disciplinary
action. I can't fault the lieutenant for rescuing the girl either, even if her
methods leave something to be desired. And, as much as I hate to admit it,
there's a time and place for preemptive action." It really did sound like
Raghavan hated to admit that, and Promise wondered whose ears that statement was being recorded for. "Cameron, if you ever quote me on that I will
deny having said it to my grave."

Suh chuckled under his breath. "Don't worry. Your secret's safe with me.
If I was a hawk it might be a different situation."

"Thank God for that." The commandant turned to face the junior agent in the room. "Agent McMaster, I'm not unsympathetic to your position in this matter. Your life was endangered and a critical operation was compromised. You have every right to be angry. However, Lieutenant Paen was off-duty, out of uniform, and operating on her own time, and her actions are protected by our Good Samaritan laws. I can't very well bust her down for coming to the aid of a fellow human being in need, nor will the RAW-MC tolerate anyone attempting to do so. Have I made myself clear?"

That was bold, Promise thought. Raghavan wasn't just speaking as one of the Joint Chiefs. He was speaking as a Marine with skin in the game, drawing a line in the sand that the RCIA dare not cross. He might as well have said, "Paen is one of ours. Come after her at your own peril."

McMaster went to speak but Suh cleared his throat, and after a long moment she reluctantly nodded.

"As for you, Lieutenant, you have a history of rushing head-on into pulser fire, and it has largely served you well. Until now. Sometimes running toward the fight is the best option, sometimes it's the only option. Teaching Marines to run toward the close fight isn't easy and you're to be commended for your bravery."

Promise heard the "but" coming and prepared herself for the official reprimand. Her career was going to survive this. She wanted to smile. She wanted to jump for joy and rub Agent McMaster's face in it. Oh how she wanted to do that. Holding it back almost killed her.

"But—"

There it was. Promise held her breath, didn't dare break eye contact with the commandant.

"—a proclivity for direct engagement must be counterbalanced with clearheaded thinking and restraint, too. I've come to believe the way we'd thrust command upon you—so early in your career and without the opportunity to look, listen, and watch—robbed you of a critical window of learning, which might have taught you the difference."

"Sir, if I may." Colonel Halvorsen raised a hand, palm out. "I'm partially to blame for—"

The commandant cut him off without saying a word and then turned his gaze back to Promise. "Lieutenant, I suppose I'm to blame as much as anyone. The Corps's manpower needs are stretched thinly as it is. We're pushing our best and brightest too fast and I'm as much to blame for *that* as anyone." The commandant sighed like the weight of the world lay upon his shoulders. "Lieutenant, I'll not see your career go down in flames simply because your superiors entrusted you with too much, too soon.

"That's why I'm placing you and Victor Company under the command of Captain Sasha Yates. Captain Yates is an outstanding officer and in need of a company and Victor Company needs a seasoned CO."

I'm sorry? Promise's jaw dropped. She couldn't help looking at McMaster or seeing the vindication on the special agent's face. Suh met her gaze directly. The sympathy on the commandant's face only made the situation worse. She didn't want his sympathy, didn't need his sympathy. All she felt was raw anger that couldn't be assuaged. Not until she had the chance to take it out on something . . . or someone.

"You'll still retain your rank in Victor Company as a first lieutenant but you'll now be the company's second-in-command. That's really how it should have been all along, particularly for someone so young in grade. Because of our manpower shortages, we've far too many lieutenants serving in captains' billets. Thankfully, Captain Yates just became available. You'll be her XO."

I'm second . . . because you don't believe I could do the job in the first place.

"I can only imagine what you must be thinking right now, and what you must think of me. I know that in time you'll—"

Disbelief washed over her. Anger followed like an aftershock. Her career had just been nuked and she was standing at ground zero. Her eyes wouldn't focus and though Raghavan was still speaking she wasn't comprehending his words. Her body swayed and her hand found the edge of the conference table, enough to steady her. She knew she was going to say or do something that would end her career. Here and now. She imagined slamming Agent McMaster into the wall, which seemed like a good place to start. She'd break a bone or two while she was at it. In her mind's ear she heard the sickening crunch of calcium and marrow colliding with the bulkhead behind the special agent. She drew great satisfaction as she pictured the agent's eyes rolling up into her head before she slumped to the deck.

Promise had not in her wildest dreams considered the possibility that Victor Company would be taken away from her. A verbal reprimand? Certainly. A formal letter of reprimand in her jacket? Maybe. Who was she fooling? *Probably.* Stripping her of command? No CO would want her after this. The commandant was as good as blackballing her.

She hadn't wanted to be an officer in the first place. She'd only accepted the field commission on Montana because the circumstances had been so dire. Had it really been just a year ago? The captain had died in combat. Because of his injuries, the XO, Lieutenant Spears, had needed regen therapy to grow a new leg. Promise had given Spears every conceivable reason why she wasn't officer material. Why he shouldn't offer her the field promotion. And there were Gunnery Sergeant Ramuel and the other noncoms in the company with more years of experience. One of them could have stepped into the command gap. To her surprise Ramuel and Spears had endorsed her promotion to the hilt. "You're my choice, Promise." The certitude in Spears's voice had almost made her believe it was true. "Officer material." And then Victor Company became *her* company and she was V Company's CO, and the powers that be had let her keep it after the Battle of Montana. Sent her to Officer Candidate School, and fast-tracked her promotion to first lieutenant.

Through it all she'd given nothing but her best to the Corps and her unit. She defended her birth world when it was the last place she wanted to be. She'd taken her people into a war-torn hell to repulse an invasion of Lusitanian Marines. Montana should have been a no-win situation. She'd risen to the occasion, against overwhelming odds, when it would have been easy to just back down. Surrender. No one really knew how close she'd come to giving up but her. It still brought her shame to think about it. She knew some of the brass didn't agree with her decisions. She'd thrown people away, they'd said. Surrendering wasn't her style. Wasn't her Marine Corps. Wasn't worthy of the sterling white beret she wore.

And this, this . . . *This is grossly unfair. I have, at every turn, done nothing but my duty, I've sent women and men to die when I had no other choice, I've found a way when no one thought it possible. Now you throw it all in my face?*

"Lieutenant Paen, are you all right?" The voice was distant, distorted by her anger. Her fists balled at her sides, ready to strike out at McMaster. Her eyes shifted to the special agent and she pictured how it would go down. McMaster's life. Her career. She was rushing toward a choice she would not recover from, and she no longer cared.

The air around her stirred and a hint of saffron filled her nose and lungs. A familiar voice waded into her thoughts, broke her concentration the way a boulder breaks the flow of a stream. Her eyes grew heavy and closed against her will. She could no longer lash out with rage, because the boulder was in the way. She had to adjust course and steer around it, only she couldn't because the boulder kept moving and blocking her path. And then it wasn't a boulder anymore but a lithe tree clothed in soft green. The tree's limbs reached out to her and took her hands. She felt rough bark and bristles stroke her skin. Then the branches weren't so rough anymore and the tree changed again, now a woman. She knew that face as if it were her own.

"I said I'd never leave or forsake you, munchkin. I know you and you don't want to do this."

Striking back is all I have left, Momma. It's all I know. It's what I do best.

"No, it's not," said her mother. Sandra Paen was standing in the room now with the commandant and the assistant director and Khaine and Halvorsen and her. She and her mother might as well have been alone. "There's always another way. Sometimes you have to strike back and sometimes you have to turn your cheek and take the blow."

Mom . . . this uniform . . . my company . . . they are all I have left.

"No, dear. You have your name, and you have the confidence of your Marines, and you have my love. I am proud of you because of whose you are. Mine. Your Montanan Marines are proud of you because of whose you are. Theirs. No one can take that from you. Not Cameron Suh. Not McMaster. Not even the commandant."

Fear, betrayal, retribution—they'd all flooded Promise's soul in near-toxic levels. But their poison wasn't strong enough anymore. Something else had taken root and was growing deep inside of her. Promise felt it sprout and spread throughout her body. Where it spread, the poison retreated. She fought the urge to lean further on the table for support, because she wouldn't give McMaster a gram of satisfaction. She clenched her fists tighter still, behind her back where no one could see them. Her vision cleared and where her mother and the stream had been only a moment before now lay a conference table of concerned faces. The gunny was on his feet, coming toward her. She held up her hand and nodded, and once again obeyed orders that tore her world asunder.

"Better," said Sandra Paen, now just a whisper in her mind. "You'll get through this. Better answer the commandant."

"Lieutenant *Paen?*"

Thank you, Momma.

"No need. Now go do what you do best." The voice faded away but it left behind the assurance that Promise was not alone. She never had been and she never would be.

"I understand, sir," Promise said like an emotionless automaton. She came to attention and met the commandant's eyes directly as her own pooled with tears. "Permission to be dismissed, sir." The emotion came anyway and Promise looked astern as her vision clouded. A solitary drop slipped out.

"Permission granted."

Promise turned and walked out of the room without another word. Once outside, she quickened her pace to the lift. She heard the gunny call out from behind her. Later, she'd try and fail to remember taking the lift down to the ground floor, passing through the inner and outer checkpoints. She'd vaguely recall saluting a colonel and a two-star and returning the courtesy from juniors and noncoms as she marched down the steps of the outer court. At the bottom of the steps she broke into a run.

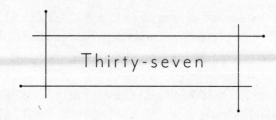

Thirty-seven

Lieutenant Colonel Price Halvorsen stood up and straightened his jacket, brushed something from his sleeve, and turned to leave the room. Demoting Lieutenant Paen like that had surprised him and it wasn't to his liking, not one bit. He didn't care for sudden changes in his command structure, particularly with little advance warning.

I'd only expected the commandant to give her an official reprimand, not take the company from her.

Not that it hadn't happened before to other battalion commanders. And with the RCIA in the mix, well . . . *At least I didn't lose Paen altogether.* His sudden affinity for Paen nearly threw him off-balance.

Halvorsen was almost to the door when he stopped. Agent McMaster acted like she might say something as she approached the door from the other side of the room. Then the moment slipped by and she was gone.

He couldn't help agreeing with the commandant's assessment of Paen's headstrongness. She had that in spades. Charging hell and high water always came with a price and Paen hadn't yet learned to count the cost. Not fully. But she'd deserved better than she'd received and she was still one of his officers, and he always fought for his own. The more Halvorsen thought the more his feet refused to walk out the door.

The colonel turned to face the commandant, who was deep in conversation with Suh. "Sir, may I have a word?"

Commandant Raghavan turned toward Suh with a that-figures look on his face.

"The room is yours for as long as you need it. We can finish up later." Suh gave a slight bow to Halvorsen and the gunny, and then a deeper one to the commandant before walking around the conference table and out of the room.

"Sirs, I'll leave you to it then," said Gunnery Sergeant Khaine before he too turned around to leave.

"No, Gunny, please stay," said Halvorsen. To Raghavan, "Permission to speak freely, sir?" His words were respectful but firm and he wanted a witness just in case.

Raghavan motioned to the chairs. "Why not." Raghavan opened his collar and massaged his eyes. "Wait one." He pulled a small device from his jacket pocket and set it on the table in front of them. "*Now*, Colonel, you may say whatever is on your mind."

Halvorsen saw that the gunny was as surprised as he. The commandant let a healthy dose of mock surprise consume his face before he gave a rueful laugh.

"Come, now, gentlemen. Consider where we are. I don't want the spooks overhearing our conversation any more than you. Believe me. Assistant Director Suh would listen in if I let him." There was no humor in his smile now. Suggesting that the assistant director of the RCIA would record an off-record conversation between the commandant of the RAW-MC and his subordinates was treading in dangerous waters. Swimming with the sharks, as they say. Halvorsen was dubious, to say the least, even in the RCIA's offices. Would Suh dare and break any number of laws in the process?

As if he'd read Halvorsen's mind, the commandant nodded yes. "Before you say anything, I want two things clear. This entire discussion is off-the-record. Understood? If it ever leaks and I find out one of you is to blame . . ."

Halvorsen dipped his head. "Yes, sir." The gunny did the same.

"Fine. Now, I'll only say this once and I'll deny to my grave having said it. Taking Victor Company away from Lieutenant Paen was a bad idea. You never heard that from me."

"Sir?" Halvorsen hadn't expected Raghavan's admission or the jammer on the table, and he quickly shifted tacks. Maybe the commandant had had no choice in the matter. That led even higher up the chain of command than he would ever have conceived of on his own. Wherever he'd thought this meeting might go, it had definitely jumped into uncharted space, to—he feared—plain-clothed civvies who passed laws instead of intel for a living, and had no idea about how to run a military. He wondered just what he'd gotten himself into. He didn't know the commandant well. The man had a reputation for being fair and approachable and that's why Halvorsen had asked for a word with him to begin with. Now he didn't know what to say and part of him wished he hadn't said anything at all.

Humor danced in the blacks of Raghavan's eyes. "Colonel. You needn't say any more. Lieutenant Paen is headstrong. We no doubt agree on that count. But, I'll take an officer I have to dial back every time over one who's overly cautious because she's afraid of making a mistake. Paen didn't deserve what just happened to her, not one bit."

"Then why, sir?" Halvorsen's question might have angered a lesser officer, and earned him a chewing-out.

"Timing, Colonel. After they benched General Granby, Paen was on *their* radar." Raghavan raised an eyebrow. "You understand? Why do you think I'm involved at all, with the career of a mere first lieutenant? Let's just say I did it for an old friend and leave it at that."

Telling, that, Halvorsen thought. *Good for her.* Paen had a rabbi somewhere in the Corps who had enough clout to pull the commandant of the RAW-MC into a meeting about the future of her career, and that list had to be very short. Maybe less than a handful of senior officers, and they probably all had stars on their collar points. *Good on her.*

"Theirs, sir?" Another bold question. *Their radar? Whose radar?* Dangerous, dangerous waters he found himself swimming in. But he was already in well over his head and the commandant could have drowned him by now if he'd wanted to. Halvorsen swallowed hard and refused to break eye contact as his brow broke out into a cold sweat.

"The . . . powers that be . . . didn't appreciate the lieutenant's actions on Montana, or that she used the stand-down codes to try and take the island. You understand? These . . . um . . . *reputed pillars* of our great republic believe some of the senior brass in the Marine Corps and the Navy and their distinguished colleagues in the pro-defense parties are courting a war with the Lusitanians. Headstrong soldiers like Paen feed into their misconceptions. Frankly, I'm inclined to agree with them, at least up to a certain point. I've never been mistaken for a hawk."

That's an understatement, Halvorsen thought. Raghavan believed in a

strong military to keep the peace, and on that point he and the commandant couldn't agree more. As to the scope of the matter, each man saw it
differently, and those differences were a yawning and impassable chasm.
Raghavan wanted a fleet force well shy of an arms race with the Lusies.
Small, lean, and mean, in other words. A one-major-conflict fleet force
capable of handling numerous small wars too. The commandant hadn't
been quiet on the matter either, and powerful winds were blowing in his
favor. He'd published several articles in *Military Times* and *Defensive Fire,*
semischolarly essays that sourced as much history as they did antiwar his-
trionics. The newsies loved him for it. He was the de facto leading voice
among the RAW-MC's "protectionist" generals, after all. Take care of the
core worlds—that was the military's chief mandate. Provide for the common defense of the RAW, *not* the whole 'verse. "It's not our job to police
every habitable planet out there. We can't afford to do it and no one realisti-
cally expects us to." Guarding the trade routes and expanding commerce, of
course. But annexing the verge systems was not in the RAW's best interests.
The Republic didn't need to keep expanding. Strategic basing rights on select worlds would do.

Hawks like General Granby, *and Promise I suppose,* the colonel thought,
believed in a strong military, so strong that no potential enemy would dare
consider threatening it. Granby believed in projecting that force as far as the
RAW's budget would take her. Her "interventionist" camp wanted more basing rights, and more planets brought into the fold, and a fleet force capable of
fighting two major wars simultaneously. "Contain the Lusies," went the mantra. Crush them in time, because in her estimation it was going to come to
that. Be willing to drop through atmo and go to the deck if and when the
time came, and Granby believed the time was at hand. The more allies the
better, which was why Felicia Granby had vocally pushed hard for an additional million mechanized Marines in the last defense authorization bill.

"Look," Raghavan said after carefully sifting his words. "Lieutenant Paen
angered the wrong people at the wrong time. Then General Granby went
and pulled her little stunt and . . . she was smart to send the lieutenant on
liberty while matters blew over."

Halvorsen's face gave him away.

"That's right, Colonel. The order came from Granby." Raghavan abruptly
stood. "Gentlemen, now you know and I bet you wish you didn't. You're dismissed. Please walk out of here and forget we ever had this conversation."

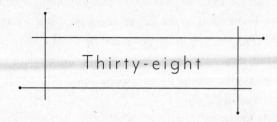

Thirty-eight

As Promise entered her quarters she banged into the door before it slid out of her way. She grabbed the door and forced it the rest of the way open, and then shoved it into its recess in the wall. The door groaned and she heard something snap. *Great. Now I'll have to call base maintenance.*

"Welcome home, roomie."

Sephora was sitting on the bed in a lotus position with a pillow and data-pad in her lap and her back to the wall, frowing in concentration. She was on Promise's bed instead of on the cot Promise had requisitioned for her, which was on the other side of the room. Sephora wasn't wearing makeup, and her baggy overshirt made her look incredibly young.

I just want to lie down. Please . . . move. Promise leaned back against the door, which had screeched into place but not completely closed. *Careful, P, or you're going to bite her head off. She doesn't deserve it.*

"That bad, huh?" Sephora raised her head but didn't look up from her screen.

"Is it just me or did someone dial up the gravity? My feet feel like mech-boots. And what is that smell?"

"You're in a lovely mood," Sephora said. "It's called a candle. The scent is Jasmine Mint Refresh. It's my good-mood candle. At least it was before you walked in." Sephora glared at her. "It calms me. Maybe you should try it."

"Maybe *you* should—" Promise cleared her throat. "—give me a moment."

She doesn't need to carry my burden. She might just put two and two together and blame herself for what happened if I say any more. I could have been busted down or booted out of the Corps altogether. But I wasn't and that's something to be thankful for. Promise raised her heel and tried to pull off a gloss but it didn't want to budge. *Come on.* The lights were too bright and she wanted to be alone and she'd never been fond of the smell of mint. Now she had a headache this big.

"Want to talk about it?" Sephora asked.

"Why does everyone keep asking me that?" Promise unbuttoned her regular-dress jacket and threw it on the foot of her bed, hoping Sephora would take the hint. Something under the bed wiggled and caught her attention. A string of auburn yarn was poking out of her craft box, sliding down the side. Then it dropped to the floor, slithered over, and coiled at her feet. Promise blinked hard but to no avail. When she tried to squash it with her heel it vanished into thin air. *I've gone mental.* It was one thing to see and talk with her dearly departed mother once in a while. Inanimate objects coming to life took her issues to a whole new level. She shook her head to clear her thoughts and succeeded only in amplifying the pounding in her skull.

"See a bug?"

No, I was trying to squash a yarn-snake thingy. Promise shook her head and winced.

"Okay, I understand," Sephora said with disappointment. "But if you ever want to . . ."

"No—it's not like that," Promise said. Wearing her problems like a badly tailored uniform wouldn't work with Sephora, and it wasn't fair to the girl. Oh how she wanted to lie down and sleep the rest of the day away, and hopefully wake with some clarity. Be alone. Sephora had her own cot, over there against the wall. Her eyes motioned toward it but the girl was clueless. Empathy and reading minds clearly weren't skills Sephora had had to exercise before. *You're not being fair, P. She's trying. You're shutting her out.*

Sephora moved over but didn't invite Promise to sit, which irritated her even more.

"I have this idea." Sephora turned the pad around.

Promise had half a mind to yank the girl off her bed and toss her across the room. The bold-script banner at the top of the datapad brought her up short.

"Stop Human Trafficking One Life at a Time." Sephora pulled her knees up and hugged the datapad to them. "While you were out I took your advice about my education. You know, about what I want to do with my life." She hesitated. "I want to make those bastards pay, so they can't hurt other girls like they hurt me. But I can't." Sephora slid the pad down her knees. "I shot that man and"—Sephora's voice wavered—"I can't do that again, not like you. No offense?"

"None taken." A two-word brush-off. *P, what is wrong with you?*

"It was just a dumb idea." Sephora shrugged and looked down at the datapad before tossing it aside.

Tango down, Lieutenant. Well done. Way to crush the girl's spirits.

"Sephora, wait. Look at me." It came out like an order to one of her Marines. Promise might as well have said "about-face."

"Sephora . . . please." She had no idea how to mother the girl, or even how to be a big sister. A friend? Maybe she could do that. *Sir, if you're there, a little help, please.* It was the sort of prayer with no faith to make it fly. One of desperation, and like usual it felt like it bounced back. She sank to the bed next to Sephora and stretched out her legs until her feet dangled over the side. The achiness in her quads told her it was long past time for a run. She really wanted to sleep and was not up for being the girl's sounding board. "I'm sorry. I'm being selfish, and insensitive, and a complete idiot."

"And?"

"And don't push your luck. Okay? *And* . . . I want to hear about your idea. My meeting went badly and I guess I'm still processing what happened."

"It was nothing."

Promise leaned over and risked a hug, one of those from-the-side jobs that gave little and expected even less in return. Sephora's flinch told her she should let go. "I'm proud of you. Big. Time. Proud."

"Whatever."

"Don't whatever me. I am proud." Promise squeezed her shoulder and didn't let go. "You've gone through . . . well, you're a survivor. Not only that, you're an overcomer too. You want to help other girls in harm's way, and give back. That's amazing. It takes courage and strength and guts to want to do that. You make me want to be a better Marine, and if you can do that for me you can do that for other girls too."

"I don't know what to say."

"Try a thank-you."

"Okay, that." Sephora leaned in a bit. Nearly cracked Promise's shell. Then Sephora stood up and walked over to her cot.

It's a start, Promise thought as her throat felt thick. *A great one. Even if she has a long way to go. I guess I do too. Here I am acting like a victim when the real victim is sitting over there. You are* not *damaged,* Promise wanted to say, but she didn't dare. Not yet. The girl had been traumatized and scared, no question about it. PTSD, for sure. *Join the club, kiddo.* That didn't make her damaged goods, not in that way.

"I'd like to hear more." Promise nodded at the datapad.

"Well, okay. I want to graduate." The words came out in a rush as Sephora began to pace about the room, hands circling the air. "Get my certificate and maybe go to college after I save some money." She swiveled to look at Promise, hands going to her hips. "Intro to Spatial Geometry is going to be a problem." Sephora crossed her eyes and mock-offed herself. "Oh, I guess I shouldn't do that, right?"

"As long as it's not your trigger finger it's okay."

"Smartass."

"You said it."

Sephora crossed her arms. "I've got a lead on a tutor. Maybe I'll do some volunteering too. I think I could be a good listener, you know, for girls like me. Maybe if I speak out someone else won't have to go through what I did. I can hurt the bastards that way . . . without the guns, right?"

"Leave that job to me, okay?" Promise's hands were starting to sweat. "I don't like to kill. Sometimes the job requires me to and I'm okay with that, particularly if it means keeping others safe. Like you."

Sephora nodded and looked out the window. Early-afternoon clouds had rolled in and light rains were expected through the evening.

"Thanks."

"Don't mention it, kid." Now her hand had a tremor, which made her angry, because it had been a while and she didn't like others seeing her that way.

"Promise, are you okay?"

If we're going to do this she might as well see what she's in for. "I'm going to let you in on one of my secrets." Promise reached under the bed and pulled out four silver styluses.

"Are those weapons?"

"No. They're knitting needles. I knit when I'm angry, or upset, or when *this* happens." She held up her hand and couldn't keep it still. It hadn't been this bad for months. "Knitting helps the tremors. It's like therapy. Want a hat?"

"Sure. Got any green?"

"You're in luck." Promise pulled her craft box all of the way out from underneath her bed and fished through the spun balls of yarn until she found a bright green speckled orb highlighted with flecks of ocher and sand. Held it up and got Sephora's nod.

"So . . . want to give me a try?"

"Huh?" Promise furrowed her brow as she cast on her stitches to each of the four needles, and then joined them together to knit in the round.

"You know, do you want to talk?" Sephora said. "I need the practice if I'm going to do this for a living. Pretend I'm your counselor." She grabbed a chair and pulled up to Promise's bed. "I'll listen while you do *that,* and take some notes, okay? You just need to let it all out, so don't go telling me what you think I want to hear."

You have no idea. Promise rolled her eyes.

"What was that?"

"You just reminded me of someone, that's all."

"I wonder who?" Sandra Paen said from the corner of the room. She was leaning against the windowsill. The blinds were raised and either Sandra's body was shimmering or the light outside was playing tricks on Promise's mind. She never knew when her mother would appear. Morning or night. Or what her mother would be wearing. At the moment it was Marine Corps regular dress and the rank of four stars, just like Commandant Raghavan of the RAW-MC had worn when he'd taken Victor Company away from her earlier that day.

Very funny, Mother. Have you come back to demote me too?

"Stop feeling sorry for yourself and talk to the girl."

By now Promise was pretty sure that Mom was really dead, dead since she was a young child on Montana, and whatever Promise was seeing now was some sort of break with reality. *Or a psychographic projection of my subconscious self in response to one or more traumatic events from my past. Whatever.* If she was sane on the battlefield—and she could run'n'gun with the best of them—she could live with a small mental-health challenge as a sideshow. To keep life interesting, of course. Notwithstanding the yarn-snake thingy, which was beside the point and so far just a one-off. *Besides, everyone is diagnosable once you got to know them, right?*

"Sounds like you and Sephora were made for each other."

The resemblances between Sephora and Sandra weren't hard to miss either, and they were more than just skin-deep too. Once you got past Sephora's nose ring and the chain that ran from it to her lip, and the buzzed hair and the tats. Both women were well built. *It isn't fair,* Promise told herself in the corner of her mind that largely sat neglected. Like her off-duty attire and her social life. Beautiful women with beautiful lines. Sephora could have been a much younger version of Promise's mother. Same generous curves and sinfully long legs. Same regal neck and near-flawless skin. Promise had gotten none of it and she wasn't a fool either. "Beauty is in the eye of the beholder" was a bunch of crap. Beauty was beauty, pure and simple, and her flat build and angular muscles just weren't.

"Are you okay?" Sephora asked. "Where'd you just go?"

Promise cleared her throat and "frogged" part of her work. The stitches ripped out fast and angry, and she lost one of her needles, which clanked to the ground. "That's just frogging great. I'm fine."

"She just read you like a book," said Sandra.

Same as you do, Momma.

"Is that such a bad thing?" Sandra asked. "Maybe you need some flesh and blood in your life."

That stopped Promise cold.

"Just think about it, Promise. So far you've approached Sephora as the girl in need. She's not the only one." Sandra blew Promise a kiss and began to fade from view. "Love you, munchkin, and I always will."

"Earth to Promise," Sephora said. "Hey, you're really starting to worry me."

Promise shook her head. "Sorry, I'm fine, just overly tired."

"No, you're not fine," Sephora said. "Be honest."

"Don't worry, munchkin, you're mostly well-adjusted where it counts." Sandra's voice was more a thought now, inside Promise's head, and her mother was singing a song from her childhood. Something about letting it go.

"Promise, you're freaking me out. Why don't you put the needles down, okay?"

Great, now I'm getting it from both ends. "Don't worry. I really am fine." *BUMED might not agree.* "You ever see ghosts from your past?" Promise put her work aside and smiled weakly at Sephora. "Like memories that won't let you go?"

"Yeah," Sephora said cautiously.

"Well, my mother is one of those memories." *I can't believe I'm going there.* "I hear her voice telling me to do this or that. Sometimes she won't shut up. Sometimes I need her voice. Does that make any sense?"

"Sometimes I hear my father's voice. He loved to sing after a long day of work. That's one of the things I miss most about him."

"I'd love to hear more about him sometime. Really. But time is in short supply at the moment. Speaking of which—" Promise scooted to the edge of the bed and clasped her hands together, elbows on her knees. "—I found you a place while I'm away."

"Why do I have the feeling that now is one of those times when *you're* going to tell me what to do and what not to do?"

"Stop reading my mind, will you?" Promise tried her best to look angry but couldn't hold the ruse. "Seriously, you're really good at that."

Sephora crossed her arms and held herself tightly. "And?"

"My unit is shipping out soon and we need to settle your living arrangements. There's no time to go out and find a place. I have an idea."

"And?"

"An officer I once served under said if I ever needed anything to comm her. She's got a huge home, her kids are all grown, and she's got a lot of time on her hands. She's actually a highly decorated general and someone I have a lot of faith in, and I think the two of you might hit it off. How would you like to go live with a great-grans?"

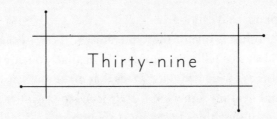

Thirty-nine

Lieutenant General Felicia Granby's country house was less than twenty minutes from the RAW-MC's Central Mobilization Command, if you flew by aerodyne. A hardwood forest guarded the general's home on all sides. From a distance it looked more like an ancient Roman phalanx than a wood: bases and branches impenetrably linked like overlapping shields. There was a single, unpaved access that meandered for several kilometers beneath a canopy of trees, and over several streams. The access wasn't a proper road by any stretch of the word. Great-Grans had stubbornly refused to cut and pave a swath across her land.

Promise and Sephora spotted the house when they were almost on top of it. It was less a home and more a small castle. Three stories of stone and wood stood beneath a tower, which occupied the northwest corner. A head-high battlement ran the perimeter of the roof with rectangular cutouts equally spaced on all four sides. Promise had to dig a bit into her history to come up with what they were called. *Crenels.* On Holy Terra, during medieval times, an archer would string her bow and rain indirect missiles from behind the battlement, or use the indentation for line-of-sight fire. The piece of artillery guarding the entrance nearly made Promise laugh. It didn't fit the period of the home at all. She'd seen something like it in the histories that predated the Republic. Terran, perhaps twenty-third century in origin. She supposed there were more surprises hidden on the grounds too.

I bet it still fires.

A mech was trimming the lawn as they circled the house pad, which lay in a sea of manicured green. A large beast sprinted from the doorway as the aerodyne settled onto the pad.

"Here we are," Promise said as she got out.

"This place is like something from a vid," Sephora said. The beast was a black and white Great Dane and he didn't slow down until the last possible moment, and then he threw his front paws up into the air and slammed Promise into the frame of the aircar. The jolt nearly knocked the air out of her lungs. Slobbery dog kisses covered her mouth. Sephora had gotten out on the starboard side of the aircar, and come around the front of it. Her hand covered her mouth and the other was pointed at Promise and her spotted friend.

"I think he likes you."

"A little help."

"Sorry, P. You're on your own."

"That's enough, mister," Promise said, pushing the dog's massive head aside. "All right, already. Get *down*." The dog pushed his nose through her feeble defenses and licked her from chin to brow and cheek to cheek.

"Come on, please?"

Sephora was laughing now. "He's huge and, um, really excited."

The dog was gyrating and Promise's shoulders were hurting because they were pinned between two massive paws and civilian-grade plexi. She was about to knife the dog's throat when the front door of the house slammed shut and a gravelly voice barked out across the lawn.

"Otis! You filthy mongrel. Get your horny tail back here this instant."

Otis cocked his head, gave Promise one more kiss, and then sprinted for the house. Great-Grans swatted his backside as he took the stairs, which sent the dog scooting into the foyer.

"Sorry about that," Grans said, tossing Promise a hand towel as she neared. A small tray was hovering behind her. "Otis is a prized stud. And he hasn't seen action in a bit." Grans gave Promise a sardonic look. Then she smiled at Sephora. "You two are the first pretty young things he's spotted in weeks."

"Ah—" Promise got her feet beneath her and toweled herself off. Though she was out of uniform her hand rocked to her brow out of habit.

"Relax, girly. I've been benched. You've been demoted. We don't need to make it any worse with all that hooey." The general reached for the tray and selected two glasses filled with amber fluid and ice cubes. "Here. It's un-sweetened. I've got crystals and local honey inside if you want to doctor it." She raised a third and said, "Cheers."

The trees swayed in a sudden breeze, branches briefly parting to reveal the access road before closing ranks to swallow it whole. Most were older than the house itself, some well into their second century. *That one must be three mechsuits across, shoulder-to-shoulder,* Promise thought. *I bet Grans has whiskers in the trees.*

"The trees are the true wealth of the place," Great-Grans said with a wave of her hand. Her work jacket was marred with dirt and grass, and a pair of gloves was folded over one of the front pockets. A wide-brim hat blocked the rising sun's rays. "Welcome to Neverfar Manor."

Sephora took a hesitant step toward the general. She'd decided on some-thing semi-modest at the last moment, much to Promise's relief. The nose ring was in and her tattoos were peeking out all over. *At least the skirt cov-ers her cheeks,* Promise thought. She exchanged looks with the general while Sephora circled in place, hand on her heart and eyes as large as full moons.

Then Grans rolled up a sleeve and stretched out her arm. A black and gray tattoo of a demon dog appeared to leap off of her skin, and a blond pinup was riding it. "That's me on the beast, long before I grayed." Grans winked, spun around, and waved over her shoulder for them to follow. "I was young once. Leave your gear, both of you. I'll have Roman get it."

Sephora turned to Promise looking positively delighted. Shielded her mouth and said, "Wow, for an old lady she's great."

"I heard that, young woman."

Sephora swore under her breath.

"I heard that too. The lieutenant and I don't care much for language so you'll kindly keep it to yourself."

"Yes, ma'am."

"Last I checked you weren't in uniform," Grans said as she reached the steps, "unless you plan on joining up. At the moment, I'm not feeling chari-table toward the Marine Corps or I'd take you to the recruiting station myself. 'Ma'am's are for uniforms. Something else, please."

Sephora gave Promise a help-me-out look. "Um, sorry, Great . . . Grans?"

"That will do, girly. That will do. Come on in."

As the door opened, they heard another aerodyne approaching at sub-sonic speeds. Promise caught sight of the craft, which looked no larger than a bird. And it was several hours early. *You've got to be kidding me?* The bird became an unidentified craft, and then a silver-sheened aerodyne like the one currently parked on Neverfar's grounds.

"I'm sorry." Promise turned to face Sephora. "I thought I had at least the morning to spend with you and Grans."

"Your new captain tried to comm you first," Great-Grans said. "I was going to tell you once we took a load off and had our tea."

"I turned off my implant," Promise said absentmindedly. "And my mini-comp." Grans gave her a reproving look though you could tell her heart wasn't in it. Technically, Promise wasn't supposed to disable her mastoid implant, ever. At least not until she retired from the Fleet Forces, and even then the Corps could reactivate it and recall her to active duty, without notice.

The first aerodyne, which was already parked on the lawn, lifted about a meter into the air and floated over to make room for the second vehicle.

"She stays outside," Great-Grans said as she ushered them indoors. "Finish your tea first. It's nothing against the captain. She's just following orders." Another stern look like the one from Grans's vid. "Sit tight while Roman transfers your gear and grabs Sephora's things from the car."

A woman got out, on the side opposite the house, and stretched her arms in the sky before coming around the aerodyne. She had a slight build and her head barely crested the top of the car. She was wearing plain clothes and her hair fell to her shoulders, and was tied to one side. Promise watched from the storm window and felt an arm slide around her shoulder. Sephora. It was an unexpected show of affection from the girl, and Promise sagged into it, reached up, and patted her hand.

They clinked glasses. "Cheers. To the bravest Marine I know."

"Thanks, kid."

"See you when you get back, roomie. Don't worry about me. I'm going to be okay. Great-Grans seems, well, really great."

"Watch your backside around Otis," Promise said.

"Count on it."

"All right, come here." It was a short, intense embrace. The tears came anyway.

Great-Grans stood in the doorway with a distinguished-looking gentleman. He wore a single-button jacket and was halfway through a cigar.

"Roman is my man candy," Grans said as she slipped an arm around his waist. Her head came to Roman Granby's shoulder. He looked pleased and gave the general a smooch on the crown of her head, and then he puffed on his cigar and blew a halo into the air.

"Ms. Paen, it's a real pleasure," Roman said. "Sephora, I look forward to getting to know you. Be right back with your things." Then he was out the door.

"All right, girly. Out you go. Mustn't keep the captain waiting."

"Thanks, Grans. I really can't say that enough . . . taking Sephora in and all."

"I'll put her to work while you're away. Stay sharp." Grans looked like she wanted to say more before she threw a sideways glance at Sephora.

Promise nodded and smiled. She and Victor Company were headed to the planet Sheol, which in the ancient Hebrew meant Hell as an actual place. There was no point worrying the girl any more than she already was.

The Marine Corps had a saying that was as old as the Corps itself: "Where do we go? To hell and back. Ua! Ua! Ua!"

Indeed. Promise looked at her new captain outside Grans's house and frowned. *Well, I'm on my way.* As she headed for the door, Otis walked up beside her and nosed her leg.

"You better stay here, boy. I know exactly what you'll do if I let you out."

Forty

Promise hesitated at the top of the steps of Grans's house, and took the grounds in one more time. She closed her eyes and inhaled the scent of the forest and grasses. Not far away, Victor Company was hot-walking their mechsuits up the ramp of a dropship, and humping gear like stevedores, their nostrils filled with pungent, hot tarmac smells.

They've got this. Besides, they've got Captain Yates now. They don't need me anymore.

A battalion-level deployment meant a lot of gear, which was why Charlie BAT had been assigned several dropships to accompany them to Sheol. Much larger than even an assault-class LAC, the large conical craft were designed primarily to ferry equipment and manpower from a parking orbit to a planet's surface. Promise had signed off on Victor Company's requisitions before she'd departed for Guinevere, and if the other companies in the battalion were deploying with as much gear, well, the battalion was gutted up, loaded for bear.

Snap out of it, P. You're an officer. Stop sulking and Marine up! A part of her just couldn't. *Even my AI could hump my gear up the ramp if it had to.* That made her feel about as worthless as an unloaded weapon.

The Republic's Artificial Corporeal-Sentience Edicts strictly regulated what AIs could and couldn't operate in the RAW Fleet Forces. They prohibited nonbiological intelligences from being fully autonomous. As long as they were slaved they were fine. AIs were prohibited from controlling assets critical to the Republic's daily functions and survival, on the military *and* civilian side. For the most part, Promise couldn't disagree, particularly when it came to prosecuting wars. War fighting was a human enterprise and tech was there to help you kill more of the enemy, not to decide which enemies to kill.

One paragraph in particular summarized what the branches Navy, Marine Corps, and Sector Guard, plus the planetary militias, the intelligence community, and local law enforcement, could and could not do with their AIs. The RAW Fleet Forces called them the "Can't-Do Edicts."

Artificial Intelligences may not:
1. Exercise autonomous control over the nets.
2. Independently operate any craft larger than an assault-class LAC, and only then as a matter of last resort, for a finite period of time, providing all human pilots are incapacitated or otherwise not available.
3. Command any unit—ground-, sea-, or space-based—capable of delivering a nuclear payload.
4. Independently man remote outposts or orbital platforms.
5. Issue orders for drones and remotely piloted platforms.

Essentially, AIs couldn't do jack without a jane's retinal scan and verbal say-so. Which to Promise's thinking begged the question: *Why have them at all?*

The Marine Corps had managed a single exemption on the nuclear question: semi-autonomous AIs for their mechsuits. Because the fiscal argument for them as a force multiplier had far outweighed the risks of using them in theater. And even mechanized Marines still needed presidential approval to deploy nukes. Even a "full-throat" AI could be tethered to a loyalty protocol, but all the Corps had gotten were Semi-Autonomous Reasoning Grunts. SARGs. Without them, the Corps would have had to bolster its ranks by a factor of ten, and specked down their armor.

The truth was that she needed her SARG to monitor the nets, track hostiles, access damage to her mechsuit, make on-the-march repairs, ready weapons (and sometimes, yes, even fire them for her), monitor her vitals, fly whiskers, and attend to myriad other details that all had to run perfectly in the background while she gave orders and stroked the trigger of her wep. In. Real. Time.

Tell that to Senator Oman and her Neo-Isolationists and see if the woman doesn't cream her skivvies.

Mr. Bond was more than just her AI-assist, Bond was safe and reliable, her danger maker with a massive upside.

Until she bought it, Bond remained a critical part of her armor, and extremely capable on its own. Still, there was no way Promise would ever trust Bond to cold-walk her armor. Marines just didn't do it as a matter of principle. Her mechsuit was hers. Bond wasn't even the copilot. An arm maybe, with mad killing skills. End of story.

Promise reached the bottom stairs as the front door banged closed behind her. A blur of a dog bounded around her legs and across the grass.

"Otis! Get back here."

She cupped her hands. "Captain, he's friendly . . ."

Captain Sasha Yates tried to sidestep the dog and ended up being knocked to the deck, facedown, instead. The first order Promise heard her CO give was a one-word scream.

"Help!"

Forty-one

MAY 21ST, 92 A.E., STANDARD CALENDAR, 0922 HOURS
REPUBLIC OF ALIGNED WORLDS PLANETARY CAPITAL—HOLD
NEVERFAR MANOR

"Otis, you filthy mongrel," Promise shouted as she ran toward the captain. Pulling Otis off Yates proved impossible given his size. The slap on his backside did the trick. She hit him a lot harder than she'd intended to, which sent the beast yelping back toward the house and out of view.

Yates rolled over, her hand over her eyes to block the sun. "Thanks a lot, Paen." They weren't in uniform but common courtesy still ruled the day and omitting Promise's rank like that was at the very least rude. Still, Promise figured the captain had just been assaulted by a mongrel, so she cut Yates some slack.

"Ma'am, I'm terribly sorry about this."

Yates ignored Promise's hand and pulled herself up. Her clothes were stained with grass, mud, and drool. The fabric over her thigh was torn; the pants were a complete write-off. "I hope the bastard is happy."

"Lieutenant Paen." Yates assessed her clothing with disgust. She looked upward and then at Great-Grans's house before turning to face Promise. "It isn't every day one gets invited to a general's home. I had hoped to say hello."

This day can't get any worse. Promise thought of several things to say in reply, and not one of them was going to defuse the situation.

"Ma'am, I'll replace your clothes. I must have left the door cracked open."

But that wasn't what the captain was aiming for. Promise hadn't even considered the setting they were in, and she should have. Had Grans? The wall of trees and the fortified home, the artillery piece and the car on the pad with the general's last name on the rear plate—all of it spoke to the general's war-hawkishness like a smartly canted beret. Otis had certainly made a statement. The grounds could not have been hotter.

Captain, would you care to pick me up at Grans's house on your way back to Mo Cavinaugh? Why hadn't she seen it before? Great-Grans had made some calls and taken care of everything. Yes, the general certainly had. And Grans hadn't come out to meet the captain either. That could only be taken one way. Yates was probably wondering how Promise had pulled it off in the first place. If she was trying to put the captain in her place by showing off a powerful benefactor, she'd just succeeded marvelously.

Yates crossed her arms. "Do you have anything to say to me?"

"Ma'am, my . . . I guess you'd call her my little sister . . . she needed a place to stay while we deploy. The general has plenty of space." Carefully put, that. Promise made to say more and then realized she was probably better off leaving it at that.

"Indeed." Yates turned toward the aerodyne as a large cloud rolled across the sky and cast its shadow over them. A bird called from the trees and then another answered it. Yates opened the door and got in. "Coming?" Promise could see the gold in Yates's eyes.

"We have a tight schedule. We'll talk on the way." The aircar's door slammed shut.

Promise should have entered first as the junior officer present. She walked around the aircar and entered from the other side. As she settled into her seat, she felt the cold frame of her GLOCK press against her side. The general had insisted she bring it, much to her surprise.

"Bring your senior with you," Grans had said over the vid comm. Promise had contacted Granby about what to do with Sephora. She'd dialed and hung up three times before letting the comm go through, because asking the general for such a huge favor was outlandish, right? Yes, Granby had told her to reach out if she needed anything. Wasn't that what people said in the moment? She had gone to hang up a fourth time when the general appeared on-screen and recognized her immediately.

"Lieutenant Paen. This is a pleasant surprise. What brings you my way?"

They'd talked a good five minutes about Promise's career. The general was up to speed on a number of matters. Her recent vacation. Her near brush with death and detention on Kies Tourosphere. Her demotion, which was exactly what Granby had called it. They'd talked about Sephora, and the general hadn't blinked. "Why don't Roman and I take her in while you're away? Get her on her feet until you return." Then Grans mentioned her senior and told her not to show up without it.

How did she know about that? Well, how did she know about the rest of my escapades? Great-Grans knows all.

"Aye, aye, ma'am," Promise said with a smile. "Gladly."

"My mother gave me my first weapon too," Granby said. "Nothing like yours, though. When it comes to firearms, I'm always game for show-and-tell."

"I look forward to it, ma'am."

Now she was in an aircar with her new CO. Swapping stories and antique firearms with the general would have to wait for another time. Time. It always came down to that. Her GLOCK was in every way a weapon displaced by time, and as much as Promise cherished it, she was never quite at ease in its presence. She'd inherited the GLOCK as a child, though at the time she hadn't known it. Quite suddenly, her mother fell ill, and by the following winter she was gone. Her death left Promise with an emotionally distant father, and a small box of things meant for her. Except her father hid the box in the attic and refused to talk about his pain. Years later, Promise found the GLOCK by accident while looking for something else. She recognized the rough-hewn trunk instantly. At the bottom she found her mother's pistol.

Her father went to his grave never knowing she'd found it. He was murdered during the raids on her homeworld, before the RAW Fleet Forces had neutralized the pirate threat operating in the sector. She ran to the Corps to start anew.

The GLOCK was all Promise had left of her mother's things. And to this day, it continued to steal her out of the present, either by displacing the present with memories of a past she'd just as soon forget, or by distracting her with questions about a future that would never be. A future with a mother.

Stop wallowing in the past, P. Focus on the here, now. Focus on your new captain. She's already angry enough with you.

They were now over water, more or less pointed toward Joint Spaceport Mo Cavinaugh, when Yates shifted in her seat. "I must confess, Lieutenant, I am at a bit of a loss for words. This situation is . . . unique. What am I supposed to do with the trenchant Lieutenant Promise Paen?"

Trenchant? Promise hadn't been called that before. She wasn't even sure what the word meant. Impetuous? Yes, she'd been called that and honestly owned the word. Headstrong, prone to rush in? Yes, and yes. A Marine who preferred direct action. Yes, yes, and yes. *But not . . .*

"You're the savior of Montana," Yates said, which only made matters worse. "A decorated Marine. Until recently, the CO of Victor Company. I was not privy to what happened prior to assuming command of Victor Company. I was only told to report for duty and that you'd be staying on as my XO." Yates gave her a piercing look. "That about sum it up?"

"Yes, Captain," Promise said.

"What happened was classified."

Promise nodded.

"But, I'm sure you have some thoughts on the matter. Off-record, of course."

"Yes, ma'am."

Yates clicked her tongue. "Lieutenant, this isn't going to work if we don't get past simple yeses and noes. I know you can't tell me some things but surely you can tell me *something.*"

She was already in enough trouble with the RCIA. Talk now and she might inadvertently hand Agent McMaster another reason to come after her. *Keep your mouth shut, P.* No doubt the colonel wanted to get on with their mission instead of dealing with a pissing match between the Marine Corps and the intelligence community. He didn't need a personality conflict between one of his company captains and that captain's lieutenant. Now Halvorsen had both. His opinion of her was already dangling by a much-frayed thread.

"I'll understand if you don't want me as your second-in-command," Promise said a moment later. "I'll ask the colonel for a transfer when we land."

They passed over a small peninsula and an old lighthouse. "I'll think about it."

The aircar banked again and the cabin filled with the scent of saffron.

"Taking the honorable way out, are we?" The voice was laced with maternal sarcasm. "In my book it's called quitting. You are better than that, Lieutenant." Promise's mother, Sandra Paen, sat on the opposite bench in the cab, facing her and the captain. Sandra's anger hit Promise cold, every bit as real as the captain's. Sandra was dressed in plain clothes cut with taste, and her shirt, belt, and pants fit her contours perfectly.

No, it's not, Mother. It's called bowing out with honor.

"That's total nonsense," Sandra said. "You've made this mess, munchkin. Now fix it."

Just like that? Promise thought.

Yes.

Promise heard the one-word response in her head as clearly as if her mother had spoken to her aloud.

"Apologies go a long way," Sandra said. "You put the woman on the defensive. Really, munchkin, what did you expect? You could have just closed the door behind you. But no, you had to sic the dog on her."

"I did not."

Sandra crossed her arms and dared Promise to prove her wrong. "Just apologize, and be done with it."

Just . . . just . . .

"Eventually, you're going to take my advice and do the right thing anyway so you might as well do it now and spare yourself the trouble."

Stop using my sense of duty against me.

Sandra faded out of view though her voice lingered a moment longer. Now she sounded like she was speaking through Promise's mastoid implant. "That's one of the things I love the most about you, dear. I'd like to think you got that from me."

Promise closed her eyes, felt dampness on her cheek, and quickly brushed it away. When she looked up, her mother was gone.

"Ma'am, about that transfer. Perhaps I was—"

Yates raised her hand. "Enough, Lieutenant. We've just met. Replacing you isn't an option. Believe me, I tried." Yates briefly turned toward her. "I'm not happy with the situation but as I see it we only have one option. Our duty."

"Yes, ma'am." Yates's words yanked her up by the collar.

"Borrowing trouble won't improve the situation."

"No, ma'am. We have enough of that already."

Yates snorted. "Agreed." Yates's right hand tapped the armrest between them. "I need your candid advice, Lieutenant. I expect you to be honest and candid, nothing less, not now or ever. If you're to be my XO you must back me to the hilt in public and speak your mind when we're alone."

"Ma'am, in that case, the captain needs a new executive officer."

"Possibly." Yates's face became unreadable. "Is that your best advice? If it is I'm disappointed. You're rattled and your jacket suggests you don't do *that* easily. Under normal circumstances, I'd kill to get an officer of your caliber."

"And now, ma'am?"

"For starters, I'd like to strangle the general's mutt."

Promise turned to the window and the terrain below. They were flying high enough for her to notice how the roads followed the natural contours of the land. They flew over an orchard and a small lake, and a sailboat far from the shore. In the distance she could see the spaceport and the outlines of several dropships and smaller shuttles nestled in their bays. There was the tower. Her unit was waiting. No, not hers anymore. What would she say to her Marines, to Yates's Marines? The situation seemed completely untenable, not to mention completely unfair. A transfer made sense. She could resign her commission. The odds of the Corps accepting that weren't . . .

"Ma'am, back at the house. I can only imagine what you must think of me. I'm afraid some of it is probably true."

Yates actually laughed. "Did you sic that four-legged bastard on me?"

"I meant you no . . . well . . . I didn't mean to . . . Ma'am, I was angry." Promise threw her hands into the air. "*I am* angry. I'm grappling with a lot of changes in my life. I'm going to get my footing back, on my word as an officer, as your executive officer. You have my word."

Yates shifted in her seat toward Promise, eyes open and thoughtful. "Tell me, Lieutenant, what's your read of this situation? I've just replaced the CO of Victor Company—you. Yet, you're still here as my XO. How do you think our Marines are going to take that?"

Ours. It was the olive branch Promise needed to snap out of it.

"I screwed up, ma'am. It's as simple as that. Battalion wants a seasoned company commander in charge of Victor Company. That officer isn't me, at least not yet. *Your* Marines deserve to know the truth, at least that much."

"Just like that?"

Promise spread her hands wide. "It's the least I can do."

"Do you always do your duty, Lieutenant?"

That nearly did it. Lit her anger off like a chem torch.

"I've struck a nerve."

Shut up, P.

"Don't agree with the powers that be, do you?"

Keep it shut, Lieutenant. Just. Keep. It. Shut. Promise imagined shoving Yates out the door as they flew.

"You must have really pissed someone off in a very high place. Been there, done that. I can relate. You'll live, believe me."

"I'll try, ma'am."

"Oh, Lieutenant, you'd pay for that one if I didn't like you so much."

Promise laughed uncomfortably.

"Lighten up, Promise. That was a joke." Yates grabbed a bottle of water from the chiller at their feet and took a long drink. "Tell me, what do you know about counterinsurgency?"

COIN? The non sequitur took Promise by surprise. "Honestly, not much, ma'am." Asymmetrical warfare. Guerrilla tactics. Textbook definitions she could spout off, which wasn't the same thing as real knowledge of the subject. COIN doctrine had been around for as long as people had been killing each other. The little guy's way of fighting back. The sum of her knowledge came from a self-paced course on the nets, part of her degree in pre-Diaspora military conflict, from the University of Salerno. She'd earned that on her own time before being field-promoted to second lieutenant. Her brain wasn't working particularly well at the moment, and it wasn't calling up the dates and names and theories. At least she recalled the big takeaway. Direct engagement, shock and awe, swamping an enemy's defenses with superior firepower—these were all ideas conventional forces understood well, and militaries throughout human history had trained for the wars they'd already fought with tactics they'd already mastered. The average jane or jack knew little else.

"It's not exactly covered at Officer Candidate School, ma'am. We tend to leave asymmetrical warfare to SPECOPS, or the spooks."

"That's a vast understatement. We don't teach our platoon commanders a lot of things in OCS, and then we send them out to garrison the rim."

A small craft broke the sound barrier nearby.

"I did a tour on Clear Harbor, which isn't more than a jump from your homeworld." Yates set the bottle of water in the nearby holder and folded her hands in her lap. "Harbor has a lot of problems for a rimworld. Poverty, crime, and lawlessness in the outer provinces. Those we expected, particularly in the first decade or two post-incorporation. The homegrown terrorists were bent on stalling incorporation, or killing it altogether. Thankfully, they weren't very organized. I was a green lieutenant when my battalion hit

Harbor's atmo, and then deployed to Forward Operating Base Nautilus. We stayed the longest five and half months of my career. We lost several dozen boots to improvised explosives and we were wearing mechsuits. One of my sergeants stepped on one. There wasn't much left to send home to his wife and child. A young boy walked up to my checkpoint and refused to turn around. I had him in my sights for several mikes when his jaw clenched and he bolted toward us. I didn't have a choice."

The thought of killing a child rattled Promise to her core.

"Lieutenant, they were all dressed the same, like every other citizen of the planet. Women, men, and even children. They struck our blind spots during patrols and disappeared into the markets. They hid behind innocents and took refuge in holy places. It was not conventional and it wasn't fair and to some degree that's what we're headed for on Sheol. Sheol doesn't have the population centers of Harbor." Yates looked down the bridge of her nose. "Be grateful for that. But it does have mines to protect, and it has the terrorists and they won't hesitate to strike from the shadows. I'm assuming command of Victor Company because of my experience on Harbor. Battalion wants someone with on-the-ground experience dealing with terrorist scum like the Greys. That's the official line and I expect you to toe it. I'm not letting you off easy. I won't embarrass you or throw you under the track in front of the unit either. You're a RAW-MC officer and my XO, and I expect you to do your duty, unless you prove you are unfit for the post. Then I *will* relieve you of it. Have I made myself clear?"

"Yes, ma'am."

"That's why I'm here, Lieutenant, and that's why you need me as your CO. That's why Victor Company needs me as its CO. Clear? Nothing lasts in the Corps, not forever. We're a dynamic breed. The situation on the ground changes all the time, the tactics we use change, the chain of command changes. I won't undermine you in front of the company. Listen, look, and learn. V Company is still a raw unit. It's still working up. Most of the company has little history with you. They will adjust. Tell your friends not to make this personal or I will. Don't think more highly of yourself than you ought. While some of what has happened to you may be personal—and I highly suspect that it is—not all of it is. The parts that matter most aren't.

"You're a RAW-MC officer, a very capable, very new officer at that. Remember who you are. Follow my orders and we will get along famously."

Forty-two

Jordas Tarakov woke at her usual time, just before Sheol's red-cloud dawn. Her sheer chemise brushed the cold floor of her high-rise apartment. The entire east-facing wall of her bedroom was constructed out of penetrator-proof plexi, from the ceiling to the floor. Outside she saw a typical Sheol morning. Heavy clouds lit by an old sun, and polluted rain with high winds projected throughout the day. Below her 367th-level view lay the tightly packed city of Nexus, a corporate enclave of modern scrapers filled with air lanes already crammed with morning traffic. Beneath the city lay a floating foundation of permastone, nearly ten square kilometers of earthquake-resistant composites that could stand up to a thirteen on the Yuka-Toomi scale. Nexus was one of the great engineering marvels of the entire sector, a "quakeproof" city on a shifting planet that refused to be tamed.

A rust-colored public transport flew past Jordas's apartment window and briefly blocked out the sun's paltry rays. A little redhead waved from one of the transport's port windows. Though the girl couldn't possibly have seen her through the reflective plexi that tiled the building, Jordas waved back anyway. Then she tapped the plexi twice to activate the nets. She whisked aside this screen and that one until she found what she was looking for.

Ah, here we are. Nexus's mayor was speaking at the 11:30 A.M. ribbon-cutting ceremony inside the terrarium. Mayor Engel's speech would last nearly an hour, because *Mayor* Engel always went long. About three thousand souls were expected to attend, after a five-klick run through the streets of Nexus. The winner would break the ribbon at the finish line outside the city's new terrarium. The Morton-Saki Tactical Firm was handling security and manning tented checkpoints along the runners' route. Armored drones would scan the skyways while humanoid sentinels patrolled the ground routes for potential terrorist threats. Random citizen scans and retinal maps were authorized. The nets reminded Jordas to please comply if stopped. The sentinels were just doing their job. "Refrain from kicking the bots, please," said a prominent loop. Another assured the body politic, "The city may be in effective lockdown but we are on low alert. Be sure to bring your rebreathers and rain shields to the run. The citywide deflector gird is only partly operational. Acid rain again. Have a fun and productive morning."

A looping vid on the Corporate Congress's daily page drew her eye to a small boy with handsome features and walnut eyes. He was pulling his mother up a set of steps to a dais inside the Nexus Interplanetary Terrarium, outside the OnWae exhibit.

A sad smile crossed Jordas's face, drawing her hand to her heart. *He's grown so much in just the last standard month.* Her affections for the boy created a dangerous conflict of interest between her personal and professional lives. If her boss found out, he'd kill her for it. Jordas clenched her teeth to a regain a measure of control. *You had to go and get attached.*

She paused the vid and lingered on the boy's eyes. *My Dietrich's eyes.* Jordas steadied herself against the plexi and drew slow, steady breaths to push aside the nausea in her gut. *He's collateral damage in a war I didn't start.* She almost believed the lie. Jordas slammed the plexi with a closed fist. *The corporate mongers have raped this planet long enough. They've grown fat from the toil and labor of the miners' guild. Sheol's wealth belongs to the system, to the people of Korazim, not to our Republican taskmasters on Hold.* She spit at the plexi, and then ordered a sanibot to clean it up.

A long, hot shower drew out some of her frustration. She dressed quickly in a red blouse, tan slacks, and thigh-rise boots, each boot lined with a holster to conceal one of a pair of identical pulse pistols within easy reach. A white headscarf, dark glasses, and her earpiece completed the ensemble. She grabbed the pack at the bottom of her closet and laid it at the foot of her bed. The sphere inside was twenty centimeters across and looked like a child's plaything. The built-in projector came preloaded with hundreds of star maps and an impressive playlist, mostly classic lullabies from the twenty-third and twenty-fourth centuries. Jordas held the globe in her hands and keyed the arming sequence. The device scanned her eyes and prints, and beeped three times.

Commander Walker Greystone's voice suddenly filled her sparsely furnished bedroom. Jordas realized the device had accessed her apartment's AI without permission. "Congratulations, Jordas. Today, you fulfill your pivotal role as a Grey Walker, in the fight for Sheol's independence from the murderous mongrels of the Corporate Congress and the mighty Republic of Aligned Worlds." Greystone's voice spoke with near-religious zeal. Once again Jordas found herself caught up in the commander's call to arms. "This planet's wealth belongs to the people of the Korazim system. We sit on a treasure trove of Mizienite that could solve our people's woes, eradicate hunger, eliminate homelessness, and replenish our damaged ecosystem. All the 'Publicans care about is their precious M-steel and their ever-expanding military-industrial complex. If it wasn't the 'Publicans it would be the Lusies, or the Terran Federation, or someone else. The time to strike is now. For Sheol, for Korazim, and for independence. Your target stands. Head there now and raze it to the ground. We'll meet you at the extraction point. To liberty, Jordas." She envisioned the commander raising a glass of malt scotch to her success. "To the blinded masses you will liberate. To the freedom your actions will bring. I salute you."

About an hour before noon, Jordas left her apartment and made her way to the ground floor of her building. She stopped at the front desk for a mask and rain shield. "Morning, Yuri."

Jordas raised her glasses and batted her grayish-blues at Yuri Foocoo. The man blushed and turned away. He had a wrestler's build and thick eyebrows. The nub of a discreet comm was just visible in his right ear.

Foocoo gave her a shy once-over. "Mm, love those boots, Jordi." Then he returned to his work, as if she weren't there. After several seconds, a low chuckle rumbled from his chest.

Jordas opened her arms wide. "All right, handsome, do I really have to ask?"

Foocoo's face lit like a floating lamp. "You're going to love these." He walked out from behind his desk and lifted his right foot. The blue-dyed monk strap matched his trousers perfectly.

Jordas squealed and clapped her hands with delight. "Splendid, Yuri. You and your shoes are the highlight of my morning. We really must go shopping together. I still want to meet the craftsman."

"The best part is the buckle on the instep. It's negatively charged to resist bacteria. You never know what you'll walk through in the course of a day."

"Humph—that seems so obvious. It's a wonder we aren't all wearing similar tech."

"Let me get your rain shield and a car." Foocoo cupped his ear and ordered her a cab.

"And a saucer, please. I'm picking up Dietrich today. We're off to the terrarium for the mayor's speech and the big run."

Jordas settled into her taxi, blew Foocoo a kiss as he closed the door, and crossed her legs for the short trip. The couch molded to her frame, and the taxi's AI offered her a beverage. She declined and looked out the window as the aerodyne rose several hundred meters, through a sheet of sour rain, into one of the lower sky-lanes. The taxi put down at the corner of Chardium and Eighth. Jordas raised her wrist for payment and her minicomp's single chirp confirmed the transfer. She got out and slaved Dietrich's saucer to her minicomp. The saucer bleeped and rose a meter on a plane of countergrav before setting off after her into the Mandrake building.

The lift opened on the sixteenth floor, and the double doors of the Children's Village greeted her. The upscale day center for preschool-aged children was a favorite among the officials of the Corporate Congress. The floor of the reception hall was monogrammed with the center's mission: LAUNCHING ONE MIND AT A TIME.

No turning back now.

Cherry Soons looked up from the reception desk with a crooked smile on her face, and motioned to the steaming cup of tea on the counter. "Right on time. There's your usual."

"Thank you, Cherry. You know you don't have to. Just because I work for the mayor doesn't mean—"

"Oh, I didn't do it for her. Nothing against Mayor Engel, mind you. Our Dietrich asked me if he could make you a cup first thing this morning when his mom dropped him off." Cherry smiled broadly. "I did it for *him*. That boy is going to break hearts."

She turned away and mentioned the first thing she could think of. "The mayor tells me a new vein in Mine Nine looks promising. If the yield is high enough, the Corporate Congress may have the funds to finally dome the city, which will make life better for all of us." The words were populist drivel and they tasted bitter in Jordas's mouth. She forced herself to say them anyway.

"Right, be back in a millisec with young Dietrich."

Hearing his name again nearly brought Jordas to her knees. She placed a hand on the countertop and closed her eyes. *You can do this. He won't feel a thing.* The *whoosh* of sliding glass doors pushed the thought aside.

"There's my little Ditti."

Dietrich Phineas Engel nearly tripped over his feet when he saw his personal bodyguard. He ran to Jordas and wrapped his arms around her leg. "Hi, Jordi. I don't want to ride today. Would you hold me, please? Hold me for days?"

"Of course, Ditti."

Jordas situated Dietrich on her hip and pressed her face into his soft skin, wiped damp eyes on his hair. *He was born without a choice. They will just kill him anyway, and our people won't mind taking their time either.* She'd seen enough in the last year to convince her of that. *Besides, look who his mother is, he'll just become like her. I'm saving him. I'm saving my Dietrich.*

The soft tone in her ear was on time. "Agent Tarakov. . . . Yes, I have him. . . . Rendezvous in ten, copy that. Tarakov, out."

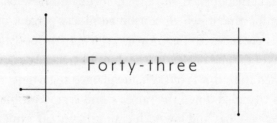

Forty-three

Sheol hung in space like an angry ball of plasma in a full-blown rage. From space, the land looked necrotic. From the surface, the clouds appeared to bleed. Mount Fhorro Tan had erupted violently, spewing ash to an altitude of fifteen kilometers, the plume clearly visible even from orbit. Slag and embers thick as heavy snow fell in all directions, as far as the naked eye could see.

"So this is what a nuclear winter looks like," remarked the somber shuttle pilot as she peered up through her cockpit's armorplaste.

The name tab on her flight suit said Jase. Her real name was Agatha Marcher. Agatha's features were as common as her surname. Except the St. August Marchers were anything but common. Hailed from the Isle of Tabor, on the capital world of Lusitane. These Marchers had served their queen for generations among the ranks of the Ministry of Intelligence, Department Five. Agatha had joined MOI-5 straight out of university as her father had before her, as seven generations of Marchers had before him, and she wasn't about to let a bit of fouled weather tarnish the family reputation.

Marcher pulled on a rebreather and heavy jacket and moved to the shuttle's hatch. The mask's comm automatically activated. "Get the crates ready to move."

Her colleagues were in the shuttle's aft compartment.

They better be hard at work. If I catch them messing around again I'll flog their pathetic hides.

"Roger that," said a male voice. "We're rolling."

Her "milk-run" shuttle was a blocky, short-range transport vehicle with a two-seat cockpit that opened into a small medbay amidships. Beyond that was the aft compartment, which consumed ninety percent of the vessel's capacity. It was packed with tied-down cargo, mostly foodstuffs from the domed gardens of the city of Nexus. The shuttle's tracked deck was designed for old-fashioned roll-on/roll-offs. That explained the whine of bearings as the first crates trundled down the ramp. Countergrav was handy. But the margin on food was low, and low-tech crates shaved off a full two percentage points of cost. Sometimes it paid to go old-school.

"Leave the small ones behind," Marcher said as she popped the forward hatch just off the cockpit. "We'll get them later. I need the fridges emptied as soon as possible. Load one on a sled for me and bring it round. We have another run to make. I'll handle the screenwork and meet you back at the shuttle within the hour."

"Roger that."

The fridges carried the most perishable items. She could easily stand in the largest of them, stretch out her arms, and turn around. The cubic meters were going to come in handy.

The ground shook and the shuttle's readouts recorded a seven-point-five on the Yuka-Toomi scale. Thanks to Combat Outpost Danny True's floating foundation of permastone it only felt like a solid three. Just a baby quake, and a mild tantrum at that. Not like the ten-point-four that had rocked the continent two days ago. That one had felt like a six and done real damage.

Marcher caught an ember in her glove and pulled a smoke out of her vest pocket. She lit up before realizing that she couldn't smoke it through the mask. Fire control was dousing hot spots as fast as they appeared. A crew ran past the nose of her shuttle toward a temporary building. *There goes the barracks,* she thought as she flicked the smoke away.

Just outside the hatch, Marcher stepped onto the ladder and descended to the deck of Pad 6. Her foot put down in hot powder and cinders. Her flight suit and boots were flame-resistant, so she wasn't worried. Unlike the city of Nexus, Danny True didn't have a deflector, which was more than enough cause to be concerned. The outpost was getting the worst of the fallout. Worst by far. Shuttles and dropships and mechsuits could operate in the ash indefinitely as long as their scrubbers held out. The temporary buildings and tents didn't have the environmental equipment to handle it.

At the rear of the shuttle Marcher saw her colleagues wearing exosuits, hefting crates onto a flatbed hauler. One waved back at her before grabbing another crate with ease. The other worker came around the shuttle pushing a sled on a plane of countergrav. *"Everything's loaded,"* he said as he pushed the sled toward her. On it lay a hermetically sealed unit as long as a tall man.

Marcher slaved the sled to the minicomp strapped to her arm. She consulted the screen to get her bearings and set off for the command center at a brisk pace.

"Stay alert," Marcher said to her colleagues as she walked away. "I don't want to be out in this any longer than we have to. And . . ." She quickly amended what she'd been about to say, because the link wasn't secure. It probably wouldn't matter. Still . . . ". . . the planet's throwing a temper tantrum. Be ready to evacuate on a moment's notice." She'd almost said "when," and she scolded herself. *Careless, very careless.* She patted her side and felt the hard outline of the disrupter in an oversized coat pocket. It was set to maximum yield. One blast could kill a man at close range, or momentarily stun a mechanized Marine.

She'd left Nexus on the half hour. Nexus's high-rises towered over the Fiskar Plain, near the holocaust's edge. Its citizens were sheltering in place while work crews struggled to bring online hastily scavenged deflector arrays. City humor bordered on the macabre. Sheoldians preferred the term "Hellions" instead, which fit the planet's general mood, particularly today. Nexus's nickname was Camp Hell-No, for two reasons. Just about everything organic refused to grow unless it was domed, and Hellions didn't complain about the weather. When you lived on Hell there was only looking up.

Except not today.

A rumble in the sky caused Marcher to look up with alarm. The sound was faint at first, and then it swelled and soon a loud roar filled the sky. *They're early.*

Visibility was so poor she knew she wouldn't catch sight of the 'Publicans before they were nearly on top of her position, which left her little time.

"Heads up. We have inbound," Marcher said over her comm. Their original plan had been to hit the morgue, which was next to the camp's walk-in coolers, using the ash for cover. Grab a spare mechsuit and be gone before its absence was noticed. A drop meant that heightened security was probably already in place. She was going to have to improvise.

"Change of plans, gentlemen. Deliver the cargo and return immediately to the shuttle. I'll meet you there in fifteen minutes. I have to take care of something first."

Marcher altered course for Pad 3. If her intel was right, a Republican LAC was preparing to put down there with a cabin full of Marines. The job only called for a suit of armor. A suited Marine would have to do.

Forty-four

Into Sheol's hellish inferno Charlie Battalion fell. Any sane being would have fled Sheol's surface on the first available ride up. But the RAW-MC wasn't known for its sanity. It was known for going to hell and back and this time the Corps really meant it. First in, first to fight, no matter the odds.

As Charlie BAT dropped, Promise refused to don her helmet, not until her stomach caught up with her mechboots. Because she knew she'd never get the smell out. Not completely. It was bumps all the way down to Combat Outpost Danny True. She sighed deeply as the dropship settled into its cradle, and only after taking a few deep breaths did she unstrap from her webbing. The mild sense of nausea that always accompanied a drop passed quickly enough. She donned her helmet and dropped the visor, and watched her HUD come online. The engines began to cycle down as canned air filled her helmet. Her jaw flexed to equalize the pressure in her ears. Thankfully light attack craft and dropship engines didn't breathe air. Otherwise, the landing would have been aborted.

"Seal confirmed," her AI said. "I'm tracking all points from Victor-Two. Victor-One will be dirtside momentarily."

"Excellent, call the roll."

Promise's Marines were out of webbing and on their mechboots before a five-count. They started "pinging in." While Promise kept one eye on them she did a visual check of all her weapons.

Her recently upgraded Kydoimos-6 Mechanized Infantry Combat

Battlesuit, or mechsuit, still didn't feel right. She'd added extra articulating plates of armor on her shanks and shoulder blades, which brought her up to 230 kilos total: skin, beegees, and armor. Without her beegees, or under-armor, her overarmor would have rubbed her raw. You didn't break in new armor as much as it toughened you up. The calluses were hard-won, aged like good wine. The added weight was throwing her balance off a bit, which meant her suit's gyroscope needed more calibrating. For now she'd have to live with the slightest list. She didn't want to think about using the head while suited, at least not until she'd installed the new latrine mods. She'd just hold it. The internal shoulder pads were still cutting into her traps and the HUD was a bit too sharp thanks to a recent upgrade.

The air still smelled funny. "Mr. Bond, I thought I told you to clean the scrubbers."

"You need to break them in, ma'am," Bond said. "Another four to six hours should do it."

Or I could just break you in, Promise thought in response.

"All right, people, look lively," she said over the company battlenet. Her heads-up display was wide-awake now, all members of her half company called and accounted for. Two toons were with her amidships, their green icons burning on her HUD, their articulating hulks the apples of her eye. Two more toons were aft of her position, out of sight in the rear compart-ment of the dropship. Four toons of five brought her up to twenty Marines total, a half-strength company. Captain Yates had designated Promise's half Victor Company Two, or Victor-Two. Victor-One was with Yates in the next dropship, which had yet to put down.

"Considering the lovely weather we're having, I doubt the Greys will try something," Promise said. "Don't count it." She drew one of her auto pis-tols loaded with high-yield penetrators and racked the slide, and then re-peated with the other before holstering it too.

"Weapons hot. Drain it, dump it, pack it up, wolf it down. We go in five mikes."

Her HUD started counting down as she bypassed the energy rifles and carbines, and grabbed a minigun from the recessed weapons rack in the starboard bulkhead. She linked the feed from the minigun to her mechsuit and carefully swung her arm from side to side to make sure the feed didn't hitch. It was on the bulky side for a heavy weapon but the captain wanted to go in as heavy as possible. About face level a second recess opened to reveal five specially designed ammunition packs. Promise selected the second hump from the right and strapped it on over her armor. She felt the magnetic locking clamps engage between the shoulder blades of her armor, and then a suited fist pounded her back twice. She turned her head and saw Private Race Atumbi grinning beside her. Promise thanked him with an energetic thumbs-up and a big smile. The young Marine beamed through his visor. He was learning, and had just knocked on her suit to tell her the hump looked green-to-go. Promise linked a second feed from the minigun to the pack, and her HUD confirmed the pack was secure and plugged into her mechsuit. The interlocking jewels of her right gauntlet undulated as she pulled the trigger of the minigun (with the safety on and the feed disabled, of course). Six conjoined barrels twirled madly about their peristeel axis. It was the most beautiful whine she'd ever heard.

"The lieutenant sure loves her weapons," Lance Corporal Kathy Prichart said over the battlenet, her armored back facing Promise's. Kathy was running a gauntlet down the row of weapons, deciding on the one for her. *"Hm . . . I don't know. A carbine would be prudent, don't you think? The atmo sucks and it'll screw with pulsed energy fire. Oh well. There's nothing in the 'verse quite like a tri-barrel."* Maxi was to her left and his carbine appeared to be jammed. Prichart had a gift for irony considering her preferred choice of rifle. The tri-barrel was as heavy as the minigun Promise had selected, and Kathy never suited up without the grossly overpowered energy weapon. Not ever.

"Look who's talking, Lance Corporal," Promise said. "Your Triple-7 isn't exactly economical."

Prichart grabbed a carbine and then changed her mind and handed it to Maxi. *"Here, this looks like your speed."* Then she hefted the tri-barrel out of its rack with both gauntlets, cradled it in one arm while stroking the barrels with the other. *"Weps aren't supposed to be economical, ma'am. They're supposed to drop targets."*

"Ooh-rah," came from a chorus of jarheads.

Promise shook her head and smiled.

The RAW-MC's battle cry was as primal as it was difficult to explain. Ask any toon of Marines what "ooh-rah" meant and you'd get three different answers back. Forward, kill, get some, make 'em pay. Yet every one of hers knew exactly what it meant. They were mostly smart enough to keep their smirks about the lieutenant's weapons to themselves too. Except for Prichart, who could get away with it.

"Ooh-rah," Promise said to herself as she squeezed the trigger of her minigun again, relishing the high-pitched howl of her six-shooter. She loved, loved, loved the sound of that weapon. The M-1306 spewed hypervelocity darts at roughly four times the speed of sound, at about five thousand rounds per mike if you asked the weapon to put out for you. Otherwise, you kept a light touch on the trigger, and held it back when it really mattered. It was an effective weapon against mechsuited infantry, lightly armored vehicles, and small aircraft, and positively devastating against skins in unpowered body armor.

The chrono on Promise's HUD ticked under four mikes to go-time.

Promise toggled the link from the hump to the minigun and felt the penetrators shunt through the feed. The weapon's status updated on her HUD, went hot. Her palms started sweating, and her suit immediately wicked the moisture away and into her suit's reclaimed water supply.

Most of her Marines had already moved toward the starboard and portside hatches, forming themselves into two predetermined columns, but a few were still selecting weapons and checking ammunition feeds. Atumbi was overstuffing his suit's compartments with throwing grenades, again. Prichart snagged a third auto pistol, but couldn't find a place to put it. Lance Corporal Nathaniel Van Peek stepped out of line and backtracked to add a carbine to his weapons mix. He already had a railgun in hand.

"Mr. Bond—run a system-wide scan and give me a verbal on my weapons mix." Promise walked through her people and joined Prichart at the front near the bulkhead hatch.

Bond read her weapons manifest like narrated nonfiction:

- "Shoulder-mounted Hordes—ready.
- "Mini-1306—ready.
- "Auto pistols—ready.
- "Triple-7 Carbine and Flexible Grenade Launcher—ready.
- "Force blade charged and ready.
- "Ammo feeds are green-to-go."

There was a momentary pause before it finished, "All systems nominal, Lieutenant."

"Very well. Run it again."

Bond didn't sigh but Promise heard the unvoiced complaint anyway.

She never ran an op without checking twice. Never. Not since that time when her HUD had died in the midst of a firefight. She hadn't had any tracers, either. She never wanted to operate blind again.

"Aye, aye, ma'am. Please stand by." Now Bond sounded put out.

Her HUD told her the pressure inside the dropship had equalized with the standard atmospheric conditions on the ground.

Because of all that ash and burning cinders in the air, energy weapons had a much reduced range of fire, which is why most of the boots of V Company had ditched their e-weapons in favor of conventional arms. Most of Promise's Marines were double-checking their FS-7.77s or Triple-7 Carbines, one of the standard duty rifles of the RAW-MC. A Flexible Grenade Launcher hugged the rifle's frame in an over/under configuration. The Triple-7's latest upgrade accepted a flexible ammo feed called a snake, which was similar to the one her Mini-1306 used. It could get tangled up—even knotted—without impairing function. In theory. The Triple-7 had its own external ammo pack too, which was squared instead of rounded, and it could engineer ammo on-the-march, from the necessary raw materials: armor-piercing; explosive; armor-piercing explosive; tracers in case your HUD glitched in battle; and more. Each of her Marines carried two backup pistols that only a mech-suited human would dare fire. Try it in skin and you'd break your arm or your skull from the recoil; you never forgot the training vid for that one. Throwing grenades. Plenty of those, and some of them got up and ran if your throw was off. The force blade was for melee, and Horde missile launchers, one perched on each shoulder, when you needed to swamp the enemy. In all, it was enough firepower to prosecute a little war.

Prichart sidestepped around Promise and returned a moment later with a second tri-barrel slung over her back and secure in webbing.

"Seriously?" Promise shook her head.

Three mikes to go-time. Kathy gave her a stern look.

"Are you finished?" Promise made sure she sounded exasperated. "We're about to pop the hatch. Now is not the time to stuff your face."

"Almost, ma'am," Prichart said with her mouth full. "Hunger waits for no jane." Prichart turned toward Promise and smiled through her visor. She canted her head toward her drink tube and pulled mightily. "Ah, better."

"Mute yourself."

"Roger that," Kathy said as a drop of goo ran down her chin.

Promise wrinkled her nose. "What is that, anyway?"

"Starch and modified proteins—all slow-release. You should tank up too, ma'am." The "ma'am" was slightly emphasized with the faintest hint of command authority, and pitched respectfully. Kathy was Promise's subordinate, not the other way around. Kathy was also Promise's guardian, and in very specific situations Kathy could disobey Promise's orders if her life depended upon it. Kathy had done it once and saved Promise's life.

"Caf will do." Promise preferred an empty stomach during an op, maybe a cup of hot caf too. The less she put in, Promise figured, the less could come out.

"First rule of survival, ma'am," Kathy added and took another loud sip, and then another slurp of goo.

"Copied that," Promise said with emphasis. Not "copy that," but *"copied that,"* because they'd had this conversation more times than Promise cared to count.

Her HUD dropped below two mikes to go-time.

Kathy pivoted on her heels to face the hatch, knees slightly flexed, ready for the jump to the deck below. *"I won't need much range in this mess,"* she said as if she'd read Promise's mind about her choice of weapon. *"Just a solid lock and a millisec to squeeze the joy. Can't leave my baby."*

"Nuh-uh," Promise said, and held out a hand. "Carbine please." The next moment a Triple-7 was sailing through the compartment toward her. Promise caught the weapon with one hand and locked it into place on Kathy's back next to her backup tri-barrel pulse rifle. "Backup, for your backup, just in case."

"Suits in motion?" Kathy asked.

"Negative, stand by for my order," Promise said, holding up a metal finger as she heard something crash behind her.

Sergeant Sindri and Private Atumbi had decided to move toward the same weapon at the same time.

"Ah, ah, ah," Maxi said over the battlenet as he snagged the last minigun from the rack. His voice sounded tinny to Promise's ears.

"You're not old enough to handle one of these, Atumbi."

Maxi being Maxi, Promise thought. His tone carried an edge instead of its usual humor, and that wasn't like him.

"Now, now, Sergeant. Give the private a break," Promise said. "He'll be a PFC before you know it."

"Good, I'll let him hold the mini then," Maxi said without taking his eyes off the minigun. He backed up a pace, spun around, and headed toward the hatch on the port side of the vessel. Took up his position as the port point man. Maxi was acting strange.

"Atumbi, take this." Promise handed the young Marine another carbine and swapped him ammo packs, and then double-checked his feed. Punched him lightly in the chestplate. "Green-to-go." She opened a private link and said, "Watch where you point it. Finger off the trigger until it's time to slag something, okay?"

"Roger that, ma'am," Atumbi said. Promise could see his head bobbing up and down inside his helmet.

"Form up," Promise barked out as she headed back toward the forward hatch on the starboard side. Kathy was already in the lead position, and Promise was grateful to have her there. Her point woman.

Captain Yates had let Promise keep Prichart as her guardian even though she wasn't the company commander anymore. The decision was unorthodox, and Promise couldn't have been more pleased. Relieved, in fact, because keeping Kathy meant she could keep an eye on her guardian. Funny, that. Kathy would have said that was *her* job. In her deepest-down, Promise couldn't stand the thought of something happening to Kathy. She'd tried dodging the fear for months, and finally had to chain it to the floor of her will. The chains rattled a lot. They'd yet to break free.

Promise said a quick prayer for Kathy and her Marines. *Sir, please keep them covered, keep them safe. If it has to come, save the beam for me.* Then she finished her morning grace.

The operational plan was straightforward. Victor-One would move to cover the north and east sections of the landing zone while Victor-Two under Promise's command covered the south and west quadrants. Maxi, Staff Sergeant Go-Mi, and Sergeant Dvorsky comprised her platoon leads. Go-Mi and Dvorsky were in the back of the dropship with the platforms. Promise opened a link with both women to confirm their toons were green-to-go too. Heard their affirmatives over her mastoid implant.

Her HUD dropped below one mike to go-time.

Forty-five

MAY 25TH, 92 A.E., STANDARD CALENDAR, 0858 HOURS
THE KORAZIM SYSTEM, PLANET SHEOL
NEXUS CITY, UPPER RIA BURROW

Jordas and Dietrich took the Number 3 tube from the Mandrake building to the corner of Lutron Boulevard and Third, arriving at the underground substation just across the street from the terrarium. They walked up a flight of stairs to the street level to find that the rain had lessened to a steady drizzle. Jordas keyed her rain shield and held Dietrich close as she stepped into the elements. The terrarium's dome curved upward more than two hundred meters, and it appeared to glow as if it was lit from within. A large crowd had gathered at the base of the dome, near the main gate. A small platform whizzed by, cutting them off. Then it altered course, swung around, and flew into her path.

"Back off," Jordas said.

The tracker reversed several centimeters. Jordas sighed and raised her glasses. A green light mapped her eyes, and then the tracker beeped and whisked away. A moment later, Mia Strauss stepped out of the crowd.

"Over here."

Agent Strauss's eyes scanned from three o'clock to nine before settling on Dietrich. She wore a muted pantsuit and working shoes, and an all-business smile. A rain shield cast an iridescent hue about her.

"Agent Tarakov, right on time. Dietrich, are you ready to see the OnWae?"

"Ready, me? Are you kidding, Mia?"

"Never kid a kidder, right, Ditti? All right, you two, stay close."

Mia escorted Jordas and Dietrich past the admission lines, to a side entrance marked STAFF ONLY. Once inside, they snaked through several well-lit corridors and up two flights of stairs to a private viewing booth deep inside the terrarium, which overlooked the main stage below. A crowd of people surrounded the stage on three sides. Peddlers walked through the assembled mass selling hot and cold treats, and nonalcoholic beverages. Jordas figured there were over two thousand in attendance, perhaps even twenty-five hundred.

"Nice, yes? Good," Agent Strauss said, and slapped her hands together. "You'll have a panoramic view of today's event." Strauss did a quick sweep of the room. Apparently satisfied, she nodded at Jordas and left without a word.

"Wow, I wanna see." Dietrich pushed out of Jordas's arms and pulled her toward the plexi window. "Oh, wow, can I have one?" He pointed to a cart laden with trinkets and inflated OnWae. "Please, please, please? I'll love you for days."

"Not now, Ditti. I'm sorry but there isn't time. Your mom is about to speak and she wants you with her. Agent Strauss will be back to get you soon. Afterward, I'll take you back to the Children's Village."

"Mia isn't fun. You take me."

"Afraid not, kiddo. Ah, don't give me that face. You'll survive." It was the wrong thing to say, and Jordas barely reached the dispenser before she threw up.

"Jordi?"

"Yeah. Just something I ate. Go back to people-watching."

Jordas wiped her mouth on a napkin and returned to Dietrich's side with a bottle of carbonated water. She looked up at the terrarium's ceiling, which was actually a dome within a dome that served two important purposes. While the OnWae were herbivores and considered quite safe to be around, they were still massive creatures. It wouldn't do for the general public to be in their vicinity. So an outer dome had been created for the public, and a much smaller inner dome was cordoned off for just the OnWae. The wall separating the two was actually more than a dozen meters thick and honeycombed with various businesses.

Jordas looked behind her and caught a glimpse of one of the OnWae launching itself from its perch high above. She looked back and down and saw the stage the mayor would soon occupy, surrounded by the residents of

Nexus. Armed guards in gray uniforms and android enforcers stood along the perimeter, forming a solid line at the front of the stage.

A woman's voice sounded in her ear. *"One minute, Agent Tarakov."*

"Copy that."

Jordas took one last look at the stage. She bent down to Dietrich's level and turned him around. "Now, let's straighten your collar and tame your hair. Hmmm, ah-ha, there. Right as Korazim rain. Now, put on your biggest smile and go get 'em."

"Who am I gonna get?"

Jordas's smile faltered. She simply nodded as Agent Strauss opened the door.

"Agent Tarakov, the mayor is ready for Dietrich."

Jordas cleared her throat. "Be right there." She pulled out the small sphere from her bag and triple-pressed two buttons, which started the device's internal countdown. "Here, I bought you a gift. It will help you learn . . . and help you remember me."

Dietrich held out his hand. "Wow, thanks!"

Jordas almost aborted the mission. Just might have if Dietrich hadn't grabbed it out of her hands. "Cool, a starsphere."

"You don't have one, right?"

"I do now."

"I . . . I just want you to know how much I love you, Dietrich. You mean the 'verse to me. Do you understand?"

Agent Strauss cleared her throat. "Jordas, we really need to go. Can it wait? Dietrich will have to leave that here."

"Can I take it with me? Please, please, *please?*"

Jordas felt something die inside of her. This was all part of the plan. Part of the commander's plan, part of why she'd infiltrated the mayor's security detail more than two years ago. The innocent-looking toy, giving it to Dietrich here, now, just before Mayor Engel's speech, knowing Ditti would want to take it with him, knowing Mia would object over security concerns. Knowing Strauss had zero patience for Ditti's tantrums. She'd carefully scripted every move.

"Mia, would you mind holding Ditti's toy for him when he joins his mom? He won't take it onstage, will you, Dietrich?"

"Nope."

"See—problem solved."

"I promise, Mia. Okay?"

Mia hesitated. "Jordas, that's not been cleared by security. You should know better."

Jordas dipped her head in apology.

"All right—hand it to me."

"You're right, of course. I'm sorry. I just couldn't . . ."

Mia pressed several buttons and played with the language setting. "I saw one of these in the window at Tiniford's and thought about buying it for my niece. Does it really project any constellation you ask for?"

"Over four hundred and twenty-five worlds," Jordas replied without emotion. "Imagine looking up at the sky from Hold or Meridian Prime or Wayland, or even from Earth before, well, you know."

"You don't sound too excited about it."

Jordas froze.

"All right, Dietrich. I'll hold *this* until after your mom's speech, okay? Then you may have it back. Do we have a deal?"

"Deal, Mia. Bye, Jordi. Oh, thank you. Love you. See you soon." He blew a kiss to Jordas as he walked toward the door.

Jordas fought to keep her composure. "Ah, Mia, I'm going to buy Ditti a souvenir. I'll meet you back here after the mayor's speech."

Mia nodded and held out her hand. "Come, Dietrich. We don't want to keep your mother waiting."

Jordas waited a few minutes before making her way to the ground level. She needed to leave the building before the event. *You need to leave now.* Instead she found herself in the stairwell and then on the ground floor and midway through the crowd. She stopped six meters from the stage as the mayor appeared.

Mayor Amelia Engel was dressed in a finely tailored silver pantsuit and six-inch cherry heels. Her blond hair was smoothed back into a bun that added severity to her already thin face. "Greetings, citizens. Thank you all for coming. This is a momentous day for our humble planet. I'm so glad you and your families decided to share it with me and my son." The mayor turned and opened her arms. "Ditti, please come out and say hello to every-one."

Jordas watched Dietrich bound across the stage, watched his wispy hair bounce with each stride. She saw Mia standing in the wing, holding Diet-rich's starsphere. She glanced at the minicomp on her wrist as it ticked below two minutes. *Jordas, what do you think you're doing?* She looked back at young Dietrich, as he waved at the crowd. His eyes found her, freezing her in place. The doubt she'd managed to push down deep slowly worked its way up, until it cracked her resolve. She scanned the sea of parents and children. A teacher and her class stood nearby dressed in matching orange shirts. She saw little Dietrichs all around her, their smiles and joy and innocence. *How can I take that from them?* When she once again looked at Dietrich, her resolve shattered. Without thinking, she began to push her way through the people, and toward the wall of security.

"Excuse me, I need to get *through*." Jordas pushed with urgency. People started turning toward her, others complaining as she shoved them aside. She inhaled deeply. "Bomb!" The crowd morphed into a panic-stricken sea as people bolted for the exits. Jordas heard a sickening crunch to her left. A young woman lay on the ground nearby, leg badly canted, a small canine whimpering at her feet.

Several armed guards moved to intercept Jordas. As she lunged for the stage, a local enforcer grabbed her arm, his hand knifing her in the throat. Jordas went down, doubled over. Couldn't breathe.

Agent Mia Strauss closed the distance between her and the mayor, pulse weapon drawn. Strauss crashed into Mayor Engel and Dietrich, taking both down. The sphere in her off hand rolled out of her grasp and crashed into the base of the dais, then rolled backward, within reach of little Dietrich.

"Keep your head down, ma'am, and shield your eyes. Dietrich, we're going to play a little game. Close your eyes and count to twenty, just like hide-and-seek. Okay?" Several agents took up flanking positions to either side of the mayor, pulse weapons tracking their line of sight. Agent Strauss reached back and produced a handful of flat metallic disks from a thigh pocket, slid several into position, and tossed the others over her shoulder. She raised her wrist. "Activate shield wall!" The disks began to glow as a charged current arched from one disk to the next, until an invisible field enveloped the mayor and her security detail.

Strauss tossed a small sphere to Agent Morg Neiliech, who threw it straight up in the air and yelled out, "Cover!," and a split second later, "Clear."

When Strauss opened her eyes, a semitranslucent barrier stood between her and the mob. She barked into her comm. "Situation Orange. I repeat, Situation Orange. Position not secure. I need immediate evac on the south lawn and a HIRT team, now! And sniffers, and a med tent for casualties. Move!"

Strauss pushed up to one knee and turned her attention to Jordas.

"Stop! Enforcer—stand down. She's one of mine." Then to Jordas, "Agent Tarakov, you made the call. Now, explain it!"

Jordas tried to respond. She grabbed her throat protectively as the guards let her go. All she could do was look at Agent Strauss in horror and guide her to the starsphere by her knee. The toy she'd given Dietrich just minutes before. Her lips formed the word "bomb," and her eyes were wide with panic.

Recognition and then shock crossed Mia's face. "Agent Neiliech, you're in command. Get them out of here and to the aerodyne. Tell flight control to shut it down and make a hole. Now! Don't wait for clearance. Just go. *Run!*"

For a man built like a warship, Agent Neiliech moved with the grace and speed of a light attack craft. He holstered his weapon, scooped up the mayor and her son, and tucked one under each arm. Turned to his subordinates and said, "Stay on me until the package is secure. What doesn't move aside goes down, clear?" Nods all around. Mayor Engel had turned pale. Dietrich looked nervous, caught between a little boy's excitement and fear. Neiliech sprang forward with his charges hugged tight, ran through the energy barrier, jumped off the stage, and bolted for the rear exit.

Agent Mia Strauss leveled her weapon at Jordas. "Why, I ought to . . . How much did you sell out for?" Her eyes bounced to the sphere. "What's the blast radius?"

Jordas rasped out words loud enough for Strauss to decipher over the comm. "Quarter klick."

"God help us."

Jordas cleared her throat hard. "Lower parking structure. Go."

"How long?"

"Twenty-five seconds."

The last thing Jordas saw was Agent Mia Strauss disappearing through a service entrance before a brilliant white flash of light brought the dome down on top of her.

Forty-six

Captain Yates commed Promise as her chrono approached go-time. *"Ready, Lieutenant?"*

"Yes, ma'am. Victor-Two is green-to-go."

"Stay sharp. This should be routine." There was a hint of doubt in Yates's voice. *"Kick your boots out first. Victor-One will follow once we touch down. Good hunting, Lieutenant. Yates, out."*

Promise did one last visual count of her Marines, which was when she noticed Atumbi's pale face. His visor was still up and his helmet's internal lights were on. And he was breathing hard. Promise opened a private link with him. "Private, nice and slow. In . . . and out. Good. Again. Now, listen to me. Stay with your platoon sergeant and you'll be fine. Pop your visor only if you have to. Even in this atmosphere you'll survive. Just don't take too long sealing up. Speaking of which, you need to do that, now."

Promise opened a company-wide channel, to all four toons under her direct command, including the two in the aft compartment of the dropship. "Watch your six and watch out for your toonmates. The air is a fogged mess. I want clean kill lanes. The ash is going to cut down visibility and screw with our thermals. Keep them off and stick with visuals. You shoot it, you own it. Whiskers won't survive long in this stew so don't bother deploying them." That meant her people wouldn't be able to use a lot of their mechanical ears and eyes to look for hostiles, and that was a real concern. Promise couldn't

see any way around it. The tiny probes were invaluable reconnaissance platforms, and if you snuck one behind an enemy's lines you could literally shoot
around corners with eyes-on-target. Except the ash in the air was throwing
off a ton of interference, and the whiskers' shielding wouldn't last long in
such a corrosive environment.

"Remember, you aren't authorized to cloak. The atmosphere is throwing
off too much interference for it to hold." The Kydoimos-6 mechsuit's recent
upgrade had included a field infantry cloak, the Witchfield. When activated, it
dampened heat and sound by slightly phasing the space around the wearer
in a null field. Given the radiation and ash in the air, the colonel had benched
it. And it was still a closely guarded secret. There was no sense showing it
off if the odds were good it wouldn't work correctly.

"Maintain visual contact with your platoon sergeants. Confirm before
firing. The Greys are known for their unpredictability, and we're off-loading
a lot of remotely piloted platforms. That's a lot of mechs and boots on the
deck, all at once. We need to get them into place quickly, and then make the
handoff to their ground-based operators. No sane civvie is going to be out
in the ash. The Greys might just try it. Verify before you fire. If it doesn't
squawk a RAW-FF I-dent and it refuses to surrender, kill it."

"*Suits in motion?*" Prichart asked again.

Promise's HUD was blinking on double zeros and she was running late.
The incident with Sindri and Atumbi had distracted her and eaten up precious time. She made a note to talk to Sindri about his timing when they
could hash it out.

"Let's make some commotion," Promise replied.

Prichart popped the forward hatch on the starboard side of the dropship
as Maxi popped the hatch on the port bulkhead. Howling winds and ash
flooded the compartment.

"Red Toon, go. Blue Toon, go." Promise gave the order while triple-checking
her weps. *Still green-to-go, just like the last time you check. Stop fretting, P.*

The captain preferred colors to 123s, so Promise's platoon was "Red
Toon," which made her "Red-One." Sergeant Sindri, as the platoon sergeant
of Blue Toon, was "Blue-One." In the aft compartment of the dropship, Black
and Gold Toons waited to debark with the third and fourth waves of remotely piloted platforms, once the perimeter was secured. It was simple
catch and release. One mechanized Marine could slave up to five RPPs to

her suit with her AI running traffic control. The captain had given them fifteen mikes to get the RPPs to their assigned positions around Combat Outpost Danny True. It had seemed like plenty of time.

Promise was quick on Prichart's six as she jumped out the hatch. *On Red-Two's six,* she thought. She tapped her suit's boosters as she dropped the ten meters to the ashy deck below. The full tug of Sheol's 1.21 gravities clawed at her suit. Ash mushroomed as her boots touched down in a hellish winter wonderland, ash as thick as the freshly fallen powder in the foothills of Montana. Van Peek was out next, and then two more Marines followed after him.

"Red and Blue, get to your positions first before you ping your assigned RPPs." Her people already knew that, but the operation was already behind and Promise didn't want one of her boots trying to rush it. "*Then* confirm the link and wait for your mechs to join you. Hold position until you hear from me."

Red and Blue Toons fanned out around both sides of the dropship to form a defensive shield shaped like a clock, with the nose of the dropship oriented to high noon. Her HUD looked like a light board of primary colors, all moving in concert, each pinprick a RAW-MC soul. There was Blue-One—Maxi—at roughly nine o'clock, on the other side of the vessel. Good. His Marines were quickly moving into position. Promise settled in at the three-o'clock position. She and Maxi were the farthest out from the dropship and they'd have the best chance of spotting something amiss. In theory.

Over her externals Promise heard the dropship groan as its aft hatch yawned open to disgorge the mechs. Tightly packed rows of surface-to-air and surface-to-surface weapons platforms began tromping down the dropship's primary cargo ramp, which was situated aft and between the craft's two massive fusion engines. They marched five-by-five, just like RAW-MC toons of mechanized Marines. No other military in the 'verse deployed platoons of five. Most preferred eights or tens, and some even twelves. Not the RAW-MC, which had always set precedent instead of following the conventional wisdom, even if it was centuries old. "Pull twice the weight with half the metal." "Lighter, faster, better." Those were the mantras. So had the tradition been since the Republic's war of independence from the Terran Federation nearly three centuries before. Toons of five, companies of forty, just like the storied "First Company" of militiamen fighters who'd rallied a planet to the cause of independence and won Hold its freedom.

The remotely piloted platforms looked like top-heavy birds affixed to armored legs. Instead of arms, each platform sported two carryalls laden with missiles or energy mounts. Bulbous noses housed onboard guidance systems and point defenses. Promise's suit reached out for her toon of RPPs as they hit the top of the ramp.

That's odd, Promise thought. The row of platforms in front of hers looked off. Two RPPs were swiveling left and right, and then one of the two deployed its weapons. Another appeared to be scanning the sky like it was targeting something. She queried her HUD to find out whose platforms were acting up. They were Bohmbair's. She'd expected better from him.

"Cut the antics, Red-Four," Promise said.

"Not me, ma'am," replied Private First Class Bohmbair, the fourth member of her toon. He was two positions to her right. Bohmbair's RPPs reached the bottom of the ramp and quickly picked up speed. *"My links are cutting in and out . . . must be the atmospheric interference."*

"Not at this range." Promise turned inward. "Bond, give me a SITREP on my links."

"Holding, ma'am. Your RPPs are forming on you, as ordered—" Bond's voice stopped abruptly. "Correction, I lost the feed for a millisecond but now have it back." Then, "Ma'am, I just lost it completely."

"What?" She opened a company-wide channel. "All toons, report to your platoon leads." Then she tightened the comm loop. "Red Toon, give me a SITREP on your slaves."

Static and snow answered her while ash accumulated between the barrels of her minigun, as if the weapon had sat in a storage room, collecting dust for years.

"Red-Three, do you copy? Lance Corporal Van Peek, do you copy? Kathy, do you read, over?"

"Lieutenant . . . links are dropping in and . . . getting significant inter . . ." Kathy was cutting in and out. There was no word from Van Peek.

Promise did a three-sixty in her suit, looked skyward; saw nothing but ashen sky. Turning back to scan the ramp, she said, "Mr. Bond, I don't think we're alone." Her formation was falling apart. The platforms were not fanning out the way they were supposed to. A toon of mechs was wandering away from the dropship and toward several nearby buildings. Maybe it was her paranoia, but that toon of mechs appeared to be flanking her position. "Bond, can you clean up the net? What's going on with my HUD?"

"The battlenet is down, ma'am. We're being jammed."

"Cycle the net. Transmit new codes. Get me Captain Yates. Do it now!"

The static continued for a split second and then the Marines in her toon were talking over each other, and then yelling over each other. At that moment a platform to Promise's three o'clock locked her up and fired.

Promise's arm jerked up, her gauntlet tensing without her express orders. Small explosions blossomed in front of her as her minigun's penetrators intercepted the first flight of missiles aimed for her. Bond's work. She'd given her AI standing orders not to wait for hers when it counted, and she'd agonized over the parameters of said orders to ensure that Bond understood when and when not to act. When and when not to fire. The platform crumpled under her continued weight of fire before going down.

Promise started counting. "One." Her HUD glitched and three icons simply disappeared. Several more changed color from green to crimson.

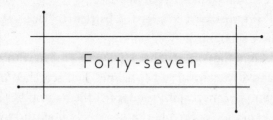

Forty-seven

For all their preparations, Charlie Battalion never planned on facing the enemy within, and here it was staring them in the face. Their own tech had turned against them.

If we don't see relief soon my people don't stand a chance. Promise spun and ducked, juked left, and squeezed the trigger of her wep.

A flight of missiles whizzed by Promise's shoulder and hammered the dropship behind her, leaving a small gash in the behemoth's side. The platforms were swarming her people from every direction, and firing on them with impunity. Grossly outnumbered, her Marines were firing back, and the dropship, nearby buildings, and the other vessels on the pad were paying the price.

Too far away to help, Promise watched one of her Marines run wildly to avoid fire. When the Marine phased out of view she wanted to rip him a new one. A split second later an armored gauntlet and then a forearm and shoulder reappeared. Because the net was scrambled Promise couldn't get a solid fix on who it was, but she was willing to bet it was one of her greenhorns who'd just activated the Witchfield. Without authorization.

Gaawd bless!

"Bond, get me a link to that Marine. She's going to get herself killed."

Given her distance from the Marine, and all the solid particles and gasses in the air, it was a small miracle that she saw the disembodied arm pumping up and down at all. As the colonel had feared, the Witchfield hadn't held, and the Marine's limb had fallen out of phase.

"All toons," Promise barked over the battlenet. "Don't cloak. I repeat, don't cloak. There's too much—"

It materialized in the corner of her HUD, streaked in with zero warning, sliced the air above the crown of her helmet, and scorched the metal as it passed by. Even in her mechsuit Promise felt the hair on her head stand at attention. The explosion rocked her in her mechboots and took her to the ground. As she pushed up, she again caught sight of the partially phased Marine. *I'm too late.* A toon of platforms had taken notice too, and as they turned toward the half-seen Marine they opened fire. The driver's helmet fell out of phase while the rest of her armor rippled in and out of view. Direct hits peeled away precious armor and speed. Now the Marine was limping, stumbling, and desperately trying to turn around and bring her weapon to bear.

A tear slipped from the corner of Promise's eye. *The hallmark of a Marine. A sister of the close fight.* Then the Witchfield failed and Promise's heart sank, and all she could do was watch death's door yawn wide open. The air swelled with enemy missile fire and explosive penetrators. She didn't have time to watch the dust settle. There was nothing left to see anyway.

Promise got to her feet and screamed, ducked, shuffled sideways, and vented her rage into an obstinate platform. That made . . .

Two.

The captain's voice broke through the chaos over a company-wide channel. *"ALCON, the platforms are comprised. Neutralize them. Rally point, here."*

Promise heard Captain Yates grunt over the battlenet and the sounds of gagged weapons fire bleeding over the comm.

A ring dropped on Promise's HUD, roughly halfway between her position and the captain's, near a small depot not far from the dropship's nose. To reach it, she'd have to plow through a lot of metal, metal that only moments before had been on her side. Unless . . .

"En route, ma'am," Promise said. "One mike, over."

"Copy that. I'm almost there." Her link to Yates terminated.

"Red Toon, converge on me." Promise spit out the order rapid-fire as she ran for the dropship. "Skim the hull. Slay the demons."

The hull of the dropship curved in along the belly, and the bottom of the curve was the only cover close enough to reach. The dropship would get her toon most of the way there. She'd hug the vessel until she had to break cover, and then sprint the rest of the way to the depot.

Fifty meters out, she spotted five shadows running through the embers, and they were headed roughly in her direction. They were almost to the depot when it exploded. Then five became two. A secondary blast picked up the survivors and threw them backward. When neither got up, Promise refreshed her HUD, locked up another platform, and cut loose a flight of missiles. She pinged both downed mechsuits and received one reply. PFC Jupiter Cervantes was down for sure. Facedown by the look of it. *And if that's Jupiter then the other Marine must be the captain.* Promise wanted to scream.

Three. New orders flowed from her mouth without hesitation. "Slipstitch to ALCON, I'm assuming command of Victor Company." Promise reverted to her callsign to minimize any confusion. "The skipper's down. Repeat, the skipper's down. To anyone who can hear me, head to the rally point."

Staff Sergeant Go-Mi's voice broke over the net. "*—tenant Paen, do you read? Lieutenant Paen, do you co—*"

"Staff Sergeant, say again, over." Promise came along the dropship's side. Go-Mi's icon barely registered on her HUD, flickered a moment, then disappeared. "Staff Sergeant, what's your status, over?"

She shuffled right, fired, skipped left, fired, flipped over a platform, and landed facing its backside. Fired and destroyed.

There's too many, and they're everywhere. I need . . . Promise pulled the carbine from her back with her off hand. *More.* Her mechsuit could handle the minigun with her dominant hand, as long as she kept it to short bursts of fire. She raked a toon of platforms as they attempted to flank her position. Pulling her arms apart, the carbine swept right and the minigun left. Dead mechs tumbled to the ground on both sides.

Three to seven dropped like falling stars.

"*—trapped, ma'am,*" Go-Mi's crackling voice broke through the net. "*— mech tripped the manual override to the blast door . . . urned and fired on us. We can't—*"

Promise watched Kathy drop two platforms and then bolt toward her position. A third mech was bearing down on her guardian's three o'clock and it appeared that Kathy hadn't spotted it. Promise tried to warn Kathy but her words only bounced back. It was the worst possible time for a bad connection. The platform opened fire and a dozen missiles raced toward

Kathy's position. Without thinking, Promise swung her minigun around and fired from the hip, prayed she didn't end up hitting Kathy instead. The air exploded as the minigun's penetrators tore across the missiles' flight path, setting the air on fire. Several projectiles still broke through and Kathy disappeared into a blanket of ash and smoke.

"No!" Promise snarled. She swung her weps around and acquired lock with the mini and the carbine. Fired. Her target folded in on itself before crumpling to the ground.

Eight.

Van Peek burst through the explosions, his railgun steadily coughing solid-core rounds into the stewed air. Somehow Kathy Prichart was bent over his shoulder and she appeared to be pounding on his backplate.

"—*down, put . . . down, put me*—" Kathy sounded crazed. Van Peek didn't set her on her feet until they were at Promise's side.

Promise took a knee while Kathy and Van Peek dropped into a guard position on either side of her. "Sergeant Go-Mi, blow a hole in the hull if you have to. There should be a crate of explosives somewhere inside the aft compartment. I need you in the fight." She still couldn't locate the captain on her HUD. "Captain, do you read, over?" If Yates was only knocked unconscious her mechsuit's triage capabilities should have had her up and running by now. Static and muffled explosions answered her. "Bond, locate her."

"Strange, I can't fix her position."

"Last known?"

"The supply depot."

"Keep trying, and get me the colonel."

"Sorry, ma'am. I'm not able to raise him either. When you cycled the codes we lost contact with the rest of the battalion."

"Keep trying."

"Roger that, ma'am."

"And launch my whiskers. All of them. Get me eyes in the sky."

Missiles burst from a cloud of smoke and peppered the deck around her, kicking more ash and chunks of the deck into the air. Kathy and Van Peek dove in opposite directions, plowed through ash up to their faceplates. Promise rolled up and sideways to minimize her profile. As she got to her feet, the force of the blast picked her up and slammed her into the dropship's hull, and the feed to her minigun died. The impact cracked the outer

shell of her helmet too, and it knocked the wind out of her lungs. She rag-
dolled to the deck, and came to rest spread-eagled on her back. Pinpricks
filled her vision and they weren't coming from her HUD. Kathy and Van
Peek were standing over her and returning fire. Above them was the belly
of the dropship. To the left was the ashen sky. She couldn't remember where
she was or what she'd been doing. Was it snowing? An oddly shaped flake
settled onto her visor. *I thought snow was white.* Then the ground shook and
bits of dirt and debris pelted her faceplate and jolted her back to the present.
Promise rolled over as a platform fell from the sky and broke apart on impact. A twisted piece of metal struck the ground a half meter away and it
might have been a foot.

Oh, right. That was trying to kill me. Promise blinked, swallowed hard.

Kathy took a knee beside Promise. *"Ma'am, we've got to go. Can do?"* Prichart tapped the trigger of her tri-barrel, and three continuous beams sliced an
advancing platform from top to bottom. She pulled her backup weapon
and split her field of fire, arms sweeping over Promise's body, her tri-barrel
parallel with the deck and her carbine to the side. *"Any time, ma'am."*

Promise pushed to her feet and rotated her back to Kathy's. Her mini lay
in the ash at her feet, its ammo feed cleanly severed. Promise racked the
weapon between her shoulder blades and drew her back up. The carbine felt
too light in her hands. Her magazines wouldn't last long.

She was seeing mostly single now and the stars in her vision had almost
faded out. *Well, make that single and a half.* She figured she'd just aim for
the center of the blur and make do.

"Kathy, I'm fine. Thanks for the cover." She assessed Kathy's MEDSYS
and exhaled in relief. Kathy's armor was intact but her guardian wouldn't
survive another hit like that, and neither would Promise, for that matter.

Her HUD glitched again. Prichart and Van Peek, who were beside her,
and Bohmbair, who was . . . Promise turned toward his position. She brought
up the magnification, doubled back, and then her eyes stopped over the smoldering hunk of metal half buried in the ash. There. *No.* She let loose with
everything she had and another mech fell.

Nine. She pulled the depleted magazine, loaded another. Felt the weapon
quake as it cycled. Then scanned for her next target.

She couldn't get a visual on Maxi or Blue Toon, but at least she had his
Marines back on her HUD. On the dropship's other side, Blue Toon was out

of position, the toon's third point a crimson blip on her HUD. Two more from Blue were glowing orange. Maxi's and Atumbi's icons were so close together they were nearly indistinguishable from each other, and they were surrounded by enemy icons.

They're fighting back-to-back. We have to get to them.

"We check Bohmbair and then head for Maxi. Don't stop for anything else."

Promise was at a full sprint before Kathy or Van Peek could protest. Multiple tangos closed upon her position. Fired. A spray of hypervelocity penetrators ravaged her armor and her carbine. Promise tossed the now ruined weapon and pulled her force blade as she entered melee range. She sliced cleanly through a nearby platform, and then rotated into a second, came out and then up, and arced downward into a third. "Bohmbair, do you copy."

She was so mad she forgot to count her kills. "Bohmbair, do you read, over?" And then she was at Bohmbair's side, knees deep in ash. She refused to look away.

Van Peek took a knee and rolled the young Montanan onto his back. "No." Bohmbair's visor was cracked and his head was an unrecognizable mess.

The grief nearly unraveled her resolve. She flashed back to their first meeting aboard RNS *Kearsarge*. Then Private Bohmbair had been so proud to join Victor Company. He'd been proud of his Montana roots and prouder still to serve under the command of the most decorated Montanan in the RAW-MC. Her. They'd shared more than just the Corps and now he was blotted from the 'verse. The bright-eyed youngster who had joined the RAW-MC because of what she'd done on Montana.

"Kathy, Nate—we need to get to Maxi. Stay on me." Then to Bond, "Activate the Banning Shield, continuous bucklers on each arm." She sprinted forward, once again leaving her guardian and Van Peek in her wake. She heard Kathy's objection over the comm and paid no attention to it.

Two cerulean energy circles blossomed around her armor, one on each forearm. They were about as large as the tire of a midsized groundcar, and while they held out, virtually indestructible. The Banning Shield had saved her life back on Montana, back when it was a one-off. The BS had encased her mechsuit in a bubble of pure energy and all but fried her fusion plant. BUWEPS went back to the drawing board and returned with the current model that every mechanized Marine Corps officer now deployed with. The new version could be used as a bubble for longer periods of time without slagging the driver's fusion plant, or it could be split into multiple smaller shields or even a shield wall to provide point defenses.

Promise raised one arm, which absorbed a burst of penetrators and then a missile. The force of the hits killed a lot of her forward momentum but didn't breach the shield, or scorch her armor. They were almost to the dropship's engines when Maxi's icon turned yellow.

Forty-eight

Promise and Kathy came around the rear of the dropship and passed through the shadow of the craft's wing. The aft ramp was extended, its end buried in snowy ash. Dead platforms were piled waist-high near the base of the ramp. True to Staff Sergeant Go-Mi's words, the blast door was down. Unless Go-Mi could restore power to the door or find an alternative way out . . .

Something dropped from the belly of the dropship, just to the side of the ramp, and then ducked behind it and out of sight. Then another something hit the deck before disappearing too. For a moment Promise thought they must be Go-Mi's people, out at last. Perhaps they'd cut through the deck plating and forced their way outside. Missile fire disabused her of that notion a split second later and nearly took her out.

"Down," Promise barked as remotely piloted platforms started pouring through the dropship's guts. Her HUD lit up with incoming. She shuffled sideways, and then pivoted and leapt over her guardian, and came down hard on one knee. Now she was between the threat and Kathy. Her shield morphed on the fly from two spheres into a flattened azure wall as tall and broad as two mechsuits, enough to shield both her and Kathy.

Promise hit the deck with such force her shield drove itself over a meter into the earth. Kathy braced herself against Promise's back as missile after missile spent itself on the shield, and then Van Peek was at her other side. "Horde launchers to full auto," Promise ordered. They arched up and over the shield, and targeted the dropship's landers and the mechs hiding beneath it. Dozens more raced to catch up, and their explosions stirred up so much ash and debris that for a moment Promise lost sight of the dropship. The sound of twisting metal was unmistakable and a sickening crunch shook the ground beneath them. Promise held her breath as the dropship listed into view. One of its landers must have failed. Then Maxi's icon turned orange and Promise's shield burned out.

"Slipstitch to ALCON. Form on my rally point." She dropped a ring into her HUD and pushed it out across the battlenet. Maxi's downed suit was at the epicenter and there was a second icon too, Atumbi's. Still green and moving, now dodging, now returning firing. Now orange.

"All points, *move!*" Then she ordered the unthinkable over the battalion battlenet. "Broken Arrow. Repeat, Broken Arrow. Direct all fire on my position!"

As Promise, Kathy, and Van Peek rounded the other side of the dropship, two light attack craft buzzed the deck overhead, stirring the ash below. Visibility was bad enough already, Promise thought. She didn't need help from above. Promise lost sight of her toonmates in the up-stir. Something blew up to her left, rained confusion and debris. She checked her HUD to gather her bearings and find Maxi's position. *Over there. Wait, now he's over there.* Her HUD was seeing ghosts and she needed hard contacts. She split the distance and ran as fast as her mechsuit's legs would carry her.

Entering clearer air, she saw a platform blow apart on her left and a second pivot upward and fire. Inbound missiles hit true, obliterating the platform and the earth below. The newly formed crater was so large that Promise had to alter course to avoid it, and she almost fell in anyway.

The LACs split and came around for another go at it. The roar of cannon fire and missiles overwhelmed Promise's externals and made her wince. Heavy penetrators ripped into the platforms with impunity, taking them by twos and fours. Several struck Promise's armor and bit deep, but at this point she didn't care. Their bellies opened and toon after toon of RAW-MC mechsuits started dropping from the LACs, five-by-fives. Promise saw their boosters light off at the last possible second prior to touchdown. The cavalry had arrived. Charlie Battalion and its god of war, Lieutenant Colonel Price Halvorsen, stomped the deck like the god's own war hammer.

Maxi's icon turned red, and Promise's father's words bled across her mind. *He gives and takes away.* Morlyn Gration had said so often to his daughter, in the good times and the bad, and even in his wife's eulogy. Promise would never forget turning eight without a mother. Yin and yang. Blessings and curses. Life and Death. The wind howled as she charged a nearby mech. Her minigun became a battering ram, and with it she punched deep into the platform's internal organs. Molycircs and synthetic goo back-sprayed her armor and doused her visor in a milky chem wash.

Promise swung the mini toward the next threat with the platform now impaled on the weapon. Because she'd burned out her Banning Shield, the platform would have to do for a shield. She rotated sideways to minimize her profile and let the platform absorb a flight of missiles and more pulser fire aimed at her. She spotted Maxi, there, flat to the deck, not fifteen meters away. Five mechsuits hot-dropped to the deck closer still, between her and Maxi. Promise turned to face them, out of ammo, out of options. *This is it,* she thought. She raised her force blade above her head and charged.

"Stand down, Lieutenant!" A window opened in her HUD, and the colonel's hard eyes appeared.

"We'll mop up these bastards." Halvorsen's voice grated over the comm. *"See to your wounded. Medevac is en route. See you when this—"*

"Sir, request permission to accompa—"

"De-nied," Halvorsen said. *"Your armor's slagged. Your company's a mess."*

It was the odd way he said "your company" that grabbed Promise's attention; otherwise she might have outright disobeyed the command. Because Victor Company wasn't hers at all and . . .

"Your people need you . . . here." The colonel's eyes were blazing mad on her HUD and focused on a target she couldn't see. His eyes target-locked and fired and for once his volcanic temper wasn't directed at her. A shared enemy had a way of turning personnel conflicts into bygones, even if the enemy—their platforms—had been friendlies just moments before. The colonel's eyes focused upon her again and he actually winked before killing the link.

The colonel was running toward the fight and he'd told Promise to stay behind. A part of her went to that dark place that believed he'd left her behind because he didn't trust her at his side. Because she was unstable and he needed steady at his side and steady was definitely not her. Her sane side said that was nonsense. His decision to leave her behind had nothing to do with her abilities and everything to do with where she needed to be most. *I'm only being realistic,* thought her dark side. *No, you're being a fool,* came a voice of reason, and it sounded a lot like her mother's. Her mind bent like a reed, and it was only Atumbi's cry for help that steeled it against the conflicting winds.

"*Lieutenant! What do I do? What do I do?*"

"Is Maxi's MEDSYS functional?" Promise asked as she turned and ran to his side.

"*Checking, ma'am. Stand by. . . .*"

Atumbi hadn't thought to check. Shock did that to a Marine, particularly one new to combat. She wasn't at all surprised.

"*It's down but I . . . I can reroute it . . . through mine. Doing that now.*"

"Access triage protocol two," Promise said. "Initiate rescue breathing. If that doesn't work we'll have to crack his suit and use the cup." She was almost to Maxi now.

"*Copy that. I'm in, wait one . . . okay, his MEDSYS is spinning up . . . accessing P-2 now . . . there, the O2 is flowing. What's next?*"

"We need a full scan of his injuries." Promise slid to her knees and linked with Atumbi's MEDSYS and found the right subroutine. "Got it." A hologram appeared next to Maxi's body. There was so much data displayed that Promise could hardly make sense of it. She reached into the holo and whisked the armor away, and then Maxi's beegees, until the virtual Maxi was down to his holographic skin. Yellows and oranges and reds ranked Maxi's injuries by priority. Promise rotated the image 360 degrees to check for external wounds.

"*What do I do?*" Atumbi started to panic again. "*His heart is blown out. The arteries are slagged. There's no use trying to jump him. We need a stasis collar ASAP or—*"

"Medevac's is one mike out," Bond said.

"Private, keep oxygen flowing to his brain." Promise laid a gauntlet on Maxi's armored chest. "Deploy his nanites and yours. Start with the wall of the heart, there." Promise stabbed deep into the projection. "Here," she said as small tendrils snaked from both of her gauntlets and into the ports on Maxi's armor. "My nanites are away. Make them count. I'll get you that collar. Fix the heart as best you can and you'll give him a fighting chance. You can do this, Marine."

The sounds of LAC engines drew her eyes skyward. Looking up, Promise spotted an assault-class LAC lined up on her position, and it appeared to be diving. Its nose-mounted minigun swung to starboard and spewed penetrators into a crumpled line of platforms. Then the minigun swung right at Promise. She threw herself over Maxi while shoving Atumbi to the side, as the rain of fire passed overhead. She hadn't seen the platform behind her, now a slagged mess. Promise raised a hand and waved at the LAC, and immediately thought what a foolish thing that was to do in the midst of a battle. Whether or not the pilot saw her gesture was beside the point. He'd just saved her life and . . .

"*Mayday, Mayday, Mayday* . . ." broke over the battlenet. The LAC tipped dangerously to the side and the sound of twisting metal filled the sky. Promise watched in horror as the LAC's midsection bubbled outward, and then contracted like a great hand had wrapped around it and squeezed. Whoever was inside the vessel couldn't have survived that. It happened so fast she wasn't even sure of what she'd seen.

The LAC fought for altitude, turned sharply, and then came back around. For a moment Promise thought the pilot had the reins.

Maxi.

"Kathy," Promise said, as she struggled to heft Maxi's lifeless body up and over her shoulder. "Help."

Her guardian was already there. Promise and Kathy looped their arms under Maxi's and ran toward the dropship. Atumbi was just a few lengths back, covering their retreat. The LAC's impact caused the ground to ripple beneath them, throwing rock and ash forward of their position. Atumbi went down and his icon disappeared from Promise's HUD.

"Boosters, now!"

Something slammed into her shoulder and she lost her grip on Maxi.

"Armor breach. Deploying smartmetal," said Bond.

She hit the deck and slid into a blanket of ash. A few moments later, she got to her feet and wiped her faceplate with the edge of her gauntlet. Over her shoulder was the downed LAC, and there wasn't much to look at. Directly ahead lay the dropship. She spotted Atumbi a dozen meters away, lying on his side in the ash.

"You okay, Private?" Promise did a quick sweep of the area. "We need to find Maxi."

"*I'm fine but my armor's slagged. I can't get up.*" Atumbi was between the dropship and Promise, so she headed his way. She was halfway to him when the dropship's aft compartment bubbled, and then collapsed in on itself, and she knew instantly that Staff Sergeant Go-Mi's people were dead.

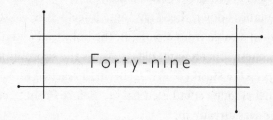

Forty-nine

Promise cradled Maxi in her arms and ran toward the approaching craft. The McHaster class shuttle drew close and began descending. KS2 was stenciled in black and gold on the shuttle's nose. From RNS *Kearsarge*. Otherwise, its hull was white space. The ramp was already dropping as it put down. Promise tapped her boosters, and landed on the ramp before it had fully extended.

A corpsman wearing a rebreather and sergeant's stripes ushered them inside. The name tab said CELLERMAN. "Lay him on the couch, there," Cellerman said in a muffled, female voice. Promise entered the cramped interior of the shuttle, and heard the hatch close behind her and the air cycling through the overhead vents to flush the fumes and particulate from the cabin. A light strobed overhead, ionizing the air. Cellerman tore off her mask and joined Promise at Maxi's side, a hypo already poised in her hand. She found the pressure point on the side of Maxi's helmet and pushed her thumb into it to retract the helmet's visor. Reaching in with the hypo, she pressed it to Maxi's neck, and then angled a cup inside until it was over his nose and mouth.

"Have to keep the oxygen flowing."

Of course. Promise heard the mechanical sounds of rescue breathing over her externals mix with the background noises of a Republican shuttle. She raised her visor and breathed the flat air of a Republican vessel. Maxi's chest rose and fell in slow cadence. Promise latched on to the rhythmic inhale/exhale pattern and matched it without thinking. Maxi's heart might be ruined but the brain was the larger concern. A collar would slow time

---

until the cutters could address the heart. They just had to get him in it. To do that they had to get him out of his armor.

"His suit's plant is down. Let's try some juice before we start cutting." Cellerman snaked a cable from a panel in the bulkhead and plugged into a port on Maxi's chest. "Lieutenant, please access the subroutine to open his armor while I prep the stasis collar?" Cellerman reached into another compartment and fished out a small medical kit. Before Promise could give the order, Mr. Bond was already in.

"Got it, ma'am. Stand by. . . ."

Maxi's suit opened with a pop. A small seam formed from the sternum to the crotch, and down the length of each arm and leg, but stopped at the joints. Then the armor retracted in on itself. Promise pulled off her gauntlets and tossed them on a nearby shelf.

"Good, I've got the helmet." Cellerman had obviously done this before.

Promise scooped Maxi out of his armor. Even with her visor up her vision was still foggy and her eyes were struggling to focus.

"Ma'am, please," Cellerman said.

She didn't want to let go, because if she did she might lose him. He felt like nothing in her arms. Her eyes flicked to Cellerman's for the truth.

"Lieutenant, we got to him in time." Cellerman looked like she understood. "You did good work."

His skin was so pale and he was cool to the touch. "Where do I put him?"

The corpsman's eyes radiated confidence and they flicked toward the opposite bulkhead, to a berth recessed into the wall. A human silhouette was drawn on the pad.

"Lay him inside the lines." Promise did as instructed, and then moved aside. A brace came up and around to immobilize Maxi's neck as multiple panels and readouts came to life.

Cellerman moved quickly, with practiced hands. She checked his eyes and pressed another hypo to his neck. A collar detached from the wall and began to spin around his head until it locked into place.

"Believe me, I've seen much worse," Cellerman said without taking her eyes off Maxi. When she pulled back, a light-blue stasis field raced across Maxi's body, and closed around his head and feet. "I have every expectation he'll pull through, Lieutenant." She put a hand on Promise's shoulder. Her smile was a great comfort. The screen above the bay was lit with Maxi's vitals, and Cellerman turned to make a few adjustments. "There. I've got this,

Lieutenant." She looked over her shoulder. "Leave the worrying to me. Looks like you have your hands full outside. Please be careful. I don't want to see you in my medbay."

"Take care of him. He's. . . ."

"They all are, Lieutenant." Cellerman pulled on her rebreather and pointed toward the hatch.

Right. Promise's visor snapped into place. "Okay." She stole one more glance at Maxi before recoupling her gauntlets. Then she was tromping down a carpet of ash. Gray powder dusted up as the shuttle leapt skyward, and boosted out of view.

"I've retrieved Bohmbair," Kathy said over the battlenet. Her voice sounded strained. *"I'll bring him in."*

"Copy that, Kathy. We'll get him home to his family." *And the rest of them too, at least the ones we can find.* Promise made a mental note to add his star to the inked canvas on her arm. She'd wear him high on her shoulder. Maybe she'd have the father saturate his star just a bit brighter than the others. That seemed fitting.

Promise surveyed the grounds of Combat Outpost Danny True, and her head began to swim. Her ears were still ringing and her suit's scrubbers were close to clogged with Sheol's atmosphere. Her minutes in the shuttle had been a breath of fresh air. The edges of her armorplaste HUD had fogged again, and her air reserves tasted burnt. There were six more sections to scan. She called for her sled and moved to the next section. Three hermetically sealed crates sat atop the sled. She hadn't found much to put in them. Even though the sled floated on a plane of countergrav, Promise felt like she was towing the weight of the world behind her. The sled hovered silently as she tromped into the next grid, marked Gamma-332.

"Mr. Bond, begin scanning."

Promise forced herself not to think about Maxi. Cellerman knew what she was doing, and worrying about him wasn't going to make a bit of difference. Her worry was like an angry hound on the edge of wide-awake. Oh, how Promise wanted to kick it in the ribs, but she knew if she did it would just bite the hand trying to feed it.

Promise's HUD tagged something in the ash near the boundary between Gamma-332 and Gamma-334, and a small claxon chimed over her mastoid implant. She walked over and knelt in the ash, stirred with her gauntlet until she struck something metal. The plate of articulating armor rippled as she pulled it out of the char. Her HUD matched the remains to Private First Class Jon Ream. Ream had been a friend of Bohmbair's. Promise wondered if the two men were having drinks in the next life. The plate was rounded and probably a piece of shank, she guessed. She turned it over and found parts of Ream fused to the shank, almost retched in her helmet. More bits of Ream turned up and went in the crates. She tripped on his faceplate several meters later.

Combat Outpost Danny True looked a lot like Ream. Fires, ash, and death surrounded her. Victor Company had fared slightly better; only sixteen casualties, fifteen of them KIAs. *Beyond the stasis collar and beyond this life,* thought Promise as she walked the scorched earth. Two full platoons hadn't even made it to the fight. Every private and PFC, corporal and sergeant, jane and jack gone. *Just gone . . . when that abomination went off in the dropship.* Promise looked around in shock. *They can't be gone. They. Can't. Be. Bohmbair and Staff Sergeant Go-Mi and Sergeant Dvorsky and . . .* Promise felt the shakes coming on. She couldn't chain her grief into something useful like a hat or a scarf—her knitting supplies had been in the dropship.

Her armor felt too tight to breathe in. Strange, that. A mechsuit was a Marine's outerwear, a jane's second skin. Promise had logged over a thousand hours in armor, and not once had she experienced claustrophobia.

Deep breaths, P. Breathe. Do it again. There you go. Just keep it together a little longer.

Her dead never stayed that way for long. She'd heard the first accusation hammering on her skull in the shuttle. Maybe it was Maxi's ghost. *Why? Why? WHY?* Now it was multiple voices. *Why didn't you save us? Why didn't you do more? Why not you?* The whys became a riotous crowd, the last one by far the worst. *Why not you?* Survivor's guilt left her with no clear answers, just like it had in times past. Why had her father died at the hands of murdering pirates? Why had she survived then and why now? She hadn't been in the Fleet Forces when the pirates struck her home on Montana. She knew enough now to realize their ship had had scanners. Her thermal print might as well have been a signal flare shot high into the sky. They'd overflown her position, and left her to watch her father's murder from what she'd believed at the time to be a safe distance. Her home had burned to the ground.

Her father had believed in more than this life, and a world beyond the grave. Problem was she couldn't test the theory without getting killed, and in the deepest-down she was scared to death of giving up this life. Because if there was a God surely His scales would weigh her deeds and find them wanting. And if there wasn't a God all she had was this life, and much of it was unfinished. She had innocents to protect and madmen like the Greys to hunt down for their crimes. That she knew she could do. *Harbinger of death. Here I come.*

"I've got a few more sections to go. Kathy, how about you, over?"

"Just finished mine. I'll be glad when this day is over." Kathy sounded close to tears.

"Understood. Retrace your steps. Make sure you didn't miss anything. Let's bring them home."

"Copy that. Circling back now. Prichart, out."

Fifty

Julius "Walker" Greystone sat with his feet propped up on his desk and a thick Johansen smoldering in his mouth. The overhead filter had broken down again and the room was as hazy as the sky above Korazim's capital city, Procyon. Walker was puffing on his second Johansen of the meeting, much to the consternation of his number-two man and his most trusted assassin. Two more cigars lay on his desk like parallel tracks, for later that afternoon. Like the one in his mouth, they were unfiltered and peppery because why bother otherwise. Walker smoked with his whole face and his thick brows rose happily as he puffed out a series of rings into the unpurified air.

"A good cigar is like making love," Walker said in a gruff, convivial voice. "It's a slow burn, all the way to the end. Isn't that right, Bella?"

Bella Antonescu was perched on Walker's desk, her legs crossed and her face schooled to hide her true feelings on the matter. She wore a tan jacket, fitted slacks, and black stiletto boots. A conventional pistol hugged each hip. Both barrels were cold but inside she was seething mad. Everyone in the Grey Walkers knew she was Walker's woman. He didn't have to make the point by embarrassing her that way. He didn't have to smoke up the room either. But that was Walker. She was his. The room was his. Forget that and you wouldn't live long in the outfit. Thankfully, Antonescu barely noticed the peppery bite of Walker's breath anymore. How could she, considering the quality of the air on Sheol? At least he'd switched to the mint-flavored Johansens during what passed for Sheol's spring, at her insistence. She'd pitched the others and presented him with the minties, and then turned her cheek and tried her best not to flinch. The blow hadn't come like it had so many times before.

"Bella, you've got the biggest pair in the world," he'd said. He'd leaned forward and cupped her hand in a rare display of affection. For all of his sixty-plus years, Walker had looked like a deprived child in the grandest department store imaginable. Years of sharing his bed had hardened Antonescu against the smell and aftertaste, even against the blows of her common-law mercenary. She didn't dare call him hers, though that's how she felt about him. Not on her life did she do that.

If Walker had an addiction, it was her: lips, hips, and barrel. She was the woman he reached for at night and the woman who listened to him snore. She'd earned the right to elbow him at twilight. Usually, he slept like a baby in her presence, and that spoke volumes. When there was a mark, Antonescu took care of it. Discreetly. She'd stopped counting her marks years ago, somewhere in the high sixties, maybe low seventies. She'd done more than a few doubles, and that wedding party Walker couldn't stand. Rigging the stretch limo's engines to fail over the water had been ingenious, all for a man who couldn't be bought.

"Commander, you better put that out before you suffocate Mouse." Antonescu leaned forward on Walker's desk and planted a kiss on his forehead.

"He's fine, aren't you, Mouse?"

Cato Tate was the outfit's small-arms expert and Walker's second-in-command. Like an ordinary house rodent, Cato liked to sit in the corner with his back to the wall, where he could see everything. Only Mouse was on his feet and leaning against the wall of the pop-up honeycombed office looking rather pale, and trying very hard not to breathe the air.

"Sure, chief," Mouse said, cupping his nose and mouth. He was small of stature and wore a too-thin mustache.

Walker kicked a wastebasket across the floor in time to catch the contents of Cato's stomach. "Fine," he said as he came to the end of his cigar and put it out on his desktop.

"You said never to do that." Antonescu was genuinely surprised. He'd nearly beaten her once for doing the same thing.

"I did, because you ruin the smoke. Letting it go out on its own is about as bad. It will never taste the same either way. Mouse, you owe me twenty-five."

"Just take it out of my pay—" Cato wiped his mouth on the handkerchief he'd pulled from his coat pocket. "—like you always do."

"Done. Open a window so I can breathe," Walker growled out. "And comm Marcus. We need to discuss some things."

Humid air rushed into the small office from a darkly lit outside. The sound of lapping water wasn't far off. The sky was black and starless. Unnatural. It had taken Antonescu weeks to adjust to living inside the dormant volcano that served as the Grey Walkers' base camp on Sheol. The lamps weren't strong enough to bathe the rocky overhead in light. They were about a kilometer underground and far enough from an active hot spot to enjoy relatively cool weather by Sheol's standards. The subterranean lake had been a bonus. They'd constructed their base by the lake's shore, because the water acted like a natural heat sink, keeping the days and nights consistent.

"Don't worry," Walker had said when they'd moved in. "There won't be activity here for at least a hundred years. The RAW will never think to look for us in a planet-sized zit." Never say Walker wasn't one for words.

It wasn't long before a broad-shouldered man approached Walker's office. Antonescu watched his outline draw near through the now-open window, and her hand slid to her sidearm. He was almost to the door before she could see the stubble on his chin and upper lip. Marcus Shoup didn't bother to knock or wipe the soles of his boots at the door. Antonescu knew he didn't bother using the safety on his weapon either, in spite of Cato's explicit orders. When you had close to one hundred armed mercenaries working for you, in close quarters, in low light, underground, upon ground that was known to shift, you didn't leave safeties off. It didn't matter if you had one in the chamber or charge in the cell. Keep it simple. Keep it safe. Marcus believed the rules didn't apply to him.

Antonescu eyed the pulser on Marcus's hip and the only empty chair in the room, which would put Marcus directly opposite Walker and Walker squarely in the sights of the barrel when Marcus sat down. She pushed off the desk and spun the chair to straddle it, which left Marcus to stand. His scowl could have stripped the smoke damage off Walker's office walls.

"How many did we lose?" Walker asked.

"Not one," Marcus said.

"How many did *they* lose?"

"Impossible to know." Marcus shrugged his massive shoulder.

"And the mechsuit?"

"Heavily damaged, but intact."

Antonescu thought she saw fear on Marcus's face. There for just a rare moment. It disappeared so quickly she couldn't be sure.

"The driver is stabilized in Medical," Marcus added. "She's got a mouth on her, that one. Keeps switching between Terran Standard and a language I don't recognize. What is an overgrown *pen-day-hoe?*"

"You mean *pendejo.*" Walker threw his head back and roared. "I haven't heard that word since I was a child."

"Fits too," said Antonescu. Walker frowned and shook his head at her, message loud and clear. *Don't.* "Well, it does," she said, and emphasized the point with her eyes.

"Say that to my face again." Marcus's weight shifted forward and both hands were clenched.

"Pen-day-hoe."

"Say that to my face one more time and I'll—"

"Enough!"

Antonescu jumped in her chair. Even Marcus blinked and took a step backward.

"Did the Marine scrub her suit before you took her?" Walker's tone was deadly calm.

"Not as far as we can tell."

"Good." Walker rocked forward in his chair. "The Lusitanians won't pay for it otherwise."

"We've hooked the armor up to our scanners but it's going to take time to crack it." Marcus looked from Walker to Antonescu. "We could try to crack the Marine instead." It was one of the few times Antonescu could remember seeing Marcus smile, and it sent chills down her spine.

"Might have to. Leave that to me." Walker gave Antonescu the look, which told her he was leaving that to *her.* Killing wasn't the only thing she was good at. Antonescu dipped her head in acknowledgment and stood to leave.

"Keep at it. The RAW-MC has developed a field infantry cloaking device." Walker stood abruptly. "Hopefully we snatched a suit with one of those because it doubles the price. I can think of more than one government that will pay handsomely to get their hands on the tech. Maybe we'll get ourselves a bidding war."

"Double-cross the Lusitanian Empire?" Antonescu said.

"No." Walker leaned forward on his desk and glared at her. "Do you take me for a fool? The Lusies funded this operation. *They* arranged the welcoming committee at Danny True. *They* gave us the pirate drive Mouse installed on the *Black Weasel*."

The *Weasel* was the outfit's only jump-capable assault-class LAC. The pirate drive made a hyperjump inside a planet's atmosphere possible. Only a madman would try something like that.

Walker's lip began to twitch. "Be that as it may, I still intend to make the Lusitanians pay for my armor." He stared at Antonescu until she looked away, before he returned his attention to Marcus. "Tell our technicians to proceed cautiously. I don't want to trip a fail-safe and end up with a lobotomized suit of armor. We're playing the Lusitanians against the Republic. But we don't want the queen mad at us. Bella, go have a chat with our Marine. Don't come back until you have what I need."

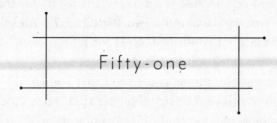

Fifty-one

MAY 25TH, 92 A.E., STANDARD CALENDAR, 1222 HOURS
THE KORAZIM SYSTEM, PLANET SHEOL
COMBAT OUTPOST DANNY TRUE

Thanks to a stiff wind washing over Combat Outpost Danny True, visibility was approaching something tolerable. And Mount Fhorro Tan had spent most of its wrath before settling down to a low rumble. In the distance, Promise saw the faint outline of the wreckage she'd come down in. She didn't even want to think about the inside of the craft, or the one that Captain Yates narrowly escaped from before it too had imploded. Both dropships looked like a crushed tin of rations, and only one weapon left that calling card. A warp bomb. The technology was bleeding-edge, and because of its inherent instability banned by every star nation in the 'verse. Leave it to a lunatic like Greystone to set one off.

Remains in tow, Promise was almost to Danny True's temporary command center when her mastoid implant crackled to life. *"Lieutenant, is PFC Cervantes with you?"*

It was the first time she'd heard the captain's voice since the battle ended. Thank God Yates was still alive. Though Promise would never admit to it, she was glad to have a CO to pass the buck to. "No, ma'am, I thought she was with you."

"She was but I can't track her. We may have a problem."

"Stand by, ma'am. Let me try." Promise opened Victor Company's unit roster and scrolled down to CERVANTES, JUPITER—PFC. "Activate Cervantes's emergency transponder, continuous squawk."

"Please state command authorization," said her AI.

"Identify Lieutenant Promise T. Paen." For a second she couldn't remember her command key, because she'd had to change it only the day before. "Ah . . . Tango-Foxtrot-Six-Gamma-Two-Two-Six-Echo-Alpha-Three-Two."

"Voice identification confirmed. Hold for retinal scan." Two seconds later: "Stand by, ma'am. Locating PFC Cervantes now."

The result was almost immediate. SIGNAL NOT FOUND.

"Wait a minute, this can't be right." Jupiter's brain-box should have been throwing off a signal of some kind. "Ping her box again."

"Negative, ma'am," her AI said. "The PFC's I-dent isn't squawking. Neither are the tags in her mechsuit."

"None of them? That's not possible."

"Same story on my end, Promise," said Captain Yates. *"Her brain-box could have been destroyed."*

Every mechsuit driver carried a surgically implanted static backup, or brain-box, at the base of her cerebellum. Its nickname was "the NCO brain," because having a sergeant of some stripe yelling at you in the background was never a bad thing at all. During combat, it recorded what the driver saw, the actions the driver took, and the outcomes she caused, for after-action reports and reviews. It could also link with the mechsuit's AI combat matrix so that if the driver was incapacitated, a jane or jack could still fight at a reduced level of combat effectiveness with an AI-assist.

A driver's brain-box also stored a unique I-dent, which could be triggered in the event that a Marine fell unconscious or was captured. Either Jupiter's brain-box was malfunctioning or it had been destroyed. *Or it's been tampered with. Theoretically, that's possible.*

"Could she have been in the dropship when the warp detonated?"

"No, she was with me," Yates answered, *"on my heels, running for the main supply depot. When it blew I was thrown clear. When I got to my feet Jupiter was gone. There was so much chaos . . ."*

"Captain, what if her armor rejected the new codes when I cycled the net? It's happened before. That might explain why we can't find her."

"That's possible." Yates sounded unconvinced. *"I hope to God you're right. Still, where is she?"*

"Did any craft depart during the attack?" Promise asked. She hadn't even thought it through. They were missing a Marine. No squawk. No remains. That didn't leave a lot of options, and Jupiter had to be somewhere. And RAW-MC mechanized armor didn't go AWOL.

"*I don't know,*" Yates said. "*Wait one while I check. Why? You don't think someone . . .*"

"I can't see how, ma'am, but we can't rule it out either."

"*You do* think someone . . . *God help us . . . stand by.*"

Promise didn't have to wait long. "*Promise, I've got a controller Lynn on the comm. He's from the Nexus Flight Authority. A shuttle on a grocery run did lift off during the attack.*" Yates paused. "*The pilot didn't have clearance and nearly plowed into one of our LACs as it fled. We were too busy to pursue. I'll patch you in.*"

Promise's HUD split into two panels. The captain's eyes filled the left screen and a frazzled-looking civilian contractor appeared on the right. His skin was yellow, very pale, and his uniform was stained and burned. Both hands were badly blistered. A black cap said NFA in bold white lettering. Nexus Flight Authority. He was sitting at a workstation and cupping an earpiece. Two holographic windows floated before him. He reached into the right-hand window and flicked the image aside, then again, and then a map appeared.

"*All right, Mr. Lynn. We know the shuttle was supposed to return to Nexus after making its run to Danny True. Any theories on where it went?*"

"*Just a minute, ma'am.*" Lynn looked off-screen. Apparently, Yates wasn't the only one relaying information.

"*Ma'am, we're trying to fix the shuttle's position as we speak. We lost it en route to Nexus. It dipped below scanners and disappeared. We fear it may have crashed. We're pulling satellite telemetry now but that will take time for us to sort through and given the atmospheric conditions I doubt it will be much help. As soon as I know more I will . . .*"

"*Don't you have an AI?*" Yates said.

"*Yes, of course.*" Lynn's eyes hardened. "*We still have to place a work order, and requisition the time. Captain, this isn't a core world with unlimited resources.*"

"*Mr. Lynn, Lieutenant Paen, my XO, is listening on the comm.*" Lynn's eyes flicked to Promise, and she realized the captain has just made her visible on the man's screen. Lynn did not look pleased. "*I've linked the lieutenant into our conversation as a witness. I suggest you do the same on your end. I need immediate access to your satellite grid. Please, patch me through.*"

"*Ma'am, that's not something I can authorize without checking with my—*"

"*Lynn, I don't have time for a pissing match between our governments.*" Promise heard the captain's deep breath over the comm. "*Mr. Lynn, I real-*"

ize this is a local NFA matter. It's your shuttle that's missing after all. I hope your people are all right. I truly do. I will do everything in my power to help you find them. But, I have a missing Marine and reason to believe that shuttle may have abducted her. If she's a hostage that changes everything. I have no desire to interfere in NFA affairs. Please, sir, my Marine was driving a latest-gen RAW-MC mechsuit worth more to the Republic than either one of us fully realizes. My suit's AI is available. I can get us both what we want. You, your shuttle and her crew, and me, my Marine."*

The Kydoimos-6 mechsuit came equipped with several classified systems. Half the drugs in the suit's pharmacope were banned on the civilian market. The software was of course military-grade tech, not to mention the mil-spec AI, which was as close to sentient as humanly possible. Promise was certain the field infantry cloaking device was Yates's primary concern. Other star nations were developing their own versions of it, but only the RAW had an operational model. Assuming the Bureau of Marine Intelligence had that right.

"If my Marine meets an untimely end and my armor falls into enemy hands how do you think that's going to reflect upon me, or you?"

"Ma'am, I don't know . . ."

"Mr. Lynn, patch me in. That's all I'm asking. I need eyes on the last known position of that shuttle. Just a look, okay. Get me that and I'll get out of your system and out of your hair, deal?"

Lynn was sweating now and his eyes were bouncing between the captain and Promise.

"Sir," Yates said with as much respect as she could muster, *"who do you think just hit us? How many were in your tower when it went up?"* Lynn's eyes dropped to his hands. *"Please, sir, help me catch the bastards who did this."*

Lynn clenched his jaw and then turned and punched something into his controls. *"I could get into big trouble for this."*

Promise's HUD chirped without warning. "Ma'am, I've got a prompt from the NFA's planetary control grid," Bond said. "And a temporary user name and password. Shall I authenticate?"

"I assume the lieutenant has an AI too?" Lynn said. *"I can only let the two of you in. No more. And you can't stay long, okay?"*

"Thank you, Mr. Lynn," Yates said. "The RAW-MC owes you and we always pay our debts."

"No, ma'am, the Greys owe us all one. I lost good friends today. Don't let them get away with this."

"I swear to you we won't. Yates, out."

The right window on Promise's HUD closed and the left grew to fill it.

"Promise, I've got the shuttle on the tower's pickups. There," Yates said. The feed streamed into Promise's HUD. There was the parked shuttle, and a work crew was off-loading crates from the cargo bay. A lone silhouette stood by the craft's nose wearing a rebreather, so facial recognition was out of the question. Probably the pilot, Promise thought. Then the pilot grabbed a gravsled loaded with a long crate and disappeared out of view. Yates advanced the vid. The pilot reappeared a dozen mikes later and helped load the crate. Weapons fire and explosions swamped the feed. The craft lifted off, and narrowly avoided colliding with one of their LACs before it flew out of view.

"That's it." Yates was calm but Promise could tell that the captain was working hard at it. *"That's the last known position and heading. Looks like the ash and smoke blinded our satcams. We have no way of knowing where she went."*

"I suggest we send a search party along the same heading and see where it leads. We might get lucky and find wreckage."

"Agreed," Yates said. *"For now it's the best we can do. I'll comm the colonel and ask for LAC support. We need all our birds in the sky looking for that shuttle. The colonel's at Nexus in an emergency meeting with Mayor Engel. There's been a terrorist attack and several hundred civilians are dead."*

"What?" Promise said. "Why am I only hearing about this now?"

"I only found out moments ago. No one's claimed responsibility. Not yet. We expect they will, soon."

Promise had no doubt who "they" were.

"There's something more going on here." Yates sighed. *"Perhaps the mayor can kick loose some civilian craft to help our search. For now, get your people a hot meal and make sure they flush the ash from everything. Then, I want them in their racks. You, too. Victor Company is grounded until further notice."*

Fifty-two

Private First Class Jupiter Cervantes began to come to. She was tied to a metal chair, and her legs were pulled apart and lashed to either side. She'd lost feeling in her feet and she desperately wanted a drink. The sound of un-rolling utensils froze her in her seat.

"This will do nicely," said a male voice. He wheeled something over on squeaky casters. Jupiter tried to crack her eyes and saw what might have been a man. The right eye wouldn't budge and the left wasn't focusing. Her tongue pushed against the wall of the right side of her mouth. Nothing. She was pretty sure the ear on that side wasn't working either. *And I don't regen.* The last time she'd gone under the knife was for the hand. It had gotten crushed by a malfunctioning bulkhead door. She'd been holding it for a friend and nearly lost her hand for the trouble, back before she'd enlisted. A civvie cutter took it and gave her a synth hand in trade. Half a year of ther-apy left her with a replacement that still didn't feel right. Occasionally, when she was really tired, she still had to think carefully to make it cooperate.

I'm going to kill the man who did this to me.

Suddenly she couldn't breathe.

"Hello, dearie." His breath smelled like spirits and ash.

He wants you to struggle. Don't.

"I need some information, pet. We can do this the easy way. Or, we can have some fun." The pressure on her throat let up enough for her to draw in a gulp of air, and a finger pushed her chin to the side. "I vote for fun." Then he went exploring.

She rammed his head with the numb side of hers. Her attacker swore and crashed into something.

When she didn't see stars she knew the worst was probably true. She'd never see the passageways of a warship the same again, or the setting of the sun, or her reflection in a still pool. She began shaking uncontrollably. Anger over the loss of her eye momentarily overrode her fear. She didn't want an optic. Science had come a long way but even the best tech still saw in digital, whereas the eye worked with the brain to blend everything perfectly. Smoothly. Not discrete. All machines saw were pixels and pieces instead of the whole.

Jupiter never saw the back of his hand coming. Stars burst across her good eye.

"Think you're cute, pet? When I'm done with you you won't be."

She felt a hand at her collar, and then cold metal against her skin, and tugging and cutting and a rush of cold air on her chest. "No." She twisted in her chair, deparate to break free from her bonds. Her vilest fear roared like a tsunami and crashed over her. "No." His hand slid beneath her beegees. "Please, *please* don't do this." Then down the curve of her belly as his other hand wrapped around her throat.

"I'll kill you. I'll cut your—"

"Not so confident, now, are you? What's that? Oh, I bet a little air would help. But this is tit for tat, dearie. I let up, I want something in return."

A door opened and footfalls echoed across the cavernous chamber. "Marcus! What the hell do you think you're doing?"

His name is Marcus. His name became a lifeline. His rough hands retreated. If she could only focus on his name, grab ahold of it, and hold on, then she wouldn't have to face what he'd just done to her. What he'd taken from her. She clung to his name as a climber hanging from a ledge about to fall to her death.

"I told you to crack the armor and get her out, not to rape her. What happened to her face?"

"It was that Lusie pilot's fault, Marcher. She hit the Marine with a full-powered disrupter blast at point-blank range. She should have stopped to look first. The helmet was damaged, cracked."

"You've been drinking. You fool."

"Marcher is lucky she didn't fry the suit's programming, or the Marine's jelly. I had to cut her out of her armor with a torch and 'Publican armor doesn't cut easy."

"Is that what happened to her eye? Did you nick her head with a torch? Walker will kill you for this."

"Only the nerve. Marcher did the rest. Thank her for that."

"I will. You're lucky you didn't take her head off. Get out. Now!"

"Hey, we've got the armor." Marcus sounded punch-drunk. "I was just having a little fun."

"Tell that to her."

"Is the commander's woman going soft?"

"Get . . . *out*."

Jupiter thought she heard the sound of lapping water in the distance. It was faint and she figured her mind was playing tricks on her.

"So, you're Walker's woman. Does he beat you too?"

Again the blow struck Jupiter's good eye and it took everything she had not to holler out in pain.

"Tough girl, huh? Keep it up and neither one will work."

Jupiter's head lolled to the side. From the corner of her eye she saw a silver oblong, and it was the size of a large man. It had arms and legs, and a horrible black stain ran the length of its torso. Her mouth opened in horror when she realized what it was.

"*Mi bebé.* My armor. You've ruined her!"

"Access codes, please. Or your situation gets very ugly, very fast."

"Service Number MM-I 171 563 149. Private First Class Jupiter Cer—"

The next blow rocked her jaw, causing her to bite through her tongue Warm blood slicked down the side of her chin, and the taste of copper filled her mouth.

"Access codes. Please."

Jupiter gave her service number and full rank in Castilian, with attitude. That earned another punch to the jaw and one to the gut. She doubled over as far as her bindings would allow her to and groaned, and spit out blood and teeth. The follow-up snapped her head backward, and to the side.

Keep this up and you're going to need two replacements, Jupiter told herself. *That won't be any way to live.*

"Careful, I don't regen." She could barely understand herself. "You buy it, you pay for it."

The woman half laughed. "I admire your spark. Tell me what I want to know and I'll spare you further discomfort. I have a hypo to take the edge off. Would you like to talk?"

She thought of Lieutenant Paen's can-do attitude and full-throat spirit, and knew the XO wouldn't rest until she found her. *Keep her talking until the lieutenant arrives. What if she doesn't arrive in time? NO, she has to. She's going to come* "I . . . take your meaning. How 'bout some water?"

"Here, this will help with the swelling so you can drink." There was a sharp prick on her neck and then the pain began to recede. "What do I get in return?" the woman asked.

"If I give you my codes my CO will know." She almost sounded like herself now. "What if I show you the back door?"

"And you get to save face, assuming I let you live. I'm listening."

Jupiter didn't answer. A burning warmth slid down her neck and back, releasing anguished muscles and joints. She let herself slump to the side and started moaning. Just about every square centimeter of her body really did hurt. She clenched her fists, once, twice, a third time just to be sure—surely her mind was playing tricks upon her—but it wasn't, and that's when she knew it wasn't over. They hadn't scanned her for synths because if they had they would have discovered her artificial hand and they would have disabled it. *Foolish mistake,* she thought. *It's going to get you killed.* She dislocated the tip of her thumb on her right hand without making a sound. With a bit of effort the tip popped, and then unscrewed to reveal a razor-thin blade. It made short work of her bindings. She moaned again to cover up the noise of fraying rope.

"Okay, my head is killing me." Jupiter forced her head to the side to expose her carotid artery. "Please. May I have another?"

She heard feet shuffling and a moment later felt cold metal pressed against her neck. She inhaled sharply as the device knifed deep with its concoction. A deeper, more penetrating burn spread across her face, down her jaw, into her shoulders and her back, and down into her abdomen. Her entire body sagged. The swelling around her good eye retreated, and her vision began to clear.

"Thank you. Have a seat." Her words were so lifeless they sounded like an off-the-shelf AI might have said them.

"All right. I'm listening."

Jupiter smiled with great effort. "Getting in is simple, really. All you have to do is trick the suit into believing you're not a threat."

"How do I do that?" the woman asked.

"Three simple steps."

"Hold on." A few moments later Jupiter heard uneven footfalls stumbling toward her and she didn't have to guess whose they were.

"Thanks a lot," Jupiter said.

"I need his brain . . . even if it is damaged. Tell me what I want to know and I swear he won't touch you again." Then to Marcus, "Make yourself useful. Kneel by her armor."

Jupiter raised her chin and turned to address Marcus. "You always do what you're told, Marcus?"

"I swear I'm going to rip your—"

"Enough! Private, I suggest you think carefully about your next words. I would hate for them to be your last."

"It's Private *First Class*." Hearing the woman sigh was worth it. Jupiter was pretty sure this was going to end badly for her. No chance she was walking out of here, not without eyes, and not if Marcus had his way. She could at least try to take them both with her, and with any luck, get a signal off to the lieutenant.

"Like I was saying, three simple steps." Jupiter took a deep breath.

"And?"

"In order . . . or you'll trigger the suit's countermeasures. Hear that, Marcus? Get ready.

"Step one is simple." She nodded toward her armor. "You just need to . . ." Seizing the woman's distraction, Jupiter brought her arms around and rocked forward in the chair, tipping it and herself into the woman. Her thumb sank into the woman's throat and she pushed it in and up just to be sure. She heard a wheeze and a small gurgle and then the woman slumped in her arms. Jupiter groped for her sidearm. There. The cold polymer frame felt like home. She drew, and aimed as best she could for Marcus, who was already backing away. When she squeezed the trigger and nothing happened she feared the weapon was bio-locked. Swearing, she racked the slide while straining her good eye to keep Marcus in her sights.

"You'll lose," she said. Her arm tracked right as Marcus moved, then right again. He stopped and started to laugh.

"You can barely see me. Just wait until I get my hands on you."

She fired until Marcus went down, and then she cut her feet loose and crawled toward his position, one hand on the ground and the other on the sidearm. Marcus lay in a pool of his own blood, breathing quick and shallow.

"You don't look so pretty, pet," Jupiter said. She frisked both legs and came up with a second pistol, two magazines, and a fixed blade. The knife slit his throat like butter.

"That's for my armor, my eyes, and for touching what's not yours."

Jupiter crawled back toward her armor and found the helmet was missing. She was close to despair when she caught sight of the visor on a low shelf. Her pharmacope was sitting next to it and she quickly grabbed it and smashed it on the floor. Cupping the helmet with both hands, she turned it around in her palms, and inched it over her head.

"Identify Private First Class Jupiter Cervantes, Rico-Epsilon-Two-Charlie-Five-Five-Niner-Charlie-Echo-Four-Six."

Blue light danced over her shattered HUD, and her hopes soared. A cardinal voice began speaking: *"Voice identification conf . . ."* Then it died in midsyllable and her HUD sparked out.

She heard shouts in the distance and the heavy footfalls of booted feet running toward her. She ripped off her helmet and upended it in her lap. Inside she found a small disk embedded in the padding of each ear. In the center of each disk was a small pin, which she depressed to make them pop out. A quick turn counterclockwise and they came away. She snapped them together and they instantly warmed in her hand.

Done.

Jupiter sagged to the ground as a bolt of energy washed over her. The homing device fell to the deck and rolled under the table. As it came to a stop it started blinking once per second.

Fifty-three

MAY 25TH, 92 A.E., STANDARD CALENDAR, 1905 HOURS
THE KORAZIM SYSTEM, PLANET SHEOL
COMBAT OUTPOST DANNY TRUE

"We've got her."

Captain Yates stormed into Victor Company's temporary barracks. The honeycomb structure was semitranslucent to take advantage of the daylight. Considering Sheol's current mood, there wasn't much of it. The cells in the wall provided enough energy for the internal lights, the utilitarian kitchen, the showers, and the head. They were all silent at the moment. Most of Victor Company had hit their racks hard. Promise had opted for the shower, hoping it would help her unknot. So far it hadn't worked.

"Where?" Promise barked over the sound of pelting water. She quickly rinsed off and mopped her hair with a towel before stepping under the blower. A column of forced air dried her in seconds.

"SOS just came in," Yates said as she jerked open a locker and drew her sidearm. It clanked on the top shelf, followed by several spare magazines. Yates stripped out of her utility shorts and shirt and grabbed the towel from the shelf below. Water hit the deck before she was in. "Jupiter triggered her backup. She's in a dormant volcano two hundred fifty klicks from here. Battalion is deploying."

"About time. Give me three mikes and I'm green-to—"

"Negative, Promise," Captain Yates said forcefully. "We've been ordered to stand down."

"What?" Promise opened the flash-cleaner and pulled out her shorty one-piece, which she'd opted for because of Sheol's heat. The standard mechsuit underarmor was cut more sparsely than the full-body version, with straps at the shoulders instead of a full tee and legs down to the calves. The vents in the underarms and back provided extra cooling. Promise stepped in and sealed up. "Then what's the hurry, ma'am?"

"The colonel wants me in the command center before he dusts off. I'm the next senior officer on post. I'll be in command while he's away. I hate this atmosphere and my teeth taste like ash." Yates gargled and spit. "I'm not standing in as the BAT-CO looking like this. It's going to be a long night and I could use the company. Why don't you join me?"

"The colonel can't do this!" Promise winced at her tone of voice. She sounded like a petulant whiner. *But he really can't do this. It's not fair.* "Why?"

"That's exactly what I said. But, I was overruled. Can you really blame him?" Yates stepped out of the shower dripping wet. "Hand me that, will you? Thanks. Promise, look, Victor Company just got smashed. We are down to nearly half strength. You saw my armor and I saw yours. They're trashed. We can't deploy in them. I was lucky to get mine off in one piece, and only with a lot of help. It's in the morgue now and I doubt the servomechs will get it online. There's no time to thaw a replacement suit. Otherwise, I'd have asked to go."

"Permission to comm the colonel, ma'am."

Yates racked her hands on her hips and sighed. "Promise, it won't do any good."

"Ma'am, *please*."

"Lieutenant." Yates's voice was as hard as peristeel. "I just got blasted by the colonel for forcing the issue. He threatened to toss me in the brig if I didn't drop it." Yates turned to her locker. She glowered at her reflection in the mirror on the door. "I suggest you do the same."

Suggest isn't the same thing as an order, Promise thought as she opened her locker.

Promise locked her hands at the small of her back, stroking a tube of gloss; popped the cap and pushed it firmly into place. It felt cool and slick in her hands and reminded her of her mother's long-ago mantra "Never leave home without your lips." The more she stroked the tube the more her nerves settled, the more she focused on the here and now, the more the shakes subsided and her voice calmed down until she was reasonably certain she had her emotions under control. She adjusted her belt and her sidearm and glossed her lips, and then turned to face Yates.

"Permission to speak freely, ma'am." She offered the tube to Yates without explanation.

"What am I supposed to do with this?" Yates brushed the offer aside.

"Battlefield makeover, ma'am."

"Are you trying to tell me something?"

The two enjoyed a brief smile, which evaporated when Promise opened her mouth.

"Lieutenant, I don't have time for this." Yates had pulled on her beegees and a pair of utility shorts, fingered her hair, and holstered her pulser in a drop-down wraparound. Then she reconsidered the tube of gloss. "Fine, hand it over." She puckered and nodded in the mirror. "Not bad." Her laughter caught Promise off-guard. "I can't believe I'm saying this. All right, Promise, go ahead. Don't say I didn't tell you so. And watch your tone of voice when you comm the colonel. Here, catch." Then Yates grabbed her rebreather and headed for the door.

Promise opened a link to the colonel with her mastoid implant and looped the captain in too. The connection went through immediately.

"Why am I not surprised? Request denied. Halvorsen, out."

Promise commed back. "Sir, I just want to—"

Died again. Opening and closing links so fast could be mildly disorienting, like spinning and spotting in a mirror. Promise focused her eyes dead ahead on the vents on her locker and commed a third time.

"I don't want to *fight*, sir—" She'd blurted that much out and the link was still open, which caused her hopes to rise. "I just want to watch."

"You have ten seconds to convince me of that because, one, I don't believe you, and two, that's all the time I have to spare. Go."

"Sir, I may be a PITA—"

"I know *you* are, Lieutenant." The colonel's voice was smiling. "I said convince me, not preach to the choir."

"I know better than to roll in a trashed can. My armor is slagged, I'm out of whiskers, my scrubbers are clogged, my shield is spent, and there's no time to thaw one of the spares. Let me ride along. I'll stay put. I'll be a good Marine until you secure the area. I've been reading through the captain's library on counterinsurgency. I've spooled up, sir. Maybe I can help you."

"Time's up." Promise kicked her locker, leaving a sizable dent in its too-thin frame. She reared back to kick it again when she realized the link was still open. "Sir?"

"*What?*"

"Sir, Jupiter is one of mine. I want to be there when we bring her out. Please."

Halvorsen sighed like the weight of the 'verse was on his shoulders. "*I won't tolerate heroics, Lieutenant. You'll stay put or I'll shoot you myself. You have fifteen mikes to get yourself and your gear aboard my LAC or I leave without you. Understood?*"

"Copy that, sir. Lance Corporal Prichart and I will meet you at the LAC. Thank you, sir. You won't—"

"*Save it . . . chrono's ticking . . . Halvorsen, out.*"

Promise twirled on her heels. "Captain?"

"*Why do I have a bad feeling about this?*" Yates's voice sounded muffled and slightly out of breath.

"Don't worry, ma'am. What could go wrong?"

Yates coughed and swore simultaneously. "*Don't make me regret this, Lieutenant.*" After a long pause, Yates said, "*Good luck, Lieutenant.*"

"Thank you, ma'am."

Promise commed Kathy and quickly filled her in on the situation. As she killed the comm link, she kicked open her footlocker and started grabbing more gear. Two tightly rolled bundles of translucent material came out first.

One for me and one for Kathy. She's gonna hate me for this.

She shook out her bundle and quickly put it on over her beegees. The material was a bit stiff, but what did you expect from nanospheroidal body armor? It was a far cry from her mechsuit, and far better than nothing.

I can't believe I'm putting this on, she thought. *Well, you got a better idea?*

The material was smooth to the touch and looked like a glorified rain slick. But it could stop a hypervelocity dart, or at least significantly slow one down. It could blunt light pulser fire in a pinch, too.

The technology behind NBA was already hundreds of years old and "dime-store" quality by current RAW-MC standards. *It was probably nickel-store class by the time the RAW was founded,* Promise thought. *Funny how the saying has far outlived the coin it was named for.* She supposed the description accurately described the truth of it. The armor was, well, cheaper than dirt. In a pinch it might just save her life and that's why Promise always kept a couple of sets on hand. It was a by-product of the twenty-first century's quest to cure Alzheimer's; made bulletproof ceramics obsolete nearly overnight. Researchers from the Weizmann Institute of Science and

Tel Aviv University had stumbled upon a beta-amyloid protein that made up the plaques found in the brains of patients suffering from Alzheimer's disease. The plaques were organic and unbelievably hard. So hard, in fact, that all sorts of interesting applications soon presented themselves. A small Israeli armament manufacturer took notice and developed a building block of beta-amyloid-A. Initial tests showed it to be substantially stronger than two standard defense materials of the day: stainless steel and Kevlar. The result was the nanosphere, which gave rise to better armor and better bulletproof glass, lightweight munitions, riot shields, unbelievably robust reading glasses (before the Terran Federation made corrective surgery a universal right in the twenty-fourth century), and improved prosthetics. Even modern-day armorplaste, the material used in shuttle and LAC cockpits and the visors of military-grade mechsuits, derived from the incredibly small, incredibly strong self-organizing nanosphere.

Promise sealed her see-through slick armor and wrapped the utility belt around her waist, and then hung a thigh holster on each side, and cinched the straps tight. Two auto pistols disappeared, and then a handful of extra magazines went into the pouches on her belt. She pulled on an ablative vest for added protection. Near the bottom of the locker was her mother's GLOCK. Promise picked it up with care.

"What are you going to do with that?" Kathy said as she rushed into the brow of the barracks. The entrance had an exterior and interior door. Kathy came in so fast the inner door opened before the brow could scrub the pocket of air it had momentarily trapped. Suddenly the barracks smelled like burnt toast. "This isn't Montana, ma'am. That is not a real wep."

Promise shrugged. "It's my good-luck charm." She pushed it into the flap of her belt against her right kidney and gave Kathy a that-settles-that look.

"Uh-huh. Just don't pull it. You'll just get yourself killed. Or me." Kathy scraped the bottoms of her boots on the entrance rug, leaving two white streaks on the mat. She pulled out a ration bar and gnawed off a hunk as she advanced toward her locker.

"Let me guess. You were at the chow hall."

"First order of survival," Kathy replied after swallowing. "Why'd you interrupt me? I had a hot plate and a corner table calling my name. Real eggs and fresh bread. And fresh berries, ma'am. *Berries.* Now all I've got is this."

"Too bad. Get your gear. Here, I'm afraid you're going to need this." Promise tossed a roll of slick armor over her shoulder. "We leave in—" She looked down at the chrono on her wrist. "—ten mikes and we need to make a stop first."

Promise swung by the weapons rack and grabbed a pulse rifle, slung it over her back, and removed a rebreather from the set of hooks above it.

"Coming?"

Kathy took in Promise's appearance. Her eyes darted from the vest to the thigh holsters and the pulse rifle, and then she looked down at the roll of armor in her hand. "We're leaving our mechsuits behind, aren't we? You actually buy this crap?"

"Yes." Promise nodded as she donned her rebreather. "And, no, at least not all of it. Hurry up. Chrono's ticking and I don't want to make the colonel any angrier than he already is."

"I'll have to leave my baby behind," Kathy complained. She puckered her lips and dug in her heels, and looked ready to disobey orders.

"You'll survive."

"You've got that right. One mike, please." Kathy put her NBA on under protest, kicked open the locker, and gutted up. One by one she laid five weapons on the bench beside the locker. Two pulse pistols and two conventional semi-autos, and a backup for her ankle holster. She pulled out her vest and put it on, and holstered the e-weps in cross-draw positions on the vest. The c-weps slid into her thigh holsters. Promise counted five pistols, and Kathy wasn't done. She slammed the lid on the locker and grabbed a grenade launcher from the door. The sling of rounds went over her head and arm and across her chest.

"What?" Kathy said. "You said to leave my armor for this. That doesn't mean I can't be armed."

Promise tossed Kathy a rebreather. "The colonel is going to pitch a fit."

The outer door parted and Promise and Kathy jogged outside into the snowy ash.

Fifty-four

"Lieutenant, what are we doing in here?"

Kathy and Promise were standing in the middle of a temporary ware-house. The walls were honeycombed like their transient barracks and the sound of machinery and the smell of industrial chemicals filled the air.

"Welcome to Charlie Battalion's short-term morgue."

"You sound chipper," Kathy said. "Why?"

"Few sights rival a row of pristine battle armor. Take a look at that." Promise pointed at the back wall, inhaled deeply, and sighed.

"Right. All I see are a bunch of virgin mechsuits."

"Exactly."

Two platoons' worth of undamaged, unclaimed suits of armor stood at attention against the rear wall. They were the battalion's reserves, and Prom-ise drank them in like a cup of gourmet caf gutted up right.

Kathy wrinkled her nose. "Smells like a motor pool to me. Oh, wait, it is a motor pool and we're deploying without our armor. Life's not fair."

If Promise had had thirty mikes she could have uploaded Mr. Bond to the onboard computer and calibrated a spare suit to her biometrics. There simply wasn't time, and she was sure the mechsuit would have been a deal-breaker with the colonel. *Good thing I'm going into battle without my armor, or I wouldn't be going at all.* Promise laughed out loud, and quickly covered her mouth. Kathy looked at her with growing alarm. Promise waved her concern away. "I'm just thinking how weird it is be deploying in skin. When's the last time we did that?"

"Um, never," Kathy said. "We're mechanized Marines."

Promise took a moment more to covet the armor. The wall of articulated plating glinted in the overhead light. From head to toe, she saw beautifully untarnished, undamaged virgin peristeel.

"Chrono's ticking," Kathy said. Her tongue started clicking like an antique wall clock. "We need to go. Colonel Halvorsen is waiting and that is not a good thing. *Capisce?*"

"Have patience, Kathy. Indulge me."

The sight of all that throw weight brought Promise's blood to a simmer, and few things could do that. There'd been a tall Montanan who'd come close and failed, only because Promise had run back to the Corps instead of into his arms. Mr. Jean-Wesley Partaine had been a man of steel with a heart of clay, and she'd let him go because her life was the Corps and his was Montana. At the moment, virgin armor was as good as it got.

"Personally, I've always found our armor a bit boring," Kathy said with a yawn. "It's sexy to drive, plain-jane to look at." Kathy picked up a boot and brushed the ash off the toe.

"Not plain. Untarnished. It's clean like armor should be."

"It's more fun when it's dirty."

After bashing heads, Promise thought. "Point taken."

Proper mechanized Marines didn't mark up their armor, or paint it loud colors, or stencil their significant other's name on the metaled butt cheek. In the history of the RAW-MC, no self-respecting toon or company or battalion of Republican Marines had deployed with war paint. If you modified anything it was the weapons mix, or the interior cushioning at the shoulders and hips, more plating here in trade for compartments, or an extra compartment there instead of armor, and you could always change your AI's voice to sound like your grandpappy or your daughter or a semi-autonomous witless mech. War paint was for the weekend warriors in the planetary militias, and delta-sierra mercenaries. Bright colors made for bright targets and you didn't paint shoot-me-heres on the hull of your ride home.

"Come on," Promise said reluctantly, walking through the semipermeable deflector shield meant to keep the ash out of the next room.

Victor Company's suits were in bay three, just through the first opening

of the main entrance. Promise and Kathy found their armor strung up in
the air. Their mechboots were about at face level and tendrils snaked from the
chest and arms, in and out of their cracked armor. Teams of servomechs
were busy scraping and washing Sheol's atmosphere out of every armored
plate.

"That's depressing," Kathy said as she gazed up at her suit. It was fouled
all over. Promise spotted three holes in the upper torso of Kathy's suit and
an ugly gash on the left shank where a missile had torn deep enough to expose the suit's internal structure. Had she not sealed the leg with smartmetal
Kathy probably would have lost it.

"I can see her bones. My poor baby." Kathy had tears in her eyes when
she turned to look at Promise. "So, mind filling me in on what we're doing?"
Kathy glanced at the chrono on her wrist. "We're about out of time."

"We don't need much. Grab your helmet, a collar, and a spare seabag."

"I thought we were leav—"

"We *are*. Our mechsuits aren't in shape for combat." An eyeless servo-
mech dropped from the overhead and beeped at Promise. It was tethered to
several cables and moved like an agitated cephalopod. "Get out of my face,"
Promise said. She slapped the metal octopus in the optic and it let out a
shrill beep and jetted into the overhead. Then she turned to Kathy. "I'm not
leaving without Mr. Bond."

Promise walked under her armor and found her helmet on a set of
shelves, cleaned and gleaming new against the far bulkhead. "Good, the
dent is gone." She opened a link to her helmet with her mastoid implant and
subvocalized her authorization.

Kathy's eyes grew wide. "You can't be serious."

"*Voice identification confirmed,*" said the standard flat-sounding AI
voice. "*Please don the helmet for retinal scan.*"

Promise spun the helmet round and quickly pulled it on, which was no
small feat without the rest of her armor. The helmet weighed almost nine
kilos, mostly because of all the armored plating over the interior shell of
battle foam. Unlike the rest of her armor, the helmet didn't have to flex or
bend around her muscles. It just had to rotate from side to side and pivot up
and down on its collar. The lack of mobility allowed the engineers to print
the helmet out of a core of foam overlaid with peristeel. Foam that could
stop at least one high-velocity penetrator if it got through the armor, or slow
it down to a survivable head wound. In theory. Promise saw Kathy through

her visor looking at her like she was out of her mind. She quickly circled her hands to tell the PFC to get with the program.

"Lieutenant, my sensors must be malfunctioning. What's happened to the rest of me?"

"Getting scrubbed." Promise looked toward the ceiling and caught her helmet as it started to roll backward, off of her head. Without the collar it wasn't seated properly and it weighed a ton. "See. We're going for a ride-along to rescue PFC Cervantes. Your body is staying put but you're coming with me."

"I haven't been briefed on the operation."

"I'm doing that now." Promise sighed, and pulled the helmet off to stuff it into her seabag. "You're to stay off comm and keep your mouth shut. But, monitor the battlenet through my implant." She felt Bond make the link. "Good. I expect the colonel will patch me in once we dust off. I want locations on our Marines and all known hostiles, and maps of the base as they update. And, I want a fix on PFC Cervantes. She's activated her homing beacon. When we land, find it."

"Lieutenant, I've just queried the company battlenet and I'm not authorized for this operation. You're listed as an observer only."

"That's right. Do we have a problem?" *I've never lied to my AI and I'm not about to start now.* Kathy pulled her helmet on. Her AI must have asked the same question, because Kathy's eyes went wide and she looked at Promise, arms spread in a what-now look.

"Technically, you're not deploying, at least not with your body. Kathy and I have no intention of disobeying our orders. *Unless we have to.* But we're not going in blind either. We need your ears and eyes to stay informed." Promise rapped the top of her helmet and sealed up the bag. "You are designed to function without your armor in emergency situations, which this is, and I'm about to enter a hot zone. I may need to wear you to defend myself. Understood?"

"I may need command authorization for this."

"You have mine . . . and Captain Yates's." *Okay, that was a stretch. But the captain did say to get my gear and Mr. Bond is an essential part of it. I need my AI.*

"Why didn't you say that in the first place?"

"Shut up, Bond."

"Shutting up, ma'am."

Promise gave Kathy a questioning look as she slung her bag over her shoulder. "We good?"

"Yup, Ms. Pie was listening in. Pie's booted and green-to-go." Kathy stuffed her helmet and with it her AI, Ms. Pie, into her bag and slung it behind her. "How are we going to explain the helmets to the colonel?" Kathy raised a brow. "Hm?"

"Grab some extra medkits from that shelf, and some rations too. You'll probably get hungry."

"Right . . . because you're just trying to be helpful." Kathy's snark failed to mask her worry. Promise nodded like she understood.

"Come to think of it, I am." Kathy grabbed a stimbar and tore off the wrapper, and offered a second one to Promise. "Just what do you plan on doing, ma'am?"

Promise stuck out a hand. *No thanks.*

"We're getting Jupiter back, no matter the cost."

Fifty-five

MAY 25TH, 92 A.E., STANDARD CALENDAR, 1919 HOURS
THE KORAZIM SYSTEM, PLANET SHEOL
COMBAT OUTPOST DANNY TRUE

The ash was barely falling as Promise and Kathy sprinted across the flight deck toward the waiting assault-class LAC. Lieutenant Colonel Halvorsen was suited up and standing at the top of the aft ramp, gauntlets on his hips. His coarse voice crackled over Promise's mastoid implant.

"Took you long enough, Lieutenant."

Promise was T minus ten seconds and didn't see the problem.

"What's with the gear?" Halvorsen was pointing at Kathy's seabag, which was bursting at the seams. Promise could see his eyes through his faceplate shift from her guardian's gear to her own.

Careful, P. Remember, a Marine never lies to her superior officer.

"Medkits, rations . . . because my guardian is a bottomless pit, small arms in case we have to defend the ship. Just the usual gear, sir." The colonel didn't need a line-by-line manifest of the bag's contents, right?

They reached the top of the ramp and the colonel still looked unconvinced. His brows nearly met as he scowled. Promise held her breath until the colonel turned around and tromped back into LAC. *"Take us up."* The ramp retracted as they hit the top and the blast door slammed down on their heels. They secured their gear in an overhead smartrack and strapped themselves into webbing. Promise tore her rebreather off and let it hang loose around her neck.

"See," Promise shouted to Kathy over the up-spin of the LAC's engines

and the chatter of Marines headed toward a hot zone. A few gave them puzzled looks before returning to their conversations. "Easy."

Kathy subvocalized through her mastoid implant. *"We're going to get
shot at . . . aren't we, ma'am."*

"Want a new lieutenant to shadow?" Promise crossed her arms, somewhat annoyed.

"Don't joke like that." Kathy smiled. *"After this op, I just might."*

Promise broke into a smile and held up a hand in apology. Kathy and
Promise started chuckling lightly. A moment later they were laughing full-
throat. A Marine next to Halvorsen motioned toward them. The colonel
leaned into view from midway up the compartment and raised an armored
finger to his faceplate. His voice boomed over his externals. "Shut it or I'll
toss both of your asses out the nearest drop ring."

"Sorry, sir. Inside joke," Kathy shouted back before she made the switch
and turned back to Promise. *"If we get shot at I get to shoot back, right?"*

"That goes without saying," Promise said.

Kathy leaned back in her webbing and closed her eyes. *"Good, I'm counting on it."*

Colonel Halvorsen's voice boomed through the LAC's compartments. "Seal
up. Lock and load. We reach the LZ in three mikes and—"

Concussions rocked the LAC's hull, interrupting the colonel's final instructions before landing. He could have spoken over the battlenet instead. He hadn't and only one explanation made sense. Her. He still hadn't
looped her in.

Colonel's got a soft spot, Promise thought. *Just not too soft.*

"Looks like a hot entry. Prep your armor for drop," the colonel added.

The pilot's voice filled the compartment a split second later. *"We're taking heavy flak. Prepare for emergency drop. I'll meet you at the rendezvous in
Sector Thirty-Four. Godspeed. Hell's teeth."* The cabin's interior lights cycled
to a low-light red as the LAC banked hard and pitched forward. Promise
heard the staccato burps of the LAC's forward minigun and the muffled
thrush thrush thrush of missiles bursting from their hard points along the
sides of the hull. She couldn't hear the point defenses striking down incoming birds with their diminutive beams, or the offensive energy mounts targeting the launchers on the ground. A Scourge-class assault LAC had both

in spades and she knew the air outside had just become a killing field. The craft shook off a direct hit and banked to the opposite side, and Promise's gut floated toward the overhead.

"Fun, right?" Kathy said as she bounced in her seat.

Promise bared her teeth as ordnance pounded the hull. Her hand reached into her pocket and retrieved her tube of lips. *Never leave home without it.* As the LAC bounced and ordnance peppered the hull, she stroked the cool metal tube, and focused on its smooth hard surface, on the cap that popped on and off. The explosions seemed to fade and she found herself thinking of Sephora. She wondered what the girl was up to. Perhaps she and Great-Grans were in the general's kitchen baking cookies. Great-Grans didn't strike her as the baking type. Then again, Great-Grans didn't strike her as the type to do much besides bash skulls.

The LAC lurched violently and the webbing cut deep into Promise's shoulders. She winced and said a quick prayer. *Sir, cover them. And Jupiter, wherever she is. Help us get her out.*

Another lurch and Promise yelped in her seat.

"You're not afraid of a little flak, are you, ma'am?"

The Marine across from her and one seat down chuckled over his externals. His faceplate was down and his eyes were lit by his HUD, and they were smiling. Promise wanted to wipe the smug right off of his face.

"No, Staff Sergeant," Promise had scanned his armor for his rank and found the embossed Vs riding the staff sergeant's chestplate, three up top and one below. The Vs were obvious to a jane or jack who knew to look for them, providing she or he was up close. Otherwise they blended in with the armor to prevent the enemy from picking off senior noncoms or officers from sniper range. "But my shoulders are screaming at me."

"Gotta love the suck," the staff sergeant said.

"Ooh-rah," Promise replied.

Several helmets snapped toward her, veteran grins plastered on the faces inside. The whites of their teeth shone brightly in the lights of their HUDs. Then the staff sergeant slammed his fist on his thigh and cried out, "We love the suck, oh yes we do."

The rest of the compartment bellowed in response, "We love it like a RAW-MC screw."

Promise saw a much younger woman who looked scared to death on the opposite side of the LAC and one seat down, and gave her two thumbs up. The woman smiled weakly and closed her eyes. The LAC shuddered violently and the woman screamed in her helmet. Her externals were off so Promise couldn't hear her, but she felt for the young woman anyway. Probably her first hot drop. *She might not be blooded.* That brought back memories. Promise caught her attention when she opened her eyes, and mouthed, *It's going to be okay.*

"Drop in one mike. Toons to your assigned drop rings," the pilot said evenly. He might as well have been ordering his meal at chop for all the emotion that was in it. "Repeat, drop in one mike. Toons to your rings."

Pairs of metal rods descended from the overhead. They were as tall as a suited Marine, and comfortably spaced for grabs-and-holds. At the bottom of each pole was a large textured grip fit for a giant's hand, or a mechanized Marine's. Two platoons unstrapped from their webbing and took their places around the rings. Five by five they circled up and gripped their drop poles, five around the forward ring and five around the aft. Promise heard their maglocks bolt to the deck. They exchanged thumbs-up and fist pumps and Promise knew the platoon sergeants were giving last-minute instructions. "Look lively. Trust your training. Stay on me." That sort of thing. Promise wished she could join them. She couldn't help thinking how unfair it was that she wasn't dropping with them. It should have been her leading one of those toons. Her dropping in first to extract her Marine. Her rushing the danger because that's what a lieutenant of Marines did.

The toon nearest her came to attention in their armor, backs ramrod straight and boots locked tight, which told Promise they were on a final countdown. Ten seconds later the deck beneath their feet pulled away, the howling wind and sky was visible beneath them. Only a thin layer of magnetic armorplaste separated them from the torrent outside. Then the armorplaste vanished and they fell through the hull and disappeared. The ring sealed and the next toon rose to take its place until just two toons of Marines remained.

The young woman she'd encouraged only moments before got up to drop, and turned to face Promise. She still looked nervous but seemed to have it under control. The single flat stripe or "runway" of a PFC stood out slightly on her armor.

"Don't worry. We'll get some for you . . . and we *will* bring PFC Cervantes home."

Promise went to speak and couldn't. Her throat felt thick, her words dissolved in an incomprehensible mush. All she could do was nod and look away. The PFC joined her toon and the deck disappeared. Without warning, flak exploded directly below the ring, and fragments struck the armorplaste shield, which cracked through but held. The light of the explosion briefly lit the overhead of the LAC. The blast knocked the PFC out of the ring. Her arms swung widely as she careered backward, into the bulkhead webbing.

Promise unclipped and grabbed a hook from the overhead. She secured it to her utility belt and ran to the Marine's aid. The LAC shook and slammed her into the opposite bulkhead. She tried to roll into the wall to blunt the blow. Her shoulder still took the brunt of it and she felt something crunch. She quickly rotated the joint, and everything appeared to be working, though not without pain. She pushed off the bulkhead and stumbled across the aisle as the *pop pop pop* of flak buffeted the LAC. Her arm looped through webbing to secure her position. Then she drew her combat blade with her free hand and cut one strap, and then another.

"You're green-to-go, PFC," Promise yelled, and pounded the young woman's shoulder, twice.

"Copy that, ma'am. I owe you one."

"Drop a Grey and we're even."

"Roger that, ma'am. With pleasure."

Promise helped her sister to her feet and back into position, which immediately seemed like a stupid thing to do. She wasn't wearing her armor. One good bounce and Promise would have more than a bruised shoulder. They were so close that Promise could see the green flecks in the PFC's eyes. Promise lost her footing and the PFC grabbed her arm to steady her as the LAC jostled them about. The Marine opposite them, a much taller man with graying eyebrows, gave her a thumbs-up. Even in the low light, Promise was close enough to see the three inverted hash marks of a sergeant of Marines on his chest.

"Well done, ma'am," he said over his externals.

"Good hunting, Sergeant," Promise said in return.

The platoon sergeant waved her backward. "Strap in, ma'am. And thanks for Montana."

She nodded her thanks, and then moved toward her seat. She removed the hook from her utility belt and was turning to sit when the armorplaste disappeared and the sergeant, the PFC, and their toon plummeted through the hull and into the flak -torn sky. Promise lunged for the webbing, just managing to grab a strap with her right hand. Her left flailed widely as the opening tried to suck her out. Her fingers started to slip as her feet lifted off the deck.

"Kathy!"

She lost her grip as the drop ring closed, and banged her chin as she hit the deck and slid feet-first into the now-closed drop ring. Her hand had web burns, her chin had deck burns, her shoulder had web cuts and was bruised, and she was pretty sure she'd just cracked a rib. Other than that she was unharmed and the LAC hadn't even touched down. *Maybe it's a good thing I didn't drop today.* Kathy was at her side in moments, helping her strap in.

"I'm okay, Kathy. Really." Promise pushed her hands away. "Stop making a fuss."

Kathy pulled a stick from her vest and held it to Promise's chin. "Hold still. This is going to hurt."

The anesthetic gel lit her on fire, but it stanched the bleeding, and then congealed into a semipermeable barrier.

"There." Kathy produced a sheath and pulled the knife out halfway before seating it properly. "Here, you might need this too."

"What's this for?" Promise grabbed the hilt of the combat blade and spun it and the sheath in her hand without thinking.

"Yours got sucked out the drop ring. But I brought a spare. Never hurts to have a backup."

"Says the girl with all the weps."

"Knives have their place too." Kathy's head jerked sideways. "Hear that?"

"What?"

"The sky's gone quiet." The LAC started its descent and the pilot's voice rang through the compartment.

"I'm setting down. The colonel said to patch you in once they'd dropped. Stand by."

Figures, Promise thought. She heard landing jets fire and felt the craft brake hard as it swept in toward the LZ. The deck shook as the LAC's engines strained against gravity. Then they were on terra firma and the engines were spinning down.

"Come on up," said the pilot. *"I've got two jump seats and a nice view. You can follow the action while I use the head."*

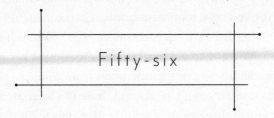

Fifty-six

Staff Sergeant Nia Tanner was bounding down a rocky corridor with her external lamps set to high beam. Flecks of crystallized minerals glinted in the walls and ceiling. So far Tanner had found a torn bag of rations and a half-dozen spent tins, all crushed except for one she found sitting upright with a piece of gum stuck to the side. She'd approached it carefully to make sure it wasn't rigged before kicking it down the corridor in disgust.

"Pigs," Tanner said as she slowed to single-time to avoid more trash.

Promise and Kathy were seated in the cockpit watching the operation from Staff Sergeant Tanner's point of view. The feed from the staff sergeant's HUD was projected on the cockpit's armorplaste. The image was snowy and Promise wondered how long the feed would last before they were down to audio only. Promise had stolen a moment to grab a hot cup of caf from the dispenser on the bulkhead just outside the cockpit before taking her seat in the pilot's chair. She adjusted the screen's resolution as best she could, leaned back, and drank deeply. An odd concoction of smells filled her nose and lungs: cinnamon spice and honey, fresh mech lubricant, and worn utilitarian Fleet Forces gray vinyl.

The cockpit's wraparound armorplaste had been grayed to block the view to the outside, and then split into three viewing panels. To Promise's left was a roster of India Company's eight toons of five, from the seniormost officer at the top to the most junior private on the bottom, and their icons were burning green. Promise spotted Halvorsen's toon and quickly found the icon of his guardian, PFC Aimee Chua. She reached up, tapped the panel, and dragged her finger up and to the left. A window opened, displaying the five points of the colonel's toon. She tapped Chua's icon and another window opened, giving her box seats to Chua's HUD. Without enlarging the window she wasn't going to get much detail. That was okay with Promise. She wanted a general sense of the operation from multiple points of view. She pulled up a staff sergeant's HUD and those of two more sergeants and piped all their voices through the cockpit's externals.

There wasn't much to hear. *"Corridor, clear. Proceeding right,"* and *"No sign of hostiles,"* and *"It's too quiet. Where is everyone?"*

Halvorsen's voice broke through the battlenet. *"Cut the chatter, stay off the net. Report up through your platoon leads."* The colonel added after a moment, *"Something's not right. Push your scanners' sensitivity to max. Proceed with caution."*

Colonel Halvorsen had brought a full company of forty boots. Upon landing, he'd deployed whiskers around the island's perimeter, and one had found a waterfall, and flown through it and discovered a craggy entrance on the other side. Staff Sergeant Tanner had entered there, nearly three mikes ago, with her toon, while a second stayed behind to guard the entrance and the trek back to the LAC.

To Promise's right was a map of the island, its beaches, and the front door Halvorsen had taken half of India Company through. I Company's captain was with him, while its lieutenant stayed on the beach, just in case. It wasn't so much a door as an old lava tube. Halvorsen had fallen through by accident and realized his good fortune shortly after hitting bottom. *"I meant to do that,"* he'd said after a string of expletives had assailed the battlenet. Of course the colonel had and no one was going to argue the point with him. Maybe later . . . over drinks . . . in a month or two when this was over and they could reminisce like punch-drunk Marines.

The map was expanding in real time as Tanner's and Halvorsen's columns scouted farther in; lines zigging this way and zagging that way, like a light pen on a datapad. Whiskers flew down corridors until they hit dead ends. Promise noted a handful that had stopped reporting altogether. There were more offshoots and chambers and passageways than probes and Marines to search them, and the ones they'd mapped seemed to meander without a pattern, except for one. Promise focused on a long blue streak running deep inside the dormant volcano. There at the tip. That was Tanner's toon, driving deep.

Promise's head snapped to the center panel at the sound of weapons fire. Tanner juked left, slammed into the rock wall, and fired at a small cannon mounted to the overhead. *"Fixed defense neutralized,"* Tanner said. A split second before the staff sergeant had fired, her HUD had dropped a circle around the cannon. A brief analysis appeared in a small window with a picture, the weapon's dimensions, and the type of ordnance fired. Promise let out a breath. Light penetrators posed no problem for a RAW-MC mechsuit. Then she noticed the height of the corridor, and her nerves kicked in. The passageway had been made by man. The cuts in the walls were clear evidence of that. The corridor wasn't wide enough for small vehicles to traverse, and the ceiling was at least three meters deck-to-overhead. Even the tallest Marines weren't that tall, which meant the Greys had cut this passageway for something else, and Promise could think of only one thing that something else could be.

"Staff Sergeant. Look lively. They got battle armor."

"Who is this?" Tanner snapped back over the battlenet.

"Lieutenant Promise Paen, Victor—"

"Lieutenant! Get off the comm," Halvorsen cut in.

"But, sir, the overhead, it's cut for—"

"Copy that. This isn't our first dance, Lieutenant. Now get off my net."

"Roger that, sir." Promise slumped in her chair and pressed her caf to her chin. She heard the burst-cough of a Triple-7 and leaned forward in her seat. Looked left and quickly confirmed the status of Halvorsen's boots. *All accounted for, all still green.* Her eyes bounced to PFC Chua's HUD and the HUDs belonging to the sergeants, and finally back to Staff Sergeant Tanner's. Tanner was nearing the end of a corridor that emptied into something huge. Massive, actually. *This could be it.* Promise started gnawing on her lip.

"Ma'am, you need to relax." Kathy was seated to Promise's right with a bowl of snacks in her lap. Unlike Promise, Kathy had reclined in her chair and propped her feet up on the copilot's panels. "The colonel's got this," Kathy added.

Deploy whiskers. You need eyes in the sky, Staff Sergeant. Promise winced when she bit into her cheek. *Why haven't you deployed your whiskers?* She was now on the edge of the pilot's seat.

Tanner reached the opening and took a knee at its mouth. Her left hand rose and made a fist, which signaled an all-stop for the boots behind her. Her right arm swept her field of fire with a tri-barrel pulse rifle. *"Jazz, give me a full-up scan of the chamber.*" Jazz was Tanner's AI, and it spoke a moment later in a voice as smooth as glass. *"Negative contacts, ma'am."*

Now do it again. Promise willed her thoughts to Tanner's ears. She inhaled and her eyes grew wide. *Tell your AI to do it again.*

"Whiskers are away," Tanner said as a tiny swarm of probes flew into the chamber, and mapped its length and width and height, and then split toward eight different exits.

"We've got tree branches everywhere," Tanner said, swearing under her breath.

"So unfair," Kathy said. Now she was squirming in the copilot's seat. The pilot was in the back using the head and the copilot was up top manning the primary turret. They'd offered their seats with their sympathies. Both warrant officers were on loan from the Navy and had told Promise and Kathy to help themselves to the caf and the view. Promise had taken the liberty of using the comm and the seat warmer too.

Promise held her breath as Tanner circled her hand and pointed forward, and then held up two fingers and pointed left, and then another two and right. Then the staff sergeant was on her feet and moving. Promise saw Marines spilling into either side of Tanner's peripheral vision. Tanner's beams went to high but didn't dent the darkness.

No, no, no . . . she didn't scan again. Promise was about to comm the staff sergeant and make it an order when she heard an audible click over the feed.

Tanner jerked to a stop. *"I've snagged something."* She looked down and flashed her lights on the ground, back and forth, and back and forth again. There. Midway through a third pass she caught sight of a thin strand of wire snagged on the instep of her right mechboot. *"Wire! Get ba—"*

The holotank erupted with light, and the link to Tanner disappeared. Promise threw her hands up without thinking, spilling hot caf all over her slick armor. She rose out of her seat, rapped her head on the panels overhead. Slammed back into the pilot's seat. "No, no, no." Her hands raced over the holopanel, shifting the screen to the next senior enlisted Marine. Promise's heart sank. She was looking through PFC Karol Makkes's HUD; two Marines were down and a third appeared to be limping. The darkness lit up with muzzle flashes and Makkes fell sideways. There was no sign of Staff Sergeant Tanner anywhere.

"Contact. Multiple signatures." The *wump wump wump* of launching

Horde missiles filled the cockpit, and Makkes's HUD momentarily whited out. A nearby explosion pelted her with debris and her HUD actually cracked. *"There's too many. I'm falling ba—"* Her voice cut out in midsentence as her icon turned crimson on Promise's display. Crimson like Staff Sergeant Tanner's entire platoon, which shifted from the center of the screen to the bottom of the roster with the mounting list of casualties.

The cockpit erupted with chatter. *"I'm hit"* and *"I can't see them . . . I can't see them"* and *"On your six, get down!"* An icon turned red from Third Platoon and then another from the Fifth. Two from the Second turned orange with critical damage. It took a moment for Promise to locate Second Platoon on the map.

Second Toon was guarding the exit, and they were all that stood between the volcano and the LAC. Promise's hand flew to the small panel on the arm of the pilot's chair. She pinged several nearby whiskers and slaved them to her controls. They immediately adjusted course and headed for the LAC's position. Promise split the center screen into three separate windows. Her eyes in the sky closed on the LAC and she saw lifeless fields of rock and large boulders and . . .

"There. See them?"

"Looks like unpowered armor." Kathy pulled her feet down and leaned toward the screen. "Wait a minute. What's that?"

Promise blinked in surprise. "It's a Clydesdale."

"A what?"

"Clydesdale Combat Suit," Promise said. "CCSes were the battle armor of the RAW-MC fifty years ago. They're big and clunky and about twice the mass of one of ours. They were melted down for scrap."

"That one isn't and it looks pissed. That thing's a monster."

Promise sent a whisker in for a closer look. The Clydesdale suit grew until it filled most of one of the center windows. It was big and black and splattered with war paint. Its name was stenciled on its massive chest. STOMP. The mercs by its side wore unpowered armor and barely came to its waist. Promise counted two Clydesdales and six mercs altogether. "Make that seven," Promise said. "There's another one." Through the cockpit door behind them they could hear the overhead turret swing around, its dual miniguns spinning up, and then the unmistakable scream of hundreds of hypervelocity penetrators per second flying downrange.

Kathy pushed out of her seat and ran toward the back of the LAC.

Promise turned around and hesitated as staccato fire broke out across the battlenet. She heard the colonel issuing orders. He'd reached the same chamber PFC Makkes had died in but from a different access way. More weapons fire, more explosions, then silence. The silence told Promise the hostiles either had been neutralized or had fallen back themselves. *"Clear"* and *"Clear"* and *"Clear,"* said three Marines she didn't recognize. A mass of icons including the colonel's had come to a stop at the mouth of the cavern. She breathed a sigh of relief as the mass shifted, and fanned out so as not to present such a large target. Then they were moving again. Fifth Platoon split left and down a previously mapped passageway while the rest stayed with the colonel. It took her a moment to realize where the Fifth was headed—back toward her, back to the LAC, back to deal with the mercs on the beach.

Promise muttered under her breath as she ran after Kathy. *I don't know how we're going to get out of this one.* Then she addressed Bond. "Get me the LAC's equipment manifest."

"I told you the helmets would come in handy," Promise said as she reached Kathy and her seabag. Kathy already had hers slung over her shoulder, and then she was headed for the forward hatch. "Got to get more throw weight," she yelled as she ran. Promise had her seabag on the deck plating and her collar and helmet out in record time. The collar was more a pair of shoulder pads with an articulating ring. The pads settled over her traps and the tops split open, and the ribs folded down to hug her upper back and chest. The pressure plates beneath them inflated and made the fit snug. Then she pulled her helmet on and rotated it. *Click.*

"Lock confirmed," said Bond. *"But not sealed."*

"Noted," Promise said. *Not sealed* meant she couldn't dive underwater without her helmet filling up, or deploy in a vacuum, and if the mercs used chemical weapons she was a goner.

Near the forward hatch was a rack of spare weapons designed to be fired in mech. The minigun was calling Promise's call sign but she knew she couldn't hope to hold the thing, let alone fire it without her armor, unless she got help, fast. Kathy was busy checking out a tri-barrel pulse rifle and grabbing extra cells. Without her mech's fusion plant to power the weapons, Kathy wouldn't get many shots out of it. And the weapon was nearly as long as her guardian was and weighed almost fifteen kilos, which was on the light side for a heavy weapon but still awfully heavy for a close-quarters fight. It was going to be a beast to lug around and fire, and it had a voracious appetite.

"It's got four spare cells, maybe five shots each. Tell me again why we left our armor?"

"Those things are designed for battle armor. It's going to vent a lot of heat. Watch yourself or you'll get burned."

"Do you have a better idea? Nothing else has a chance of taking down one of those monsters."

A list of gear began rolling across Promise's HUD. "I've got the LAC's equipment manifest . . . and an idea." Promise's eyes locked on a tier of data, second column over and third row down. She sent the file to Kathy's HUD. "Rack that wep and follow me." Kathy looked insubordinate and muttered something under her breath. They were running again, this time with Promise in the lead, through another bulkhead door and toward the rear of the craft. They passed beneath the overhead turret and Kathy had to cup her ears against the onslaught of blistering rapid fire. They ran past the engine room and into a small maintenance locker. A wall of shelving housed translucent bins of spare parts, all sealed and bolted down in case of turbulence or a loss of artificial gravity. On the opposite wall were two service bays, and each housed a yellow exosuit.

"You've got to be kidding me," Kathy said.

"We're improvising."

"They're not even half mechs. They're not even armored."

"They'll do."

"They're exosuits, Promise. Just metal bones and actuators. We won't last long in those things."

"Actually, exosuits are quite robust. They can absorb some damage. At least a little." Promise bit her lip. "Maybe. Stop worrying or you'll make me nervous."

"Just remember who's guarding your backside."

"Saddle up, Marine. You want to live forever?"

Promise approached the nearest exo and turned around. She double-checked her web vest and her pistols to make sure they wouldn't get caught or crushed by the exo and smirked as Kathy unstrapped both of her ankle holsters. You backed into an exosuit just like you did your armor, except it wasn't nearly as form-fitting and its performance left a lot to be desired. It was like a two-dimensional skeleton without a head. You had to bring that with you. There were ribs and metal bones for arms and legs and powered joints and a pair of metal boots that looked pretty good, all things considered. She slipped her feet in and frowned when nothing happened. Her armor always greeted her with a warm hug and moisture-wicking hospitality. *This* was nothing but a pile of junk. But it didn't come with a built-in head, fore and aft connections that rubbed you raw. She reached across with her right arm and pulled a small control panel from the bulkhead, which swung outward on a cantilever. "Let's see. . . . Mr. Bond, I'm in need of your expertise." She pulled up the exo's subroutines. "Can you link with this thing?"

"You know full well what my capabilities—"

"Shut up, Bond, and make the link. While you're at it, check the manual, see if Kathy can plug the tri-barrel into her exo's fusion plant. She'll need power to run it if we want to live long. If this thing has a governor, disable it. I mean to kill terrorists, not load cargo." She heard a muffled explosion from amidships, which shook the deck plating beneath her feet, and then the turret fell silent. "How long?"

"*Stand by.*"

Promise appraised the exosuit with impatient eyes. She was strapped into a powered skeleton, and the thickest bone couldn't be more than three centimeters at its thickest point. She doubted that was going to blunt a direct hit from a heavy pulse weapon, let alone protect her from missile fire. She jerked upright as the insides of the boots molded to her feet. *About time.* A bit tight but it would do. Her head snapped left as metal hoops closed on her arm like the rings on a casket of beer. She got a wicked pinch on her thigh as the loops closed on her legs, all the way down to her calves, and she was pretty sure the suit had just claimed its kilo of flesh. Finally she was in. The chestplates locked into place last, covering most of her torso. The gauntlets were hanging nearby. She pulled them on and flexed the fingers one by one. The touch felt pretty good. Promise tried to take a step and nothing happened.

"Why isn't this thing working?"

"*I'm still initializing, ma'am. You aren't authorized for the stevedore. I had to hack its net and upload your biometrics. Stand by.*"

The exosuit began to hum and Promise felt a strange sensation ripple through her torso and extremities.

Another explosion rocked the hull.

"There's no time. How long?"

"*Stand by.*"

"You already said that."

"Now, Lieutenant."

Promise was pushing against the exosuit's dead weight for all the good it was doing, because the exo was still tethered to the bay by clamps, so when the power kicked in and the clamps let loose her right leg leapt forward and she stumbled out of the bay, and nearly crashed into the opposite bulkhead. She pulled herself upright and turned around to face an amused Kathy Prichart.

"Ready yet?"

"Half mike, ma'am," Kathy said over her externals. *"I'll catch up."*

Promise dashed out of the maintenance room, up the length of the LAC toward the forward hatch. She reached for the minigun as the LAC took another hit. "Better test the feel first." It was a good thing she did, because the pulse rifle she tested on got crushed in her hand. "Right. Let's try this again." She switched hands and cracked the rifle's stock. "Hmmm." She tossed the broken weapon in the air and caught it like an egg. "Better."

Promise reached for the minigun and carefully wrapped the exo's hands around the barrels, slowly squeezed until she had a solid grip. She lifted and wrapped her trigger hand around the grip and stock, and tapped the trigger carefully. Promise strapped into the specially made ammo pack, activated the ammo feed, and toggled the safety to fire.

"Bond, patch me into the LAC's externals. I need to know where they are."

Her HUD split into two windows. The upper showed a 360-degree wrap-around, while the bottom displayed a shot of the port and starboard sides of the LAC, just forward of the engines, and a shot to the rear of the craft. A hostile in unpowered armor was placing something on the side of the LAC, at about where the starboard engine began. The armor was thick and blocky and made the wearer look like a high-tech gladiator. The rain slick Promise was wearing wasn't going to hold up long against armor like that, which said nothing of the Clydesdales out there. Promise clenched her jaw and keyed the forward hatch on the starboard side just as Kathy bounded into view.

"Lieutenant, wait one. I just need to grab a wep. I'll cover you."

"There's no time." The hatch flew open and Promise leapt through.

Fifty-seven

Promise rotated forward as she fell, and she didn't have the boosters or stabilizers to autocorrect that. A black blur broke her fall as she came down. She heard a sickening crunch over her externals, and a woman's voice let out a bloodcurdling scream. With the exosuit on Promise figured she probably weighed north of one hundred kilos. Getting to her feet, she checked on her victim. The woman's screams were now a drunken sort of moan and she was barely conscious. Part of her helmet was missing and an awful gash ran down the side of her face. Blood spurted from where her shoulder and hip had been only moments before. Had there been time Promise would have pressed a hypo to the woman's neck, and only then moved on.

"Three o'clock," Bond said. "Three contacts, fifty meters out, rounding the nose of the LAC, and they're moving toward us. The lead element is a Clydesdale."

Bless.

One last glance at the wounded mercenary and she was running toward the fight. She started counting. *One.* And that kill didn't really count in her book because she hadn't meant to kill her. Neither was she sorry for it. The Clydesdale wouldn't go down so easily.

Three red icons blipped on her heads-up display, moving in formation. Her HUD labeled them Echo-One, Echo-Two, and Echo-Three. Promise reached back and grabbed the stock of the pulse rifle that was slung to her back as the trio came into view. She tapped the panel situated forward of the trigger assembly and activated the rifle's self-destruct sequence, set the countdown for a seven-second count. Then she increased her speed and hurled the rifle with three seconds to spare. It slammed into the hostile to her left as it blew. One red icon disappeared from her HUD. Promise took a running leap just as the Clydesdale fired at her. Sailing through the air, she kicked the stevedore's boots out in front and realized the moment she did so that her trajectory was off. Instead of a solid hit she caught the merc across the jaw with her bootheel. The merc went down, which left the Clydesdale. She rolled into the crash to blunt the fall and came up running as fast as her exosuit would carry her toward a nearby boulder. The Clydesdale was slow to rotate. It got off a shot and her shoulder took the hit. Burning pain followed, but not enough to slow her or the shoulder down. She reached the boulder and came around its other side to more trouble. Instead of a right arm the Clydesdale had a massive cannon, and it was pointed at her.

That's three, she said. *And you're going to be four . . . as soon as I figure out how . . .*

"*You're target-locked, ma'am,*" barked her AI at the same moment her HUD registered the launch.

Promise spun to her backside and around the boulder as the shell shrieked past her and detonated in the background. She juked to the other side as the Clydesdale recalibrated and fired again. Then she was out in the open and moving laterally, angling in to close the distance. Back and forth in no discernible pattern while her minigun vomited hundreds of hypervelocity darts. The mini's barrels started glowing red-hot, but Promise didn't let up on the trigger until the Clydesdale's arm was ground down to a useless stub of metal. The Clydesdale took a step backward and raised its maimed limb. She charged the overgrown mechsuit as two shoulder-mounted missile pods spit out their payload at near-point-blank range. Promise was out in the open and on a berserker charge, so there was no way to dodge them all. Her minigun strafed the air, cutting down two missiles. More went wide and exploded in the dirt nearby. Two birds struck her in the chest and shoulder. The exo's feeble frame and Promise's suit of nanospheroidal body armor shrugged off the worst of the blows. Blistering heat seared her neck and chest as she flew through the air. She did her best to roll into the fall as her minigun broke away and spun end over end, far out of reach. She slammed into a smaller boulder and slid to the deck.

Her HUD was offline, her faceplate cracked, and all she could see was dirt. Her left arm was bent upward at an awkward angle against the boulder, and she couldn't move a muscle.

"The exo's offline. Can you reboot?"

Her AI didn't answer.

"Bond!"

Promise felt the earth shudder beneath her as the Clydesdale approached. A massive boot put down by her head, filling what vision she had.

"Lady, you've got the biggest pair in the 'verse. I'll give you that before you die."

Her HUD flickered, and then spun up. Her heart soared when she heard Bond speak. "I'm online, ma'am."

"I need power, now."

"Your fusion plant was damaged in the fall," her AI said. "Switching to reserves. They won't last long."

Promise pushed against the boulder and rolled onto her back as the Clydesdale's knee came up. The earth shattered where she had been just a moment ago. The Clydesdale stomped again. Promise barely got both gauntlets under the massive boot, and stopped it short of crushing her chest.

"You're only delaying the inevitable. I'm bigger than you, stronger than you, and—"

"It doesn't matter," Promise said over her externals. There, on her HUD, Lance Corporal Kathy Prichart was approaching fast. A burst of energy struck the Clydesdale, but its armor held. The Clydesdale stepped back and turned to face the new threat, which gave Promise time to get to her feet. She watched Kathy berserker-charge, firing a tri-barrel in one hand and a carbine in the other. The Clydesdale staggered under the weight of fire, and almost tripped over Promise as it backed up. Still it didn't go down, and then it fired another salvo of missiles at Kathy. Kathy seemed to anticipate them and juked right, and then she stroked the trigger of her tri-barrel, which tore through the Clydesdale's knee. One of the Clydesdale's missiles caught her in the shoulder and took the arm off at the elbow, and the tri-barrel with it. Kathy and the Clydesdale both went down.

Promise was on her feet again, and it was now or never. She crashed into the back of the armored brute. The helmet was so large it was all she could do to loop her arms around the visor. She just managed to hook her fingers together, and squeezed with all the energy the exosuit could spare.

"Three percent power, ma'am."

"Divert every joule to the arms."

Promise feared it was too little too late. The driver's good hand came up and tried to swat her off, the torso rotating wildly as it got to its knees. She held fast, felt something give. Crack. She focused all her energy there.

"No, no, get off! I'm going to ki—" Metal whined and the driver screamed as the helmet bent inward. The blood went everywhere.

"Four."

Promise ran to Kathy's side as the exosuit's power reserves dropped below one percent. What was left of the chestplates opened and the bands on her arms withdrew. She pulled off the gauntlets and tossed them as she stepped out of the exo, and knelt by Kathy's side. Kathy's forearm was missing and the flesh above the elbow joint looked like shredded meat.

Kathy looked over at her arm in an obvious state of shock. "Uh-oh, P. That's not good. Definitely not." Kathy winced and arched her back in pain.

"Hold on, Kathy," Promise said. She tried to recall the little bit of first-aid training she'd received. She was used to working with her mechsuit's triage capabilities and her pharmocope. She didn't have either at the moment and she was north of rusty when it came to field medicine. *Access the scene. Is it safe?* Promise looked around. *Check. Am I safe?* She checked her HUD, and the nearest hostile—make that three—was on the other side of the LAC. *Safe enough. Check. Access the victim. Breathing? Check. Bleeding? Double check.* She had to stop the bleeding. Most of the exosuit's arm was missing. Jagged bone was visible and Kathy was lying in a pool of her own blood. Kathy's head lolled to the side and her eyes glazed over. Promise drew her fixed blade and staked it to the ground. She tore off her utility belt, grabbed the knife, and cut off a small swath, which she pushed between Kathy's teeth. "Kathy, you've got to bite this. This is going to hurt."

Kathy bit down on the fabric and turned her head.

Promise made an incision at one end of the belt and fed the other through it to create an improvised tourniquet. She slipped the tourniquet over the stump, just beneath the shoulder, audibly counted to three, and pulled. Kathy's back arched again as she screamed.

Several seconds later Kathy turned to her with unfocused eyes. "Am I going to make it, P?"

It could go either way, so Promise wasn't lying when she said, "Yes. I'm counting on it." She was simply betting on the best possible outcome. Life. Promise pulled a small pouch from a pocket on the arm of her beegees, and dumped the contents into Kathy's mouth. "Nano pills. Never leave home without them."

Nano pills were a cheap, efficient way to pump the body full of nanorobotic medics. They were a far cry from regen and a no-other-option corpsman's best friend. In the short run, the nanobots would help seal the wound while freeing the body to divert the bulk of its resources to red-cell production. They'd also minimize the risk of infection until Kathy received medical attention. The pills also included a powerful neuroinhibitor to keep Kathy comfortable, and a cocktail of synthetic hormones to rapidly increase the body's production of erythrocytes.

"*Three hostiles are approaching from the rear of the craft,*" Bond warned.

Promise looked up as another Clydesdale rounded the LAC and came into view.

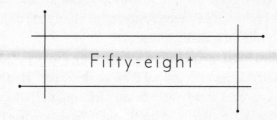

Fifty-eight

The Clydesdale didn't bother aiming at her as its massive boots closed the distance, and then it slowed to a walk and stopped. Promise's sidearms wouldn't begin to dent armor like that, and her fixed blade would break before it made so much as scratch against tempered peristeel. Promise stood and raised both hands to her helmet. She rotated the helmet and felt the collar give, and then pulled it over her head.

"Ma'am, I strongly advise against that," Bond said.

"Duly noted. It doesn't matter anymore. Keep your recorder on." Promise set the helmet down, visor toward her enemies, and let her hands fall to her sides. A man and a woman, each in unpowered armor, came up on either side of the Clydesdale, their weapons were trained on her.

"Now, now, the boss wants this one alive." The voice sounded digitized and carried the weight of command. *"If she moves, I'll kill her. Casmir, go and cuff her."*

Casmir's eyes never left Promise's as he lowered his rifle. He came around the Clydesdale, handed the weapon to his shorter colleague. The woman had a severe face and thin lips that were curled upward behind her visor. Casmir's face was unreadable behind his as he turned to face Promise. He was wearing either heavy polymer with peristeel-reinforced meshing—Promise guessed it was that by the looks of it—or, if the Greys hadn't had the chits for that, maybe a much thicker version of nanospheroidal body armor. Either way, it was more than adequate protection against what she had at her disposal. And Casmir was covered in it, head-to-toe. Except for his face, which was shielded by a visor. *That's armorplaste for sure.* She caught a glimpse of the hollow of his neck between his chestplate and helmet. His Achilles' heel. Promise actually smiled.

Casmir pulled his sidearm before approaching Promise. "Ma'am, I don't want any trouble. Cooperate and we'll make this easy." He stopped about four meters away, eyes steady as a beam and singularly focused on her. There was a sense of familiarity in them, and if Promise wasn't mistaken he looked a bit uncomfortable. "Pull your sidearms. Toss them over there." He gestured with the barrel of his pulse pistol.

Promise kept eye contact as she wrapped her hand around the grip of her left sidearm. Pulled slowly. Casmir had said "ma'am," and he was being all professional. No bawdy humor. Zero threats. *Interesting.* She drew and tossed the pistol underhanded, and then cocked her head. "How am I doing? You're former military, aren't you?" Her weapon landed well out of reach, and cartwheeled twice before coming to rest on its side.

Casmir's mouth tightened. "Now the other one." His eyes bounced to the remaining semi-auto on her hip, which she drew and tossed too. "Good, now turn around with your hands clasped behind your head."

Promise stayed put. "How long were you in for?"

"Turn *around.*"

Good. She'd gotten to him if only a little bit, caught him off-guard, and the more distracted he was the easier killing him was going to be. Promise put her back to Casmir and saw her mother's GLOCK lying next to Kathy's good side.

"You don't have to do this," Promise said over her shoulder. It was a low blow aimed at whatever modicum of honor the mercenary still had left.

"Shut up . . . and do what you're told."

"*Casmir, chrono's ticking. Move it!*" said the disembodied voice driving the Clydesdale .

Promise heard Casmir's boots disturb the rocky soil as he approached.

Her GLOCK had been tucked into the flap against the small of her back, and it must have fallen out in her rush to help Kathy. Kathy had pushed herself up to a seated position against a nearby rock, and her color had largely returned. The arm was still oozing but now a translucent sheen covered the bone and exposed tissues. That was the nanobots at work. Kathy's eyes were focused too. Another few minutes and the nanobots would have the wound completely sealed. Promise's eyes bounced from the GLOCK to Kathy's face, and then back to the GLOCK. Her eyes went wide, filled with understanding. Kathy's right hand crawled to the pistol and covered it, and she slowly pulled it to her side, tucking it between her leg and the ground. Promise mouthed the words *On three.* Kathy nodded.

Her weight rocked to the balls of both feet. Promise mouthed the word *Two.*

Now Casmir's hand was on Promise's wrist.

One.

She spun around and knifed Casmir's throat with a spear hand, hitting him in the Adam's apple. Casmir coughed and raised his hands to protect his throat. It was a reflexive move, and Promise seized it, and brought her hand up and wrapped it around Casmir's weapon. Her trigger finger covered his as she guided the barrel up and under the visor of Casmir's helmet. Squeezed the trigger. The angle of the blast was a bit high. Casmir's eyes rolled backward in his head as he fell limp in her arms.

The woman in unpowered armor snapped her rifle up and returned fire. She didn't have a clear shot at Promise and ended up hitting Casmir in the back instead. Then Promise heard her GLOCK's report shatter the air, six shots in all before she got off her own. The woman staggered backward. Promise heard the thunderclap of rounds seven and eight. Promise brought Casmir's pulse pistol up and double-tapped the trigger, her sights on the woman's visor. Scored direct hits. One more and she'd be through. Kathy's ninth round hit the woman in the throat, just above the chestplate and below the protective strap on her chin, and plowed through the hollow of her neck. The woman staggered backward, dropping her rifle as her hands went to her throat. Promise dumped Casmir's body and was running toward the Clydesdale before the female mercenary hit the ground.

Promise went for the discarded pulse rifle. It was her only chance of taking the Clydesdale down. Whoever was driving that thing was slow on the take. Promise closed the distance, firing at the Clydesdale's helmet with Casmir's pulse pistol, which was like throwing stones at a giant. She faked left. The Clydesdale spread its arms wide, to cover either side, which left its front temporarily unguarded. She got off three more shots before she was almost on top of the armored beast, and then she dove to the left and rolled underneath its massive arm. Her hand shot out and wrapped around the cool stock of the rifle. As she came up she pivoted on her feet and brought the weapon to bear, and aimed at the Clydesdale's neck, at the weak point. The collar. A split second more and she would have gotten off the shot. The Clydesdale's arm swung back and sent her flying through the air. The landing knocked the wind out of her lungs. Her head hit hard and her vision burst with rainbow colors. The last thing she remembered was ash and clouds and what might have been the outline of a Republican LAC and numerous silhouettes dropping from its belly. Then the blackness consumed her.

Fifty-nine

MAY 26TH, 92 A.E., STANDARD CALENDAR, 1312 HOURS
RNS *NITRO*, PLANET SHEOL, GEOSYNCHRONOUS ORBIT, DAYSIDE

Promise woke in the low light of the medbay of RNS *Nitro* to a rhythmic *beep beep beep* by her head. The intake above her howled as it drew up the air. She heard slippered feet shuffling across the deck. A voice spoke. She couldn't tell if the words were meant for her, and they were garbled. Then clearer. Then, "Better get Captain Yates." Promise opened her eyes to a blurred face and a penlight. "Sorry, Lieutenant. Hm. Not bad . . . all things considered. Try not to sit up, okay?" The faint inhale/exhale of a breathing machine hummed in the background. Promise tried to sit up anyway. Her side screamed immediately and told her it was best not to. Then she remembered why it hurt.

A suit of Clydesdale armor had tried to stomp her to death. She saw the metal boot mere centimeters from her skull, and the aggressive tread that had almost ground her into paste. She remembered thinking, *This is it.* The merc had pulled back when Kathy charged. Then Kathy was on the ground bleeding, her arm torn off, and Promise was at her side administering first aid. Her exosuit had lost power and they'd been surrounded. Another suit of Clydesdale armor towered over her. After that the details got fuzzy. She probed her side and inhaled sharply. *But I'm still here. Guess that means someone else got him. Kathy?* Promise's head snapped up, her heart in her throat. The room started to swim and bile filled her mouth. There, to her right in the next bay over, was a sleeping Lance Corporal Kathy Prichart. Promise breathed a sigh of relief. Kathy's left arm was a bandaged stump and her face was badly cut. Otherwise she looked okay. Promise took a deep breath before letting her head fall back into the pillow.

The *beep beep beep* didn't let up. "Can someone please shut that *off*?" She rolled to the side to investigate. Dared to open her eyes. A flat-screen monitor showed the outline of her body and there were an inordinate number of orange highlights from her cracked head to her broken toe. *A lot of damage. Here we go again,* Promise thought. She tried wiggling her foot. The screen indicated major damage. Strange that it didn't hurt at all. That was something.

She had a skull fracture, on the right side this time to match the one she sustained on the left side during her battles on Montana. *Which explains why my head is pounding, again. Okay . . . that's serious . . . my last one wasn't too bad and my brain recovered just fine. I'll live.*

Her leg had taken damage; the kneecap had split in two. *My leg's been hurt worse than that. That's what quickheal is for. What else?*

She had broken ribs. *Tell me something I don't know,* Promise thought as she probed her side. They were wrapped tightly and she didn't feel much like breathing, and the *beep beep beep* was still harassing her.

"Please, shut that off before I get up and do it myself." She heard movement, and then silence.

She had a lacerated kidney. *Fine, I'll piss red until I don't.*

Her left wrist was broken in three spots and she was missing her . . . "You've got to be kidding me," Promise said aloud. She raised her right hand and saw double for a moment. Saw the bandage and more fingers than she actually had on one hand. When it all came into focus she felt like punching someone in the jaw. Her middle finger was MIA, nothing but a stub, and her brain was telling her it was still there. She even swore she could feel it bend around a phantom trigger, but where flesh and bone had been before she'd fallen unconscious there was only recycled air now. *If the driver of the Clydesdale isn't dead already I'm going to kill him myself.*

"Just noticed that, huh." Captain Yates drew up beside Promise's bed. "Promise, you are one crazy jane and a glutton for punishment." Yates turned toward the monitor and pursed her lips. "How are you feeling?"

"Fine," Promise said. "Well, I'll *be* fine." She didn't know how to take the crazy jane comment. *What is that supposed to mean?* The captain couldn't possibly know she heard voices in her head, or that she talked to her dead mother on a semiregular basis. *Could she?* Promise wondered. Then Yates's stern façade cracked.

"Lighten up, Lieutenant. That was a joke. Maybe the doc needs to do another scan of your jelly."

Promise forced a smile. "I'm just glad to be alive."

"You and the lance corporal probably saved the pilot and copilot's life by going out there in exosuits. Probably saved the LAC too. You did good work on Kathy's arm. Otherwise, she would have bled out." Yates's eyes grew as wide as saucers. "I can't believe you actually fought a couple of Clydesdales in exosuits. *Exosuits.* God knows what might have happened if those metal behemoths had intercepted Second Platoon after the colonel ordered them to secure the LAC. Something tells me they wouldn't have fared nearly as well as you did. Why is that?"

"Ma'am?"

"Some Marines have a knack for the improbable." Yates pulled up a chair and sat down. "When I heard you'd fought in an exo I shook my head. 'Sounds like Lieutenant Paen' is what I actually said. Then I replayed what happened. I watched the vids. The LAC's pickups captured most of the exchange, and your helmet got a decent shot of it too." Yates gave her a skewed look. "At one point, you were shooting with your off hand. Did you realize that?"

"About the helmet, ma'am. I was just—"

"Violating orders. I know. You were told to leave your armor behind."

"Technically, I did. Ma'am."

"Promise, I've already endorsed your actions. So has the colonel, by the way. Where'd you learn to shoot like that?"

"I'm sorry, ma'am. Come again?"

"Really, Lieutenant. The fake modesty is getting old. When you took the merc's pulse pistol from him, um, after you shot him with it, it was in your left hand. Then you fired at his partner with your off hand and as near as I can tell from the vid you didn't have time to aim."

"Ah . . ."

Yates cocked her head. "That was a compliment. I've tried to improve my off hand for years. I qualify with my left . . . barely. That was some nice shooting, Lieutenant. Not as nice as the lance corporal's. Prichart used your senior to hit the one chink in the woman's armor."

"Ah . . ."

"A 'Thank you, ma'am' will do. Do you always carry your senior into battle?"

"Right. Ah . . ."

"You're impossible. You know that?" Yates sat back and crossed her arms. "I've nominated you and Kathy for the Silver Star. I was filling out the screenwork for the Medal of Honor, for *you*, but the colonel reminded me that you are persona non grata with some powerful people in the Congress. We don't want to paint too large a bull's-eye on your back. I told the colonel you'd already taken care of that. Still, he has a point. Sorry." Yates's eyes were seas of emotion. Equal parts humor and mist. Yates turned away and cleared her throat.

"Ma'am, I already have a Silver Star," Promise said.

Yates nearly choked on her words. "I know. You've accumulated quite the collection of glittery."

"I didn't mean it that way, ma'am."

"Promise, I know what you meant. At least I think I do." Yates took a hard look at her, like she was making up her mind or searching for something. She laid a hand on Promise's shoulder and squeezed before pulling back. "Sometimes you try too hard, Lieutenant. You need to learn to relax." Yates looked across the medbay. Promise followed her eyes to the bed at the far end of the compartment. She had to sit up a bit to see who was in it. Jupiter.

"How is she?"

"That's complicated," Yates said.

"What happened?"

Jupiter was intubated, and her head was heavily bandaged. Her arms were tied down too. Private Atumbi was sitting at her side, and both of his hands were wrapped around one of hers. Promise looked back at the captain and saw the rage in her eyes.

Yates took a deep breath, leaned forward, and gripped the side of the bed with both hands, her eyes on Jupiter. "They got away . . . at least Greystone did." Yates's words were barely above a whisper. "We lost Jupiter's armor too. The Greys had a jump-capable LAC. One of ours was pursuing when the bastards jumped out at four thousand meters elevation."

Shock registered on Promise's face. You just didn't do *that*. The calculations to enter jump-safe space were complicated enough. Throwing a planet's gravity well into the mix, and the local atmospheric conditions, and the unexpected jolt of turbulence—any one of the three could throw your calculations off by a wide margin and dump you in a part of the 'verse you didn't want to be in. Like the center of a star. "Greystone is a madman. The jump created a massive shock wave. Our LAC lost its countergravity matrix and barely made it down. If there'd been a city below . . ."

"Before I blacked out, I swore I saw a LAC coming down."

"That was Captain Spears and Golf Company. It's their LAC that crash-landed when the Greys jumped out. Captain Spears's Marines reached you just in time. He took down the Clydesdale himself and he personally put a beam through the driver's head when the merc refused to surrender. Spears worked the Clydesdale over with his mechboot. You'd have thought it was personal the way he went off on that thing.

"Spears commed me from the surface to check on you. He said to tell Lieutenant Paen he'd put his new leg to good use and that you'd understand." Yates cocked a brow.

Promise tried not to laugh because her side hurt so badly. "Captain Spears lost a leg on Montana, back when he was a lieutenant." Promise nodded and smiled. "He got regen, and rehab, and I got field-promoted and put in charge of his company."

"Ah, and Lieutenant Paen was born. So I have him to thank for all the trouble you've caused me."

"Something like that," Promise said. "What about Golf Company?"

"Thankfully, Golf Company came through with zero casualties. Some bruises and broken bones but nothing that won't mend. G Company is on the surface now, guarding Combat Outpost Danny True. Sometimes it doesn't pay to be a mechanized Marine."

"What about Jupiter?" Promise asked.

"They . . . hurt her, Promise, deeper than a bullet ever could." Yates swallowed and looked away. "They . . . she killed her attacker and triggered her homing beacon. We found her unconscious. Half naked after . . . She'd lost an eye and the nerves on half of her face were gone. Last night she came to, and she wouldn't stop screaming. She pulled the line from her arm, and tried to gouge out her good eye. Atumbi has been at her side nonstop. He's read to her and wiped her brow and told her it's going to be okay. She was awake this morning, briefly, but she's heavily drugged. He's a good jack."

The full implications of what Jupiter went through hit Promise like a maglev.

Yates looked away. "Jupiter was my guardian, Promise. She was *my* protector and look where it got her." Yates closed her eyes and shuddered. "She's headed home, to Hold, tomorrow. So are you and Kathy. So am I. We all are."

"Hold? Ma'am, I don't understand. We just got here."

"And now we're leaving on the *Nitro*. She jumps out in the morning." Yates's voice turned flat, lifeless. "You're missing one finger and most of a second, on your dominant hand—your trigger finger—and you've got broken bones and substantial organ damage, and your second traumatic brain injury of your career. Most of your injuries will heal in a matter of weeks, but you're still looking at multiple regen treatments and therapy for the hand, and that's at least a couple of months. Kathy's in for twice as long for the arm because she doesn't regen, and I'm probably being conservative. And Jupiter. Well, only time will tell."

I can still shoot with my left. It probably doesn't matter now. "What about Victor Company?"

"Victor Company is down to half strength. Again. A year ago it was nearly decimated on Montana when you went to the mat with the Lusies."

"Ma'am, we were up against—"

"Now hold on, Lieutenant. I'm not criticizing your actions. Keep your mouth shut and hear me out."

Promise hated when she wore her emotions on her sleeve. She could lock them down in combat easy. That was no problem. Or push them aside when they'd taken casualties and the explosions and shell shock were overwhelming, and her Marines needed her to tell them what to do. Put her under the microscope and she lost all perspective, and wore her feelings like a festered wound, raw and oozing for all to see. Victor Company had been through a lot, and much of that was on her shoulders, and it always would be. Her orders had sent Marines to die. And not just any Marines either. Hers. They'd followed her orders because they'd trusted her to get them in and then get them out. Every death felt like a failure on her part. She didn't need to be reminded about it by her superiors. Promise knew that wasn't Yates's point at all. *It sure feels like it is.* The unit had pulled through before, buried its dead, welcomed new boots, and reorganized. Victor Company had done its best on Sheol when a knife in the back had nearly done it in. Promise was proud of her boots. She'd asked as much of them as any commander could hope for.

"For now, the company is returning to Hold." Yates met Promise's eyes directly. "This time the unit's losses are on me. I'm responsible for what happened on Sheol. This was not your fault." Yates's voice wavered. "It's mandatory counseling for everyone and extended special passes. Our people need to see their loved ones and find some sense of normalcy. Beyond that, we'll see."

"Captain, there's more, isn't there. What aren't you telling me?"

Yates met her gaze evenly. "I wasn't going to say *anything*. It's the colonel's job and I was glad to leave him to it. Look," she said, opening her hands. "The company is a mess. Too much trauma does something to a unit. Jupiter tried to kill herself when she came to. Yesterday, Corporal Youseff from Third Platoon hanged himself in the head. Maxi found him just in time, and cut him down before it was too late. That young man suffered brain damage and he may not recover. Do you know why he did it? PFC Bohmbair was his best friend."

And Bohmbair died on my watch.

"Marines from the other companies in the battalion are talking about us like we have a death wish. Some of the religious types think we've been cursed. Like the snake on our unit patch. Maybe they're right. I don't know anymore. The colonel believes the company should be disbanded, at least for now. The final decision isn't up to him, but if I'd had to guess, it's probably going to happen. What else can we really expect?"

"I expect to do my duty, ma'am. It's just talk and superstition and it's all nonsense."

"Not if people believe it, it isn't. The wounds are real. Promise, the Pythons have run their last op. You're to be reassigned. All of us are. The colonel already made some transfers to shore up the holes in his remaining units. Most are staying behind, on Sheol. Lance Corporal Van Peek went to Golf Company under Captain Spears. Fourth Toon needed a new heavy-weapons expert. Atumbi went with him and you'll be happy to know he just made PFC, too. Sergeant Margolease is the new platoon sergeant in India Company, Third Toon. The gunny is headed back to Hold to teach at the School of Infantry. For now, it's back to Hold with you and Kathy too, for rehab. You'll both be reassigned to a new unit at a later date, once you're off the wounded list."

"Ma'am, what about you?"

"I'm headed back to Hold to assume command of Lima Company, Charlie Battalion." Promise nodded. That meant the captain wasn't going too far from home and that she'd be back. "I asked to take you with me, but was told no. You won't be cleared for duty in time. My new lieutenant is already working up my Marines back on Hold. I'll be there for a month and then it's back to Sheol to bring the battalion up to full strength."

"Thank you, ma'am," Promise said. "Your faith in me means a great deal."

"We haven't worked together long, and we've had our differences. But I've come to respect you, Promise. I still believe you're brash and ill-tempered. Inspite of that, there's no one I'd rather have covering my six in a firefight. Just remember to hold your tongue and don't say everything that comes to mind. Okay? Do that and you'll be fine."

"What about Maxi?"

"Sergeant Sindri stays with me. He will command Lima Company's Fourth Platoon. I need a veteran like him to keep watch over all the unblooded cubs I'll be inheriting. Lima is going to be as green as they come; probably greener than the Pythons were before we deployed to Sheol."

Yates looked at her chrono and yawned. "I need to get some rack time." She stood and arched her back, and looked over her shoulder. "So do you. First you have some visitors. I hope you don't mind."

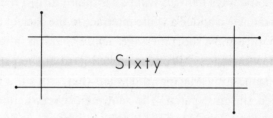

Sixty

MAY 26TH, 92 A.E., STANDARD CALENDAR, 1322 HOURS
RNS *NITRO*, PLANET SHEOL, GEOSYNCHRONOUS ORBIT, DAYSIDE

Suddenly Promise's bed was surrounded by a wall of Marines dressed in beegees and somber expressions.

Race Atumbi held out his hand first. He was wearing the single gold flat stripe or runway of a newly minted private first class, set against khaki flash, on both shoulders of his beegees. His unit patch was noticeably absent. She supposed that made sense with Atumbi's reassignment. The revelation still stung. Victor Company—aka the Pythons—had paid for their nickname in blood. Knowing the name wouldn't continue created a swirl of confusing emotions inside of Promise, and she had no idea how she was going to sort through them. *Guess I'll have time for that later while I convalesce. Right now I've got a promotion to celebrate.* Promise was happy for Atumbi. Sheol was his first deployment and he'd already been through so much death and destruction. Promise saw confidence rising up in the young man, and something told her he'd forever shed the nickname "Trip." She could tell by the way he held his shoulders back and how he held his head high; those attributes hadn't been there before. Maxi cleared his throat and nodded toward Atumbi's outstretched hand.

"Ma'am, it's been an honor." Atumbi hesitated when he realized he'd just tried to shake the lieutenant's bum wing. He quickly stuck out his left.

"Congratulations, Private First Class. You deserve it."

Atumbi beamed and cleared his throat. "This is for you, Lieutenant." He pulled something from the pouch on his utility belt. It was his missing unit patch, the python coiled around a warship, constricting it to death. Promise's eyes started to mist up against all of her objections. "I wasn't a Python for long, ma'am, but in some ways I always will be." Promise turned the patch over as her vision blurred. He'd added a white interface to the back of the patch, and added his signature and a short message: *Semper paratus*, always faithful.

"Thank you, Race. I . . ." Promise looked hard at the patch and swallowed. It was something Marines did when they sent off a beloved commander. Signed the unit patch. The sentiment overwhelmed her. She'd lost Victor Company—she'd lost the Pythons—when Captain Yates was put in charge. The patch should have gone to the captain, not to Promise. Her hand closed around the patch, knowing she didn't really deserve it.

"It's okay, Promise," Yates said from the corner of the room. Promise hadn't realized the captain had stayed. "They asked me if it was okay. This entire situation has been, well, it's been less than optimal, and the Pythons never really were mine to begin with. What happened to you wasn't right. The way they took the company from you—I see that now." Yates looked a bit flushed. "*Your* Marines, well, they followed me but they admired you. Here, I signed mine too. After all, the Pythons were yours first."

One by one, they each said good-bye. Lance Corporal Van Peek mock-punched Promise in the arm before handing her his patch.

"Thanks, Nate."

Sergeant Jesus Margolease hung back a bit and Promise had to urge him forward. "I feel like I'm intruding, ma'am. I was a last-minute replacement, you know."

"I'm glad you came to say good-bye. Good luck in I Company."

The gunny passed shots to toast the occasion. "Gunny, what is in this?" Promise said as she took hers in hand and ran it under her nose.

"An energy drink, I believe, with some restoratives and vitamins. You don't think the doc let me in here with the good stuff, do you?"

They all shared a good laugh over that, and the gunny added his patch to the growing pile. "Gunny Ramuel, Godspeed" was written in bold lettering on the back. Ramuel wrapped her hand in both of his massive paws. "I won't be too far away, Lieutenant. You need anything you comm me or just drop by, understood?"

"Yes, Gunny."

They chatted a few minutes more and then each Marine departed with a final handshake and a warm smile. Promise was nearly worn out by the time they left. And then there was just Maxi.

"Well, P, it's been a good run."

"Almost six years, right?" Promise said in a thick voice.

Maxi nodded and looked at the unit patch in his hand. He seemed reluctant to give it to her, and when he did his face became flushed. It said, "Sergeant Sindri, I was the lucky one."

"I didn't know what to write. . . ." Maxi looked down at his boots.

"You said it better than I ever could. I was the lucky one. We've been through a lot, Maxi. And you've been the best friend I could have hoped for." Promise grabbed a tissue by her bedside. "This isn't good-bye, okay? Just see you later. Take good care of Captain Yates. Comm me before you deploy with your new company."

"Will do, P. You get better and get back in a mechsuit, soon."

"Roger that," Promise said.

As Maxi walked out of the room a piece of her heart walked out with him. She heard stirring from the other side of the bed and turned over to see Kathy awake and staring at her with puffy eyes. Kathy yawned, gave her a puzzled look, and then glanced at the mound of unit patches on top of Promise's bedsheet.

"What'd I miss?" Kathy's stomach rumbled like one of Sheol's volcanoes. "What's for breakfast? I'm starving."

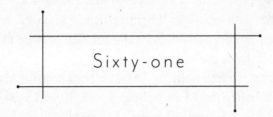

Sixty-one

Heavy rain pelted the windows of Neverfar Manor. The weather was unseasonably wet and humid, and dark-gray clouds had blunted the morning light. Promise gazed out the kitchen window of Lieutenant General Felicia Granby's country home as raindrops streaked down the checkered windowpane. It wasn't much of a way to pass the time, but she didn't have anything better to do, and she'd volunteered to man the oven until the timer beeped. Sephora and the general's husband, Roman, were playing a game of chance in the den. The general had opted for her morning paper by the bay window and a cup of hot tea. The weather didn't seem to be an issue for any of them. For Promise it was another reminder of everything that had gone wrong in the past two months. That, and she was bored out of her mind.

Promise yawned and checked the muffins, again. She pulled several mugs from the cabinet to her left and placed them on the waiting tray.

The past six weeks had been uneventful, which was putting the best possible spin on six of the longest weeks of Promise's military career. She was overrested and overfed (her sides had thickened noticeably). Rehab had gone according to plan but was still taking too long. Her new trigger finger still wouldn't follow orders. Her brain was issuing the right commands and her nerves were firing downrange and hitting targets, but the muscle memory wasn't there yet. Her doctor had told her to be patient with the finger, and he'd finally approved her return to light duty. A desk job and screenwork caught up with every officer eventually. She'd yet to be reassigned because she was still on the injured-service-members list. All that added up to a lot of "still"s. Promise was itching for action.

She'd commed Twelfth Regiment's senior personnel officer during the first week of her convalescence on Hold, before she was released to Joint Spaceport Mo Cavinaugh's Health and Wellness Center for physical therapy. At first getting through had been easy. "Lieutenant, I'll let you know as soon as you're reassigned." Then a week passed and then two. So she called again. "I'm sorry. I don't have anything for you yet. Please be patient." After that her calls went unreturned. She met the SPO's AI, named Charles. Charles was always polite and the SPO always busy. Eventually Charles stopped answering her comms.

"Charles, I know you're getting my messages. Call me back, please." How far she'd fallen to have to grovel at the feet of an AI. "I'm about to be cleared for duty. You *know* how to reach me." Promise began to wonder if she'd ever see the inside of a mechsuit again.

That's when she'd started calling daily. Then a vid had arrived from Lieutenant Colonel Halvorsen himself. His sit-tight-and-wait speech made her suspicious and her mind kept going to a dark place. "BUPERS is juggling a lot of boots right now, and has more pressing matters than deciding the fate of a lowly bar. You're still wounded. Stop fretting. Get better and give them time. Don't make me return to Hold and kick your ass." By this time she was visiting the range three times a week. Her range sessions were the highlights of her otherwise ho-hum life. Requalifying at fifteen meters, slow fire, with the standard-issue pulse pistol put a skip in her step. It was a temporary high. The doc wouldn't let her back in a mechsuit for three more weeks, which meant no Heavy Pistols or tri-barrels or miniguns or anything remotely fun. Life wasn't fair. Thankfully she still had her GLOCK and the doc didn't know about it and what he didn't know about couldn't hurt him. It was only a matter of time and training before her trigger finger stopped anticipating the break and pulling her shots high, and to the left.

Sephora had seen to her every need, and visited her in the hospital when she wasn't working, and cooked for Promise when she returned to their quarters (she still hadn't found a place off-base yet). Sephora had found a job at a local pet store that ran an adjacent veterinary clinic and pet rescue, and she was also volunteering at a women's shelter several times a month. She'd even taken in a stray named Striker. The speckled mutt had taken up residence at the foot of Promise's rack.

Sephora's laughter pulled Promise out of her thoughts and to the open doorway to the den. Promise crossed her arms and leaned against the door frame. Cinnamon and flour and brewing caf and the smells of a well-used kitchen swirled with the pungent scent of burning firewood as soothing instrumental music played in the background.

Sephora and Roman were seated near the hearth at a small table fashioned from a large tree stump. It was ornately carved and lacquered, and small tiles were scattered across its surface.

"This game is impossible," Sephora said, raising her hands in frustration. She was struggling to remember all the names of the scoring combinations of the game, all the melds and matches, pongs and kongs and chows, and the special tiles that earned you bonuses. The tiles were fashioned from small rectangular bits of carved bone and inlaid with traditional Chinese symbols and characters, some primary colors, others white with space-black script. The fireplace crackled with blazing hardwood.

The general looked up from her morning paper from her chair by the window. "That set cost Roman a small fortune. He couldn't just order a facsimile. No, he had to have the real deal and for that we had to find an antiquities dealer and pay twice the price. We could have fully automated our home for half as much."

Sephora's eyes went wide. "You've got to be kidding me. What's this worth?" She tossed one of the smooth rectangles into the air. Roman caught it and added it to her hand.

"Dear, need I remind you about the cannon I bought you for our anniversary, the very one sitting outside the front door? We could have purchased a nice aerodyne and hired a personal driver for what that monstrosity cost. But, no, you had to have an authentic twenty-third-century Terran M-86 GALANT-C Field Cannon with a functional gravplate and the original cup warmer."

Great-Grans started to laugh as Promise walked into the room with a tray of breakfast items: mixed-berry muffins, fresh fruit, a carafe of juice, and of course one of fresh-brewed caf.

"What did I miss?" Promise said as she set the tray down and prepared the table for Grans, Roman, and Sephora to join her.

"Grans and Roman were just bickering about money while I got my butt kicked at mahjong." Sephora threw Promise a help-me-out look. "Want to play the winner?"

"Oh, no you don't," Promise said as she poured herself a cup of caf and added cream and sugar, stirred, and sipped appreciatively. "Yum. I'm not getting suckered into a no-win situation. You may lose to Roman *for* me."

"Thanks a lot." Sephora leaned on the tree-stump table with her chin on her hand and started to pout. "A little help."

"Here," Roman said. He arranged a few tiles for her, pulled one from Sephora's hand and one from the wall. "Ah, a dragon. You're in luck." He rotated a second dragon tile until it was oriented just right. "There. You're doing pretty well. You just need two more tiles."

"Why do I have the feeling I'm not going to get them?"

"Because—" Roman worked quickly and looked up at Sephora with a twinkle in his eye. "—you're not."

"Those are honor tiles, right?" Sephora said. The rare pattern included all four winds: north, south, east, and west.

"Very good. *Mahjong.*" Roman couldn't have been more pleased. "Would you like to play again?"

"No."

Promise clinked her caf mug with a butter knife. "I hate to interrupt your fun but breakfast is served."

"She seems to be doing well," Great-Grans said. Promise and Grans were at the front of the house by the bay window. The rain had stopped and the sun had pushed through the clouds. Sephora and Roman had seized the opportunity to take Striker and Otis for a walk through the wood.

"They seem to get along well too," Promise said.

"Roman has that effect on strays. He's a good man." Grans turned to Promise and motioned to the chairs nearby. "Why don't you take a seat? There's something I've been meaning to discuss with you."

"All right," Promise said. The way Grans said "sit" sounded more like an order and less like a polite request. Now her stomach felt like it did when she was dropping through atmo toward a target.

"I'm getting back into uniform. The commandant commed me two days ago and offered me a job I couldn't refuse."

"Really, ma'am. That's fantastic news. Congratulations." Promise couldn't have been more pleased for her. "May I ask what the new job is?"

Grans's smile consumed her face. "I'm taking over Force Space-Reconnaissance."

Promise sat up a bit straighter, and her shock must have bled through clearly, because Grans's smile grew into the biggest she'd ever seen. Her internal scanners detected an opportunity and oh how she *needed* an opportunity right now. *And Grans is talking SPECOPS.*

"It's a star down. Technically, I'm being demoted to major general." Gran's eyes danced with mischief. "There's no better place for a war hawk like me than special operations. You heard what happened to Senator Oman?"

The non sequitur momentarily caught Promise off-guard. Yes, she had read something in the nets about a campaign-finance scandal involving several members of the Neo-Isolationist Party. She nodded but didn't say a word. Allowed the twinge of smile to creep out. The Conservatives had smelled blood, and maybe that had something to do with Great-Grans's very fast rise to grace.

Grans looked her in the eye. "Ready to play Great-Grans says?"

Here it is. Promise swallowed hard. She'd volunteered after all, during Victor Company's workup. And you didn't say no to Grans if you knew what was good for you.

"I want you to come with me. The next training class starts in three months. I *know.* That gives you little time to prepare. If you want another month or two you've got it. Just say the word. Either way I want you to try out. No guarantees, mind you. You'll have to earn your wings like everyone else."

Marine special operators earned wings. It was the one symbol in the RAW-MC that always garnered respect, regardless of the rank you held.

The Republic of Aligned Worlds Marine Corps Force Space-Reconnaissance companies were the elite units in the Corps. SPACECON companies operated behind enemy lines and in direct-action operations. SPACECON Marines were all-around janes and jacks: masters of vacuum, land, and sea; planetary-insertion specialists; heavy-weapons experts; experts in pararescue and hostage rescue tactics . . . just to name a few. And their armor was the best in the 'verse. You didn't dare compare SPACECON armor to the RAW-MC's standard-issue mechsuit. For one thing, Space-Recon operators were neural-linked with their mechsuits. They had ports at both temples and they jacked into their armor. Their AIs got up close and personal thanks to the "neural clasp." And there was the matter of the SPYADR or Synthetic Poly-Appendage Driver's Rig. A SPYADR mechsuit wasn't an add-on or something strapped to the back of a mechanized Marine like a rucksack or external pack. No, SPYADR armor was built from the skeleton out around a highly specialized arachnid-like frame. Drivers learned to integrate the SPYADR's limbs with their own, and thanks to the neural link they literally became one with their mechsuits and their AIs. They could issue commands with a thought, and scuttlebutt said they even felt their armor's pain.

"A SPYADR driver?"

"Yes." Grans's eyes crackled with energy. "When do you want to start your schooling?"

There was a time, not that long ago, when Promise thought she might have said no. Back before she'd been field-promoted. She'd enlisted to get away from her birth world shortly after her father's murder. A fresh start where no one knew her name was what she'd been after, and for a time she'd found it. Nearly five years passed in the Corps with little fanfare. Antipiracy duties let her knock heads and stop bad men from doing bad things to good people who needed defending. She'd made good in her toon, and followed the regular promotional tack. Then she became a noncommissioned officer and then a platoon sergeant. Life seemed to be on track and she was genuinely happy. Then she'd deployed to Montana, where everything changed.

Since Montana I haven't really owned my own life. That made her smile, because it wasn't exactly true. Enlisting in the RAW-MC wasn't for the independent soul. Civvies exercised self-autonomy and got to decide what they wanted to be when they grew up. Marines did what Aunt Janie told them to, where she told them to do it, when she told them to do it, how she told them to do it, until their service was paid in full.

In a sense, Promise had never been master of her own destiny, and she knew it.

No, the general didn't ask me to try out. She'd asked me when *just like Auntie Janie. I'm being handled, again.* A big part of her resented that. A bigger part of her wanted in. Wanted the challenge of making it with the best, and if you wanted to operate with the best you joined Space-Recon.

"By the way, Kathy's in too. We like to keep our officers and guardians together. No guarantees. Assuming you both graduate, you'll be assigned to-gether to a company and Kathy will stay with you as your guardian, at least until she 'ranks out.' That won't happen for a couple of years."

"What about Maxi?"

Grans shook her head. "I actually pulled his jacket. He's a good Marine, just not what we're looking for in SPACECON. But you are." The general offered her hand. "Congratulations."

Promise looked intently at the hand. Shaking it would be a game changer. For her and for Sephora. She looked out the window and realized she couldn't up and abandon the girl.

"Don't worry, Promise. She'll be taken care of. I've already spoken with Roman about it. Sephora has a home here if she wants it. If not, we'll be here for her if and when she needs help. That girl has grown on us. We won't let anything happen to her. And, let's be honest. You're not the stay-at-home type, are you?"

Promise hated to admit it, but the general had read her like a book. *And isn't this what I was after? Action? A target to shoot. A place to belong. So what are you waiting for, P?*

"Space-Recon sounds good, ma'am." Promise took the general's hand. "Three months will do."

Epilogue

PEACE IN OUR TIME NOT LIKELY

Excerpted from an interview with Queen Aurilyn II of the Lusitanian Empire, in an exclusive with John Kagame of the *Lusitanian Register,* after her speech from the throne, regarding the Republican question and the heightening cold war between the LE and the RAW, August 5, 92 A.E.

JOHN KAGAME: Your Majesty, I'm going to come right out and say what the commoner on the street is thinking. We're headed for open hostilities with the Republic of Aligned Worlds, and God help us if it comes to that. God help our sons and daughters who will pay the highest price if our two star nations come to blows. Do you think you can pull us back from the brink?

QUEEN AURILYN II: (the queen's smile fades) Pull us back? I think about that every day, John. I don't have a daughter or son of my own, but I have cousins and nephews and I worry for them, and I worry I might have to send them into harm's way. Daily they consume my thoughts and prayers. I will do whatever I can to keep them safe, to keep them home.

But, pull us back? That was your question. And you know me, John; I don't dodge the tough ones. I fear the answer is no, at least not entirely, because that would mean I'm dealing with rational actors, and a star nation that acts in good faith toward us. The Republic of Aligned Worlds won't even call itself an empire, this in spite of its annexation of numerous verge worlds, some against their will, and all in the name of peace. Their president says preemptive action has saved lives, and prevented wars. What rubbish. Preemptive action has lined the Republic's coffers with the wealth of other worlds—that's what's happened. Consider the planet Sheol, in the Korazim system. The Republic is in bed with the system's corrupt government. Together they are raping the planet, and the citizens of the Korazim Sector aren't seeing a single solitary chit of benefit. Why? I think you and I both know the answer.

The Republic of Aligned Worlds may have a president instead for a queen, but the Republic is every bit as much an empire as we are. We've built ours with open hands, not a closed fist, from a coalition of willing planets. We wish to avoid hostilities with the RAW at all costs. We mean no planet ill will. But . . . I cannot say that of the Republic . . . not with the level of confidence I wish I felt . . . and believe me I would like to very much believe as much of the Republicans as I know is true of my Lusitanian subjects.

JOHN KAGAME: Would you talk a bit about your government's obligations to the private sector. You've taken a lot of interstellar heat on this matter over the past year, much of it from the Republic.

QUEEN AURILYN II: Between our realms, the Republic of Aligned Worlds claims to hold the moral high ground on this particular issue, particularly in its system of government and its relationship between the government and the markets. We're the monarchists after all, even though we are a constitutional monarchy. I am bound by the constitution as much as you, John. But never mind that. We're the autocrats and tyrants because we have a queen—me—and a hereditary aristocracy, and because our lords and ladies own a substantial share of our lands and enterprises. To be fair, we have to watch that. Too much government ownership is a bad thing. I'll grant the Republic a small point on the matter. But their senators and congresswomen point their finger at us and say, "Look, the 'Lusies' don't believe in free markets or the common man rising above it all. Their system is rigged. Their titles are passed in utero. The rich will always be rich, the titled entitled, the poor nothing more than worker bees."

John, it's all utter nonsense. At the very least it's a gross distortion of who we really are. I would say something else but you're going to broadcast this and children will be listening. . . . At least we are honest about how we run our government. It's crass to put it this way—I doubt you'll be surprised to hear me say it, you do know me well enough by now—our government and our private sector are in bed together, and I say why shouldn't they be as close as a married couple, two equals with overlapping and oftentimes mutually aligned interests. Shouldn't our lords and ladies and their families have a major stake in the government and in the private sector? After all, the peers of the realm are often the ones who fuel the economy by risking their fortunes. They create hundreds of millions of jobs in the process, they sit on the boards of our most prestigious firms and know the ins and outs of our government too, which means they can legislate and regulate from real-world experience. The peers know how to make money and they know how to stay out of the way so others can make it too. They pay the lion's share of our taxes that care for our truly poor, taxes that fund our military, taxes that pay for myriad other things like air traffic control and clean power and interplanetary commerce; all necessary to our way of life and without which the empire simply couldn't survive.

Of course our commoners can rise very high in our political and private sectors. We do have a House of Commons, and the Commons control the purse strings. Think on that. Can a commoner become queen? Well no, of course not, but the king was plucked off the street when I asked him to marry me and I'd say it's worked out rather well for him. Oh, and consider this: Among our top one hundred firms, fifty-five are owned by women and men—by families no less—with no title other than president or CEO. That speaks for itself.

JOHN KAGAME: All excellent points, Your Majesty. What about the Republic's office of the president? Can't anyone aspire to the highest position in the RAW? Surely you see the point, Your Majesty.

QUEEN AURILYN II: (the queen smiles and shakes her head, no) Seeing isn't believing, John. Supposedly anyone can rise to the highest office of the land in the Republic of Aligned Worlds. The Republic likes to trot that out whenever it's feeling particularly uppity. Anyone, no matter their station at birth or genetics or ancestry, can become president of the Republic of Aligned Worlds. Utter rubbish again! The truth is their president and cabinet, Senate and House, and High Court and all their NGOs and un-elected bureaucrats, are bought and paid for by their lawyers and lobbyists and their shadow corporate congress, all behind closed doors . . . and against their own laws I might add.

At least we are open, honest, and transparent about giving our peers a significant stake in the governance and the economic prosperity of the Lusitanian Empire and all her member worlds. The Republic, well, I dislike using the word "liars." The bar for that must be very high. You do take my point.

GLOSSARY
(not at all exhaustive)

A.E. after Earth

AI artificial intelligence

ALCON all considered

ANDES Android Enemy Soldier, but commonly used to refer to android sentinels, friendly or foe

APER armor-piercing explosive round

Armorplaste a clear, high-strength, military-grade polycarbonate material (pronounced armorplasty); sometimes shortened to "plaste"

Aye yes

Aye, aye "I understand and will comply"

Bag-drag to be transferred, or to ship out

BAT-CO battalion commander

BATRON battlecruiser squadron

Beegees the underarmor worn by mechsuit drivers, which prevents chafing while "suited" and affords the wearer some protection against small-arms and energy fire; beegees are acceptable attire in place of utilities while aboard ship and sometimes referred to as a "body glove"

BMR Battlefield Mapping Reticule (projects a compressed three-dimensional display of energy signatures into the wearer's field of view)

Bravo Zulu well done

BUMED Bureau of Medicine, or Bureau of Medicine and Surgery

BUMIL Bureau of Military Intelligence. BUMIL is the shortened form of BUMILINT (BU-MIL-INT), with "Intelligence" omitted and understood, and is the source of many jokes in several military traditions. In the Republic of Aligned Worlds, for instance, BUMIL also refers to the collective intelligence communities of the entire military, including NAVINT

(Naval Intelligence) and MARINT (Marine Intelligence). One may insult the military's intelligence—BUMIL—without specifically disparaging a particular branch of service.

BUPERS Bureau of Personnel

BUWEPS Bureau of Weapons Development

CAR short for "carbine," a long arm with a shorter barrel than a rifle

CIC Combat Information Center, or Combat Intelligence Center

Civvie a civilian

Civvies civilian clothes

Comm communications device (adjective, verb, or noun)

COMSEC communications security

Copy as in "copy that"—or "I heard what you just said"

Crossed Anchors and Charger the official emblem and insignia of the Lusitanian Imperial Navy

CRURON cruiser squadron

CZ cruiser

Deck the floor or surface of the earth

Delta sierra DS, or "dumb shit"

Eve or Echo-Victor-One, a code name for a female prisoner

EWO Electronics Warfare Officer

Ferrocrete a military-grade material that is poured to make roads and landing pads for light attack craft and shuttles

FGL Flexible Grenade Launcher, capable of firing an assortment of explosive ordnance

Fighting hole a defensive position dug into the ground

FOB forward operating base

Fruit Salad also called glittery; medals and service ribbons worn by uniformed military

FTL faster than light

GEHAK Gravitic-Enhanced High-Altitude Bunker-Killer

GLOCK a popular twentieth-century semi-automatic firearm created by Gaston Glock that revolutionized the small-arms industry with its polymer frame; became known as the "plastic gun"

Gunny nickname for a gunnery sergeant (but not for a master gunnery sergeant)

HALO High-Altitude, Low-Opening (e.g., "HALO drop"; "HALO jump")

HAWC Health and Wellness Center

HG heavy gravity (e.g., "HG world")

HMS His/Her Majesty's Ship, used before the name of space-faring war-ships

Horde missiles small antipersonnel/antiarmor missiles launched in pack-ets, or "hordes," that are designed to swamp an enemy's defenses

HUD heads-up display

HV hypervelocity (e.g., "HV round")

HVT high-value target

ILW Independent League of Worlds, a now-defunct coalition of non-aligned planets in the Rim, or verge. The planet Montana initially led the league before joining the Republic of Aligned Worlds. After Montana's departure, the ILW fell apart.

J-CIC Joint Combat Intelligence Command

JSA Justification for System Activation (which is a PITA to fill out)

Klick kilometer

KZ kill zone

LAC light attack craft, the workhouse of most space Marine Corps. A LAC is typically a system-bound (i.e., non-jump-capable) craft capable of in-terplanetary and atmospheric flight. There are several classes of LAC, which range widely in size. Most warships carry a small complement of LACs to support their Marine detachments.

LE Lusitanian Empire, a constitutional monarchy with a hereditary king or queen as the head of state, a lower House of Commons composed of elected officials, and an upper House of Lords

Liberty authorized free time ashore or off-station that is not counted as leave

LIDAR or LiDAR, a remote sensing technology from the twentieth century that measures distance by illuminating a target with a laser and analyz-ing the reflected light; the terms originated as a combination of "light" and "radar"

LOS line of sight

Lusie a derogatory term used by Republicans and citizens of other star na-tions when referring to the Lusitanians (from the LE)

LZ landing zone

MARINT Marine Intelligence

MBP mini Bi-Polar rifle, an electromagnetic projectile launcher (an elec-tromagnetic rail gun)

Mechsuit mechanized suit of battle armor. Before the advent of powered armor, the word "mechanized" referred to soldiers equipped with armored vehicles. Mechsuits are roughly humanoid with interlocking plates of armor that protect the driver. Modern militaries prefer a plug-and-play platform and semi-autonomous AI assists.

MEDSYS medical emergency triage system

Mess dress uniform worn at formal occasions and roughly equivalent to civilian black-tie

Mike minute

Mike-mike millimeter

MOI Ministry of Intelligence

MOLLE Modular Lightweight Load-carrying Equipment (pronounced "molly")

MOS Military Occupational Specialty

MRS Mobile Recharging Station (for handheld energy weapons); also Misses

NAVCOM Navigation and Communications

NAVINT Naval Intelligence

NCO noncommissioned officer

Ninety-day wonder an officer commissioned in a military branch after an unusually short training period

Noncom noncommissioned officer

OCS Officer Candidate School

Overhead ceiling of a building or ship

Peristeel an alloy used to make mechsuits, small land and aerial craft, and warship armor

PF platform or space station, often but not always a military installation

PFC private first class

Pharmacope a Marine's personal bank of drugs, typically implanted in the thigh; a mechsuit's MEDSYS contains a backup

'Publican a derogatory term used by Lusitanians when referring to Republicans (from the RAW)

Rack bed

RAW Republic of Aligned Worlds, a democratic republic of worlds that won its independence from the Terran Federation in 2481 C.E.

RAW-FF Republic of Aligned Worlds Fleet Forces, an umbrella term referring to the collective military branches of the Republic: Marine Corps, Navy, and Sector Guard

RAW-MC Republic of Aligned Worlds Marine Corps

Regular dress roughly equivalent in form and function to a civilian business suit

Rim the outskirts of human civilization—a rim planet or rim world is typically poor and nonaligned, often plagued by rampant poverty and lawlessness; the term is often used interchangeably with "verge," although it is considered a derogatory term by rimworlders

RNS Republican Naval Ship (or Republican Naval Warship—with "war" being understood), used before the name of Republican space-faring warships

Roger as in "Roger that"—or "I understand what you just said"

RPP Remotely Piloted Platform

SAC Standard Atmospheric Conditions

SAM a surface-to-air or ground-to-air missile

SAR search and rescue; also, "sounds about wrong"

SARG Semi-Autonomous Reasoning Grunt, a mechsuit driver's AI assist

Scuttlebutt gossip or a rumor

Seabag a duffel bag

SECCOM Sector Command

Semper Fidelis "Always Faithful" or "Always Loyal"

Semper Paratus "Always Ready," the official slogan of the RAW-MC

Seraph, globe, and anchor the official emblem and insignia of the RAW-FF

SERE Survival, Evasion, Resistance, and Escape school

SITREP "situation report"

Skipper nickname for the captain of a warship or the captain of a company of Marines

Skivvies undergarments, including skivvy shirts and skivvy drawers

SNCO staff noncommissioned officer

SNEAK Stealth-Navigation-Evasion-Adaptation-Kill suit

Snotty cruise an ensign's first mission after successfully completing her or his officer's training, often at a service academy

SOP standard operating procedure

SPECOPS Special Operations Forces, or Special Operators, or Special Forces

Striker sniper

Tango down target eliminated or neutralized

TF task force; also, Terran Federation, the first and largest star nation in the 'verse (Terrans consider the abbreviation a veiled insult)

UAV unmanned aerial vehicle; broadly used to mean a drone that can operate in atmospheric conditions as well as in vacuum

Utilities designed for wear in the field, the standard working uniform for deployed and most garrison Marines and Sailors

Vacsuit garment capable of withstanding harsh environments, vacuum, and the extreme cold of space; often worn inside warships and small craft during combat as a precaution in case of loss of atmospheric containment and necessary for extravehicular activities

Verge derogatory term for the outskirts of human civilization—a "verge" planet is typically poor and nonaligned, often plagued by rampant poverty and lawlessness; the term is often used interchangeably with "Rim"

VTOL Vertical Takeoff and Landing vehicle

Webs short for "webshorts" and "webvests," loose-fitting clothing with MOLLE gear woven into the fabric

Whisker a small drone used for reconnaissance by many militaries and clandestine services across the 'verse

WILCO I have received your last message, understand it, and "will comply"

Wolf a "blooded" Marine (i.e., a Marine who has killed in combat)

XO executive officer, the second-in-command of a military unit

INDOMITABLE

The Chronicles of Promise Paen,
BOOK TWO

W. C. Bauers

A TOM DOHERTY ASSOCIATES BOOK
NEW YORK

INDOMITABLE

Copyright © 2016 by William C. Bauers

A Tor Book
Published by Tom Doherty Associates
175 Fifth Avenue
New York, NY 10010

www.tor-forge.com

Tor® is a registered trademark of Macmillan Publishing Group, LLC.

The Library of Congress has cataloged the hardcover edition as follows:

Bauers, W. C., author.
    Indomitable / W.C. Bauers.—1st ed.
        p. cm.
    "A Tom Doherty Associates Book."
    ISBN 978-0-7653-7544-5 (hardcover)
    ISBN 978-1-4668-4730-9 (e-book)
 1. Space warfare—Fiction.   2. Women marines—Fiction.   3. Space warfare.   4. Women marines.   I. Title.
    PS3602.A9358 I53 2016
    813'.6—dc23

                                                2016285197

ISBN 978-0-7653-7545-2 (trade paperback)

Our books may be purchased in bulk for promotional, educational, or business use. Please contact your local bookseller or the Macmillan Corporate and Premium Sales Department at 1-800-221-7945, extension 5442, or by e-mail at MacmillanSpecialMarkets@macmillan.com.

First Edition: July 2016
First Trade Paperback Edition: April 2017

Printed in the United States of America

0 9 8 7 6 5 4 3 2 1